Dodger

ALSO BY TERRY PRATCHETT

The Carpet People

The Dark Side of the Sun

Strata

THE BROMELIAD TRILOGY:

Truckers

Diggers

Wings

THE JOHNNY MAXWELL TRILOGY:

Only You Can Save Mankind

Johnny and the Dead

Johnny and the Bomb

Nation

Good Omens (*with Neil Gaiman*)

The Long Earth (*with Stephen Baxter*)

THE DISCWORLD SERIES

The Color of Magic

The Light Fantastic

Equal Rites

Mort

Sourcery

Wyrd Sisters

Pyramids

Guards! Guards!

Eric

Moving Pictures

Reaper Man

Witches Abroad

Small Gods

Lords and Ladies

Men at Arms

Soul Music

Feet of Clay

Interesting Times

Maskerade

Hogfather

Jingo

The Last Continent

Carpe Jugulum

The Fifth Elephant

The Truth

Thief of Time

The Amazing Maurice
and His Educated Rodents

Night Watch

The Wee Free Men

Monstrous Regiment

A Hat Full of Sky

Going Postal

Thud!

Wintersmith

Making Money

Unseen Academicals

I Shall Wear Midnight

Snuff

Where's My Cow?
(*illustrated by Melvyn Grant*)

The Last Hero: A Discworld Fable
(*illustrated by Paul Kidby*)

The Art of Discworld
(*illustrated by Paul Kidby*)

The Illustrated Wee Free Men
(*illustrated by Stephen Player*)

The Wit and Wisdom of Discworld
(*with Stephen Briggs*)

THE DISCWORLD GRAPHIC NOVELS

The Color of Magic

The Light Fantastic

TERRY PRATCHETT

Dodger

HARPER
An Imprint of HarperCollinsPublishers

Library of Congress Cataloging-in-Publication Data is available.

ISBN 978-0-06-200949-4 (trade bdg.) — ISBN 978-0-06-200950-0 (lib. bdg.)

12 13 14 15 16   LP/RRDH   10 9 8 7 6 5 4 3 2 1

❖

First Edition

*To Henry Mayhew for writing his book,
and to Lyn for absolutely everything else*

CHAPTER ONE

In which we meet our hero and the hero
meets an orphan of the storm and comes
face to face with Mister Charlie,
a gentleman known as a bit of a scribbler

THE RAIN POURED DOWN on London so hard that it seemed that it was dancing spray, every raindrop contending with its fellows for supremacy in the air and waiting to splash down. It was a deluge. The drains and sewers were overflowing, throwing up—regurgitating, as it were—the debris of muck, slime, and filth, the dead dogs, the dead rats, cats, and worse; bringing back up to the world of men all those things that they thought they had left behind them; jostling and gurgling and hurrying toward the overflowing and always hospitable River Thames; bursting its banks, bubbling and churning like some nameless soup boiling in a dreadful cauldron; the river itself gasping like a dying fish. But those in the know always said about the London rain that, try as it might, it would never, ever clean that noisome city, because all it did was show you another layer of dirt. And on this dirty night there were appropriately dirty deeds that not even the rain could wash away.

A fancy two-horse coach wallowed its way along the street, some piece of metal stuck near an axle causing it to be heralded by a scream. And indeed there was a scream, a human scream this time, as the coach door was flung open and a figure tumbled out into the gushing gutter, which tonight was doing the job of a fountain. Two other figures sprang from the coach, cursing in language that was as colorful as the night was dark and even dirtier. In the downpour, fitfully lit by the lightning, the first figure tried to escape but tripped, fell, and was leaped upon, with a cry that was hardly to be heard in all the racket, but which was almost supernaturally counterpointed by the grinding of iron, as a drain cover nearby was pushed open to reveal a struggling and skinny young man who moved with the speed of a snake.

"You let that girl alone!" he shouted.

There was a curse in the dark and one of the assailants fell backward with his legs kicked from under him. The youth was no heavyweight but somehow he was everywhere, throwing blows—blows that were augmented by a pair of brass knuckles, always a helpmeet for the outnumbered. Outnumbered one to two as it were, the assailants took to their heels while the youth followed, raining blows. But it was London and it was raining and it was dark, and they were dodging into alleys and side streets, frantically trying to catch up with their coach, so that he lost them, and the apparition from the depths of the sewers turned around and headed back to the stricken girl at greyhound speed.

He kneeled down, and to his surprise she grabbed him by the collar and whispered in what he considered to be foreigner English, "They want to take me back—please help me. . . ." The lad sprang to his feet, his eyes all suspicion.

On this stormy night of stormy nights, it was opportune then that two men who themselves knew something about the dirt of London were walking, or rather, wading, along this street, hurrying home with hats pulled down—which was a nice try but simply didn't work, because in this torrent it seemed that the bouncing water was coming as much from below as it was from above. Lightning struck again, and one of them said, "Is that someone lying in the gutter there?" The lightning presumably heard, because it sliced down again and revealed a shape, a mound, a person as far as these men could see.

"Good heavens, Charlie, it's a girl! Soaked to the skin and thrown into the gutter, I imagine," said one of them. "Come on. . . ."

"Hey you, what are you a-doing, mister?!"

By the light of a pub window that could barely show you the darkness, the aforesaid Charlie and his friend saw the face of a boy who looked like a young lad no more than seventeen years old but who seemed to have the voice of a man. A man, moreover, who was prepared to take on both of them, to the death. Anger steamed off him in the rain and he wielded a long piece of metal. He carried on, "I know your sort, oh yes I do! Coming down here chasing the skirt, making a mockery of decent girls, blimey! Desperate, weren't you, to be out on a night such as this!"

The man who wasn't called Charlie straightened up. "Now see here, you. I object most strongly to your wretched allegation. We are respectable gentlemen who, I might add, work quite hard to better the fortunes of such poor wretched girls and, indeed, by the look of it, those such as yourself!"

The scream of rage from the boy was sufficiently loud that the doors of the nearby pub swung open, causing smoky orange light to illuminate the ever-present rain. "So that's what you call it, is it, you smarmy old gits!"

The boy swung his homemade weapon, but the man called Charlie caught it and dropped it behind him, then grabbed the boy and held him by the scruff of his neck. "Mister Mayhew and myself are decent citizens, young man, and as such we surely feel it is our duty to take this young lady somewhere away from harm." Over his shoulder he said, "Your place is closest, Henry. Do you think your wife would object to receiving a needy soul for one night? I wouldn't like to see a dog out on a night such as this."

Henry, now clutching the young woman, nodded. "Do you mean *two* dogs, by any chance?"

The struggling boy took immediate offense at this, and with a snakelike movement was out of the grip of Charlie and once again spoiling for a fight. "I ain't no dog, you nobby sticks, nor ain't she! We have our pride, you know. I make my own way, I does, all kosher, straight up!"

The man called Charlie lifted the boy up by the scruff of his neck so that they were face-to-face. "My, I admire your attitude, young man, but not your common sense!" he said quietly. "And mark you, this young lady is in a bad way. Surely you can see that. My friend's house is not too far away from here, and since you have set yourself up as her champion and protector, why then, I invite you to follow us there and witness that she will have the very best of treatment that we can afford, do you hear me? What is your name, mister?

And before you tell it to me, I invite you to believe that you are not the only person who cares about a young lady in dire trouble on this dreadful night. So, my boy, what is your name?"

The boy must have picked up a tone in Charlie's voice, because he said, "I'm Dodger—that's what they call me, on account I'm never there, if you see what I mean? Everybody in all the boroughs knows Dodger."

"Well, then," said Charlie. "Now we have met you and joined that august company, we must see if we can come to an understanding during this little odyssey, man to man." He straightened up and went on, "Let us move, Henry, to your house and as soon as possible, because I fear this unfortunate girl needs all the help we can give her. And you, my lad, do you *know* this young lady?"

He let go of the boy, who took a few steps backward. "No, guv'nor, never seen her before in my life, God's truth, and I know everybody on the street. Just another runaway, happens all the time, so it does; it don't bear thinking about."

"Am I to believe, Mister Dodger, that you, not knowing this unfortunate woman, nevertheless sprang to her defense like a true Galahad?"

Dodger suddenly looked very wary. "I might be, I might not. What's it to you, anyway? And who the hell is this Galahad cove?"

Charlie and Henry made a cradle with their arms to carry the woman. As they set off, Charlie said over his shoulder, "You have no idea what I just said, do you, Mister Dodger? But Galahad was a famous hero. . . . Never mind—you just follow us, like the knight in soaking armor that you are, and you will see fair play for this damsel, get a good meal, and, let me see . . ." Coins jingled in the darkness. "Yes, two shillings, and if you do come, you will perhaps improve your chances of Heaven, which, if I am any judge, is not a place that often concerns you. Understand? Do we have an accord? Very well."

Twenty minutes later Dodger was sitting close to the fire in the kitchen of a house, not a grand house as such, but nevertheless much grander than most buildings he went into legally; there were much grander buildings that he had been into illegally, but he never spent very much time in them, often leaving with a considerable amount of haste. Honestly, the number of dogs people had these days was a damn scandal, so it was, and they would set them on a body without warning, so he had always been speedy. But here, oh yes, here there was meat and potatoes, carrots too, but not, alas, any beer. In the kitchen he had been given a glass of warm milk that was nearly fresh. Mrs. Quickly the cook was watching him like a hawk and had already locked away the cutlery, but apart from that it seemed to be a pretty decent crib, although there had been a certain amount of what you might call *words* from the missus of Mister Henry to her husband on the subject of bringing home waifs and strays at this time of night. It seemed to Dodger, who paid a great deal of forensic attention to all he could see and hear, that this was by no means the first time that she had cause for complaint; she sounded like someone trying hard to conceal that they were really fed up and trying to put a brave face on it. But nevertheless, Dodger had certainly had his meal (and that was the important thing), the wife and a maid had bustled off with the girl, and now . . . someone was coming down the stairs to the kitchen.

It was Charlie, and Charlie bothered Dodger. Henry seemed like one of them do-gooders who felt guilty about having money and food when other people did not; Dodger knew the type. He, personally, was not bothered about having money when other people didn't, but when you lived a life like his, Dodger found that being generous when in funds, and being a cheerful giver, was a definite insurance. You needed friends—friends were the kind of people who would say: "Dodger? Never heard of 'im, never clapped eyes on 'im, guv'nor! You must be thinking of some other cove"— because you had to live as best you could in the city and you had to be sharp and wary and on your toes every moment of the day if you wanted to stay alive.

He stayed alive because he was the Dodger, smart and fast. He knew everybody and everybody knew him. He had never, ever, been before the beak, he could outrun the fastest Bow Street runner, and now that they had all been found out and replaced, he could outrun every peeler as well. They couldn't arrest you unless they put a hand on you, and nobody ever managed to touch Dodger.

No, Henry was no problem, but Charlie—now, oh yes, Charlie—he looked the type who would look at a body and see right inside you. Charlie, Dodger considered, might well be a dangerous cove, a gentleman who knew the ins and outs of the world and could see through flannel and soft words to what you were thinking, which was dangerous indeed. Here he was now, the man himself, coming downstairs escorted by the jingling of coins.

Charlie nodded at the cook, who was cleaning up, and sat down on the bench by Dodger, who had to slide over a bit to make room.

"Well now, Dodger, wasn't it?" he said. "I am sure you will be very happy to know that the young lady you helped us with is safe and sleeping in a warm bed after some stitches and some physic from the doctor. Alas, I wish I could say the same for her unborn child, which did not survive this dreadful escapade."

Child! The word hit Dodger like a blackjack, and unlike a blackjack it kept on going. A child—and for the rest of the conversation the word was there, hanging at the edge of his sight and not letting him go. Aloud he said, "I didn't know."

"Indeed, I'm sure you didn't," said Charlie. "In the dark it was just one more dreadful crime, which without doubt was just one among many this night; you know that, Dodger, and so do I. But this one had the temerity to take place in front of me, and so I feel I would like to do a little police work, without, as it were, involving the police, who I suspect in this case would not have very much success."

Charlie's face was unreadable, even to Dodger, who was very, very good at reading faces. Solemnly, the man went on, "I wonder if those gentlemen you met who were harassing her knew about the child; perhaps we shall never find out, or perhaps we shall." And there it was; that little word "shall" was a knife, straining to cut away until it hit enlightenment. Charlie's face stayed totally blank. "I wonder if any other gentleman was aware of the fact, and therefore, sir, here for you are your two shillings—plus one more, if you were to answer a few questions for me in the hope of getting to the bottom of this strange occurrence."

Dodger looked at the coins. "What sort of questions would they be, then?" Dodger lived in a world where *nobody* asked questions apart from: "How much?" and "What's in it for me?" And he knew, actually *knew*, that Charlie knew this too.

Charlie continued. "Can you read and write, Mister Dodger?"

Dodger put his head on one side. "Is this a question that gets me a shilling?"

"No, it does not," Charlie snapped. "But I will spring one farthing for that little morsel and nothing more; here is the farthing, where is the answer?"

Dodger grabbed the tiny coin. "Can read 'beer,' 'gin,' and 'ale.' No sense in filling your head with stuff you don't need, that's what I always say." Was that the tiny ghost of a smile on the man's face? he wondered.

"You are clearly an academic, Mister Dodger. Perhaps I should tell you that the young lady had—well, she had not been well used."

He wasn't smiling anymore, and Dodger, suddenly panicking, shouted, "Not by me! I never done nothing to hurt her, God's truth! I might not be an angel but I ain't a bad man!"

Charlie's hand grabbed Dodger as he tried to get up. "You never done nothing? You, Mister Dodger, *never done nothing*? If you *never done nothing* then you must have done *something*, and there you are, guilty right out of your own mouth. I'm quite certain that you yourself have never been to school, Mister Dodger; you seem far too smart. Though if you ever did, and came out with a phrase like 'I never done nothing,' you would probably be thrashed by your teacher. But now listen to me, Dodger; I fully accept that you did nothing to harm the lady, and I have one very good reason for saying so. You might not be aware of it, but on her finger there is one of the biggest and most ornate gold rings I have ever seen—the sort of ring that means something—and if you were intending to do her any harm, you would have stolen it in a wink, just like you stole my pocketbook a short while ago."

Dodger looked at those eyes. Oh, this was a bad cove to be on the wrong side of and no two ways about it. "Me, sir? No, sir," he said. "Found it lying around, sir. Honestly intended to give it back to you, sir."

"I can assure you that I believe in full every word you have just uttered, Mister Dodger. Although I must confess my admiration that in the darkness you not only were able to see the form of a pocketbook, but also so readily decided that it belonged to me; really I'm quite amazed," said Charlie. "Settle down; I just wanted you to know how serious we are. When you said, 'I never done nothing,' all you were doing was painting the whole of your statement with negativity, crudely but with emphasis, you understand? Myself and Mister Mayhew are cognizant of the generally unacceptable state of affairs throughout most of this city, and by the way, that means we know about such things and endeavor in our various ways to bring matters to the notice of the public, or at least to those members of the public who care to take notice. Since you appear to care about the young lady, perhaps you could ask around or at least listen for any news about her; where she came from, her background, *anything* about her. She was badly beaten, and I don't mean a domestic up-and-downer, a slap, maybe. I mean leather and fists. *Fists!* Over and over again, according to the bruises, and that, my young friend, wasn't the end of it!

"Now there are some people, not you of course, who would say we should go to the authorities, and this is because they have no grasp at all of the realities of London for the lower classes; no grasp at all of the rookeries and the detritus of decay and squalor that is their lot. Yes?"

This was because Dodger had raised a finger, and as soon as he saw that he had got Charlie's full attention, the boy said, "Okay, certainly it can be a bit grubby down some streets. A few dead dogs, dead old lady maybe, but well, that's the way of the world, right? Like it says in the Good Book, you got to eat a peck of dirt before you die, right?"

"Possibly not all in one meal," said Charlie. "But since you raise the subject, Mister Dodger, for your two shillings, and one more shilling, quote me one further line from the Bible, if you please?"

This was something of an exercise for Dodger. He glared at the man and managed, "Well, mister, you have to goeth, yes that's what it says, and I don't see no shilling yet!"

Charlie laughed. "'You have to goeth'? I'll wager that you have never attended church or chapel in your life, young man! You can't read, you can't write; good heavens, can you give me the name of one single apostle? By the look on your face, I deduce that you cannot, alas. But, nevertheless, you came to the aid of our young lady upstairs when so many other people would have looked the other way, and so you will have *five* sixpences if you undertake this little task for me and Mister Mayhew. So ask around, search out the story, my friend. You may find me by daylight at the *Morning Chronicle*.

Do not look for me anywhere else. Here is my card if you should need it. Mister Dickens, that's me." He passed Dodger a pasteboard oblong. "Yes, you have a question?"

Dodger looked more uncertain now, but he managed to say, "Could I see the lady, sir? 'Cos I never really clapped eyes on her—I just saw people running away, and I thought you fine gentlemen was with them. I ought to know what she looks like if I'm going to ask questions around and about, and let me tell you, sir, asking questions around and about can be a dangerous way to make a living in this city."

Charlie frowned. "At the moment she looks black and blue, Dodger." He thought for a moment and went on, "But there is some merit in what you say; the household has been turned upside down by this, as you must understand. Mrs. Mayhew is getting the children back to sleep and the girl is in the maids' room for now. If you are to go in there, make sure your boots are clean, and if those little fingers of yours . . . You know the ones I mean, the kind I am aware of that are adept at finding other people's property in them, and 'Oh, dear me, and stone the crows,' you had no idea how it got there. . . ." He trailed off. "Do not, I repeat *not*, try that in the house of Mister Henry Mayhew."

"I'm not a thief," Dodger protested.

"What you mean, Mister Dodger, is that you're not *only* a thief. I will accept, for now, your story about how my pocket-book ended up in your hands . . . for now, mind you. I note that the slim crowbar you have about your person is designed for opening the lids of drain covers, from which I deduce that you are a tosher, a grubber in the sewers—an interesting profession, but not one for a man hoping for a long life. And so I wonder how you still survive, Dodger, and one day I intend to find out. Don't come the innocent with me, please. I know the backside of this city only too well!"

Although he gasped at this and protested that he was being spoken to as if he was a common criminal, Dodger was quite impressed: he'd never before heard a flash geezer use the term "stone the crows," and it confirmed his view that Mister Dickens was a tricky cove, the sort who might bring a lot of nastiness down on a hardworking lad. It paid to be careful of flash geezers like him—else they might find someone to do something with your teeth, with pliers, like what happened with Wally the knacker man, who got done up rotten over a matter of a shilling. So Dodger minded his manners as he was led up and through the dark house and into a small bedroom, made even smaller by the fact that the doctor was still there and by now was washing his hands in a very small bowl. The man gave Dodger a cursory glance that had quite a lot of curse in it and then looked up at Charlie, who got the kind of smile that you get when people know you have money. Just as Charlie had surmised, Dodger hadn't had a day's proper schooling. Instead, his life had mostly been spent learning things, which is surprisingly rather different, and he could read a face much better than a newspaper.*

The doctor said to Charlie, "Very bad business, sir, very nasty. I've done the best I can; they're pretty decent stitches if I say so myself. She is, in fact, a rather robust young woman

---

* Contrary to what he had said to Charlie, Dodger could read, having had some tuition from Solomon the watchmaker, his landlord, and the *Jewish Chronicle*—but it was never in anyone's interest to tell anybody anything that they didn't need to know.

underneath it all and, as it turned out, has needed to be. What she needs now is care and attention and, best of all, time—the greatest of physicians."

"And, of course, the grace of God, who is the one that charges the least," said Charlie, pressing some coins into the man's hand. As the doctor left, Charlie said, "Naturally, Doctor, we will see that she gets good food and drink at least. Thank you for attending, and good night to you."

The doctor gave Dodger another black look and hurried back down the stairs. Yes, you had to know how to read somebody's phizog when you lived on the cobbles, no doubt about it. Dodger had read the face of Charlie twice now, and so he knew that Charlie had little liking for the doctor any more than the doctor did for Dodger and, from his tone, Charlie would be more inclined to put his trust in good food and water than in God—a personage who Dodger had only vaguely heard of and knew very little about, except perhaps that He had a lot to do with rich people. This, generally speaking, left out everybody Dodger knew (except for Solomon, who had negotiated a great deal with God somehow, and occasionally gave God advice).

With the man's ample bulk out of the way, Dodger got a better look at the girl. He guessed her age at only about sixteen or seventeen—although she looked older, as people always did when they had been beaten up. She was breathing slowly, and he could see some of her hair, which was absolutely golden. On an impulse he said, "No offense meant, Mister Charlie, but would you mind if I watched over the lady, you know, until dawn? Not touching or nothing, and I've never seen her before, I swear it—but I don't know why, I think I ought to."

The housekeeper came in, casting a look of pure hatred at Dodger and, he was happy to see, one that was not much better toward Charlie. She had the makings of a mustache, from below which came a grumble. "I don't wanna speak out of turn, sir. I don't mind keeping an eye on another 'author of the storm,' as it were, but I can't be responsible for the doings of this young guttersnipe, saving your honor's presence. I hope no one will blame me if he murders you all in your beds tonight. No offense meant, you understand?"

Dodger was used to this sort of thing; people like this silly woman thought that every kid who lived on the streets was very likely a thief and a pickpocket who would steal the laces out of your boots in a fraction of a second and then sell them back to you. He sighed inwardly. Of course, he thought, that was true of *most* of them—nearly all of them really—but that was no reason to make blanket statements. Dodger wasn't a thief; not at all. He was . . . well, he was good at finding things. After all, sometimes things fell off carts and carriages, didn't they? He had never stuck his hand into somebody else's pocket. Well, apart from one or two occasions when it was so blatantly open that something was *bound* to fall out, in which case Dodger would nimbly grab it before it hit the ground. That wasn't stealing: that was keeping the place tidy, and after all, it only happened what? Once or twice a week? It was a kind of tidiness, after all, but nevertheless some shortsighted people might hang you just because of a misunderstanding. But they never had a chance of misunderstanding Dodger, oh dear no, because he was quick, and slick, and certainly brighter than the stupid old woman who got her words wrong (after all, what was an "author of the storm"? That was barmy! Somebody who wrote down storms for a living?). Nice work if you could get it, although strictly speaking Dodger always avoided anything that might be considered as being work. Of course, there was the toshing; oh, how he loved that. Toshing wasn't work: toshing was living, toshing was coming alive. If he wasn't being so bloody stupid, he would be down in the sewers now, waiting for the storm to stop and a new world of opportunity to open. He treasured those times on the tosh, but right now Charlie had his hand firmly on Dodger's shoulder.

"Hear that, my friend? This lady has you bang to rights, and if you emulate Genghis Khan in this household and I hear of it, then I will set some people I know onto your tail. Understand? And I will wield a weapon that Genghis himself never dreamed of and aim it straight at you, my friend. Now I must leave the stricken young lady in the care of yourself, and the care of you to Mrs. Sharples, upon whose word your life depends." Charlie smiled and went on, "'Author of the storm,' indeed; I must make a note of that." To the surprise of Dodger, and presumably to the surprise of Mrs. Sharples, Charlie took out a very small notebook and a very short pencil and quickly wrote something down.

The housekeeper's eyes gleamed with a cheerful malignance as she regarded Dodger. "You can trust me, sir, indeed you can. If this young clamp gets up to any tricks, I shall have him out of here and in front of the magistrates in very short order, indeed I will." Then she screamed and pointed. "He has stolen something of hers already, sir; see!"

Dodger froze, his hand halfway to the floor. There was a very anxious moment.

"Ah, Mrs. Sharples, you indeed have the eyes of—how can I say . . . Argos Panoptes," Charlie said smoothly. "I happened to notice what the young man was picking up and it has been by the bed for some time—the girl had been clutching them in her hand. No doubt Mister Dodger was concerned that it should not be overlooked. So, Dodger, hand it over, if you please?"

Wishing earnestly for a piss, Dodger handed over his find. It was a very cheap pack of cards, but there had been no time to look at it with Charlie's eyes on him.

Charlie got on Dodger's nerves, but now the man said, "A children's card game, Mrs. Sharples; rather damp and rather juvenile, I would consider, for a young lady of her age. Happy Families—I have heard of it." He turned the pack over and over in his fingers and said at last, "This is a mystery, my dear Mrs. Sharples, and I shall put it back into the hands of someone who will move heaven and earth to take that mystery by its tail and drag it into the light of day; to wit, Mister Dodger here." With that, he handed the cards back to the astonished Dodger, saying cheerfully, "Do not cross me, Dodger, for I know every inch of you, I will take my oath on it. Now, I really must go. Business awaits!"

And Dodger was certain that Charlie winked at him as he went out of the door.

The night passed fairly quickly because so much of it had already slid away into yesterday. Dodger sat on the floor, listening to the slow breathing of the girl and the snoring of Mrs. Sharples, who managed to sleep with one eye open and fixed on Dodger like a compass needle that steadily points north. Why had he done this? Why was he freezing on this floor when he could have been snug and curled up by Solomon's stove (a marvelous contraption, which could also be a furnace if there was a lot of gold to melt)?

But the girl was beautiful under her injuries, and he watched her as he turned the damp pack of stupid grubby cards over and over in his hands, staring at the girl whose face was a mass of bruises. The swine had really done her up good and proper, using her like a punchbag. He had given them some handy smacks with his crowbar, but that was not enough—by God, it was not enough! He would find them, he surely would, and see the bastards in lavender. . . .

Dodger woke up on the floor in a semigloom illuminated by just one flickering candle, totally disoriented until he recognized his surroundings, which included Mrs. Sharples in her chair, still snoring like a man trying to saw a pig in half. But more importantly there was the sound of a very small and trembling voice, saying, "May I have some water, if you please?"

This caused in Dodger a near panic, but there was a jug of water on the basin and he filled a glass. The girl took it from him very carefully and motioned for more. Dodger glanced at Mrs. Sharples, refilled the glass, handed it to the girl, and whispered, "Please tell me your name."

The girl croaked, rather than spoke, but it was a ladylike croak, such as might be made by a frog princess, and she said, "I must not tell anybody my name, but you are most kind, sir."

Dodger was aflame. "Why were those coves beating you up, miss? Can you tell me *their* names?"

Once again there was the sorry voice. "I should not."

"Then may I hold your hand, miss, on this chilly night?" It was, he thought, a Christian thing to do—or so he had heard. Slightly to his amazement, the girl did indeed reach out and take his hand. He clasped it and very carefully looked at the ring on her finger, and thought: A lot of gold here, and a crest; oh my word, a boy can get into trouble with a crest. A crest with eagles on it and foreign lingo. A ring that meant something, Charlie had said; a ring that somebody most certainly wouldn't want to lose. And somehow those eagles looked rather vicious.

She noticed his interest. "He said he loved me . . . my husband. Then he let them beat me. But my mother always said that if anyone got to England, they would be free. Do not let them take me back, sir—I do not want to go."

He leaned over and whispered, "Miss, I ain't no sir, I'm Dodger."

Sleepily, the girl said in what Dodger figured was a German accent, "Dodger? One who dodges, which is to say, moves about a lot? Thank you, Dodger. You are kind, and I am tired."

Dodger just managed to catch the glass as she slumped back into the pillows.

CHAPTER TWO

In which Dodger meets a dying man and
a dying man meets his Lady;
and Dodger becomes king of the toshers

As THE BELLS TOLLED five o'clock, Mrs. Sharples woke up, making a noise that could best be expressed as *blort!* Her eyes filled with venom when they alighted on Dodger and subsequently scoured the room for indications of malfeasance.

"All right, you young castle, you have had your nice warm sleep in a Christian bedroom, as promised—and, as I suspect, for the first time. Now just you get out of here, and mind! I shall be watching you like a fork until you're out of the back door, you mark my words."

Nasty and ungrateful oh those words were, and she was as good as them, marching him down the grubby back stairs and into the kitchen, where she flung open the door with such a force that it bounced on its hinges and slammed itself shut again, much to the amusement of the cook, who had been watching the performance.

As the door hung there reproachfully, Dodger said, "You heard Mister Charlie, missus, he is a very important man, and

he gave me a mission, and I have a mission so I reckon, and a missionary gets a bite of breakfast before he is slung out into the cold. And I don't think Mister Charlie would be too happy if I told him about the lack of hospitality you've shown to me, Mrs. Sharp Balls."

He had mangled her name offensively without a thought, and was rather pleased, even though she appeared not to have noticed. The cook, however, had, and the laugh she laughed had a sneer in it. Dodger had never read a book, but if he had ever done so, he would have read the cook just like it—and it was amazing how much you could glean from a look, or a snort, or even a fart if it was dropped into the conversation at just the right place. There was language, and there was the language of inflections, glances, tiny movements in the face— little bits of habit that the owner was not aware of. People who thought that their faces were entirely blank did not realize how they were broadcasting their innermost thoughts to anyone with the gumption to pick up the signs, and the sign right now, floating in the air as if held by an angel, said that the cook did not like the housekeeper, and the dislike was sufficient enough that she would make fun of her even though Dodger was standing there.

So he carefully made himself look a little more tired and a little more frightened and a little more pleading than usual. Instantly the cook motioned him toward her, saying in a low voice, but not so low that the housekeeper couldn't hear it, "Okay, lad, I've got some porridge on the boil—you can have some of that, and a piece of mutton that's only slightly on the nose, and I daresay you've eaten worse. Will that do you?"

Dodger burst into tears; they were good tears, full of soul

and fat—there was a certain amount of body to them—and then he fell on his knees, clasped his hands together, and said, with deep sincerity, "God bless you, missus, God bless you!"

This shameless pantomime earned him a very large bowl of porridge with a very acceptable amount of sugar in it. The mutton wasn't yet at the stage when it was about to start walking around all by itself, and so he took it thankfully; it would at least make the basis of a decent stew. It was wrapped in newspaper, and he shoved it in his pocket very quickly for fear that it might evaporate. As for the porridge, he pushed the spoon around until there was not one drop left, to the obvious approval of the cook, a lady it might be said who wobbled everywhere one could wobble when she moved, including the chin.

He had written her down as an ally, at least against the housekeeper, who was still glaring at him balefully, but then she grabbed him sharply by the hand and shouted, much louder than necessary, "Just you come down here into the scullery and we'll see how much you have stolen, my lad, shall we?"

Dodger tried to pull out of her grip, but she was, as aforesaid, a well-built woman—as cooks tend to be—and as she was dragging him, she leaned toward him and hissed, "Don't struggle. What are you, a bloody fool? Keep mum and do as I say!" She opened a door and dragged him down some stone steps, into a place that smelled of pickles. After slamming the door behind them, she relaxed a little and said, "That old baggage of a housekeeper will swear blind that you must have picked up a lot of trinkets when you were here last night, and you may be sure that the picker-up of said trifles will be that lady herself. Therefore it would be very likely that any

friendships you have made here will vanish like the morning dew. The family are decent sorts, always a soft touch for a hard-luck story from a broken-down artisan or fallen woman who would like to get up again, and I've seen them come and go. Quite a lot of them are genuine, let me tell you, I know."

As politely as possible, Dodger tried to remove her hands from his person. She seemed to be patting him down rather more than was warranted and with a certain enthusiasm and a gleam in her eye.

She saw his expression and said, "I ain't always been this old fat baggage; I fell once and bounced back up again. That's the way to think about it, lad. Anyone can rise if they have enough yeast. I was not always like this; oh, you would be amazed and probably quite amused—and I might say in one or two cases embarrassed."

"Yes, missus," said Dodger. "And would you please stop patting."

She laughed, causing an oscillation of chins, and then rather more solemnly said, "The kitchen maid told me that the talk is that you helped save some sweet girl from ruffians last night, and I know, I just *know* you will get blamed for something unless I show you the lay of the land. So, little fellow, you just give Aunty Quickly here anything you is thinking of running away with, and I will see it gets put back where it belongs. I like this family and I won't have them robbed, even by a lively lad such as yourself. So if you own up now, all sins will be forgiven and you will walk out of here without a stain on your character, although I wish I could say the same about the stains on the rest of you." Her nose wrinkled as she took in the state of his trousers.

Smirking, Dodger handed her one silver spoon, saying, "One spoon, and only because I was still holding it when you dragged me down here!" Then he pulled out the pack of cards. "And this, missus, was handed to me by Mister Dickens."

Nevertheless, but with a grin, the cook patted him down again right there and then, finding his knife, his brass knuckles, and his short crowbar; she pointedly ignored them but also made him take his shoes off for inspection, whereupon she winced at the smell, with a hand theatrically over her nose, and made it clear that she wanted him to put them on again as quickly as possible. She said cheerfully, "Not got nothing up your jacksie, yes? Wouldn't be the first to have tried. No, I ain't going to look; you've got more meat on your ribs than most of your type, which means you are rather innocent, or very clever; I trust that it is the latter, and would be most surprised if it is the former. Now what we'll do next is that I'll drag you upstairs, shouting at you like the scum you are, so that the old baggage can hear. What I shall shout is that I've searched you thoroughly at risk to my own health and are throwing you out absolutely empty-handed. After that I will kick you out the door on the toe of my boot for the look of the thing, and then I'll get on with my work, which will be all the more enjoyable when I think of the nasty old boot seething like a cauldron of bees." She gave Dodger a long look as if sizing him up and said, "You're on the tosh, ain't you?"

"Oh yes, missus."

"A lot of work for not much money, so I hear."

Never tell anybody everything. So he said, "Oh well, I don't know, missus, I just makes a living."

"Now, come on, let's do the pantomime for them as is

surely listening, and off you go, but remember—come and see Quickly if you ever feel the need for a friend. I mean what I say; if I can ever help you, you just have to whistle. And if I knock on your door in hard times, don't leave it shut."

Outside, the sun was hardly visible in the smoke, mist, and fog, but that was the clear light of day for somebody like Dodger. A bit of sunshine was okay, he would agree, because it helped your clothes dry, but Dodger liked the shadows and, if possible, the sewers, and right now something in him wanted the solace of darkness.

So he crowbarred the lid of the nearest drain cover and dropped onto what wasn't all that bad a surface down below. The storm last night had been kind enough to make the sewers just that bit more bearable. There would be other toshers down there, of course, but Dodger had a nose for gold and silver.

Solomon said his dog, Onan, had a nose for jewelry. Indeed, Dodger was happy to give him the honor, because you had to feel sorry for the poor creature, who was really quite embarrassing at times, but for some reason the dog's pointy little face did actually light up whenever he smelled rubies. Sometimes Dodger would take him down into the gloom with him, and if Onan's amazing nose found wealth down there in the darkness, then when they got back home Solomon would give him extra chicken gizzards.

Dodger wished he had the dog with him today—for Onan had ears so good that he could hear a sudden shower miles upstream, and would bark accordingly—but he had started in the wrong area without the time to go and fetch him, so he had to make do the best he could, which after all was pretty good at that. If you were smart on your feet, like Dodger, you'd have grabbed your loot and been up in the fresh air long before the first surge of storm water came down the sewers.

But it was as if last night's storm had emptied the sky. It was as calm as a millpond down in the tunnels today: small puddles here and there, with a little trickle down the center of the sewer. After the storm, it mostly smelled like, well, wet dead things, rotten potatoes and bad air—and these days, unfortunately, shite. This always infuriated Dodger. From what Solomon told him, some coves called the Romans had built the sewers to keep the rainwater flowing down to the Thames instead of pouring into people's houses. But these days toffs here and there were getting pipes run from their cesspits into the sewers, and Dodger thought this was really unfair. It was bad enough with all the rats down here, without having to make certain you didn't step in a richard.*

A fair amount of light filtered down from the gutters through the drain covers, which themselves had holes in them to keep the water from running away, but really, being a tosher meant that you felt around—with fingers, and toes sometimes—for all those little *heavy* things that would get caught up on the crumbling brickwork as the water went past. But you had to search with your mind and your instinct as well, and that was the soul and center of being a tosher—old Grandad had taught him that, telling him that it could get so much a part of you that you could smell the gold even among the richards.

*Cockney rhyming slang, short for Richard the Third, which rather happily rhymes with another interesting word.

Dodger didn't know much about the Romans, but the sewers they had built were old and in a general state of falling to bits. Oh, gangs came down here to patch things up occasionally, but it was always a case of a bit of work here and a bit of work there, seldom anything very substantial. The work gangs—who were handed an official job occasionally, shoring up and repairing bits of the ever-crumbling sewers— would chase you off if they found you, though they were not as young as Dodger, so he could easily leave them behind. Besides, they were working men with working hours, and a tosher might work all night on a good night, feeling in those little places where a brick had fallen out of the wall, or the floor was not level. Best of all were the places where the water would swirl around in a little whirlpool, causing pennies, sixpences, farthings, half farthings, and—if you were very, very blessed—sometimes even sovereigns, half sovereigns, and crowns to collect; maybe even brooches, silver hatpins, eyeglasses, watches, and golden rings. They would all swirl around in this dark carousel, a great spinning ball of sticky mud which, if you were a lucky tosher and believed in the Lady of the Toshers, then you—yes, you—might be the lucky tosher who one day found a ball of mud like a big plum pudding. This was that wonderful thing known to the toshers as the *tosheroon*, which when you smashed it open would deliver unto you a fortune of a lifetime.

Dodger had found all of those things separately at some time or other, and occasionally one or two together in a little nest in a crack, which he would make a note of in his head and, of course, return to again. But while he could often come back with some goods that would make Solomon smile, he had never come across that great pie of dirt and jewels and money that was the key to a better life.

But, he thought, what better life was there than a life on the tosh, at least if you were a Dodger? The world, which meant London, was built for him, just for him; it worked in his favor as if the Lady had meant it. Gold, jewels, and currency were heavy and got trapped easily, while dead cats, rats, and richards tended to float, which was a good thing because you never like to tread in a dickie—thank goodness they floated. But, Dodger mused, as he almost absentmindedly but very methodically felt his way along the sewer, taking care to cover his favorite traps while at the same time keeping an eye out for any new ones, whatever would a tosher do if he got hold of such a thing as a real tosheroon? He knew them, the tosher lads, and when they had a good day, what did they do with their loot? What did they do with all the hard-earned money they had splashed through the muck for? They drank it, and the bigger the amount, the more they drank. Maybe if they were sensible ones, they'd put a bit aside for a bed for the night and a meal; in the morning they would be poor again.

There was a *clink* under his fingers! That was the sound of two sixpences together in the spot he called Old Faithful—a good start.

Dodger knew that he had the edge on the other toshers; that was why he had broken every tosher rule and gone into a sewer during the storm, and it would have worked too if it hadn't been for that fight and what had followed. Because if you had your eye to business, you could see places in the sewers where a tosher could hang on in a bubble of air while all around him the world raged. He'd found a good one, and while it was damned chilly, he would have been the first one down in this vicinity to reap the harvest of the night. Right now he had to hurry because other toshers would be coming up the sewers toward him, and suddenly there was a glint in the gloom as the sun caught something. It went away instantly, but he had marked it in his mind, and so he worked his way carefully to where his head told him the glint had been and found a pile of muck on a little sandbank where the outflow of a smaller sewer flowed into this one; it was still dribbling.

There it was—a dead rat, and in its jaws what looked like a gold tooth but turned out to be, as it happened, a half sovereign gripped tightly in the teeth of Mister Rat. You never, if you could help it, touched a rat, which was why Dodger carried a little crowbar with him down there. Using it together with his knife, he levered the nasty little jaws open and flicked the half sovereign out. Balancing the coin on the blade of his knife, he held it up to the trickle coming down the wall, giving it something of what you might call a wash.

May every day be as good as this! Who would be a working-man on such a day? A skilled chimney sweep would have to work for a week to get the money he had picked up today. Oh, to be a tosher on a day like this!

Then he heard the groan. . . .

Dodger edged his way round the rat and into the smaller sewer, which was half choked with debris—much of it pieces of wood, some of them sharp as knives—and all the other detritus that had last night been dislodged. But to Dodger's astonished gaze it appeared that most of the debris was a man, and that man did not look well; there was nothing very much where one eye should have been, but the other one was opening now, and it looked Dodger in the face. It stank, the face Dodger looked into, and he shuddered, because he knew it.

He said, "That's you, Grandad, isn't it?"

The oldest tosher in London looked as if he had been tortured, and Dodger almost threw up when he saw the rest of him. He must have been working by himself, just like Dodger, and got caught up when the flood came down, and there would have been everything in it, anything that someone had thrown away or lost or wanted to hide and dispose of. A lot of it had apparently smashed into Grandad, who was nevertheless trying to sit upright, covered in bruises, bleeding and colored with all sorts of nastiness such as only a flooded sewer could provide.

Grandad spat mud—at least, Dodger hoped it was only mud—and said weakly, "Oh, it's you, Dodger. Good to see you in such fine fettle, in a manner of speaking; you're a good lad, I always said so, smarter than I ever was, see. So what I want you to do now, right now, is to get a pint of the worst brandy you can find, and bring it back down here and pour it down this thing what used to be my throat, right?"

Dodger tried to pull some of the stuff away from the old man, who groaned and mumbled, "Trust me on this one. I am banged about like nobody's business, fool that I am, and at my age too! Should have known better, silly old fool. I reckon I have eaten more than my peck today and so it's time to die. Be a lovely lad and get me the liquor right now, there's a good boy; there's a sixpence and a crown and five pennies in my right hand, and they're still there 'cos I can feel it, and that is all for you, my lad, you lucky boy."

"Here," said Dodger, "I'm not taking anything from you, Grandad!"

The old tosher shook his head, such as was left of it, and said, "Firstly I ain't your grandad really, you boys only give me the name just 'cos I'm older than what you lot are, and by the Lady you *will* take my stuff when I'm gone, 'cos you are a tosher and a tosher will take what he finds! Now, I knows where I am and I knows there is a bottle shop just around the corner, up there downstream. Brandy, I said, the worst they've got, and then remember me fondly. Now piss off right now, or be followed by the curse of a dying tosher!"

Dodger came out of the next drain cover at a run, found the rather greasy bottle shop, bought *two* bottles of a brandy that smelled as if it could cut a man's leg off, and was back climbing down the drain almost before the echoes of his leaving Grandad died away.

Grandad was still there, and was dribbling something cruel, but there was almost a smile when he saw Dodger, who handed him the first open bottle, which he threw down his throat in one long glug. Some of it spilled out of his mouth as he beckoned for the other, saying, "This will suit me right enough, oh yes indeed, just the way a tosher should go." Then his voice dropped to a whisper, and with his one relatively good hand he grabbed at Dodger and said, "I *saw* her, lad; the Lady, standing large as life just where you are now, all crimson and gold and shining like the sun on a sovereign. Then she blew me a kiss and beckoned to me and scarpered, only in a ladylike way, of course."

Dodger didn't know what to say but managed to say it

anyway. "You've taught me a lot, Grandad. You taught me about the Lady of the Rats. So look, get the taste of the sewer out of your mouth, and then I reckon I can pull you out of here to somewhere better. Let's give it a try, *please?*"

"Not a chance, lad. I reckon if you were to pick me up right now, I'd fall to bits, but if you don't mind you will find the time to stay with me for a little while." In the darkness there was another liquid noise as Grandad took a further draft of the fiery brandy and went on, "You was a bloody good learner, I will say that for you; I mean most of the lads I see doing it just don't have the nose for toshing, but it done me good all these years to see how you was treating toshing like one of them professors going through all them books. I seen you just look at a whole pile of shite and your eyes would twinkle like you *knew* that there was definitely something worthwhile under there. That's what we do, lad—we find value in what them above throw away, what they don't care about. And that means people too. I seen you toshing, lad, and knew you had toshing in your blood, just like me." He coughed, and bits of his broken body moved in a rather ghastly dance. "I know what they call me, Dodger—king of the toshers. The way I see it, that's you now and you have my blessing on it." What was left of his mouth smiled. "Never did know who your dad was, did you, lad?"

"No, Grandad," said Dodger. "Never knew and probably neither did my ma; don't know who *she* was neither." Water dripped off the ceiling as Dodger stared at nothing much and said, "But you were always Grandad to me, I certainly know that, and if you hadn't given me the knowing of the toshing, I would never have found out about all of them places down here in a month of Sundays, like the Maelstrom and the Queen's Bedroom and the Golden Maze and Sovereign Street and Button Back Spin and Breathe Easy. Oh yes, that place saved my bacon a dozen times when I was still learning! Thank you for that, Grandad. Grandad . . . ? Grandad!"

Then Dodger was aware of something in the air, or perhaps the subtle sound of something that had been there and then gently ceased to be so. But there was still something there; and as Dodger leaned over, he felt something carried on the last breath and was simply hovering as Grandad said, from wherever he was now, "I can see the Lady, lad, I can see the Lady. . . ."

Grandad was smiling at him, and went on smiling until the light in his eyes faded, when Dodger then leaned down and respectfully opened the man's hand to take the legacy that was duly his. He counted out two coins, which he solemnly placed on the dead man's eyes because, well, it was something you had to do because it had always been done. Then he looked into the gloom and said, "Lady, I am sending to you Grandad, a decent old cove who taught me all I know about the tosh. Try not to upset him 'cos he swears something cruel."

He came out of the sewer as if Hell and all its demons were following behind him. Suspecting that it might well be so, he ran the short distance to Seven Dials and the comparative civilization that was in the little tenement attic where Solomon Cohen lived and worked and did business in a small room above a flight of stairs, which being high up gave him a view of things that he probably did not want to see.

CHAPTER THREE

Dodger gets a suit that is tough
on the unmentionables,
and Solomon gets hot under the collar

IT WAS RAINING AGAIN as Dodger got to the attic, a dreadful somber drizzle. He fretted outside while the old man went through his convoluted process of unlocking the door, then spun Solomon round when he hurtled through. Solomon was old enough and wise enough to let Dodger lie in a smelly heap on the old straw mattress at the back of the attic until he was ready to be alive again, and not just a bundle of grief. Then Solomon, like his namesake being very wise indeed, boiled up some soup, the smell of which filled the room until Onan, who had been sleeping peacefully beside his master, woke up and whined, a sound like some terrible cork being twisted out of an awful bottle.

Dodger uncoiled himself from the blanket, gratefully took the soup that Solomon handed wordlessly to him, and then the old man went back to his workbench with its pedal-powered lathe, and soon there was a homely, busy little noise that would have made Dodger think of grasshoppers in a field, if he had ever seen a grasshopper or, for that matter, a field. Whatever you thought it was, though, it was comforting, and as the soup did its work of recovery and the grasshoppers danced, Dodger told the old man, well, everything—about the girl, about Charlie, about Mrs. Quickly and about Grandad—and Solomon said not one word until Dodger was empty of words of his own, and then he murmured, "You had a busy day, bubele, and a great shame about your friend, Grandad, mmm may his soul rest comfortably."

Dodger wailed, "But I left him there to be eaten by rats! He told me to!"

Sometimes Solomon talked as if he had just woken up and remembered something; a curious little mmm sound that came out something close to the chirping of a little bird, heralding what he had to say next. Dodger never really understood what the automatic mmm stood for. It was a friendly noise and it seemed to him that Solomon was winding up for the next thought; you got used to it after a while and missed it when it wasn't there.

Now Solomon said, "Mmm, was that any better or worse than being eaten by worms? It is the fate of all mankind, alas. You were with him when he died mmm, his friend? So that is a good thing. I have met the gentleman in the past, and I suppose he must be mmm oh, thirty-three? A very good age for a tosher and from what you say he saw his Lady. Sad to reflect that I myself am mmm fifty-four though thankfully in good health. You were lucky to meet me, Dodger, just as I indeed was lucky to meet you. You know about keeping clean and about putting money by. We boil water before we drink it, and I'm pleased to say I have mmm made you aware of the possibility of cleaning your teeth, which is why mmm, my dear, you still have some. Grandad died as he had lived and so you will remember him fondly but not mourn unduly. Toshers die young; what else can you expect if you spend half your life messing about in mess? You never see a Jewish tosher, you can't be a kosher tosher! Remember fondly your friend Grandad, and learn what lessons you can from his life and death." And the grasshoppers continued to dance, sizzling as they did so.

Dodger could now hear a fight down in the street somewhere. Well, there was always a fight; fights sprouted up like a fungus, usually because a lot of people all pushed together in these wretched, dirty slums ended up not just at the end of their tether but right off it completely. He had heard people say that the drink was behind it all, but well, you *had* to drink beer. Yes, too much of it made you drunk, but on the other hand water out of the pump might quite likely make you dead, unless you boiled it first and had the money for coal or wood. That had to wait its turn, after the food and the beer (usually the other way around).

He thought, I believe that Grandad had the death he wanted. But surely no one should want a death like that? I can't say it would do for me. There was suddenly another thought: If that isn't what I want, then what is it I should strive for? It was a surprising little thought, one of those that hangs around out of general view until it pops up like a wart. He placed it behind his ear, as it were, for future deliberation.

Solomon was talking again. "Mmm, as for your Mister Charlie, I've heard of him down at the synagogue. He is a sharp cove, he is, sharp as a razor, sharp as a snake, so they tell

me. They say he can take one look at you and he's got a perfect study of you, from the way you talk down to the way you
pick your nose. He is in with the police too, as tight as a tick
with them, so now old Solomon is thinking, why did a man
like him give a job of police work to mmm a snotty-nosed
tosher like you? And it is snotty—I know you know how to
use a wipe mmm, I taught you how; just sucking it down
and spitting it out on the pavement is distasteful. Are you
listening? If you don't want to end up like poor old Grandad,
then you'd better end up like somebody else, and a good start
mmm would be to *look* like someone else, especially mmm if
you are to do this work for that Mister Charlie. So while *I* am
making the dinner, I want *you* to go to see my friend Jacob,
down at the shonky shop. Tell him I sent you, and that he
is to dress you from head to toe with decent schmutter for
one shilling, including boots, and mind you mention that last
word. Maybe you could think of it as spending part of your
legacy mmm from the late Mister Grandad? And while you're
about it, take Onan with you—he could do with the exercise,
poor old thing."

Dodger had started to argue before he realized that this
would be stupid. Solomon was right; if you lived on the
streets, that's where you died, or perhaps, as in the case of old
Grandad, underneath them. And it seemed the right thing
somehow to spend part of his gift from Grandad—and the
bounty from the sewers—on smartening himself up a bit,
and it *would* help to look better if he was to try this new line
of work. . . . He liked the idea of more specie from Mister
Charlie. Besides, if you were going to help a lady in distress,
it paid to look smart while you were doing so.

He set off, trailed by Onan, who was overjoyed at going out in daylight, and you just had to hope that he didn't get carried away. For all dogs smell—this being a chief, nay essential, component of being a dog when being able to smell and be smelled is of great importance—but it had to be said that Onan not only smelled like every other dog; he introduced a generous portion of Onan smell into the mix as well.

They headed for the shonky shop to see Jacob and, if Dodger remembered correctly, Jacob's rather strange wife whose wig, however you looked at it, never quite seemed to be right. Jacob ran a pawnshop as well as the shonky shop, and Dodger knew that Solomon suspected that Jacob also bought things without troubling himself where they came from, although he never said why he suspected that.

The pawnshop was where you took your tools if you were out of work, and where you bought them back again when you were back in the job, because it's easier to eat bread than eat hammers. If you were really skint, you popped your unnecessary clothes too; well, at least some of them. If you never turned up to buy them back, they would go into the shonky shop, where Jacob and his sons worked all day sewing and mending and cutting and seaming and generally turning old clothes into if not *new* clothes, at least into something *respectable*. Dodger found Jacob and his sons quite friendly.

Jacob greeted Dodger with an expensive grin, which is one where the seller hopes that the buyer is going to buy something. He said, "Why, it's my young friend who once saved the life of my oldest friend, Solomon, and—put that dog outside!"

Onan was tied up in the little yard behind the shop with

a bone to worry at—and good luck to him in that endeavor, Dodger thought, since any bone that got given to a dog in old London town had already had all the goodness boiled out of it for soup. This didn't seem to trouble Onan all that much, and so he snuffled and crunched in happy optimism, and Dodger was ushered back inside, made to stand in the very small space available in the middle of the shop, and treated like a lord going to one of the nobby shops you found in Savile Row and Hanover Square, although quite probably in those places the clothes you put on hadn't already been worn by four or five people before you.

Jacob and his sons bustled around him like bees, squinting at him critically, holding up only slightly yellow "white" shirts in front of him and then whisking them away before the next tailor was magically there, holding up a pair of highly suspect pants. Clothes spun past, never to reappear, but never mind because here came some more! It was: "Try these, oh dear no"; or, "How about this? Certain to fit, oh no, never mind, plenty more for a hero!"

But he hadn't been a hero, not really. Dodger remembered that day three years ago when he had been having a really bad afternoon on the tosh, and it had started to rain, and he had heard that somebody else had picked up a sovereign just ahead of him so he was feeling angry and irritable and wanted to take all that out on someone. But when he was back on the foggy streets, there had been two geezers kicking the crap out of somebody on the pavement. Quite possibly, in those days, when his temper was more liable to explode into a spot of boots and fists, if some little wheel in his head had turned the wrong way, he might have helped *them*, just to get it out of his system. But as it happened the wheel turned the other way, toward the thought that two geezers kicking an old cove who was lying on the ground groaning were pox-ridden mucksnipes. So he had waded in and laid it on with a trowel, just like last night, hadn't he indeed, panting and kicking until they cried uncle and he was too tired to chase them.

It had been a madness born of frustration and hunger, although Solomon said it was the hand of God, which Dodger thought was pretty unlikely since you never saw God in those streets very often. Then he had helped the old man home, even if he was an ikey mo, and Solomon had brewed up some of his soup, thanking Dodger fulsomely the whole time. Since the old boy lived by himself and had a bit of space to spare in his tenement attic, it all worked out. Dodger ran the occasional errand for Solomon, scrounged wood for his fire, and, when possible, pinched coal off the Thames barges. In exchange, Solomon gave Dodger his meals, or at least cooked whatever it was Dodger had *acquired*, coming up with dishes much better than Dodger had ever seen in his life.

He also got much better prices for the stuff Dodger came back with from the toshing; the drawback of this was that the old Jew would always, *always* ask him if what he was buying was stolen. Well, stuff from the sewers was definitely okay—everybody knew that. It was money down the drain, lost to humanity, on its way to the sea and out of human ken. Toshers, of course, didn't count as humanity—everybody knew that too. But in those days Dodger was not above a bit of thievery, getting stuff you could say was extremely dodgy and totally not, as Solomon would say, "kosher."

Every time the old man asked him if this stuff was just

from the toshing, Dodger said yes, but he could tell by the look in Solomon's eyes when the old man thought that he was not telling the truth. The worst of it was that Solomon's eyes invariably got it right. He would take the stuff anyway, but things would be a little bit chilly in the attic room for a while.

So now Dodger generally nicked only stuff that could be burned, drunk, or eaten, such as the stuff on market stalls and other low-hanging fruit. Things had warmed up after that, and besides, Solomon read the newspapers down at the synagogue, and occasionally there would be sad little pieces in the Lost and Found column from somebody who had lost their wedding ring or some other piece of jewelry. And it was jewelry that was more to be valued, well, because it *was* the wedding ring, wasn't it, and not just a certain amount of gold. There were often the magic words "Reward to finder," and with a certain amount of careful negotiation, Solomon pointed out, you could get rather more for it than you would get from a fence. Besides, you would never take it to a kosher jeweler, because they would set the police on you even though you'd merely "found" it, not stolen it. Sometimes honesty was its own reward, said Solomon, but Dodger thought it helped if some money came with it.

Money apart, Dodger found he felt happier on those days when he had indeed been able to bring somebody back in touch with some treasured necklace or ring, or any other trinket that they held dear; it made him walk on air for a while, which was indeed a cut above what he was normally treading on in the sewers.

One day, after a kiss from a lady who had recently been

a blushing bride and whose wedding ring had unfortunately come off her finger while she was getting into the carriage to go to her new home, he had said to Solomon, because some of the other toshers had been teasing him a lot, "Are you trying to save my soul?" And Solomon, with a little grin that was never far from his face, said, "Mmm, well, I am exploring the possibility that you may have one."

That little change in his habits, which helped glue together the relationship with Solomon, meant that he didn't—unlike some of the other toshers—have to shiver in doorways of a night, or hunker down under a piece of tarpaulin, or pay for the dreadful stinking ha'penny rope down at the flophouse. All Solomon wanted from him was a bit of company in the evenings, and occasionally the old man tactfully required Dodger's companionship when he was going to see one of his customers and therefore carrying mechanisms, jewelry, and other dangerously expensive things. In the vicinity, news of Dodger's mercurial personality had got about, and so he and Solomon could travel entirely unmolested.

As jobs went, Dodger thought Solomon's was pretty good. The old boy made small things—usually things to replace things, precious and treasured things that had gone missing. Last week Dodger had seen him repair a very expensive musical box, which was full of gears and wires. The whole thing had been damaged when some workmen had dropped it as the owners were moving house, and he had watched the old man handle every single piece as if it was something special— cleaning, shaping, and gently bending, slowly, as if there was all the time in the world. Some ornamental ivory inlays had been broken on the rosewood cabinet, and Solomon replaced them with little bits of ivory from his small store, polishing it up so neatly he said that the lady he had done it for had given him half a crown over and above his normal charge.

Okay, sometimes some of Dodger's chums called him Shabbos goy, but he noticed that he ate better than any of them, and cheaper too, since among the market stalls Solomon could haggle even a Cockney until the man gave in—and Heaven help any stallholder who sold Solomon short weight, bad bread, or rotting apples, let alone a boiled orange and all the others tricks of the trade, including the wax banana. When you took into account the good and healthful eating, the arrangement was not to be sneezed at, and Dodger never liked to catch a cold.

When Jacob and his sons had got through with the dance of the flying pants, shirts, socks, vests, and shoes, they stood back and beamed at one another in the knowledge of a job well done, and then Jacob said, "Well now, I do not know. Upon my word, what magicians we are, ain't we? What we have created here, my sons, is a gentleman, fit for any society if they don't mind a slight smell of camphor. But it's that or moths, everybody knows, even Her Majesty herself, and right now I reckon, my dears, that if she walked in this door, she would say, 'Good afternoon, young sir, don't I know you?'"

"It's a bit tight in the crotch," said Dodger.

"Then don't think naughty thoughts until it stretches," said Jacob. "I'll tell you what I'll do. Seeing as it's you, I will throw in this excellent hat, just your size if you padded it out a bit so it ain't covering your ears, and I reckon the style will soon be all the rage again." Jacob stood back, mightily pleased with the transformation he had achieved. He put his head on one side and said, "You know, young man, what you need now is a very good haircut and then you will have to poke the ladies off with a stick!"

"Solomon helps me cut it when it gets too hot and I want things to cool off a bit," said Dodger, upon which Jacob gave the kind of explosive snort that only an offended Jewish tradesman could make, even more expressive than a Frenchman on a very bad day. Generally speaking, if it had to be written down, it would begin with something like "phooieu" and end with a certain amount of spittle in the general vicinity.

Jacob wailed, "That's not a haircut, my boy. You look like you've been sheared! As though you've just got out of the clink! If Queen Victoria saw you *then*, she'd probably call out the runners. Take my advice, next time go to a proper barber! Take the advice of your old friend Jacob."

And so, in company with the dog Onan, who was still optimistically carrying his bone in his jaws, Dodger walked back into the world. Of course, shonky was shonky, however you looked at it; it might just do, but it wasn't the full shilling. What around here was? Nevertheless, Dodger felt all the better for the new clobber, even with the associated crotch problem and a certain prickling under the arms, and it was certainly better than anything else he owned and hopefully worthy of the girl from the storm.

He walked back to the alley and climbed up the rickety stairs to the attic, where Solomon greeted him with "Who are you, young man?"

On the table, spread out, were the contents of the Happy Families game. "Mmm, very interesting," said Solomon.

"This is a remarkable and mmm somewhat deadly device you have presented to me. It is mmm deceptively simple, but dark clouds soon gather."

"What?" said Dodger, looking at the brightly colored cards laid out on the table. "It looks like something for kids—though nothing like the Happy Family man and his wagon, which is strange. It's just a kids' game, ain't it?"

"Alas, yes it is," said Solomon. "I shall expand on my little theory. Every player is dealt a hand from the pack of cards, and the object appears to be to put together one complete family, *the happy family*, simply by asking one of your opponents if they have a particular card. It would seem a cheerful game for children, but in fact, if they only did but know it, the parents are setting the child on the way to be a poker player or, worse, a politician."

"What?"

"Allow me to elucidate," said Solomon, and after a glance at Dodger's blank face, "I mean *explain*, young man. It appears to go like this. In order to mmm get your happy family, you have to choose one family, and so you might as it were choose to collect all of the mmm baker family. You might think that all you need do is simply wait until it is your turn again, and boldly ask somebody to give you the next card you were looking for. It might be Miss Bun the baker's daughter. Why? Because mmm when the cards were dealt out at the start of the game, you had already got Mister Bun the baker, and so his daughter would be a step in the right direction. But beware! Your opponents might mmm, if you keep simply asking for a Bun, in their turn start asking *you* for a member of the Bun family; they may not be collecting the Buns themselves, but possibly they intend to get together a whole set of the mmm Dose family, the head of which is Mister Dose the doctor. They are asking you for a Bun when they need a Dose, because they had noticed your interest in Buns, and despite their longing for a Dose would rather use their turn mmm to put you off track while at the same time deprive you of a precious Bun!"

"Well, I would just lie and say I hadn't got it," said Dodger.

"Aha! As the game lumbers to its conclusion, your ownership of the disputed Bun will come to light, mmm yes indeed! And it will be a very sad day for you. You have to tell the truth, because if you don't tell the truth, you will never win the game. Thus this terrible battle wages, as you decide to forsake Buns now and see if your salvation might lie mmm in collecting the family of Mister Bung the brewer, despite the fact that your family is teetotal. You hope to put at least one of your enemies under a false impression of your real intentions, while all the time you must suspect that every single one of them, no matter how innocent mmm they appear to be, are trying by every strategy they can think of to foil your plans! And so the dreadful inquisition continues! Son learns to deceive father, sister learns to distrust father, and mother is trying to lose in order to keep the peace, and it is dawning on her that her children's facial expressions of fake desire or optimism to put others off the track might mmm trick an opponent into thinking in the wrong direction."

"Well," said Dodger, "that's like haggling in the marketplace. Everybody does it."

"And so the game comes to a conclusion, undoubtedly with tears before the end, not to mention shouting and the slamming of doors. In what way then does this make a family happy? Exactly what has been achieved?" Solomon stopped talking, his face very pink and upset.

Dodger had to think for a moment before he said, "It's only playing cards, you know; it's not as if it's important. I mean, it's not real."

This didn't satisfy Solomon, who said, "I have never played it, but nevertheless a child playing with their parent would have to learn how to deceive them. And you say this is all a game?"

Dodger thought again. A game. Not a game of chance like the Crown and Anchor man, where you might even walk away with a pocket full of winnings. But a game to play as a family? Who had *time* for family games? Only babies, or children of the toffs. "It's still just a game," he protested, and received one of Solomon's stares, which if you were not careful would go right through your face and out the back of your head.

Solomon said, "What's the difference when you are seven years old?" The old man had gone red, and he waved the finger of God at Dodger. "Young man, the games we play are lessons we learn. The assumptions we make, things we ignore, and things we change make us what we become."

It was biblical stuff, right enough. But when Dodger thought about it, what *was* the difference? The whole of life was a game. But if it was a game, then were you the player or were you the pawn? It seeped into his mind that maybe Dodger could be more than just Dodger, if he cared to put some effort into it. It was a call to arms; it said: *Get off your arse!*

The one thing you could say about this dirty old city, Dodger thought as he headed out of the attic, strutting along in his new suit with Onan at his heels, was that no matter how careful you were, *some*body would see *any*thing. The streets were so crowded that you were rubbing shoulders with people until you had no shoulders left; and the place to do a bit of rubbing now would be the Baron of Beef, or the Goat and Sixpence, or any of the less salubrious drinking establishments around the docks where you could get drunk for sixpence, dead drunk for a shilling, and possibly just dead for being so stupid as to step inside in the first place.

In those kinds of places you found the toshers and the mudlarks, hanging out with the girls, and that was really hanging out because half of them would have worn the arse out of their trousers by now. Those places were where you spent your time and your money so that you could forget about the rats and the mud that stuck to everything, and the smells. Although eventually you got used to them, corpses that had been in the river for a while tended to have a fragrance of their very own, and you never forgot that smell of corruption, because it clung, heavy and solid, and you never wanted to smell it again, even though you knew you would.

Oddly enough, the smell of death was a smell with a strange life of its own, and it would find its way in anywhere and it was damn hard to get rid of—rather, in some respects, like the smell of Onan, who was faithfully walking just behind him, his passage indicated by people in the throng looking around to see wherever the dreadful smell was coming from and hoping it wasn't from them.

But now the sun was shining, and some of the lads and lasses were drinking outside the Gunner's Daughter, sitting on the old barrels, bundles of rope, hopeless piles of rotting wood, and all the other debris of the riverside. Sometimes it seemed to Dodger that the city and the river were simply all the same creature except for the fact that some parts were a lot more soggy than others.

Right now, in this tangled, smelly, but usually cheerful disarray, he recognized Bent Henry, Lucy Diver, One-Armed Dave, Preacher, Mary-Go-Round, Messy Bessie, and Mangle, who despite whatever else was on their minds all said what people everywhere said in those circumstances when one of their number turned up wearing clothes that might be considered to be a cut above their station. Things like: "Oh dear, what is this pretty gentleman then?" and "Oh my, have you bought the street? Cor, don't you smell nice!" And, of course: "Can you lend us a shilling? I'll pay you on Saint Never's Day!" And so on, and the only way that you can survive in these circumstances is to grin sheepishly and put up with it, knowing that at any moment you could stop the merriment; and stop it he did.

"Grandad's dead." He dropped it on them out of the sky.

"Never!" said Bent Henry. "I was toshing with him only the day before yesterday, just before the storm!"

"And I saw him today," said Dodger sharply. "I saw him die, right there in front of me! He was thirty-three! Don't nobody say he ain't dead, 'cos he is, right? Down below Shoreditch around about the Maelstrom!"

Mary-Go-Round started to cry; she was a decent sort, with an air all the time of being from somewhere else and having only just arrived here. She sold violets to ladies during the season, and sold anything else she could get the rest of the time. She wasn't all that bad at being a pickpocket, on account of looking very much like an angel what had been hit on the head with something, so she wasn't suspected, but however you saw her, she had more teeth than brains, and she didn't have many teeth. As for the others, they just appeared a bit more miserable than they had before; they didn't look him in the eye, just stared down at the ground as if they wished that they weren't there.

Dodger said, "He gave me his haul, such as it was." Feeling awkwardly as if this was not enough, he then added, "That's why I came here, to buy you all a pie and porter to drink his health." This news appeared to raise the spirits of all concerned more than somewhat, especially when Dodger reached into his pocket and disembogued himself of sixpence that magically became tankards all round of a liquid so thick that it was food.

While these were being emptied with variations on the theme of "glug," Dodger noticed that Mary-Go-Round was still sniveling, and being a kind sort of cove, he said softly, "If it's any help, Mary, he was smiling when he went; he said he'd seen the Lady."

This information apparently didn't satisfy, and in between sobs Mary said, "Double Henry stopped off just now for some grub and some brandy, seeing as how he'd just had to pull another girl out of the river."

Dodger sighed. Double Henry was a waterman, constantly paddling his way up and down the Thames looking for anyone who wanted transport. The rest of Mary's news was unfortunately quite familiar. The gang of people who were more or less his own age that Dodger met most often were a tough bunch, and so they survived; but the city and its river were harsh indeed on the ones who didn't make the grade.

"He reckoned she'd jumped off the bridge in Putney," said Mary. "Probably up the duff."

Crestfallen, Dodger sighed again. They usually were with child, he thought: the girls from faraway places with strange-sounding names like Berkhamstead and Uxbridge, who had come to London hoping it would be better than a life among the hayseeds. But the moment they arrived, the city in all its various ways ate them and spat them out, almost always into the Thames.

That was no way to go, since you could only call what was in the river "water" because it was too runny to be called dirt. When the corpses came to the surface, the poor old water-men and lightermen had to gaff them and row them down to the coroner of one of the boroughs. There was a bounty for turning over these sad remnants to the coroner's office, and Double Henry had told him once that sometimes it was worthwhile to take a corpse quite a long way to get to the borough that was paying the most, though it was generally the coroner at Four Farthings. The coroner would post notice of the dead person and sometimes, Dodger had heard, the notice got into the newspapers. Maybe the girls' bodies would end up in Crossbones Graveyard, or a paupers' burying ground somewhere else, and sometimes, of course, as everybody knew, they would end up in the teaching hospitals and under the scalpels of the medical students.

Mary was still sniveling, and in a conversation made up

largely of blobs of snot said, "It's so sad. They *all* have long blond hair. All the country girls have long blond hair and, well, they are also, you know, innocent."

Messy Bessie intervened with, "I was innocent once. But it didn't do me any good. Then I found out what I was doing wrong." She added, "But I was born on the streets here, knew what to expect. Them poor little innocents never stand a chance when the first kind gentleman plies them with liquor."

Mary-Go-Round sniffed again and said, "Gent tried to ply me with liquor once, but he ran out of money and I took most of what he had left when he fell asleep. Finest watch and chain I ever pinched. Still," she continued, "them poor girls wasn't born round here like the likes of us, so they don't know nothing."

Her words reminded Dodger of Charlie. Then his thoughts turned to Sol and what *he* had voiced earlier. He said, as much to the open air as anything else, "I should give up on the tosh-ing. . . ." His voice trailed off. Now he was talking to himself more than to anyone else. What *could* I do? he thought. After all, everybody has to work, everybody needs to eat, every-body has to live.

Oh, that smile on the face of Grandad; what had he seen in that last smile? He had seen the Lady. Toshers always knew somebody who had seen the Lady; nobody had ever seen her themselves, but nevertheless any tosher could tell you what she looked like. She was quite tall, had a dress that was all shiny, like silk; she had beautiful blue eyes and there was always a sort of fine mist around her, and if you looked down at her feet you would see the rats all sitting on her shoes. They said that if you ever saw her actual feet, they would be rat claws. But Dodger knew that he would never dare to look because supposing they were; or even worse, supposing they weren't!

All those rats, watching you and then watching her. Just maybe—he never knew—it would take only one word from her, and if you had been a bad tosher, she might set the rats on you. And if you were a very good tosher, she would smile on you and give you a great big kiss (some said a great deal more than just a kiss). And from that day on you would always be lucky on the tosh.

He wondered again about those poor wretched girls who'd jumped. Many of them, of course, were with child, and then because the barometer of Dodger's nature almost always gravitated to set "Fair," he let go that chain of thought. Generally speaking he had always tried to keep a distance between himself and grief; and besides, he had pressing business to attend to.

But not so pressing as to prevent him from raising his mug and shouting, "Here's to Grandad, wherever the hell he is now." This was echoed by all concerned—quite possibly, knowing them, in the hope of another round of drinks. But they were disappointed because Dodger continued, "Will you lot listen to me? On the night of the big storm, somebody was trying to kill a girl—one of them young innocents you was just talking about, I reckon—only she ran away, and I sort of found her, and now she is being looked after." He hesitated, faced with a wall of silence, and then carried on again, losing hope. "She had golden hair . . . and they beat her up, and I want to find out why. I want to kick seven types of shite out of the people who did it, and I want you to help me."

At this point Dodger was treated to a wonderful bit of street theater, which with barely a word being spoken went in three acts, the first being: "I don't know nuffin'," and the next, "I never saw nuffin'," and finally that old favorite, "I never done nuffin'," followed at no extra cost by an encore, which was that tried and tested old chestnut, "I wasn't there."

Dodger had expected something like this, even from his occasional chums. It wasn't personal, because nobody likes questions, especially when perhaps one day questions would be asked about you. But this was important to him, and so he snapped his fingers, which was the cue for Onan to growl—a sound that you could have expected might come not from a medium-size dog like Onan but from something dreadful arising from the depths of the sea, something with an appetite. It had a nasty rumble to it, and it simply did not stop. Now Dodger said, in a voice that was as flat as the rumble was bumpy, "Listen to me, will you? This is Dodger—me, right, your *friend* Dodger. She was a girl with golden hair and a face that was black and blue!"

Dodger saw something like panic in their eyes, as if they thought that he had gone mad. But then Messy Bessie's big round features seemed to shift as she struggled with the concept of something unusual, such as a thought.

She never had many of them; to see them at all you probably would need a microscope, such as the one he saw once in one of the traveling shows. There were always traveling shows, and they were ever popular; and in this one they had this apparatus you could stare into. You looked down into a glass of water, and when your eye got accustomed you started to see all the tiny little wriggly things in the water, bobbing up and down, spinning and dancing small jigs and having such fun that the man who ran the traveling show said it showed how good the Thames water was if so many tiny little creatures could survive in it.

To Dodger, Bessie's mind seemed to be like that—mostly empty, but every now and again something wriggling. He said, encouragingly, "Go on, Bessie."

She glanced at the others, who tried not to look at her. He understood, in a way. It didn't do to be known as somebody who told you the things they saw, in case those things included something someone did not want to get about. There were, around and about, people much worse than mudlarks and toshers—people who were handy with a shiv or a cutthroat razor and had not a glimmer of mercy in their eyes.

But now, in the eyes of Messy Bessie, there was an unusual determination. She didn't have golden hair—not much in the way of hair at all, in fact; and such as it was, the strands that remained were greasy and tended to roll themselves into strange little kiss curls. She fiddled with a "curl," then looked defiantly at the others and said, "I was doing a bit of mumping in the Mall, day before the storm, and a nobby coach went past with its door open, you see, and this girl jumped out and had it away down the street as if she was on fire, right? And two coves dropped off the thing, right, and legged it after her, spit arse, pushing people out of the way like they was not important." Messy Bessie stopped, shrugged, indicating that that was that. Her associates were idly looking around, but specifically not focusing on her, as if to make it quite clear that they had nothing to do with this strange and dangerously talkative woman.

But Dodger said, "What sort of coach?"

He kept his focus on Bessie, because he just knew that if he didn't, she suddenly would get very forgetful, and what he got, after some churning of recollection on Bessie's part, was: "Pricey, nobby, two horses." Messy Bessie shut her mouth firmly, an indication that she didn't intend to open it again unless there was the prospect of another drink. It was quite easy for Dodger to read her mind; after all, there was such a lot of space in there. He jingled the remaining coins in his pocket—the international language—and another light went on in Bessie's big round sad face. "Funny thing about that coach; when it went off there was a, like, squeal from one of the wheels, nearly as bad as a pig being killed. I heard it all down the road."

Dodger thanked her, sliding over a few coppers, and nodded at the rest of them, who looked as if a murder had just taken place there and then.

Then suddenly, Messy Bessie, the coins in her hand, said, "Just remembered something else. She was yelling, but I don't know what, on account of it being in some kind of lingo. The coachman too—he weren't no Englisher neither." She gave Dodger a sharp and meaningful look, and he handed over an extra couple of farthings, wondering as he did so if he could reclaim some of this necessary expenditure from Mister Charlie. He would have to keep a tally though, because Charlie was definitely not the kind of man you could run rings around.

As he walked away, Dodger wondered whether he should go and see the man; after all, he had important information now, didn't he? Information that had cost him money to acquire—a considerable amount of money, and possibly worth a bit more too if he put a shine on it. Although he knew it really wouldn't be sensible to get ambitious about the amounts paid to start with. . . .

He fumbled in his pocket, a receptacle that contained anything that Dodger could punch into it. There it was: the oblong piece of card. He carefully put all the letters together, and the numbers too; for after all, everybody knew where Fleet Street was. It was where all the news-papers were made, but to Dodger it was a halfway decent toshing area with one or two useful other tunnels nearby. The Fleet river itself was part of the sewer, and it was amazing what ended up in there. . . . He recalled with pleasure that once when he was exploring there, he had found a bracelet with two sapphires in it, and on the same day also a whole sovereign, which made it a lucky place, given that a decent haul from a day's toshing could often be as low as a handful of farthings.

So he set off, Onan still trotting obediently behind him. He walked on, lost in thought. Of course, Messy Bessie wasn't the sort to come up with something so helpful as a crest such as might have been seen on a nobleman's coach, and it dawned on Dodger that in any case, if the coach was doing such dirty deeds as taking young ladies to places they shouldn't be going to, someone might not want to put their crest on it. But a squeaky wheel would go on speaking until somebody did something about it. He didn't have much time, and that was all he had to go on, in a city with hundreds of coaches and other miscellaneous conveyances.

It is, he thought, probably going to be a little bit difficult, but if I have anything to do with it, the squeaky wheel will get the grease, the grease being Dodger. And possibly, he entertained in the privacy of his own head, the men involved might form a close acquaintance with the comfort of Dodger's fist. . . .

CHAPTER FOUR

Dodger discovers a new use
for a Fleet Street spike
and gains a pocketful of sugar

FLEET STREET WAS ALWAYS busy, day and night, because of all the newspapers, and today the Fleet was not so much running as oozing along the open drain in the center of the street. Dodger had heard stories about the Fleet sewers, especially the one about the pig that escaped from a butcher's shop one time and got down there and then into everywhere else, and since there is so much to eat in a sewer if you are a pig, it became enormously fat and nasty. Perhaps it would have been fun then to go and find it; on the other hand perhaps it wouldn't have been—those things had tusks! But right now, the only monsters in Fleet Street, he had been told, were the printing presses whose thumping made the pavement shake, and that demanded to be fed every day with a diet of politics, 'orrible murders, and death.

Of course, there are other events, but everybody liked an 'orrible murder, didn't they? And everywhere along the street, men were pushing trolleys and piles of paper, or running fast holding tight to smaller bits of paper in a terrible urgency to explain to the world what had happened, why it had happened, what should have happened, and sometimes why it hadn't happened at all, when in fact it did happen after all—and, of course, to tell everyone about all the people who had been 'orribly murdered. It looked a bustling place to be, and now he had to find the *Chronicle* in all of this, hampered by the fact that he wasn't very good at reading, especially big words like that.

In the end, a printer in a square hat pointed the way, while giving him a look that said, "Don't you dare steal anything here." A bit of a slander to Dodger's way of thinking, since toshing wasn't stealing—surely everybody knew that? Well, they did if they were a tosher.

He tied Onan to a rail, confident that nobody would steal him because of the peculiar smell, and walked up the steps to the *Morning Chronicle*, where he was understandably stopped by one of those men whose job it is to stop the kind of people who need stopping. The man looked as though he enjoyed his job, and he had a hat to prove it, and the face under the hat said, "Nothing here for the likes of you, boy, you have no business here and you can go and do your thieving somewhere else, you and your dreadful suit. Hah, looks like you've got it off a dead man!"

Dodger carefully did not change his expression, but stood up straight and said, "My business is with Mister Dickens! He gave me a mission!" While the man stared at him, he pulled out of his pocket Charlie's visiting card, and said, "And he gave me his card, and told me to meet him here; can you get that into your head, mister?"

The doorman looked daggers at him, but the name Dickens apparently had an effect here for some reason, because another man with a busy look came and stared at Dodger, stared again at the card, looked back at Dodger for one last stare, and said, "You might as well come in then; don't steal anything."

Dodger said, "Thank you, sir, I will try my very best not to."

He was ushered into a crowded little room filled with desks and clerks, all looking busy with that same sense of frightful importance he had seen out in the street. The clerk at the nearest desk—who looked like the cove in charge of all the rest—watched him like a frog watches a snake, his hand very close to a bell.

Dodger sat down on a bench by the door and waited. Already the fog was rising—it always was by this time of day—and it was creeping in now through the open door. It was like an airborne River Thames, coiling and shimmering as if someone had emptied a bucket of snakes over the street. Mostly it was yellow; often it was black, especially if the brickyards were working. The nearest clerk got up, gave Dodger another scowl, and very pointedly closed the door. Dodger gave him a happy smile, which obviously annoyed him; this was, after all, the point.

But there was nothing very much here to "find," anyway. Just paper, just lots of paper and cabinets and mugs and the smell of tobacco and books with pieces of paper stuck inside them, where somebody wanted to keep his place. But what Dodger noticed were the spikes on every clerk's desk. What was that all about? Each one was sticking right up in the air; there was a piece of wood at the bottom, but why put a spike twelve inches long sticking up where it could do somebody a terrible mischief?

Pointing at the nearest, he said to one of the clerks, in the tones of a simple lad who was only asking a question in the innocent pursuit of knowledge, "'Scuse me, mister, what's this all about, then?"

The young man sneered at him. "Don't you know anything? It just keeps the desk more tidy, that's all. In newspapers, the spike is where you put something that you have finished with or don't need anymore."

Dodger gave this information his attention and said, "Why don't you just throw the stuff away, instead of cluttering up the place?"

The clerk gave him a withering look. "Are you stupid? Supposing it turns out later that it was important? Then all we'd have to do is find it on the spike."

The other clerks looked up briefly while this was going on, and then they got back to doing whatever it was they did, but not before glaring at Dodger to make certain he knew that he was not very important here and that they were. He noticed, though, that their clothes weren't much better than his shonky stuff, although there was no point in saying so.

And so Dodger resigned himself to waiting. Right up until the moment a man with a mask over half of his face barged past the doorman—who had apparently just gone for a piss in the alley, as he was stumbling back, fumbling with the buttons on his trousers—and pushed into the room. The villain pointed a large knife at the head clerk and said, "Give me your money or I'll gut yer like a clam. And nobody move!"

It was a large knife—a bread knife, with a serrated edge, perfectly okay in a house where someone wanted to carve up a loaf and probably, Dodger thought, not too bad either for carving up a person. But in the horrified silence he realized that the most frightened person in the room was the man with the knife, who was glaring at the clerks and taking no notice at all of Dodger.

Dodger thought: He is not sure what to do, but he is sure that he might have to stab one of these noodles who are staring at him and wetting their pants—and he pretty well knows that if he does that, he will end up in Newgate Prison, swinging from the gallows. These thoughts arrived in Dodger's head like a railway train, and were followed in the caboose, as it were, with the recollection that he knew that voice and its accompanying smell of bad gin. And he knew that the man wasn't a bad sort, not really, and he knew what had turned him to this kind of deed.

He did the only thing possible. In one movement he grabbed the spike from the desk and let the pointy bit just prick the man's sweaty neck. Keeping his voice low and cheerful, he whispered to the wretched would-be thief, so quietly that the clerks wouldn't hear, "Drop the knife right now and run for it; either that or you will be breathing through three nostrils. Look, it's me, Dodger—you know Dodger." Then out loud he said, "We will have none of this around here, you bastard!"

He almost breathed the man's relief, and certainly breathed an awful lot of gin fumes as he dragged him out of the place and into the fog. The clerks began to yell blue murder while Dodger shouted out loudly, "I'll hold him, don't you worry about that!" He carried on walking the man out at speed, past the red-faced doorman and into the nearest alleyway, where he dragged the would-be thief—who, it could be said, was somewhat handicapped by his wooden leg, which had a little metal piece on the end of it—along a few yards and pushed him into a dark corner.

The alley smelled like alleys everywhere: largely of desperation and impatience—and now also of Onan, who had vented his spleen and other things in protest, adding to the aromas of the alley a medal-winning stench. Blessedly, the fog made a kind of blanket over them. It stank, of course, but so did the man whose trousers were so lively that quite probably they could have gone for a walk all by themselves.

Dodger heard with relief the sound of the knife being dropped to the ground. He kicked it into the shadows, then heaved the man by his collar and hustled him to the other end of the alley, crossed the street, and pulled him into a corner.

"Stumpy Higgins!" he said. "Blow me down if you aren't the dumbest thief I've ever met. You know, next time you come up before the beak, you will end up with the screws swinging on your ankles, you bloody idiot!" He sniffed and groaned. "Cor blimey, Stumpy, what a mess you are, ain't you? Do you ever take a wash? Or ever stand out in the rain or even change those trousers?" He looked into two eyes full of cataracts and sighed. "When did you last eat?"

Then Stumpy muttered something about not wanting to be a beggar, and Dodger nearly gave up on him, but the vision of Grandad was still in his mind.

"Look, here's sixpence," he said. "That should get you a

decent bite and a space in the flophouse, if you don't drink it all up. Okay, you poor old bugger, now off you go—no one else is chasing you, so just keep on moving and get out of the neighborhood. I've never seen you before in my life, I don't know who you are, and by the look of you, Stumpy, neither do you, you poor old devil." Dodger sighed. "Look, if you're going to hold up something, the time to get grogged up is after the business, not before, right?"

And that was it. Dodger went back to the *Chronicle* offices and there was a copper there already when he arrived, and the clerks were giving the man the particulars of the aforesaid Stumpy, which at the moment did not include the wooden leg. By the sound of their babbling, Stumpy was a lot more fearsome than Dodger knew him to be, and apparently his bread knife had become a real honest-to-God sword too. The policeman was trying to take down details, being hampered by the chattering of the clerks and the fact that he wrote things down very slowly, all the while keeping an eye on Dodger, because although the policeman might not have been that good at spelling he was very good at recognizing the likes of Dodger.

He knew what was coming, and here it came as the policeman poked a thumb in his direction and said, "This gentleman was an accomplice, yes?"

The clerks looked at Dodger, and somewhat reluctantly their chief said, "Well, no, in fact to tell the truth he threatened the miscreant with a spike and chased him away."

Dodger was beginning to really dislike the policeman, because the man said brightly, "Oh, so this man here had a weapon as well?"

The chief clerk said, "Well, no, I mean it's a spike, we have one on every desk."

There was a creak on the stair by the door and a voice said, "This young man is working for me, Constable, and may I say that Mister Dodger has my full confidence. It would appear that he is a hero of epic proportions, having saved the *Chronicle* from the depredations of such a terrible creature as the one that I've just heard spoken about—possibly he should have a medal of some kind; I will speak to the editor. In the meantime, gentlemen, Mister Dodger has confidential information for me, and I would like to take him over to the coffeehouse to hear what he has to say. So if you will, in fact, excuse the both of us, we will depart."

With that, Charlie nodded to the policeman and walked down the steps, an amazed Dodger following him. Onan padded behind, ever optimistic that Dodger might be taking a route through the foggy streets that could involve a bone. Life for Onan often didn't produce the rewards he wanted; and as Dodger tied him to a lamppost, it became clear that this was going to be one of those times. Again. Dodger resolved to get him a decent bone at the earliest opportunity.

He hadn't tasted coffee before, but Solomon said it was nothing but mud, and in any case he couldn't afford it. The coffeehouse was full of the stuff, full of people and full of chatter and, above all, full of noise.

Charlie pushed Dodger onto a chair, sat down beside him, and said, "Nobody is going to hear what you say here, because in here everybody is always talking at once, and the ones who aren't actually talking are thinking about what they are going to say next and waiting for their turn. Is there any point in my asking you for the truth about that delicious little episode, or should we perhaps just let a veil of mystery fall over it? Have you ever heard of a cove called Napoleon, by any chance? Do take more sugar, and when you have finished the bowl they will bring another one; these new sugar lumps are all the go, aren't they?"

Dodger stopped feverishly pushing sugar into his pockets and said, "Napoleon, yeah, Froggy general, that's why we've got old sweats begging on the streets, sometimes with a knife, yes?"

"Well," said Charlie, "he was famous among other things for saying that what he looked for in his French generals was luck; and you, Mister Dodger, are all luck, very lucky, because something about that little escapade smells to me as bad as an extremely old cheese. I think I know you, Dodger, so I will indeed recommend to my editor that some little honor, possibly including a half sovereign or two, might be in order—although I will try and persuade him not to put your name in the newspapers, because I suspect that doing so could mean you having some little trouble finding friends in the future, since helping the police would not look good on your curriculum vitae in those shadows you frequent. You are lucky, Dodger, and the more you help me, the luckier you will become." His fingers strayed to his pocket and the unmistakable jingle of coins could be heard. "What have you found out?"

Dodger told him about the coach and the girl, with Charlie listening carefully to everything he said.

When he had finished, Charlie said, "So she saw no crest on the coach? What kind of foreign accent? French? German?"

Much to Charlie's surprise, Dodger said firmly, "Mister Charlie, I know about what's on coaches and I know to recognize most lingos, but you see that in this I'm just like you—I'm dealing with an informant who isn't bright enough to know everything or notice much."

Charlie looked at Dodger in the way that somebody would look at some sad accident and said, "You, Dodger, are what is known as a tabula rasa—Latin for a clean slate; you are smart, indeed, but you have so very little to be smart about! It grieves me, it really does, although I do see that you have had the sense to get some new clothes, the best a shonky shop could provide." He smiled when he saw Dodger's expression and went on, "What? You don't think the likes of me would know what a shonky shop is? Believe me, my friend, there are very few depths in this city that I haven't plumbed as a matter of business. But on a lighter note, I expect you will like to hear that the young lady you rescued is recovering. I believe that no one has yet reported her missing—though there are indications that she is not some street waif, so her disappearance *should* have been reported. You understand? Although as yet she cannot speak very well—she seems incapable of explaining what may have happened to her—she does appear to understand English. As a matter of fact, I believe she is a foreigner—a very *special* foreigner, although I cannot tell you why I think this may be the case. And I suspect there is some excitement about this in high places. The crest on her ring is providing an interesting line of inquiry, and my friend Sir Robert Peel is being rather circumspect, leading me to believe that there is a game afoot. As you know, I write for newspapers, but not everything a newspaperman knows gets into print."

A game, Dodger thought. He had to get into this game and win it. But what kind of game would lead to a girl being beaten like that? *That* kind of game he would have to stop. In the noise and smoke of the coffeehouse, under his breath, he said a prayer to the Lady, feeling somewhat embarrassed as he did so: "I ain't never met you, missus, but you knew Grandad and I hope he's with you now. Well, I'm Dodger, and Grandad has made me king of the toshers, and a little bit of help from yourself would certainly not go amiss. Thanking you in anticipation, yours, Dodger."

Although the din in the coffeehouse was so great now that he could barely hear himself think, let alone hear any reply or what else Charlie had to add, Dodger managed to say, "Well, if nobody has reported somebody missing, it may just be that they either don't know they are missing or hope to find the missing person before somebody else does, if you catch my meaning?"

"Mister Dodger, you are a find! Between ourselves, I rather like the police, although I suppose that you do not; but what I really like about them is the concept they have, well, some of them, at least, that the law should apply to everybody, not just the poor people. I know the rookeries do not like the police; generally speaking, you will find in high places people who dislike them even more." He paused. "And you tell me your informant told you she was escaping from a carriage and pair, and a swell one at that. Find me that carriage, my friend, and who has lent their carriage to that vicious day's work, and the world might be a better place, especially for you."

There was a jingling again and Charlie put two half crowns on the small table, and smiled when they disappeared into

Dodger's pocket in one movement.

He said, "Incidentally, my colleague and friend Mister Mayhew and his wife would very much like to meet you again, and may I suggest sometime tomorrow? They are given to believe that you are an angel, albeit one with a dirty face, with a sweet nature and possibly useful career ahead of him; whereas I, as you know, regard you as a blaggard and scallywag of the first water, full of guile and mischief, the kind of smart lad who would do anything to reach his goals. But this is a new world, we need new people. Who are you really, Dodger, and what is your story? If you don't mind?" He looked at Dodger quizzically.

Dodger did mind, but the world seemed to be moving fast, and so he said, "If I tell you, mister, you won't tell anyone else, promise? Can I trust you?"

"On my honor as a journalist," said Charlie. Then after a pause, he added, "Strictly speaking, Dodger, the answer should be no. I am a writer and a journalist, which is a very difficult covenant. However, I have high hopes and great expectations of you and would do nothing to get in the way of your progress. Excuse me. . . ." Abruptly, Charlie took a pencil and a very small writing pad out of a pocket and scribbled a few words on it before looking up again with a slightly embarrassed smile. "I'm sorry about that, but I do like to write a line or two before the words escape me. . . . Now, please do continue."

Uneasily, Dodger said, "Well, I was brought up in an orphanage. You know; I was a foundling, never knew my mother. I wasn't a very big kid neither, and there was a lot of bullies around when I grew up. So I used to dodge about a bit, keep out of the way, as it were, because some of the bigger boys laughed about my real name; and if I complained, they beat me to the ground when the superintendent wasn't looking. But that stopped after a while when I got bigger, and then they picked on me again, didn't they just! And there I was, and I thought, I ain't 'aving this no more and when I got up, I grabbed hold of a chair and I set about me." He paused, treasuring that moment when all sins had been punished; even the superintendent hadn't been able to get a hold on him. "So I finished that day out on the streets, when life really began."

Charlie listened intently to the carefully abridged version of this biography and said, "Very interesting, Dodger, but you haven't told me your name." Shrugging, because there seemed no hope for it, Dodger told Charlie his name, expecting laughter and getting no more than "Oh, I see. Yes, of course, that would explain quite a lot. Naturally, my lips will remain sealed on this issue. Although could I venture to ask you about your life subsequently?"

"Is this going to be written down in your little notebook, mister?"

"Not as such, my young friend, but I am always interested in people."

Never tell nobody nothing they don't need to know. That was what Dodger believed. But he had never before in his life found an outsider who could so easily wriggle his way inside, and therefore in this world that seemed to be changing direction all the time, he decided not to be coy.

"Well," he said, "I got 'prenticed to a chimney sweep, being a skinny youth, see, and after a while I ran away, but not before coming out of the chimney into a bedroom, a swell bedroom, and coming out with a diamond ring what I nicked off the dressing table. And I tell you, sir, best move I ever made that was, 'cos the chimneys ain't no place for a growing lad, sir. The soot it gets in everywhere, sir, *everywhere*. Into every cut and scrape, sir, and it's perilous stuff; does very nasty things to your unmentionables, and I know because I've seen the lads who stayed on and they were in a very bad way, but thanks to the Lady I got right out of it." He shrugged, and went on, "That's how life was. As for the diamond ring, when I fenced it, the fence saw that I was a likely lad and pointed me in the way of being a snakesman, sir, which is—"

"I know what a snakesman is, Mister Dodger.* But how did you get from there to toshing, may I ask?"

Dodger took a deep breath, breathing in the ashes of the past. "I had a little difficulty concerning a stolen goose and got chased by the runners, just because I had feathers all over me, and so I hid out in the sewers, see? They didn't even follow, on account of being too fat and too drunk, in my opinion. Then I found out about toshing and, well, that's it, sir, all of it, more or less."

He watched Charlie's face for an expression more than a noncommittal stare, and then Charlie appeared to wake up and said, "And what would you do if you had had a different name, Dodger? A name such as Master Geoffrey Smith, for example, or Master Jonathan Baxter?"

* A small man or boy who could wriggle into little, open windows or fanlights—especially fanlights, which were often open—to get into buildings, then let in his associates to join him in stealing everything that could be stolen.

"Dunno, sir. Probably been a normal person, sir."

At this, Charlie smiled and said, "I rather believe that you are an unusual one, my friend."

Was that a real smile on Charlie's face? You couldn't be sure with Charlie, and so that was unresolved as they left the coffeehouse and went their separate ways, Charlie to go wherever he went and Dodger to make his way back, delighting Onan by buying him a juicy bone from a butcher just before the man closed for the night. Onan carefully carried it home in his mouth, dribbling as he did so.

Not a bad day, Dodger thought as he walked up the stairs to the attic room. Finishing with more money too, not to mention a pocket full of sugar lumps.

CHAPTER FIVE

The hero of the hour meets
his damsel in distress again,
but wins a kiss from a very enthusiastic lady

SOLOMON WAS STILL AT work at his little lathe when Dodger came up the stairs. It was always strange to watch Sol working; it was as if he had disappeared. Oh yes, he was there, but mostly his brain was lodged in his fingertips, paying no attention to anything other than what he was very carefully doing until it seemed all part of some kind of natural process, as gentle as grass growing. Dodger envied him that peacefulness, but it wouldn't suit him, he was sure.

Sol's choice of clobber wouldn't suit him either, oh no. When he went to the synagogue, the old boy wore baggy pantaloons and a ragged gabardine coat, summer and winter; and when safely back in his lair in the attic, even longer pantaloons from who knew where, with a vest which—give him his due—was generally always as white as could be achieved. On his feet he chose to wear some very carefully embroidered slippers acquired in foreign parts where Solomon had at some time or another apparently lived and, possibly, from which he had escaped with his life. Then, of course, there was his apron, with a very big pocket in the front so that any small fiddly and expensive items that rolled off the workbench would be caught in it.

There was an appetizing smell coming from the cauldron on the stove—Mrs. Quickly's mutton being put to good use—that automatically made Dodger lick his lips. Dodger never knew how Solomon managed it; the old man could make a delicious dinner out of half a brick and a lump of wood. When he'd asked him one day, Solomon had replied, "Mmm, I suppose it was all that wandering in the wilderness; it makes you do the best you can with what you've got."

Dodger lay awake on his mattress for most of the night, and lying awake was very easy to do; often there were fights back down in the yards when the blokes came home, and then the screaming babies and terrible rows—the whole cacophony that was the lullaby of Seven Dials. Happy families, he thought. Are there any? And over and above the streets there were the bells, clanging out all over the city.

Dodger stared at the ceiling, thinking about the coach. Messy Bessie probably wasn't going to be any more help, and so it seemed to Dodger that the only way to find out more was to continue to ask questions, in the hope of coming to the attention of people who didn't like questions being asked, and especially didn't like questions being answered. He bet they would know a thing or two.

Where to start, where to start? A squeaky wheel, and a nobby coach. Did it have a crest on it? Maybe one with eagles? Perhaps the girl would remember more if he saw her again . . . ?

Well, he thought, Mister Mayhew wants to see me and so does his wife, and perhaps a smart young man could smarten himself up and try to put some kind of shine on his boots and wash his face before going to see them, in the hope that a good lad might at least come out of the meeting with something more than a cup of tea, perhaps something to eat. And who knows; possibly, if he was very good and very respectful, he would be allowed to see the girl with the wonderful golden hair again.

Because you cannot switch cunning off when you want to, Dodger's own cunning treacherously prompted him: maybe they will give you some money as well, for being a good boy. Because he thought he knew the kind of people Mister and Missus Mayhew were; amazingly every now and again you came across nobby folks who actually cared about the street people and were slightly guilty about them. If you were poor, and possibly took the trouble to scrub up as best you could, and had no shame at all and could also spin a hard luck story as well as Dodger could—though, frankly, he didn't really *need* to make up one, since his life, as he had very nearly truthfully described it to Charlie, had included big dollops of hard luck anyway—why, then they would practically kiss you, because it made them feel better.

Lying there in the darkness and thinking about the girl, Dodger felt somewhat ashamed to be thinking only of what he could make out of it, for surely saving the girl was in itself a kind of reward. But he was only a little bit ashamed, because you had to live, didn't you?

Uncomfortable, he turned over and thought about Charlie, who seemed to think that Dodger was some kind of a pirate king, and when you thought about it, Charlie was playing a little game of his own. Every lad wants to be considered a wide boy, a geezer, right? Dodger thought. 'Cos it makes you feel big. For Charlie, words were a kind of complicated game and it might not be a game Dodger knew well, but it was still a game—and he, Dodger, was pretty good at the game of surviving.

Staring up at nothing, he thought about Grandad, dying with a smile on his face in the sewers and in all that the sewers contained. It would be a long time before he ever went into the Maelstrom again. Rats were small, but there were a lot of them, and more and more when the news got around. He would leave a week or two at least before he would return to the place where the old man had died. Died, he reminded himself, where he wanted to be.

Then there was Stumpy, who'd had two legs until a cannonball hit him when he was fighting somewhere in Spain.

And here he was, and suddenly now Charlie's words were clinging to him, changing his world—a world where one moment you are happily on the tosh, then quick as a wink coppers might call you a hero and you are wandering around in nobby houses. Not the person you had been when you woke up. It was like some great big spring was tugging at him—and maybe, perhaps sooner rather than later, a boy has to decide what kind of man he is going to be. Is he going to be a player or a playing piece . . . ?

In the gloom, Dodger smiled and went to sleep, dreaming of golden hair.

In the morning, as clean as he could be, Dodger headed to the house of Mister Mayhew. By daylight, the man's house looked pretty good; not a palace, but the place of somebody who had enough money to be called a gentleman. The whole street looked like that, smart, ordered, and clean. There was even a policeman patrolling it, and much to Dodger's surprise the policeman gave him a little salute as they passed. It wasn't anything much, just a flick of the fingers, but up until now a policeman in a place like this would have told him to go somewhere else sharpish. Emboldened, Dodger remembered the way that Charlie talked and saluted the constable back, saying, "Good morning, officer, what a fine day it is to be sure."

Nothing happened! The copper strolled slowly past him and that was that. Blimey! In a hopeful mood, Dodger found the house. He had learned at an early age how to hang about the back doors of houses on the swell streets, and also—and this was important—to get known as a spritely lad. He had realized that if you were an urchin, then it might help to treat it as a vocation and get really good at it; if you wanted to be a successful urchin you needed to study how to urch. It was as simple as that. And if you are going to urch, then you had to be something like an actor. You had to know how to be chatty to everybody—the butlers and the cooks; the house-maids; even the coachmen—and in short become the cheerful chappie, always a card, known to everybody. It was an act and he was the star. It wasn't a path to fame and fortune, but it certainly wasn't the road to Tyburn Tree and the long drop. No, safety lay in having one talent that you can call your own, and his lay in being Dodger, Dodger to the hilt. So now he walked round to the back door, hoping he might perhaps run into Mrs. Quickly the cook again and come away once more with a pie or another piece of mutton.

The door was opened by a maid, who said, "Yes, sir?"

Dodger straightened himself up and said, "I'm here to see Mister Mayhew. I believe he is expecting me—my name is Dodger." No sooner had he said this than there was a clang from somewhere beyond, and the maid panicked a little as maids do (especially when they met Dodger's cheerful grin) but she visibly relaxed as she was replaced by Dodger's old friend Mrs. Quickly, who looked him up and down critically and said, "My word, ain't you the toff and no mistake! Pray excuse me if I do not curtsy, on account of me being all but up to my armpits in giblets."

A moment later the cook came around the door again, this time unencumbered by the bits of the insides of animals. She shooed away the maid, saying, "Me and Mister Dodger is going to have a little chat, so go and see to the pig knuckles, girl." Then she gave Dodger a hug involving a certain amount of giblet, wiped him down, and said, "You are a hero of the hour, my little pumpkin, yes indeed, they were talking about it at breakfast! It seems that you, you little scallywag, single-handedly stopped that *Morning Chronicle* being overrun by robbers last night!" She gave Dodger a saucy smile and said, "Well, I thought to myself, if that is the self-same young man I met the other day, then the only way he would stop anything being stolen would be to put his hands behind his back. But now it appears that you fought a battle with some robbers and chased them to kingdom come, so they say. Just fancy that! Next thing you know they will be asking you to be the Lord Mayor. If that is so, I would like you to take me as your Lady Mayoress—don't worry, I've been married lots of times and know how it is done." She laughed again at his expression and, more soberly, said, "Well done, lad. We'll get the girl to take you upstairs to the family, and you be sure to come down here again when you go, because I might have a little bundle of food for you."

Dodger followed the maid up a flight of stone stairs to a door, to the magic green baize door between the people who clean the floors and those people who walk on the floors—the upstairs and the downstairs of the world. Actually, what he found was a kind of pandemonium, with a husband and wife as unwilling referees in a dispute between two boys over who had broken whose toy soldier.

Mister Mayhew grabbed him and nodded to his wife, who could only smile frantically at Dodger from the middle of this tiny war as he was hurried into her husband's study. Henry Mayhew offered him an uncomfortable chair and sat down opposite him, saying immediately, "It is a pleasure to make your acquaintance again, young man, especially in the light of your intervention yesterday evening of which Charlie has informed me." He paused. "You are a most interesting young man. May I ask a . . . few personal questions?" His hand reached for a notebook and pencil as he spoke.

Dodger was not used to this sort of thing: people who wanted to ask him personal questions such as "Where were you on the night of the sixteenth?" normally damn well asked them without permission, and also expected them to be answered with equal speed. He managed to say, "I don't mind, sir. That is if they ain't too personal." He stared around the room while the man laughed, and he thought: How can one man own this much paper? Books and piles of paper were on every flat surface, including the floor—everywhere on the floor, but *neatly* on the floor.

Now Mister Mayhew said, "I imagine, sir, that you were not actually christened? I find the idea unlikely. Mister Dodger is a name you . . . came by?"

Dodger settled for a variant on honesty. After all, he'd been through all of this with Charlie, and so what he delivered was a slightly abbreviated version of "the Dodger story," because you never told anyone everything. "No, sir, was a foundling, sir, got called Dodger in the orphanage because I move fast, sir."

Mister Mayhew opened the notebook, which Dodger looked at with suspicion. The pencil was poised over the paper, ready to pounce, so he said, "No offense meant—it makes me come over all wobbly if things gets writ down, and I stops talking." He was already scouting the room for other exits.

However, much to his surprise, Mister Mayhew said, "Young man, I do apologize for not asking your permission. Of course I will not make further notes without asking you. You see, I write things down for my job, or perhaps I should say my vocation. It is a matter of research—a project on which I have been engaged for some time now. I and my colleagues hope to make the government see how terrible conditions are in this city; it is, indeed, the richest and most powerful city in the world, and yet the conditions here for many may not be far removed from those in Calcutta." He noted that there was no change in Dodger's expression and said, "Is it possible, young man, that you do not know where Calcutta is?"

Dodger stared for a moment at the pencil. Oh well, there

was no hope for it. "That's right, sir," he said. "Do not have a clue, sorry, sir."

"Mister Dodger, the fault is not yours. Indeed," Mister Mayhew continued, as if talking to himself, "ignorance, poor health, and lack of suitable nutrition and potable water see to it that the situation gets ever worse. So I simply ask people for a few details about their lives, and indeed their earnings, for the government cannot fail to respond to a careful accumulation of evidence! Curiously, the upper classes, while generally very gracious in the amount of money that they give to churches, foundations, and other great works, tend not to look too hard below them, apart from occasionally making soup for the deserving."

The thought of food once again got Dodger's stomach rumbling. It must have grumbled enough for Mister Mayhew to hear, because the man was suddenly flustered and said, "Oh my dear sir, you will be very hungry, of course; I anticipated this, so I will ring the bell and get the maid to bring you some bacon and an egg or two. We are not rich, but thankfully we are not poor. It must be said that everybody has a different calculus on this matter, however, because I have met people who I would have thought were among the most extreme of the poor, who nevertheless protest that they are jogging along nicely, while on the other hand I have known men who live in very large houses on really good incomes to consider themselves one step away from debtors' prison!" He smiled at Dodger, as he rang the bell, and said, "How about you, Mister Dodger, who I believe is a tosher as well as dabbling in other lines of ad hoc business when the opportunity arises? Do you consider yourself rich, or poor?"

Dodger knew a trick question when he saw one. Mister Mayhew, he considered, was probably not as darkly sharp about the world as Charlie was but it wouldn't pay to underestimate him; and therefore he took refuge in the last resort, which was honesty. He said, "I reckon me and Sol aren't really the poor, sir. You know, we're doing a bit of this and a bit of that and we do pretty well, I think, compared to many, yes."

This seemed to pass muster, and Mister Mayhew looked pleased. He glanced at his notebook and said, "Sol being the gentleman of the Jewish persuasion with whom Charlie tells me you share lodgings?"

"Oh, I don't think he needed any persuading, sir. I think he was born Jewish. At least, that's what he says."

Dodger wondered why Mister Mayhew laughed, and he wondered too how it was that Charlie knew enough to tell the man where he lived when Dodger himself couldn't seem to remember telling him. But that didn't really matter, because he could hear the sound of the servant just outside the door, and the rattling of a tray. A rattling like that meant that it was heavy—always a good thing. And, as it turned out, it was. Mister Mayhew said that he had already had breakfast, so Dodger tucked into bacon and eggs at considerable speed.

"Charlie has high hopes of you, as you know," said Mister Mayhew, "and I must confess my admiration at the fact you have put yourself out for our young lady, especially as, I understand, you had never met before. I will take you to see her shortly. She seems to understand English, although I fear that her mind has been disturbed by the nature of her ordeal and she seems unable to give an account of the dark events that appear to have befallen her."

Most unusually for Dodger, he looked at the food in front of him without instantly finishing it up, and instead said, "She was very scared. She's been married to a cove who treated her rotten and that's a fact. And . . ." Dodger was about to say more but hesitated. He thought: She's hurt, yes; she's frightened, yes; but I don't reckon she's lost her mind. I reckon she's biding her time until she finds out who her friends are. And if I was her, badly beaten though she be, I reckon that I would find it in myself to appear a little worse off than I was; it's the rule of the streets. Keep some things to yourself.

Dodger felt the man still watching him, and sure enough Mister Mayhew said, "So if you don't mind . . . where were you born, Mister Dodger?"

He had to wait until Dodger had finished the plateful of food and licked the knife on both sides. Then Dodger said, "Bow, sir, though don't know for sure."

"Would you mind telling me about your upbringing . . . how you came to be a tosher?"

Dodger shrugged. "Was a mudlark for a while first, 'cos, well, that's the kind of stuff you like as a kid—it sort of comes natural, if you know what I mean, mucking about in the river mud picking up bits of coal and suchlike. Not bad in the summer, bloody awful in the winter, but if you are smart you can find a place to sleep and earn yourself a meal. I done a bit of time as a chimney sweep's lad, like I told Charlie, but then one day I began toshing and never looked back, sir. Took to it like a pig to a muck heap, which is pretty much the same. Never found a tosheroon yet, but I hope to do so before I die."

He laughed and decided to give the very serious-looking

man something to think about, and so he added, "Of course I found practically everything else, sir—everything what folk throw away, or lose, or don't care about. It's amazing what you can find down there, especially under the teaching hospitals, oh my word yes! I can walk from one side of London to another underground, come up anywhere I like, and I'll tell you, sir, you won't believe me sometimes, sir, beautiful so it is! It's like walking through old houses sometimes, the slopes of the stairs and stuff growing on the walls—the Grotto, Windy Corner, the Queen's Bedroom, the Chamber of Whispers, and all the other places we toshers know like the backs of our hands, sir, once we've washed them, of course. When the evening light strikes and comes off the river, it looks like a paradise, sir. I can't expect you to believe it, but so it does."

Dodger paused and considered what he had just said, common sense meaning that he wouldn't tell a man with a poised pencil about stealing things and being a snakesman and a thief; that sort of revelation was fine for someone like Charlie, but for the likes of Mister Mayhew it seemed more sensible to put a shine on things.

"One time I even found an old bedstead down there. And it's amazing how the light finds a way in," he finished, and smiled at Mister Mayhew, who was looking at him with an expression halfway between shock and puzzlement, with perhaps a tiny bit of admiration.

Now the man said, "One last thing, Mister Dodger. Would you mind telling me how much you glean from your labors as a tosher?"

Dodger had pretty much expected something like this. He

instinctively halved the amount of his earnings, saying, "Well, there's good days and there's bad days, sir, but I reckon I might earn as much as a chimney sweep, with every now and again a little windfall."

"And are you happy in your occupation?"

"Oh yes, sir. I go where I please, I ain't answerable to anybody, and every day is a sort of adventure, sir, if you get my meaning?" And in order to boost his bona fides as an upstanding young gentleman he added, "Of course, sometimes I find something down there that someone has lost, and it does my heart good to give it back to them." Well, it was technically true, he thought to himself, even if a few shillings did come into the picture.

After a while the man cleared his throat and said, "Mister Dodger, thank you for that insight. I see that you have finished your breakfast to the extent that the plate positively shines, and now perhaps it is time to let you meet our guest again. Have you ever had such a thing as a bath? I must say that, considering your calling, you look reasonably clean."

Dodger smirked at this. "That's because of Solomon, sir, the cove what I live with. He is a devil for dirt, sir, on account of being one of the chosen people. And yes, there is a bath in the back room, sir—one of those little ones you stand in, kind of like washing yourself down with a rag, sir, and soap too, my oath, yes. I heard someone say cleanliness is next to godliness, but I reckon Sol reckons that cleanliness gives godliness a run for its money."

Mister Mayhew was staring at Dodger like a man who has found a sixpence in a handful of farthings. Now he said, "You amaze me, Mister Dodger; you appear to be a brand plucking himself from the burning. Please do follow me."

A minute later Dodger was ushered into the rather dark maids' room upstairs. The golden-haired girl was sitting upright on one of the beds, like somebody who has just got up; and the room was suddenly bright from the girl's smile, at least in the depths of Dodger, whose heart, somewhat corroded, was beating fast.

Mister Mayhew said, "Here is the young lady, who I'm glad to say is making progress." He gestured to the other person in the room. "This, of course, is my wife, Jane, whom I believe you met earlier but have not been introduced to as yet. My dear, this is Mister Dodger, the savior of damsels in distress, as I believe you know."

Dodger wasn't sometimes certain that he understood what Mister Mayhew was saying, but he thought it would be sensible to point out, just in case there would be trouble later, "There was only one damsel in distress, sir—if the damsel means a lady, of course. But just one, sir."

Mrs. Mayhew—who had been sitting beside the girl, a soup bowl and spoon in her hand—stood up and held out her hand. "One damsel in distress, indeed, Mister Dodger. How foolish of my husband to believe that there might be more than one." She smiled, and so did her husband, and Dodger wondered if he had missed some kind of joke, but Mrs. Mayhew hadn't finished yet.

Dodger knew about families, and husbands and wives; often, wives helped their menfolk who sold stuff on the streets like baked potatoes and sandwiches—although baked potatoes were always a treat—and whole families worked at the game. Dodger, who had the eye for this sort of thing, watched the families and watched their faces and watched how they spoke to one another, and sometimes it seemed to him that although the man was the master, which was of course only right and proper, if you watched and listened, you would see that their marriage was like a barge on the river, with the wife being the wind that told the captain which way the barge would sail. Mrs. Mayhew, if not being the wind, certainly knew when to apply the right puff.

The couple smiled at each other, and Mrs. Mayhew said sadly, "I'm afraid that the dreadful beating this young lady had—and I suspect had not endured for the first time—has in some way tangled her wits, so unfortunately I cannot introduce you properly. 'Simplicity' will suffice for a name, a good Christian name, until we know more. The name belonged to an old friend of mine, and so I am fond of it. She is quite young and one must hope that she will heal rapidly. At the moment, however, I keep the curtains mostly closed to keep out as much as possible of the noise of carriages in the streets—they appear to make Simplicity fearful. However, I'm glad to see that her physical faculties seem to be coming back slowly and the bruises are fading. Unfortunately I am led to believe that her life in recent times has not been . . . pleasant, although there are signs that at one time it may have been rather more . . . agreeable. After all, surely somebody must have cared for her to give her that wonderful ring she wears."

Dodger didn't need to know the precise code that passed between Mister Mayhew and his wife, but he could see that much of it consisted of meaningful looks from one to the other, and one of the messages was: better not to talk about a valuable ring in front of this lad.

He said, "She gets worried when she hears carriages, does she? What about other street noises, like horses or honey wagons*—they tend to rumble a lot?"

Mrs. Mayhew said, "You are a very astute young man."

Dodger blushed, and said, "I'm sorry, missus, but my best trousers are in the wash."

Without any change of expression, Mrs. Mayhew said, "No, Mister Dodger, I meant that you are very quick to understand things, and you are a man of the world, or should I say London, which is practically the same thing. I know that Mister Dickens is optimistic that you may be able to help us solve this little mystery." She exchanged another glance with her husband and said, "I assume you know that there was another most unpleasant aspect to this whole Satanic business." She hesitated, as if trying to move unpleasant thoughts in her mind, then said, "I believe you are aware that the young lady was . . . she was . . . she lost . . ." Mrs. Mayhew rushed out in embarrassed confusion, leaving the room suddenly silent.

Dodger glanced at Simplicity and then said to Mister Mayhew, "Sir, if you do not object, I would very much like to talk to Simplicity alone. Possibly I can also help her eat her soup. I have a feeling she might be capable of talking a little to me again."

"Well, it would be unseemly to leave a young lady alone in a bedroom in your company."

"Yes, sir, and it's unseemly to beat a lady half to death and

---

* Around about the time of Dodger, most sewerage in London went into septic tanks, or cesspits. The tanks were emptied out and the contents taken away by honey wagons.

try to drown her, but that wasn't me, sir. So I think, sir, in the privacy of this house, you might allow the rule to be a little more . . . human?"

There was the sound of Mrs. Mayhew hovering on the landing and Henry Mayhew, suddenly bewildered, stirred and said, "I will leave the door open, sir. If Miss Simplicity agrees."

His words were instantly followed from the bed with the unmistakable tones of Simplicity, saying, "Please, sir, I would very much like to have a Christian word with my savior."

True to his word, Mister Mayhew did leave the door slightly ajar, and so, awkwardly for once, Dodger sat down on the chair that Mrs. Mayhew had vacated and smiled nervously at Simplicity, who returned the smile with considerable interest. Then he picked up the soup spoon and handed it to her, saying, "What is it that you would like to happen next?"

Her smile broadening, Simplicity very gently took the spoon, put it to her mouth, and drank the soup. Speaking quietly, she said, "I would like to say that I want to go home, but I have no home now. And I have to know who I can trust. Can I trust you, Dodger? I think I might be able to trust a man who has fought valiantly for a woman he doesn't even know."

Dodger tried to look as though this was all in a day's work. "You know, I'm quite sure you can trust Mister and Missus Mayhew," he said.

But much to his surprise, she said, "No, I'm not sure. Mister Mayhew would prefer that you and I were not talking, Dodger. He seems to think that you would take some kind of advantage of me and I believe the word for that is"—she hesitated for a moment—"is incongruous! You saved me, you fought for me, and now you are going to do me harm? They are good people, no doubt, but good people, for example, might think that they should deliver me to the agents of my husband because I am his wife. People can be very exact about that sort of thing. And no doubt a man would turn up with something very official and signed with a very impressive seal, and they would obey the law. A law that would see me taken away from the country where my mother was born and back to a husband who is embarrassed by me and does not dare defy his father."

Her voice grew stronger and stronger as she spoke, but, Dodger suddenly realized, she was also sounding more and more like a street girl—someone who knew how to play a game. The slight Germanic accent had gone and the vowels of England were in her tone, and she was doing what every smart person did, which was to never tell anybody anything that they didn't need to know.

But he could not place her accent. He knew about other languages, but as a decent Londoner he vaguely disapproved of them, knowing full well that anyone who wasn't English was obviously an enemy sooner or later. You couldn't hang around the docks without picking up, if not the languages, at least the sounds the languages made, and so if you listened carefully, a Dutchman spoke differently from a German, and you could always tell a Swede, of course, and the Finns yawned at you when they were speaking to you. He was pin sharp on telling one language from another but had never bothered to learn any of them—though by the time he was twelve he knew the words that meant "Where are the naughty ladies to be found?" in a variety of languages, including Chinese and several African ones. Every wharf rat knew those; and the naughty ladies might give you a farthing for setting a gentleman's footsteps in the right direction. As he grew older, he realized that some people would say that was, in fact, the *wrong* direction; there were two ways of looking at the world, but only one when you are starving.

There were sounds of stirring on the landing and he immediately stood up, spry as a guardsman, and practically saluted a very surprised Mister Mayhew and his wife.

"Well, sir, madam, I've had a nice little chat with the girl. As you say, she seems frightened by the sound of coaches. Perhaps if I could take her out for some air, she could see that the coaches that pass your house are just ordinary coaches . . . ? And so, if you don't mind, could I take her out for a walk?"

This caused such a silence that he realized it was probably not a sensible idea. As he thought this, he suddenly also thought, I'm talking to this gent like I'm his equal! It's amazing how a shonky suit and a plate of bacon and eggs can make a man feel set up! But I'm still the lad who got up this morning as a tosher, and they're still the gent and his missus who got up in this big house, so I need to be careful, else they'll suddenly decide I'm a tosher again and chuck me out. He added to himself, though, in a voice that seemed quite daring, "I don't have no master, nobody can give me orders, I ain't wanted by the peelers and I ain't never done nothing to be ashamed of. I ain't got as much as them, oh my, not by a long chalk, but I am no worse than they are."

Mrs. Mayhew hesitated and then said, very carefully,

"Well, I am quite certain that sooner or later Simplicity must get out in the fresh air, so perhaps that could be arranged, Mister Dodger. But I am sure you will understand that it could only take place in the presence of a chaperone. You must see that leaving her just with a young man—however valiant he may be—is something that would be very much frowned upon in polite circles. We must be adamant in this respect, although, of course, I believe that your intentions are entirely innocent."

Mister Mayhew looked as embarrassed as his wife, and Dodger, still trusting his luck, in his most ingratiating voice, said, "Well, dear Mrs. Mayhew, I can promise you that there will not be any hanky-panky, because I do not know what panky is and I've never had a hanky. Only a handkerchief."

For a moment her steely glare melted again and Mrs. Mayhew said, "You are a very forward young man, Mister Dodger."

"I certainly hope so, Mrs. Mayhew, indeed sometimes I think I am being pulled forward through no fault of my own. However, Mrs. Mayhew, I am sure you will agree with me that being forward is better by far than being backward. And I believe I care for Miss Simplicity. I was thinking too that we all want to find the coves who beat her up, so if I walked about with her in the town, she might see or hear something that could give me a clue. I know that the carriage she escaped from made a noise that I, for one, haven't heard on a carriage wheel. So what I say is: find the carriage, find a clue."

Mister Mayhew looked at his wife and said, "You are commendably eloquent, Mister Dodger, but we—that is my wife and myself—feel there could be other aspects to this situation."

Dodger straightened up. "Yes, sir, I fear there may be, and I rather think so does Charlie. I don't know what an eloquent is, but I do know London, sir, every dirty inch and where it's safe to go and where it's not safe to go. Everybody knows Dodger, sir, and Dodger knows everybody. So Dodger will find out what you want me to find out."

"Yes, Mister Dodger," Mrs. Mayhew said. "I'm quite certain that is true, but my husband and I feel that we stand in loco parentis to this young lady, who appears to have no one else to care for her, and so the social niceties must be observed."

Dodger, who didn't know what a loco parentis was, shrugged and said, "Right you are, missus, but I will be passing this way again tomorrow just after lunch." He added, raising his voice a little, "In case anyone should change their mind."

Mister Mayhew caught up with him just as he reached the kitchen and said, "My wife is a little highly strung right now, if you know what I mean."

All that Dodger could find to say was "No, I don't," and like two gentlemen they left it at that, and he shook hands with Mister Mayhew and hurried through the kitchen door, his head still reeling with the way they seemed to let him speak out. Wait till he told Sol!

The cook did not look surprised when he came into the kitchen. She said, "Well, my lad, ain't you the rising star, hobnobbing with your elders and betters! Good for you! I reckon what I see in front of me now is not just another tosher but

a smart young man for whom the world is an opportunity."
She handed him a greasy package, saying, "Money is tight
here these days—things are a bit worrying all round, and of
course you won't know it but we got rid of the second maid.
If things get any worse, I reckon Mrs. Sharples will be next,
no loss, and then I suspect that it will be me, although I can't
see my lady working down here. But I done you a package
of leftovers—some cold potatoes and carrots, and a nice piece
of pork."

Dodger took the package, and said, "Thank you very
much. I'm very grateful to you."

This caused Mrs. Quickly to throw her arms open in an
attempt to cuddle him. "Spoken like a true gentleman. I
couldn't possibly expect a little kiss . . . ?" she asked hopefully.

And so Dodger kissed the cook—a rather pneumatic lady
who kissed at some length—and when he was allowed to
break free, she said, "When you rise up high, remember them
as live lowly."

CHAPTER SIX

*In which sixpence buys a lot of soup,
and a foreigner's gold buys a spy*

THE EMBARRASSMENT OF THIS followed Dodger all the way back home, as did a certain aroma of giblets. Somehow he wasn't quite as certain of who he was now—a kid from the sewers, or somebody who chats with the gentry—although he knew enough to understand that Mister and Missus Mayhew were not exactly all that much like gentry, even with their house and servants. It was certainly better than anything Dodger had lived in, but the place was just a bit shabby here and there. Not really dirty, but just enough to indicate that money was perhaps tight in this household, like Mrs. Quickly said, so every penny had to be counted.

Mrs. Mayhew had been worried too, and Dodger rather felt that the worry was somehow built in, and not just about Simplicity. He shrugged it off. Maybe that's how it goes? he thought. The more you've got, the more worried you become, just in case you lose it. If money gets a bit short, then you might be worrying about losing your nice house and all those pretty little ornaments.

Dodger hadn't ever worried too much about anything beyond the important things—a decent meal and a warm place to sleep. You didn't need a house full of little ornaments (and Dodger was a great one for noticing little ornaments, especially the kind that could be picked up very easily and shoved into a pocket at speed and sold again almost as fast). But what was the point of them? To show that you could afford them? How much better did that make you feel? How much happier were you really?

The Mayhew household had been doing its duty in a stiff kind of way, but it didn't appear to be very happy—there had been a kind of tension there that he couldn't quite fathom, unhappiness riding on the very air—and in a strange way that made Dodger feel a little unhappy himself, and he wondered why. Unhappiness was a state of mind generally alien to him. Who had the *time* to be unhappy, after all? He was often pissed off, fed up, even angry, but these were just clouds in the sky; sooner or later they passed. They never lasted long. But as he walked aimlessly away from the Mayhews', it seemed that he was dragging other people's worries with him.

He felt that the only cure for something like this would be to go down into the sewers, because if you had to be down in the dumps, you might as well have a feel around and see if you could find sixpence. He would have to go and get changed—the shonky outfit was the finest and smartest he had ever worn, and it would never do to go to work in, would it?

But . . . Simplicity. He couldn't stop thinking about her. Wondering who she might be, and who might know what had happened to her and why. And who had *hurt* her, of course. He really, really *needed* to know that now. And in this crowded town there would always be somebody to overhear anything that a body said.

The police wouldn't know *anything*, of course—that was because no one in their right mind ever talked to the peelers. One or two of them were okay, but it didn't pay to trust them. However, people talked to Dodger, good old Dodger, especially when he loaned them a sixpence, to be repaid on Saint Never's Day.

And so, on his winding way back to the attic to change, a route not just roundabout but with swings and slides as well, he found time to lounge around chatting to the dregs of the earth; and to the Cockneys, who sold apples and who liked nothing better than to gang up on the peelers for a real old-fashioned, no-holds-barred war in which any weapon was fair game. He spoke to the street traders, trading on the smallest of margins; and he chatted to the ladies who hung about doing nothing very much but were always happy to meet a gentleman with money who would be generous to a girl, especially after his drink had been spiked—after which he could have the luxury of a long voyage down the Thames to places far, far away where he would possibly meet interesting people, some of whom might even endeavor to eat him, by all accounts. If a gentleman was very unlucky—or upset someone like Mrs. Holland on Bankside—he would do the journey down the Thames without a boat. . . .

Then there were the men offering games of Crown and Anchor, which at least had the benefit of being winnable if you were sober enough and the dice rolled your way—unlike the other game you might be offered by a cheery man who owned nothing more than one flat wooden board on which were three thimbles and one pea. On that little battlefield you would indeed bet some money on the whereabouts of said pea, relying on your keen eyesight to keep track of it as the thimbles turned and spun under the hands of the cheerful chattering man. You would never, *ever* guess right, because where the pea really was was known only to the cheerful man and God—and probably not even God was certain. If you had drunk enough, you would try again and again, betting more and more, 'cos sooner or later, even if you simply guessed, it was *surely* bound to be under the one you guessed. But sadly, it never would be, ever.

Finally, of course, there was the Punch and Judy man, running his puppet show that was even more of a hoot these days now that there was a policeman for Mister Punch to beat with his stick. The kids laughed, and the adults would laugh, and everyone would laugh as the laughing Mister Punch screamed, *"That's the way to do it!"* in that squeaky voice of his, like some terrible bird of prey . . . or the wheels of a coach.

You knew when you grew up that Punch was the man who throws the baby out of the window and beats his wife. . . . Of course, such things did happen: certainly the beating of the wife, and as to what might happen to the baby, that might not be the subject for children—not a happy family.

Now Dodger, into whose mind was creeping a dreadful shining darkness in which lay a wonderful girl with golden hair, had to restrain his fists from knocking out that damned shrieking puppet as he passed the stall. He felt himself shiver for a moment and brought himself back down to earth. He *knew* all this, had known it for*ever*. But Simplicity . . . well, Simplicity was someone he could maybe do something about. And that something wasn't just for Simplicity; it was for himself too, in some funny way he couldn't quite work out yet.

Better though, if he wanted to see things that didn't make him feel sick or angry, he would find the men whose dogs could do tricks, or the men who lifted heavy weights, or the boxers—bare knuckles, of course.

But today, today Dodger was asking questions. And he had done his best. He had spoken to two ladies waiting for a gent. He had chatted to a Crown and Anchor man, who knew him by name, and even the man who lifted weights who had grunted with pleasure. On one occasion he even reminded somebody of the sixpence he had loaned to him because of his poor old mummy and subtly said, "Oh no, don't bother, I'm sure you will find a way to repay me someday." In short, Dodger moved over the face of the world—or at least that part encompassed over the stews of London—spreading Dodger like a cat spreads piss and leaving little questions in the air. So that if ever somebody heard a coach that screamed, they might just have a word with Dodger; and even better, he thought, if someone *owned* a coach that screamed, maybe screamed like a gutted pig, he might want to sort it out with the man who was asking all those questions. It was like throwing bread crumbs into a stream to see if something would rise; the drawback of this method, Dodger knew, might be that what would rise would be a shark.

Then he remembered the Happy Family man. He hesitated after this thought and wondered where and when he had last seen the Happy Family man and his wagon; probably on one of the bridges, where there was always such a lot of passing trade. It was quite magical, the happy family—that little cart with its odd menagerie of animals all living so peacefully together. He would have to take Simplicity to see it as soon as possible—she would surely enjoy it. Then he realized he was crying, seeing again inside his head a beautiful face that looked as if it had been pushed down some stairs. Somebody had done that to her, and as he wiped his nose with a rag, he vowed that one day he would indeed take her Mister Punch and back him up to a wall somewhere and most surely make him mind his manners.

But now he was startled by somebody tugging at his trouser leg, and he looked down irritably at a couple of kids maybe five years old or six perhaps, looking up at him with their hands out. It wasn't the kind of tableau he needed to see right now, but both of them had one hand held out while the other one was firmly grasped by their friend. He remembered doing that sort of thing once upon a time, but only to people he had thought of as wealthy—although when you are hungry and five years old, everybody has got more money than you. In his smart clobber, of course, he didn't look like a tosher no more. He told himself, you still are a tosher, but not just a tosher, and right now you are going to be a gentleman to the tune of sixpence.

So he led the kids to the stall run by Marie Jo, who dispensed nourishing soup to all and sundry who could put down a few farthings—perhaps even less if she was in a generous mood.

Marie Jo was one of the good ones, and there weren't enough of them. Among the tales that people told about her was that she had once been a famous actress over in Froggy parts, and indeed there was always, even in these days, something fey about her, something mercurial. According to rumors, she was once married to a French soldier who got shot in some war or other, but fortunately not before he had whispered to her the whereabouts of all the loot he had picked up in his many campaigns.

She, being a decent sort, despite the fact of being married to a Froggy all them years, had set up this stall, which was one you could trust: trust for no rats in the soup, trust for no things worse than rats, trust her not to sell soup that had bits of cats and dogs in it. Marie Jo's soup was full of lentils and other odds and ends; slightly scruffy perhaps, but taken all together it did you good and kept you warm. All right, there may occasionally have been a bit of horse, that being the Froggy way, but it just meant you had a slightly more nourishing soup. It had been said that even some of the grand eating places these days would give Marie Jo leftovers, knowing that they would be going on her stall. Apparently, people said, her French wiles twisted the nobby chefs around her little finger, but "Well done, her," everyone said, because it all went in the great big pot that she stirred all night, pausing only to dip the ladle in for the next customer; and what you paid was what she reckoned you ought to pay, and because people didn't like to see her shake the ladle at them for being greedy, nobody haggled.

And so, when Dodger turned up with the two kids in tow, she looked him up and down and said, "Well now, aren't we in the money, Dodger, and who did you steal that from?" But she was laughing, perhaps because both of them could surely remember the time—years ago before her hair was so white—when Dodger himself was very small and had hung around near her stand with one hand out, looking very sad and very hopeful, just like the pair he was delivering.

He said, "Nothing for me, Marie Jo, but feed up these two today and tomorrow to the length of sixpence please?"

The expression on her face was strange. Like the soup she sold, it was full of everything, but mostly it was full of surprise. But this was the street, and she said, "Let me see your sixpence, young Dodger." He plonked it on the stall, where she looked at it, looked at him, looked at the kids who were very nearly drooling with anticipation, then looked back at Dodger, who was red with embarrassment, and she said quietly, "Why, oh why, well now, here's the thing and no mistake, what am I to do?" Then her face broke out into wrinkly smiles as she said, "For you, Dodger, I will feed the little buggers today and tomorrow, maybe the next day too, but oh my word what has happened? Glory be! The world has gone upside down while I wasn't looking! Don't tell me that you have been going to church—I'm sure the confessional would not be big enough to hold everything you've got to say! And lo, what is this? My little Dodger has grown up to be an angel."

Marie Jo pronounced his name "Dodgeurr," which sent little silver messages passing up and down his spine every time he heard it. Marie Jo knew everybody, and all about everybody, and now she looked at Dodger with a dangerous smile, but you always had to play her game, so he smiled back and said, "Now don't you go saying those things about me, Marie Jo! I don't want nobody to whiten my name! But well, I was a kid once, you know what I mean? Mind, if you keep tally of what you feed them, I'll see to it you get the cash later, trust me."

Marie Jo blew him a little kiss with the smell of peppermint in it, lowered her voice, leaned forward, and said, "I'm hearing all kinds of things concerning you, my lad. Careful how you tread! One of them was the little fracas you had with Stumpy yesterday. He's boasting about it, you know." She lowered her voice still further. "Then there was a gentleman. And I know a gentleman when I see one. He was asking about someone called Dodger, and I don't think it was because he wanted to give you a present. He was an expensive kind of gentleman."

"He wasn't called Dickens, was he?" said Dodger.

"No, I know *him*—Mister Charlie, the reporter man, knows the peelers. One of you insufferable English, though. If I had to guess, my friend, this gentleman was more like a lawyer." Then, as if nothing had happened, she turned to the next customer without a further glance.

Dodger wandered on, meeting somebody he knew on every street corner, with a bit of banter here and a bit of conversation there, and every now and then asking a little question—not very important really, just as a sort of afterthought, concerning a girl with golden hair escaping from a carriage into the storm.

Not that *he* was interested, of course; it was just something he had heard, in a round and about way as it were, not for any special reason, of course. It was just good old Dodger, and everybody knew Dodger, wanting to know about the coach and the girl with the golden hair. He would have to be careful how he walked, but so what? He always was. And right now he was at the bottom of the rickety staircase that led up to the tenement attic.

Home, where Solomon was, as usual, at work. He always was; he was never *hard* at work—he was always soft at work, almost always on tiny things that needed tiny tools and considerable amounts of patience, and a gentle hand, as well as, sometimes, a large magnifying glass. Onan was curled up under his chair, as only Onan could curl.

The old man took his time relocking the door, then said, "Mmm, a busy day again, my friend, I hope it has proved fruitful?" Dodger showed him the largesse from the kitchens of the Mayhews, and Solomon said, "Mmm, very nice, really very nice and a fine piece of pork, I see; possibly a casserole later, I think. Well done."

Some years ago, after he had brought home a piece of pork that had remarkably tumbled out of a kitchen window and right into the innocent hands of Dodger, who had merely been passing by, Dodger had said to Solomon, "I thought you Jews were not allowed to eat pork, right?"

If Onan was the king of curling up, Solomon was a prince of the shrug. "Strictly speaking," he had answered, "that may be so mmm, but another set of rules applies. Firstly, this is a gift from God and one should never refuse a gift given freely, and secondly, this pork appears to be quite good, better than usual, and I am an old man and I am mmm very hungry. Sometimes I think that the rules made centuries ago for the purpose of getting my excitable and bickering forebears across the desert cannot easily be said to apply in this town with its rains, smogs, and fogs. Besides, I am an elderly man and I am quite hungry, and I have mentioned this twice, because I think it is very relevant. I think in the circumstances that God will understand, or He is not the God I know. That is one of the mmm good things about being Jewish. After my wife was killed in that pogrom in Russia, I came to England with only my tools, and when I saw the white cliffs of Dover, alone without my wife, I said, 'God, today I don't believe in you anymore.'"

"What did God say?" Dodger had asked.

Solomon had sighed theatrically, as if he had been put upon by the question, and then smiled and said, "Mmm, God said to me, 'I understand, Solomon; let me know when you change your mind,' and I was really pleased with that, because I'd had my say and the world was better, and now I sit in a place that is rather dirty, but I am free. And I am free to eat pork, if God so wills it that pork comes my way."

Now Solomon turned back to his work. "I am making sprockets, my boy, for this watch. It is engrossing work requiring considerable coordination of hand and eye, but also in its way the work is very soothing, and that is why I look forward to making a sprocket or two. It means I'm helping time know what it is, just as time knows what I will become."

There was silence after that, apart from the reassuring noises of Solomon's tools, and that was just as well because Dodger didn't know what to say, but he wondered whether all that was because Solomon was Jewish or because Solomon was quite old, or both, and so he said, "I want to do a bit of thinking, if that's all right with you? I'll get changed, obviously."

This was because Dodger was certain he did his best thinking on the tosh. It had rained a bit last night, but not too much, and now he wanted some time with nobody else in it.

Solomon waved him away. "Take your time, boy. And take Onan too, if you would be so kind. . . ."

A little while later, a little way away, the lid rose on a grating and Dodger dropped comfortably into his world. It wasn't too bad, because of the rain, and because it was still daylight there were echoes, oh yes, the echoes. It was amazing what the drains picked up, and voices could echo along for quite a way. Every sound left its dying ghost, bouncing who knew how far?

Then, of course, there were the noises from the street; sometimes you could follow a conversation if it was near a drain, people talking away totally oblivious to the tosher hiding below. Once he had heard a lady get out of a carriage, stumble and drop her purse, which opened. Some of the money, as the luck of the tosher would have it, rolled into the nearest drain. Young Dodger had heard her cries, and the curses to the footman who she said hadn't been holding the door properly, and he followed the sound already down in the sewer to where, falling like manna from Heaven, one half sovereign, two half crowns, a sixpence, four pennies, and a farthing dropped almost into his hands.

At the time he had been quite indignant about the farthing; what was a grand lady with a coachman doing with one farthing in her purse?! Farthings were for poor people, and so were half farthings!

You didn't often get days as good as that, but it was nighttime when the sewers became strangely alive. Toshers liked nights with a bit of moonlight. If they went down there then, they sometimes carried a dark lantern—one of the ones with the little door so you could shut off the light if you didn't want to be seen. But those came expensive and were cumbersome, and toshers sometimes had to move fast.

It wasn't only good honest toshers down there in the dark, though, oh no and dearie! There were rats too, of course—it was their natural home, and they didn't particularly want to meet you and you didn't want to meet them—but after the rats came the rat catchers, trapping rats for the dog fights.

And then you got down to the really dreadful things. . . .

There were still plenty of places in the city where the sewers were open and aboveground, and where some of them were pretending to be rivers; this meant that anything that could float or anything that could roll could be dropped or trapped in them in the dead of night. A sensible tosher stayed away from those areas, but there were other people who used the privacy of the sewers for purposes of their own—they were the kind of people who normally wouldn't go out of their way to do a horrible thing to a tosher, but on the other hand they were the kind of people who might just do so if the mood took them, just for a laugh.

They liked a laugh. . . .

Dodger's thoughts shot back onto what Marie Jo had told him. Someone who looked like a lawyer was asking after somebody called Dodger. And Marie Jo was a very shrewd lady; otherwise she wouldn't have survived.

These thoughts spread out in his brain like the incoming tide (always a nuisance to toshers near the Thames). And an answer sprang back at him.

This was his territory; he knew every sewer in the length and breadth of the city, every little hidey-hole that could barely be seen unless you knew where to look, the places that were half blocked off and nobody knew they were there. Honestly, he could navigate by the smells themselves and he knew exactly where he was right now. If someone is looking for me, he thought, if I'm going to have to fight someone, I must see to it that it's on my patch. I'm Dodger; I can dodge down here.

Right now, the air in the tunnel was more or less sweet—well, in comparison to the things that weren't sweet at all, with the possible exception of Onan who had, of course, brought his own particular odors with him. Dodger gave the two-tone whistle that every tosher knew and listened for a reply; there was none, and so, at least for now, he had this area all to himself, as he so often did.

Almost without thinking he picked up a tie pin and a farthing within a couple of yards; luck was with him, and he wondered if it was because he had just done a good deed. As he thought this, Onan began to snuffle and whine and worry at something in a broken-down pile of old bricks. Dodger suddenly heard a *clink* as Onan's nose knocked something loose. Now the dog had something golden in his jaws—a gold ring with a big stone in it! Worth at least a sovereign!

Good old Onan! And thanks to the Lady. But things happened, or didn't happen, and that's all there was to it, Dodger knew. You could drive yourself mad thinking otherwise.

In the gloom, listening to the sounds of the world above,

hunting through the tunnels, Dodger was in his element and Dodger was happy.

Elsewhere, others were not. . . .

There were many candles in this room, but none of them illuminated the face of the man seated by the tapestry. This considerably disconcerted the man known to his special clients as Sharp Bob—most certainly not the name he used when dealing with more ordinary legal affairs. He always liked to see whoever it was who was employing him; on the other hand, he also liked gold sovereigns, and they didn't worry him at all—he was always pleased to see them. He could see two of them now; a lamp in the darkness before him showed them shining on a low table. He hadn't picked them up yet, because he thought, if I pick them up before that incredibly toffish voice tells me to, for a certainty I might just have my knuckles rapped, or worse.

He didn't like this place. He hadn't liked having to spend some time in that rattling coach with a blindfold over his eyes and a man with a foreign accent sitting opposite him who had threatened to do him a mischief if he tried to take it off. He didn't like working for men with foreign accents, when it came down to it. Not to be trusted. Not like doing business with a good, honest God-fearing Englishman—Sharp Bob knew how to deal with *them*. He didn't like the way the journey here had been all around the houses either, doubling back and constantly changing direction like a thief on the run. Nor did he like the fact that after this interview he would have to go through the whole business again.

This place was plush—that was certain; it even smelled

plush. Occasionally people walked past behind him and that made him angry too, because he dared not turn his head. Creepy stuff. He had been here for ten minutes, waiting for whoever it was who had just walked silently over to a chair on the other side of the flames—a fact he knew only because the padded leather chair had complained with that little farting noise that only the very best padded leather chairs gave off when sat upon. Sharp Bob knew a good chair when he heard it, for he had been in the houses of the mighty before, though not on business such as this.

Now there was a stirring, and the someone behind the flames who was anxious not to be seen was about to talk. At this point Sharp Bob realized that the really anxious one was himself, and he had a terrible premonition that he would sooner or later have to pass water.

He nearly did when the hidden voice said: "Also, Mister Sharp Robert, I believe you told us that your men would have no difficulty in dealing with one simple girl. And yet, my friend, it would appear that she has twice escaped you and you were able to catch her only once. This does not, I am sure you will not blame me for pointing out, appear to be a very good record, wouldn't you say?"

There was something in the voice that disturbed Sharp Bob. It was English, but not quite English; as if a foreigner had learned English absolutely perfectly, but hadn't been able to include all the little usages that a native-born speaker would have picked up. In fact, as English, it was too good. Too perfect. Lacking the slurs and imperfections that the native users sprinkled on their conversations. He sat in his puddle of darkness—and fortunately nothing else at the moment—and said, "Well, sir, we expected a girl, but that lady had a punch on her that knocked out one of my boys. And one of them's been in the ring, sir! She was fast and clever, sir, fighting like anything, and you did say that you wanted her back and on the boat in one piece. Unfortunately my boys, quite frankly, sir, also wanted to get home in one piece. They say there never was a girl like that who kicked and spat and punched like a good 'un, and I've got one lad now who walks funny and is sporting a black eye, and another who had two of his fingers torn off. I mean, the first time she took us by surprise, but that time she just ran and they got her back in and tied down in your coach. Of course, after that we were too late for the boat, which is why we were bringing her back to you."

Sharp Bob was feeling on very shaky ground at the moment because, after all, it had hardly been his fault.

"Just as I told your colleague earlier, sir," he went on, "everything would have been all right on the second try, but she kicked the door out and jumped off in the middle of that terrible thunderstorm. Your coachman couldn't stop the horses, sir, not in that rain. Very unusual circumstances. Difficult to predict."

In the silence there was the sound of a page turning and a voice said, "And apparently, Mister Sharp Robert, a person called"—the pages rustled—"Dodger actually wounded your two men, very nearly drowning one in a gutter. It seems to me that we should perhaps have employed him instead."

The man who liked to think of himself as Sharp Bob but wasn't feeling all that sharp right now said, "I can still be of some help, sir, bearing in mind that you already owe me quite a lot for having tracked her down in the first place. I believe you have had my bill for that for some time . . . ?"

The speaker ignored the latter part of this statement, saying instead, "I would like to assume that you have some news pertaining to this little difficulty. I understand there was something further about this troublemaker? Do be so kind as to enlighten me, will you?"

Sharp Bob said, "He has been asking around, sir, and being very what you might call methodical about it, sir."

Sharp Bob was satisfied with "methodical" as a description, but not pleased when the voice said, unnecessarily sharply in his opinion, "Good heavens, man, surely you can use your own initiative, can you not?"

Sharp Bob knew what an initiative was, but right now he was certain he hadn't got one. Hopefully he said, "The body asking the questions ain't just any nobody, if you get my drift; he's got *contacts* on the street, which makes things a little more difficult."

The voice sounded angry, and that did not sit well with Sharp Bob's bladder. Things got no better when out of the dark the voice came back with "Is he working for a policeman—what you call, I believe, a peeler?"

A peeler! What a word to use to a troubled gentleman of fortune. The bloody, bloody peelers. You couldn't bribe them, you couldn't make friends with them—not like the old Bow Street runners—and mostly the new boys were war veterans. If you had been in some of the wars lately and come back with all your bits still attached to your body, then that meant you were either a hard man or very, very lucky. Bloody Mister Peel had sent them scurrying about like busybodies and no mistake, and they wouldn't take no for an answer, and mostly they wouldn't take any answer at all from anyone unless it was: "It's a fair cop, I'll come quietly, sir." You cried uncle, you cried aunt, you cried your eyes out the moment you fell foul of the peelers, and the bleeders wouldn't even help you put them back, and they drank like fish and roared like the Devil, and weren't friends with anybody—and that, amazingly, included the nobs. It *certainly* included those on the fringes of the legal business, like himself, who had relied on the old Bow Street boys who were, well . . . understanding, especially when money jingled.

What could you do with men like the peelers, who respected nobody except Sir Robert Peel himself? The very thought of them was just another problem for Sharp Bob's bladder to cope with. A certain amount of fear trickled down his leg as he said carefully, "No, sir, not for the peelers, sir. He's a bloke, sir, although he is really more of a geezer, sir, if you catch my meaning?"

This led to a frosty silence, which was followed by, "I do not intend to catch anything of yours, Mister Bob. What is a geezer?" The word was said as if the speaker was pulling a dead mouse out of their soup, or more accurately, half a dead mouse.

Sharp Bob, who in these circumstances realized that only half of his name was accurate, was struggling now. Didn't everybody know what a geezer was? Of course they did! Well, every Londoner did, anyway. A geezer was . . . well, a geezer! It was like asking: What is a pint of beer? Or, what is the sun? A geezer was a geezer; although it did occur to Bob that he would have to do some work on the definition before he answered the dangerous voice in the darkness.

He cleared his throat again and said, "A geezer now, well, a geezer is somebody that everybody knows, and he knows everybody, and maybe he knows something about everyone he knows that maybe you wished he didn't know. Um, and well, he's sharp, crafty, um, not exactly a thief but somehow things find their way into his hands. Doesn't mind a bit of mischief, and wears the street like an overcoat. Dodger now . . . well, Dodger's a tosher as well, which means he knows what's going on down in the sewers too—a tosher, sir, being somebody who goes down there looking for coins and suchlike that may have been lost down the drain." This mention of drains seemed to make Sharp Bob somewhat more uneasy as he continued to move uncomfortably and added, "What I'm meaning to say, sir, is that he is a central kind of cove, you might say—makes the place a bit more interesting, if you know what I mean? And he's been seen mixing with some nobby types recently."

Sweating hard and still squirming on his seat, Sharp Bob awaited judgment. Above the frantic beating of his heart he thought he could hear faint whispering beyond the wall of fire. So there was more than one person in the room with him! He squirmed even more—this was not going well.

Eventually, the voice said, "We do not have any interest in interesting people; they can be dangerous. However, if this Dodger is asking questions about the girl, then he might either find her or know where she is now, and so therefore I require you to make certain that he is watched at all times, do you understand? And, of course, it goes without saying that there should be no way that he can know that he is being spied on. Do I make myself clear, Mister Robert? Because I generally do. This is a very delicate matter, and we will be *extremely* disappointed should matters not be brought to a happy ending. I don't intend to expand here, but I'm sure you will understand what an ultimate failure ultimately entails. We want that girl, Mister Robert. We want her back.

"Incidentally, Mister Robert, one of my associates will now take you gently by the arm and lead you to a place where you can, as it were, find some relief. You may take the sovereigns as a token of good faith and we rely on you to deserve them."

A foreigner's gold, Sharp Bob thought, was as good as anyone else's, but you could get into trouble with foreigners, and he would be glad when all this was over.

After taking up the sovereigns and being allowed the blessed relief of the jakes, Sharp Bob was bundled back into the wretched coach, which by the feel of it trundled him all around London again before he was rather rudely pushed out close to his office, his mind busy with what he knew about the lad called Dodger.

One of the invisible gentlemen who had been sitting in the dark leaned down and, switching to his native tongue, said to the interlocutor, "Are you *quite* sure about this man, sir? After all, we *could* get the Outlander? I have made inquiries and he is free at the moment."

"No. The Outlander is sometimes very messy, dangerous; it might become . . . political, if it was known that we had called him in. We would prefer to avoid causing an . . . incident. No, the Outlander is the last resort. I have heard about what he did to the family of the Greek ambassador—it was entirely uncalled for. I won't dream of sending for the likes of him, until every other avenue has been fruitless. If this troublemaker persists in his troublemaking, or brings others into the affair . . . well, then, we may need to reconsider. For now, however, let us continue to use this Mister Robert Sharp. It surely can't be all that difficult, can it, for him to find a girl for us? To follow a grubby little guttersnipe? We can always get rid of him later if he becomes an . . . embarrassment."

CHAPTER SEVEN

Dodger gets a close shave
and becomes a hero (again!);
Charlie gets a story—and a pair of ruined trousers

DODGER GOT BACK HOME and cleaned his face and hands while Solomon dished up the pork casserole. Solomon never said much about his time wandering around other countries, but he had certainly learned cookery on the journey, using spices and herbs that Dodger had never heard of.

Dodger had once asked Solomon why he had chosen to come to England, and Solomon had said, "Mmm, well, my dear, it seems to me that in the pinch most governments settle for shooting their people, but in England they have to ask permission first. Also, people don't much mind what you're doing as long as you're not making too much noise. Mmm, I like that in this country." He had paused. "Once, when I was running away, as usual, I recall I met a rather hairy young man who told me that one day all that sort of thing would be swept away. We were hiding from Cossacks at the time. Occasionally I mmm wonder what happened to young Karl. . . ."

After the meal, which was delicious, Solomon and Dodger

took Onan for his walk while the sun chased the horizon. It was an education to see Solomon locking up. The steps to the attic were narrow and rickety, just like the rest of this place and more or less like everywhere else, but it was when you got inside the attic you noticed the differences—the steel reinforcement around the door, the lock that looked simple but was very complicated indeed, having been made by Solomon himself. It would have taken a small army to break in, and Dodger himself even had to give a special knock before Solomon would open his door. He had asked Solomon why he went to all this trouble, and the old man had said, "A lesson learned, my friend," and left it at that.

Now the streets looked a little like a fairyland under the honey glow of the evening sun although, it must be said, only a little. But the sun seemed to heal the city of the argy-bargy and insults of the day, although there were still a few stalls, their owners lighting up flares as the light dwindled. All was calm and placid—but you knew that this was merely the shift change, because the night people followed the day people as, well, night follows day, although day, generally speaking, doesn't pick night's pockets.

The two of them had a beer from a bottle shop, sharing some of it with Onan while Dodger told Sol about Onan's find in the sewers, and how he was planning to return to the Mayhews' house to take Simplicity for a walk if possible the following day. Tired out, they finally headed back to the attic.

On the way Dodger noticed something quite brilliant shining through the filthy air and said, "What's that, Sol? Is it an angel?"

It was said more in fun than anything else, but Solomon

said, "Mmm, my experience of angels is somewhat limited, my boy, although I do believe they exist mmm; however that particular angel, if I am not mistaken, is the planet Jupiter."

Dodger squinted at it. "What's that, then?" Sol was always telling him stuff, but this was definitely something new.

"You don't know? Jupiter is a gigantic world, much bigger than the Earth."

Dodger stared. "Do you mean that Jupiter is a world with people living on it?"

"Mmm, I believe astronomical science is uncertain on that point mmm, but I assume there must be, because otherwise what would be the purpose of it? And if I may expand mmm, I will tell you that it is only one of a number of planets, which is to say worlds, moving around the sun."

"What? I thought the sun went round us. I mean, you can see it doing it, it stands to reason."

Dodger was puzzled, and the careful voice of Solomon said, "Mmm, there is no doubt about it; the fact has definitely been established. It might also amuse you to know that the planet Jupiter has four moons, which travel around it just like our moon travels around the Earth."

"What do you mean? I thought you just said we go round the sun. So where does the moon go, then? Not round the sun too?"

"Indeed, the moon circles the Earth and together they circle the sun, and indeed mmm I can assure you about the moons of Jupiter, because I witnessed them through a telescope when I was in Holland."

Dodger thought his head would explode. What a thing to

find out. You get up, you walk around, you think you know everything there is to know, and suddenly it turns out that up in the sky everything is spinning around like a top. He felt almost indignant that he hadn't been let into the secret before, and as they continued their walk, he listened hard as Solomon imparted as much astronomy as he could remember, a process that ended when Dodger said, "Can we get to any of these worlds?"

"Mmm, very unlikely—they are a long way off."

Dodger hesitated at this and said, "As far away as Bristol, maybe?" He had heard of Bristol, apparently a big port but not as big as London.

Solomon sighed and said, "Alas, Dodger, it is much, much farther away than Bristol; it is even much farther away than Van Diemen's Land, which I believe is the farthest you can go from here, it being on the other side of the world."

It seemed to Dodger that everything he was told by Solomon stuck him like a silver pin, which didn't hurt but filled him up with a sort of fuzz. He was beginning to see a world that stretched far beyond the tunnels beneath the streets—a world that was filled with things he didn't know. Things he hadn't even known he didn't know until now. Things he realized with a jolt that he *wanted* to know about. He wondered too if maybe Simplicity might be even more interested in a man who knew this kind of thing—and he realized how much he was looking forward to seeing her again.

As they climbed the stairs, Solomon said, "If you were better at your letters, Dodger, I might interest you with the works of Sir Isaac Newton. Now let us get in—I am beginning to feel the damp. Mmm, you asked me about angels earlier, which are mmm messengers, so I suspect that means anything that brings you information may be considered to be an angel, my dear Dodger."

"I thought they were supposed to be messages from God?"

Solomon sighed as he began the business of unlocking his door. "Mmm, well now," he said, "if one day you gave up messing about in . . . well, mess, I might talk to you about the works of Spinoza, a philosopher who might broaden your mind—because, as far as I can see, there's plenty of room— and pass on the nature of atheism, which most certainly questions the belief in God. As for me, some days I believe in God, and some days I do not."

Then Dodger said, "Is that allowed?"

Solomon pushed the door open and then fussily began locking it up again behind them. "Dodger, you fail to under-stand the unique arrangements between Jewish people and God." He looked over at Onan, and added, "We are not always in agreement. You ask about angels. I speak of people. But who, for instance, are humans to sanction love to them-selves alone? Where there is love, there must mmm surely be a soul; yet curiously the Lord appears to believe that only humans have souls. I have explained to Him at length why He should mmm reconsider His stance on the matter, especially since, quite some time ago and before I met you, I was once confronted with an agitated gentleman possessed of a belief that all Jews should die, and also of a very large metal bar—a circumstance may I add that I was not mmm unfamiliar with in any case. Onan, who wasn't much more than a puppy at that time, valiantly bit him in the unmentionables, thereby distracting him so that I could lay him low with a little trick that I had mmm learned in Paris. Who can say that action wasn't done out of love, especially since in doing his very best to keep me from harm, Onan received for his selflessness the heavy blows that possibly made him the dog he is today. Mmm, and now I am rather tired, and I intend to put out the light."

In the gloom Dodger rolled out his mattress; Onan watched him eagerly, in the hope that this might be one of those nights when it was chilly enough for Dodger to want a rather smelly dog sharing the thin mattress with him. His gaze held that unconditional love that only a dog can have—a dog with a soul, surely. But Onan was irredeemably a dog, which made his metaphysics considerably less complicated than those of humans, although sometimes he had a slight crisis in that he had two gods to worship: the old one who smelled of soap, and the young one who smelled deliciously of just about everything else—at least when he got back from toshing, when to the senses of Onan Dodger was like a rainbow stuffed with kaleidoscopes. Now the hopeful dog riveted Dodger in the somewhat distressing sincerity of his love, and Dodger gave in; he always did.

The little room was silent and dark, apart from the slight snoring of Solomon, the gray light that managed to filter through the dirty window, and the smell of Onan, which in some peculiar way could almost be heard.

Outside in the street, one man watched, though he wished there were two men, because one man by himself could so easily be one dead man in the morning, if indeed the dead can find themselves dead, which was one of those philosophical conundrums that Solomon liked.

Up in the attic Dodger slept, and in his dreams he listened to the planets rolling overhead, interspersed occasionally with visions of the girl with golden hair.

Dodger got up even earlier than Solomon the next morning; usually, if he had no plans for the day, he would lounge under the blanket until Onan licked his face, and you never wanted that to happen more than once.

Solomon said nothing, but Dodger noticed his little smile as he made the soup that would do duty for breakfast today. It was true that with Solomon's magic and his contacts in Covent Garden, he could make mere gruel into a very elegant soup that Dodger believed could hardly be bettered any-where, even by Marie Jo. And right now, Dodger put down his spoon.

"That was very nice, thank you, Sol, but now I have to go."

"Mmm, not without shining your boots you are not. You are almost a gentleman now, at least in very poor light-ing circumstances, and you are on a mission of mmm great importance, and so you must look your best, especially this afternoon when you go and see Miss Simplicity again. It can be difficult enough as it is to be a member of the chosen peo-ple in this city without being accused of sending a lad like you out without appropriate schmutter; people will be going back to throwing stones at the building again! Mind you don't get that suit dirty—I want to see you back here later with not one mark on it. Now, your boots, boy." Solomon opened one of his strongboxes and handed Dodger a small metal container, saying, "This is the proper boot polish, the real thing, even smells nice mmm, not like that dratted pig fat you use! You will expend some elbow grease shining your shonky boots until you can see your somewhat shonky face in them, which leads me on to the next thing that you are going to have to do, because you will see that your face needs almost as much work as your boots, since you didn't mmm wash properly last night."

Before Dodger could object, Solomon continued, "And then you will realize that what you tend to think of as your hair is in fact something worse than mmm a Mongolian's breeches, which are noisome things indeed, for the hair and bits of yak; indeed, I believe yak milk is what they use on their hair for special occasions. And so, since I don't want to have to flee to yet another country mmm, after you have got yourself spruced up and looking like a Christian—because, my dear boy, the chances of you ever looking Jewish are thankfully small—I suggest you go and find yourself a proper barber for a haircut and a professional shave, not mmm from an old man whose hands get shaky when he's tired."

Dodger could shave himself in a lackluster kind of way—even if, truthfully speaking, there wasn't really all that much to shave yet—but he had never had a proper official haircut in his life. He would generally just do it himself, slicing off handfuls of hair with his knife, using Solomon as a kind of clever looking glass since the old boy just stood in front of him and told him whereabouts to slice next. This left something to be desired, possibly everything, and then he would have to have a go with the nit comb, which was uncomfortable to say the least, but it stopped the itching. It was great to see the little buggers dropping out onto the floor too, where he could jump up and down on them, knowing that for the next few days, at least, he was not going to be a nitwit.

He plunged his hand into his scalp now, a technique that Solomon called the German comb, and he had to admit that Sol was right—there was considerable room for improvement up there above his eyebrows. So he said, "I know where there's a barbershop. I saw it the other day when I was in Fleet Street."

He had enough time, he thought, as he applied the aforesaid elbow grease to his boots, along with the newfound boot polish. Solomon, standing over him to make certain he did it properly, said that he had bought the polish in Poland. There seemed to be no end to the countries that Solomon had visited and left at speed; it wouldn't do to force him to go to another.

Dodger now remembered how Solomon had once taken a pepperbox pistol from one of his strongboxes. "What do you want that for?" he had asked. And Solomon had said, "Once bitten, twice shy. But not that shy . . ."

When the boots were cleaned to the old man's satisfaction—and he was not easily satisfied—Dodger sprinted in the general direction of Fleet Street. The streets were warming up, but he felt clean, even if there was a certain question mark over the shonky suit: it was making him itch like mad! It looked wonderful, and he wanted to be all nonchalant and wide as he walked up the street, but this was rather spoiled by the fact that every spare minute he was scratching somewhere about his person. It was an itch that wanted to move about, a playful itch, and it wanted to play hide and seek, at one point being in his boots and then turning up behind his ears, and just as quickly finding its way into his crotch, where on the whole it was rather difficult to do anything about in public. However, he decided that going faster might help, and so he arrived, slightly breathless, at the barbershop he had noticed yesterday and for the first time glanced at the little nameplate, which he eventually deciphered as: MR. SWEENEY TODD, BARBER-SURGEON.

He stepped inside the place, which appeared to be empty until he spotted a pale and rather nervous-looking man who was sitting in the barber's chair and drinking a beverage of what turned out to be coffee. The barber sighed as he saw Dodger, dusted down his apron, and said with brittle cheerfulness, "Good morning, sir! An excellent morning! What can I do for you today?" At least he *tried* to make this greeting cheerful, but you could see he didn't have it in him. Never had Dodger seen such a woebegone face, apart from the time when Onan disgraced himself more than usual by eating Solomon's dinner while the old man's back was turned.

Mister Todd was definitely not a naturally cheerful personality; the gloom was apparently laminated to him and he was obviously more built by nature to be someone like an undertaker's mute, whose job it was to follow the coffin of the deceased, looking respectably mournful but not saying a word because that would cost tuppence extra. It wouldn't have been so bad if Mister Todd hadn't tried to ignore this by pretending to be cheerful; it was like putting rouge on a skull. Dodger was fascinated. Perhaps all barbers are like this? he thought to himself. After all, I'm only asking for a shave and a haircut.

With some misgivings, he sat down in the chair and

Sweeney swirled a white sheet over him in a way that would have been called theatrical if, indeed, Sweeney had really known how to do it the first time. At this point, Dodger became aware of a dull, persistent smell coming from somewhere. It had the flavor of decay and it mingled with the smells of soap and jars of various lotions. He thought, well, this isn't a butcher's shop, so I just bet his landlord has gone and knocked a way from the privy to the sewers—I really wish they didn't do that sort of thing.

A lot of the sheet ended up around Dodger's neck, to be whisked aside by the luckless Sweeney with lots of apologies and assurances that it wouldn't happen again. It did. Twice. Next time it fell around Dodger in a way that both of them could live with, and the sweating Sweeney turned his attention to the job at hand. At some time, somebody must have told Mister Todd that a barber, in addition to tonsorial prowess, should have memorized practically a library of jokes, anecdotes, and miscellaneous rib-ticklers, occasionally including—should the gentleman in the chair be of the right age or nature—ones that might include some daring remarks about young ladies. However, the person who had given him this advice had simply not calculated on Sweeney's terrible lack of anything that could be called bonhomie, cheerfulness, ribaldry, or even a simple sense of humor.

Nevertheless, Dodger noticed he did try. Oh my, how he tried, stropping his razor while messing up punch lines and, horror of horrors, laughing at the joke that he himself had so clumsily executed. But at last the razor was sharp enough for Sweeney and then there was the matter of the shaving foam, which the man attended to just as soon as he had laid the razor down so that its gleaming edge faced north, all the better to maintain its sharpness.

Dodger, helpless in the chair, watched in something like awe, his mind springing to and fro from the spectacle of the barber's preparations to a pleasing image of the admiration he hoped would appear on Simplicity's face once she saw him scrubbed up so well, oh my, a proper young gent. Now he could see that the man's hands had scars on every finger, although this slight problem barely showed up because Sweeney was briskly whisking up the shaving foam with all the manic enthusiasm of a circus clown. The stuff was falling out all over the place, and here and there, because it had been so suffused with air as to make it practically dirigible, it was floating away on the breeze as if it wanted to get out of there as much as Dodger did right now—especially since he was aware of that smell, that heavy and unpleasant smell, gradually permeating the shop.

"Are you feeling all right, Mister Todd?" he said. And, "Your hands are shaking a little bit, Mister Todd."

The barber's face looked like steel, if steel could sweat, and he was swaying back and forth with his eyes like two holes in the snow, looking far away but at something else, somewhere else. Dodger began stealthily to extricate himself from the cloth while keeping a sharp eye on the man. And, oh dear, and now Mister Todd started to mumble, the words blurred as they tried to get out one after the other, some of them so urgent to get away from the swaying man that they overtook themselves.

Then Sweeney was between Dodger and the door to the street, waving the gleaming razor like a bride just after her

wedding, straining to see who is going to catch the bou-
quet. . . .

Dodger, hoping that his heartbeat could not be heard, said
calmly, "Tell me what you see, Mister Todd; it sounds terrible. Can I help you?"

Bang bang went his heart, but Dodger ignored it.
Unfortunately, so did Sweeney Todd, whose mutterings
began to take on something vaguely if erratically understand-
able. Moving gently, so very gently, Dodger slowly eased
himself out of the chair and to his feet, and he thought,
opium, maybe? He sniffed, wished he hadn't—no alcohol on
the man's breath either. He said in as kind a voice as he could
muster, "What is it you are looking at, Mister Todd?"

"They . . . they keep coming back. Yes, yes, coming back,
trying to take me away with them. . . . I remember them. . . .
Do you know what a cannonball can do, sir? Sometimes they
bounce, very funny, ha, and then they are running along the
ground, and then some lad . . . yes, some lad fresh from the
farm in Dorset or Ireland, with his head full of lies about combat, and in his pocket a badly drawn picture of his girlfriend,
who might have let him tickle her fancy because he was the
brave warrior off to fight Boney . . . This young warrior sees
that dreadful cannonball rolling along on the turf like it's a
game of skittles, and so like a bloody idiot he calls out to his
mates, such as have survived, and he decides to give it a big
kick, not knowing how much force there is still left in the
ball. Which is quite enough to take off his leg, and not just
his leg. Barber-surgeon, that's me, the surgeon bit on the
battlefield being somewhat akin to butchery, but slightly better paid. . . . And I see them now . . . the broken men, the

handiwork of God twisted into terrible shapes, terrible . . . and here they come . . . here they come, just as they always come, our glorious heroes, some seeing for those with no eyes, some carrying those with no legs, some screaming for them with no voice. . . ."

All the time the razor danced and weaved, hypnotically, back and forth, while Dodger slid slowly toward the sweating man.

"Not enough bandages, not enough medicines, not enough . . . life . . ." Sweeney Todd mumbled. "I *tried*. I never pointed the weapon at another man, I just tried to help, when the best help you can give is the gentle knife, and yet still they come . . . they come here now, all the time . . . looking for me. . . . And they say they aren't dead, but I know they are. Dead, but still walking. Oh! The pity of it, the pity . . ."

Now Dodger's hand, which had been following the twisting flight of the erratic blade, gently gripped the hand that held it, and it seemed to Dodger that he could see those soldiers himself, so hypnotic was the sway of the razor, and he could feel himself being dragged toward some terrible outcome until the inner Dodger, the bit that wanted to survive, woke up, saluted, took control over Dodger's arm, and neatly and carefully lifted the razor out of Sweeney Todd's hand.

The swaying man didn't even notice it go. Still staring into a place where Dodger did not want to see, he simply let it go and slumped down over the chair, foam settling around him softly.

Only then did Dodger realize that they weren't alone, because while he had been halfway in the dream world of Sweeney Todd, there in the doorway—and being remarkably quiet for their kind—were two peelers, sweating and staring at him and poor Mister Todd. One of the peelers said, "Holy Mary, mother of God!" and both men jumped back as Dodger folded up the razor and shoved it into his pocket out of harm's way. Then he turned back, smiled cheerfully at the peelers, and and said, "Can I help you gentlemen?"

After that, the world went mad, or at least more mad than it had been before. Dodger was surrounded by people, and the little room was lousy with peelers, brushing past him to the back of the shop, and then he could hear the rattle of a lock, the thud of a boot, and, in the distance, some terrible swearing. A gust of corruption of graveyard proportions swept through the shop to cries from the crowd, leaving Dodger suddenly feeling rather queasy and, for some reason, a bit annoyed that he hadn't had his haircut.

There was the sound of police whistles outside and more peelers flooded into the shop, two of them then grasping the recumbent and possibly insensible Mister Sweeney Todd, who had tears running down his face. He was rushed out again, leaving Dodger on a chair in the epicenter of a hubbub that was loud enough to be considered a hubbub with at least an extra hub, not to mention bub. Faces watched him from every direction, and there was a gasp every time he moved, and in his rather troubled state he dimly heard the voice of one of the peelers who had just emerged from the cellar saying, "He just stood there. I mean, he just stood there, eyeball to eyeball with the man, not blinking at all, just waiting for a moment to grab the wretched weapon! We didn't dare say a word, 'cos we saw the malefactor was in some kind of dream, a dream in the mind of a man flourishing a dreadful weapon!

What can I say? I beg you, ladies and gentlemen, do not go down into the cellar. Oh no, 'cos if you do, you might see something that you really would not like to see. Stop them, Fred! Calling it dreadful carnage would not do justice to the crimes. You must trust me on this—I was a soldier once. I was at Talavera and that was bad enough. When I went down there I threw up, so I did, all over the place. I mean, well, the stink! No wonder the neighbors had been complaining! Yes, sir, you sir, can I help you?"

Blearily, Dodger saw Charles Dickens arrive on the heels of the peelers. Charlie said, "My name is Dickens, and I know young Dodger here to be a most excellent and trustworthy individual; he is also the hero who saved the staff of the *Morning Chronicle* just the other evening, and I'm sure you have all heard of that."

Dodger began feeling rather better now, especially as there was tremendous applause, and he brightened up still further when he heard somebody in the crowd shout, "I propose we make up a subscription for this young man of such exceptional valor! I pledge five crowns!"

He tried to get to his feet at this point, but Charlie Dickens, who was bending over him, pushed him gently back down into the chair, bent down until his lips were very close to Dodger's ear, and whispered, "It would be in order to groan a little in response to your terrible encounter, my friend. Trust me as a journalist; you are a hero of the hour, again, and it would be a pity if an unguarded comment at this juncture spoiled things." He leaned an inch closer and whispered, "Listen to them shouting out how much they will pledge to the hero, and so I will carefully get you to your feet and take you to the magnificent offices of the *Chronicle*, where I will pen an article the likes of which has never been written before, since possibly the time of Caesar."

Charlie smiled. Rather like a fox, Dodger thought, in the spinning, roaring, suddenly baffling world. Then he inched still closer, and said, "Incidentally, my intrepid friend, it would interest you to know that I have been told just now that Mister Sweeney Todd used his razor to slit the throats of six gentlemen who came to him earlier this week for a haircut and a close shave. But for your almost magical response, you would have been the seventh of them. And these were my best trousers!" These words were shouted, or more accurately screamed, because Dodger had thrown up his breakfast all over Charlie.

Sometime after, Dodger was seated at the long table in the editor's office of the *Chronicle*, wishing he could be on his way to see Simplicity. Opposite him was Charlie, who was somewhat less angry now since, being a man of means, he had acquired another pair of trousers and sent the other ones to be cleaned. The inner wall of the office was one of those half-height affairs so that people passing by in the newsroom could see what was happening, and now, how they *did* pass by. And linger too, with every writer, journalist, and printer finding an excuse to see the young man who, according to the magical telegraph of the streets, had wrestled to the ground the terrible Demon Barber of Fleet Street.

Dodger was getting rather annoyed about this. "I hardly touched 'im! I just pushed 'im gently down and took the wretched razor off 'im, that's all! Honest! It was as if he had been taking opium or something, 'cos he was seeing dead soldiers—dead men coming toward him, I swear it, and he was talking to them, like he was ashamed that he couldn't save them. God's truth, Mister Charlie, I swear I was seeing them too, come the finish! Men blown all to pieces! And worse, like men *half* blown to pieces and screaming! He wasn't a demon, mister, although I reckon he may have seen Hell, and I ain't a hero, sir, I really ain't. He wasn't bad, he was mad, and sad, and lost in his 'ead. That's all of it, sir, the up and the down of it, sir. An' that's the truth you should write down. I mean, I ain't no hero, 'cos I don't think he was a villain, sir, if you get my drift."

Then there was silence, somehow filled by Charlie's gaze, in this polished little room. A clock ticked and, without looking, Dodger could feel the employees still taking every opportunity to look at him, the unassuming and reluctant hero of the hour. Charlie was staring at him, occasionally playing with his pen, and at last the man said, with a sigh, "Dear Mister Dodger, the truth, rather than being a simple thing, is constructed, you need to know, rather like Heaven itself. We journalists, as mere wielders of the pen, have to distill out of it such truths that mankind, not being godlike, can understand. In that sense, all men are writers, journalists scribbling within their skulls the narrative of what they see and hear, notwithstanding that a man sitting opposite them might very well brew an entirely different view as to the nature of the occurrence. That is the salvation and the demon of journalism, the knowledge that there is almost always a different perspective from which to see the conundrum."

Charlie played with his pen some more, looking uncomfortable, and went on, "After all, my young Dodger, what exactly are you? A stalwart young man, plucky and brave and apparently without fear? Or possibly, I suggest, a street urchin with a surfeit of animal cunning and the luck of Beelzebub himself. I put it to you, my friend, that you are both of these, and every shade in between. And Mister Todd? Is he truly a demon—those six men in the cellar would say so! If they could but speak, of course. Or is he the victim as you would like to think of him? What is the truth? you might ask, if I was giving you a chance to speak, which at the moment I am not. My answer to you would be that the truth is a fog, in which one man sees the heavenly host and the other one sees a flying elephant."

Dodger began to protest. He hadn't seen no heavenly host; no elephant neither—he didn't actually know what one of those was—though he'd put a shilling on the fact that Solomon had probably seen both in his travels.

But Charlie was still talking. "The peelers saw a young man face down a killer with a dreadful weapon, and for now that is the truth that we should print and celebrate. However, I shall add a little tincture of—shall we say, a slightly different nature?—reporting that the hero of the hour nevertheless took pity on the wretched man, understanding that he had lost his wits due to the terrible things he had witnessed in the recent wars. I will write that you spoke very eloquently to me about how Mister Todd himself was a casualty of those wars, just as were the men in his cellar. I will make your views known to the authorities. War is a terrible thing, and many return with wounds invisible to the eye."

"That's pretty sharp of you, Mister Charlie, changing the world with a little scribble on the paper."

Charlie sighed. "It may not. He will either hang or they will send him to Bedlam. If he's unlucky—for I doubt he would have the money necessary to ensure a comfortable stay there—it will be Bedlam. Incidentally, I would be very grateful if you could attend at the premises of *Punch* tomorrow so that our artist, Mister Tenniel, can draw your likeness for the paper."

Dodger tried to take all of this in, and said finally, "Who are you going to punch?"

"I am not going to punch anybody; *Punch* is a new periodical magazine of politics, literature, and humor which, if you don't know, means something that makes you laugh, and possibly think. One of the founders was Mister Mayhew, our mutual friend." Charlie's jaw dropped suddenly, and he scribbled down a few words on the paper in front of him. "Now off you go, enjoy yourself, and please come back here as soon as you can tomorrow."

"Well, if you will excuse me, sir, I have another appointment anyway," said Dodger.

"*You* have an *appointment*, Mister Dodger? My word, it seems to me that you are becoming a man for all seasons."

As Dodger hurried off, he wondered exactly what Charlie had meant. He would be damned if he was going to ask him, but he would find out as soon as possible. Just in case.

CHAPTER EIGHT

A young man takes his young lady
for a constitutional walk;
and Mrs. Sharples comes to heel

DODGER MADE HASTE TOWARD the house of the Mayhews
while in his mind he saw the cheerful face and hooked nose
of Mister Punch, beating his wife, beating the policeman, and
throwing the baby away, which made all the children laugh.
Why was that funny? he thought. Was that funny *at all*? He'd
lived for seventeen years on the streets, and so he knew that,
funny or not, it was real. Not all the time, of course, but
often when people had been brought down so low that they
could think of nothing better to do than punch: punch the
wife, punch the child, and then, sooner or later, endeavor to
punch the hangman, although that was the punch that never
landed, and, oh how the children laughed at Mister Punch!
But Simplicity wasn't laughing. . . .

Running faster than he had before, Dodger arrived, if you
put any reliance on all the bells of London, just about the time
people would have finished their lunch. Feeling very bold,
he walked up to the front door—he was, after all, a young

gentleman with an *appointment*—and rang the bell, stepping backward when the door was opened by Mrs. Sharples, who gave him a look of pure hatred and, since she then slammed the door, couldn't have got a receipt from him.

Dodger stared at the emphatically closed door for several seconds and thought, I don't have to believe what just happened. He pulled himself upright, brushed the dust off his coat, and grabbed the bell pull for the second time, till at last the door was opened once again by the same woman. Dodger was ready, and even before she had finished opening her mouth he said, "This morning I defeated the Demon Barber of Fleet Street, and if you don't let me in we will see what Mister Charles Dickens has got to say about it in his newspaper!" As the woman ran down the hall he shouted after her, "In big letters!"

He stood waiting by the open door, and very shortly after this he saw Mrs. Mayhew walking toward him with a smile of a woman who wasn't sure that she should be smiling. She came a little closer, lowered her voice, and said, in the tones of one almost certain that she was going to be told the most enormous lie, "Is it *really* true, young man, that you were the one who this morning defeated the most dreadful of villains in Fleet Street? The cook told me about it; and apparently, according to the butcher's boy, the news is already the talk of London. Was that *really* you?"

Dodger thought of Charlie's fog. Thought of wanting to see Simplicity again, and did his best to look suitably bashful and heroic all at the same time. But he did manage to say, "Well, Mrs. Mayhew, it was all a sort of fog."

It seemed to work, for Mrs. Mayhew was speaking again.

"Somehow, Mister Dodger, you will not be surprised that Simplicity herself, subsequent to your recent call, has made it quite clear to us that she would like to go out in the sunshine for a constitutional walk with you, such as you suggested previously. Since it is such a fine day, and she herself seems well on the way to being restored, I cannot find it in me to deny her this wish. You will of course, as we said before, have to be in the charge of a chaperone."

Dodger let a little silence reign and then forced it to abdicate. He attempted to make the small noise that Solomon produced when he was trying to make conversation more pleasant and intimate, and said, "Mmm, I am most grateful, madam, and while I'm on the subject, if you don't mind, I would like someplace where I can sit quietly while Simplicity is getting ready. I have a few aches and pains that I need to deal with."

Mrs. Mayhew was suddenly all motherly. "Oh, you poor dear boy!" she said. "How you must be suffering. Are you very badly wounded? Shall I get somebody to bring the doctor? Do you need to lie down?"

Dodger hastened to stop her turning this into something dreadful and said, still slightly breathless, "Please, no, just a nice quiet room where I can sort myself out for a minute or two, if you don't mind. That will do me fine."

Shooing him before her like a hen with one chick, Mrs. Mayhew guided him down the corridor and opened a door into a room that had white and black tiles everywhere and a wonderful privy, not to mention a washbasin. Complete with jug.

Once he was left alone and unseen, Dodger did indeed

use the water to do something at least to his hair, which fortunately had not felt the ministrations of Mister Todd, and generally slicked himself down and made use of the privy. He thought, Well, I've made myself a hero to Mrs. Mayhew, but it's all about Simplicity, isn't it? And Simplicity herself, it appeared, had totally understood what he had said the previous day and indeed was very keen on the walk.

Dodger had never heard the expression "the end justifies the means," but when you had been brought up like him, its principle was nailed to your backbone. So after a discreet interval during which he essayed an occasional groan, Dodger turned himself into a hero and strode out of the privy ready to meet his young lady.

Mrs. Sharples was waiting in the hallway, and this time she looked at him nervously, which you certainly should do when you're looking at a man who is in the news, and what news! Since it had been such a good day, Dodger was generous enough to give her a little smile, and got a little simper in exchange, which suggested that hostilities, if not entirely forgotten, were at least temporarily suspended. After all, he was the wounded hero now, and that had to count for something, even to someone like Mrs. Sharples.

However, he noticed when she took a small book off the hall table that it was one of those that some people used for jotting things down, the ones with a tiny little pencil attached to them by a piece of string. That meant she thought she might have *occasion* to write things down, and Dodger—who had always kept a significant distance between himself and the alphabet—started to wish that he had perhaps spent more time getting to grips with the irritating business of reading as opposed to picking at the letters slowly one at a time. Too late, too late, and now there was a certain amount of movement upstairs and Mrs. Mayhew came down, holding Simplicity by the hand and descending very carefully, making sure that every foot had found the right place before the next foot joined it. This took some time, about a year by Dodger's reckoning, until they were both standing in the hall.

Mrs. Mayhew gave him what you might call an inadequate smile, but Dodger looked just at Simplicity and realized that Mrs. Mayhew had been very careful to provide her with a bonnet and a shawl which covered quite a lot of her face, and therefore most of the bruises, which were already losing some of their color. And just as Dodger looked at her, Simplicity beamed at him, and it was indeed a beam, because the bonnet made a sort of shield around her, so that the center of her face seemed highlighted.

He held out his hand and said, "Hello, Simplicity, I'm so glad you've decided to come for this little walk with me."

Simplicity held out her hand, grasped his very lightly, and said . . . nothing that Dodger could hear; and her head turned very slightly so he could see the bruising to the throat, and that burden that he was carrying almost without noticing now whispered to him, *"You will make them pay!"* In that moment, he thought he saw in Simplicity's eye a glint like a falling star shining as it fell to earth; he had only ever seen one, a long time ago and a long way away on Hampstead Heath, and he had never seen another one since, because you don't get many shooting stars when you are a tosher. But she hadn't let go of his hand, which was extremely pleasant but not practical, unless he wanted to walk backward.

In the end, Dodger carefully let go and trotted around to grasp her other hand, all in one movement, with no harm done, leading the way gently to the gate, tiptoeing through the very small front garden, where a few roses attempted to make a difference. You saw this more and more these days, he thought; people with enough money at last to live in a decent area set about trying to make their tiny little bit of land look like a very small version of Buckingham Palace.

He didn't often walk slowly in London; after all, he was Dodger, dodging here and there, and never there long enough to get caught. But now Simplicity was holding his arm and he was aware that she needed his support, which slowed him down, and that somehow also slowed his thinking so that the bits came together neatly, instead of in a hurry. He turned and looked at Mrs. Sharples, walking behind them. It was early afternoon and around here it was pleasant to walk, and in this bright light he felt curiously happy and at home with the girl on his arm. She kept in step, and every time he glanced at her she smiled at him, and there was a peace that you didn't get in the rookeries until one in the morning when the dead had stopped screaming and the living were too drunk to care. Suddenly it didn't seem to matter whether Simplicity recognized anything important or not; it was enough that they were out for this walk together.

Yet there was a part of Dodger that would always be a dodger, and it guided his eyes and ears around, listening to every footstep, looking at every face and watching every shadow, calculating, figuring, estimating, judging. Now he turned his attention to old Soft Molly, whom he could see approaching.

For a long time Soft Molly had been a puzzle to Dodger, because he had never been able to make out where the flowers came from that she sold in the streets—little nosegays, all very delicate and fine. One day the old lady, who had a face that was a playground for wrinkles, told him where she got them from, and after that he had never thought about the cemeteries in the same way. She had made his flesh creep, but he reckoned perhaps that when you were so very old that you were older than some of the people buried beneath your feet, and therefore deserving of some respect yourself, he could see why it would make sense to you to "borrow" some of the blooms scattered on the headstones of the recently deceased. It was hard to see where the harm was, and if you thought about it, the flowers stolen from the dear departed who, it must be said, could hardly be able to smell them now, were nevertheless keeping the old dear alive.

It was a sad thought, and a horrible picture, that Molly would spend time in the graveyard at night methodically collecting floral wreaths to be carefully unraveled in the heart of darkness and lovingly made into little posies for the living. In the scales of the world, how much did it matter that the dead had been robbed of the flowers they could never have seen when, for one night at least, poor old Soft Molly, who had as far as he could tell just one tooth, was still living. Besides, he thought, some of those wreaths looked like a florist shop all by themselves so would barely miss a few blossoms, and that thought made him feel a bit better.

That was why he gently pulled Simplicity with him as the old girl crouched on the pavement, looking pitiful and not having to try. He pressed sixpence, yes a *whole* sixpence, on a little bundle of fragrant blooms. And if the dead turned over in their graves, they were generous enough to do it quietly, and besides, the exercise would do them good.

When he handed them to Simplicity, all he could find to say was "Here is a present for you," and she said, she actually said, "Oh, roses!" He was certain of it. He saw her lips move, he saw the lips become a rose as they pronounced the words and then close, and even Simplicity seemed surprised to have heard the words, while deep in his heart, once again, Dodger wanted very much to hurt somebody.

Then she said, "Please, Dodger, I heard them talking. I am very grateful to Missus and Mister Mayhew but . . . it is as I feared. I heard them say that they will be very pleased when I am sent back, to the safety of my husband." The look on her face as she said it was pure terror.

Dodger turned to glance at the housekeeper, who was some way behind them, still clutching her notebook, and whispered, "I believe that despite everything you are not quite as ill as you appear, yes?" There was a silent "yes." To which he more or less silently said, "Don't let them know. Trust me, I'll see to it that you go somewhere else."

Simplicity's face shone as she said quietly, so that only he could hear, "Oh, Dodger, I am so happy to meet you again. I burst into tears every night when I remember that storm and how you drove away those terrible men who were"—and here she hesitated a little—"so unkind, shall we say."

The softness of that speech pierced Dodger's heart, orbited right round him, and came back and did it again. Was she truly beginning to believe him when he said he wanted to help her? Believe that he wasn't playing some kind of game?

"I know I should not hate," she continued, "but for them, yes! Because of them I must not use my proper name, and I dare not tell anyone it—not even you, not yet. For now, I *must* remain Simplicity, although I do not believe that I am very simple."

But although the sun was still shining and the honey was still in the air, Dodger had an inkling that somebody other than Mrs. Sharples was watching them; someone was *following*. He knew this simply because on the streets you learned to notice these things almost out of the back of your head—someone with a hand out, or maybe a peeler. You didn't get to become a geezer if you didn't have eyes in your arse, and it helped if you had them on the top of your head too. Surely now, someone was following them; and it had to be someone with a mission: a mission of their own.

He cursed himself for not thinking about this, but really you can't be thinking of everything when you are a hero. He thought, well, that was quick work—he'd only been asking questions on the street yesterday. Someone was in a great hurry. But right now he did nothing about it and strolled along at a steady pace, a simple young man taking his young lady for a little constitutional walk, without a care in the world, while inside his head the wheels turned and the troops were called up, plans were made and angles sought.

Whoever it was was keeping their distance, and whatever happened Dodger was certain that he ought to make sure nobody knew where Simplicity was living. Whoever they were, they weren't at the moment confident enough to attack him right here, especially not with Mrs. Sharples in tow; that disapproving look of hers would have been worth a battalion to the Duke of Wellington.

And so all three of them walked on happily, just like normal people, until he heard the voice of the old baggage saying, "I think this is quite far enough, young man, and so I insist that we rephrase our steps. Simplicity's condition is still very delicate, and you will do no service to let the cold find its way to her."

Her voice did not seem as unpleasant as he had heard it before, and so he guessed that the only hope was to take her into his confidence. He reached out and, much to her surprise, pulled the woman toward them, and whispered so, "Ladies, I believe there is a gentleman following us who means somebody harm. It may be Simplicity or it may be, well, me. For the love of God, and your job, I implore you now, without saying a word, to turn at the next corner and wait while I send the cove about his business."

To his amazement Mrs. Sharples whispered back, "I have misjudged you, young man. And if the bastard puts up a fight, pray kick him in the unmentionables, good and proper. Do him up bad!" Then her face returned to its usual expression of low-grade dislike for all and sundry.

Simplicity snorted and said, "Dodger, if you can, put him in the gutter."

Dodger saw Mrs. Sharples's look of surprise, but Simplicity was standing up straight and right now looked as though she was ready for a fight.

Puzzled, but somehow reassured for the moment, Dodger watched as the women barely missed a step as they walked on, and then when the time was right he turned the corner sharply into an alleyway and let the ladies pass him. He waited, his back to the wall so that when the man stepped around carefully, Dodger had him by the throat and had brought his foot straight upward to a place that would jangle, being rewarded with a groan. Then he pulled the man upright again and dragged him so close that he could smell the sweat. And there was slightly more light so he could now see him as well as smell him.

"Oh my word, Dirty Benjamin, as I live and wish I couldn't breathe. Down for a little stroll among the toffs, ain't you? What's your game today? 'Cos you have been following me a step for a step over the last seven corners I have traveled, and on one of them I crossed over my own steps. Funny, ain't it, that you should have the same roundabout journey in mind, you nasty, nasty little man. A spy! Jesus, you stink like a five-day dog, you wheeze like a pig in difficulty, and if you don't say something soon, so help me God, I will give you a pasting, see if I don't."

At that moment it occurred to him that the man was unable to say anything because Dodger's other hand was on his throat. And, indeed, Benjamin looked as if he was about to explode. Dodger loosened his grip a little, and pushed the luckless Benjamin farther into the alley.

The alley was narrow, and no one else was around, so Dodger said, "You know me, don't you, Benjamin, even in my smart new clobber? Good old Dodger, who will never do you a bad turn if he could do you a good one. I thought you were my friend, I really did. But friends don't spy on friends, do they?"

Dirty Benjamin stood frozen in front of Dodger, and after a bit of effort managed to get out, "They is saying as you killed that barber, you know the one with all them dead bodies in his cellar, yeah?"

Dodger hesitated. Life was so much simpler in the sewers, but he had learned something lately, which was that the truth was indeed a fog, just like Charlie said, and people shaped it the way they wanted it to go. He had never killed anybody, ever, but that didn't matter, because the fog of truth didn't want to know that poor Mister Todd had been a decent man who saw so many terrible things in the service of the Duke of Wellington that his mind had become as twisted as the corpses of the men they placed in front of him. The poor devil was indeed more of a candidate for Bedlam than for the gallows, though any man with any sense but no money—oh, not those of the poor who did go to Bedlam—would choose the hangman any day. But the fog of truth didn't like awkward details, and so there had to be a villain, and there had to be a hero.

Although it was a wretched nuisance, right now at least it could make itself useful, and so he looked at Dirty Benjamin sternly and said, "Something like that, but not all that. Now, if you are my friend you will tell me why you were following me, because if you don't I will make cold meat of you."

It was a rotten thing to do to Benjamin, who he knew of old as a snowdropper, who mostly stole ladies' underthings off clotheslines—being a man of no ambition whatsoever apart from being alive tomorrow—and ran errands for anyone who had some money and was bigger than him. He was the kind of person who would make a body want to wash their hands after meeting him; the man was a worm. Yes, all he did was wriggle. He was one of the lost souls, one of the people who were behind the door when God went past; they just grazed on the world, hardly disturbing it a bit, and were always scared of something.

Right now, Dirty Benjamin looked very scared, and Dodger relented, saying, "Well, maybe it won't be cold meat, because I know you, Ben, and I'm sure you're going to tell me who sent you to follow me, am I right? If you do that, I won't hurt you."

Both Dodger and his captive turned as the shadows changed to reveal Mrs. Sharples peering round the corner with Simplicity next to her. The housekeeper said, "I am sorry to interrupt your little concussion, gentlemen, but I think it is time for us to go home, if it's all the same with you?"

Dodger turned back to the hapless villain in front of him. "Benjamin," he said sternly, "I have no beef with you. This is your last chance. Tell me who you are working for and why, and I will never let on it's you."

Dirty Benjamin was crying, and not just crying by the smell of it. He slid to the ground in a pitiful heap.

And Dodger leaned over and whispered, "I have in my hand the razor of Sweeney Todd the barber, and at the moment I haven't opened the blade. But it calls to me; it calls to me to use it. . . . So now, Benjamin, I strongly suggest you tell me who you are working for. *Do you understand?*"

The words came out so fast that they tumbled among themselves. But Dodger made out: "It was Harry the Slap from Hackney Marshes, but the word is there's important coves wanting to know where you are, and if you've got some girl with you. That's all I know, honest to God. There's some kind of reward out."

Dodger said, "Who set up the reward?"

"Don't know. Harry the Slap never told me nuffin', just to tell 'im. Promised me a cut of the profit, so he did."

Dodger stared at the face. No, he wasn't lying. Benjamin was easy meat, and so he said, "Well, Benjamin, as a friend, I rely on you not to tell Harry the Slap that you have seen me." There was a frantic nodding of the head from the wretched little man on the ground. "And, of course, there is just one other thing I must do. I did say that I would not harm you but *this*"—and he swung his boot—"is from Mrs. Sharples. Sorry, but she asked me to."

He was rewarded with a deep groan from Benjamin and, amazingly, a huge and horrible grin from Mrs. Sharples, who said, "Well done, young man, do it again!"

Dodger thought, this is time to be the man who saved the world from Mister Sweeney Todd. So he said quietly, "Simplicity, and you too, Mrs. Sharples, listen. I have reason to fear that there are people who are searching for Simplicity to do her harm and therefore I am going to remove her from the kind embrace of the Mayhew household. Although I don't doubt that they *are* kind to her, it makes me shiver, it does, to think of you opening the door to them very nasty coves."

"But she is in their care, Mister Dodger," Mrs. Sharples insisted.

Dodger opened his mouth, but the noise he heard was Simplicity speaking. Not loudly, but not a whisper either, and she said, "I am a married woman whose husband turns out to be a weak and stupid boy, Mrs. Sharples, and I believe that Dodger is right in this instance. So I suggest we make our way back to the house as soon as possible."

"Yes, indeed," said Dodger. "I am sure you would be in agreement, Mrs. Sharples?"

Mrs. Sharples looked down at Dirty Benjamin and said, "What are you going to do about him?"

Dodger said to Benjamin lying on the ground, "Listen, my friend, I know who you are, and I know where you live, don't I just! Still collecting corsets, are you? Trust me that what you are going to do as soon as you are fit to stand is start walking up the road there, and you will go on walking as fast as you can in that direction as long as possible and you will not, repeat *not*, turn round to look behind you until it's absolutely dark, understand? Because you know me and I am Dodger. The *new* Dodger. I'm the Dodger what done up Mister Sweeney Todd. The Dodger what has his razor now! And if you do the wrong thing by me, I'll come up through the floor one night with it and make certain you never wake up."

There was a groan from Benjamin, who said, "I ain't never clapped eyes on you, mister, and by God I wish I ha'n't. You'll have no trouble from me."

They began to walk back to the house by a roundabout route, and it wasn't until he saw the kid selling newspapers and screaming, "'Orrible murder! Read all about it! Valiant hero to the rescue!" that Dodger fully realized how life would be getting even more complicated.

At last the little gate to the Mayhew household was back in front of them, and he quickly cased the area for spies and found none. Then he opened the gate for Simplicity, who said, "Thank you very very much, my dear Dodger," and she blew him a kiss, which made no sound at all, except that in his head the belfries of London all clanged at once in one great peal.

The interview with the Mayhews, husband and wife, went rather more smoothly than Dodger had dared hope, especially since he carefully told them how someone was clearly looking for Simplicity—the kind of person, he said, who he would not like to come knocking at their door.

"And so," he concluded, "if you would be so kind, help Miss Simplicity with such packing as she has, help us find a growler, and I will take her forthwith to Charlie, where we will be safe enough to discuss the next move. And please, Missus Mayhew, Mister Mayhew, we will not need a chaperone."

"I feel I must object," said Mrs. Mayhew. "It is hardly seemly. . . ."

Dodger opened his mouth to answer, but Simplicity stepped forward and gave Mrs. Mayhew a kiss and said, "Jane, I'm a married woman and I can stand up and say that my husband wants me as a slave or otherwise dead. I will go with Dodger. The choice or blame is mine, and I would not like to think that any harm came to this household because of me."

They stared at her as one might stare at a dog that has just sung a song, and then suddenly common sense blossomed and Mister Mayhew said, "Dear Mrs. Sharples, can you please get a cab while you, dear, help our guest—her baggage is rather spartan—and be ready for the coach to come."

Now it seemed to Dodger that the coach could not come too soon. And indeed when one did rattle up, without any bidding Mister Mayhew pressed a half crown into Dodger's hand.

"Well done, sir, very well done!"

When the cab was rattling its way to Fleet Street, Simplicity said, "My dear Dodger, why did you rescue me in the rain?"

This bowled him over, but he managed to say, "Because I don't like people who bash up other people who ain't got anybody to bash back on their behalf. I had too much of that when I was a kid, and besides, you were a girl."

The tone of her voice changed as she said, "In fact, a woman, Dodger. Did you know that I lost my baby?"

This flustered Dodger, who managed, "Yes, miss, I mean missus. Very sorry not to have been there earlier."

"Dodger, you came out of the drain like a god. Who could have come up any faster?" And this time the kiss didn't need to be blown. She delivered it directly, as it were.

Charlie was not at the *Chronicle*, but inside his office there was a boy, one of the numerous boys employed by the paper to run around with other bits of paper, looking very important as they did so. This one, though, stared at Dodger as if he was the Archangel Gabriel and whispered hoarsely, "Is it true that you throttled the monster with his own necktie? Oh, can you write down your name on this bit of paper for me, please? I am making a scrapbook."

Dodger stared at the boy's slightly grubby face, which, like his clothes, made it perfectly clear that this was a building with a lot of ink on the premises. He was at a loss and therefore took refuge in the truth, saying, "Look, kid, he was just a very sick old man, right? He thought he was killing dead men who were coming back to haunt him, and I never laid a finger on him, right? I just took the razor off him and the peelers took him away and that is that, do you hear?"

The lad backed away a little and then said, "You are only

saying that because you are modest, sir, I am sure. And Mister Dickens says that if you was to turn up here again today, looking for him, you could find him in the Houses of Parliament, on account of the fact that he is doing a bit of court reporting today. Mister Dodger, he said he'd tell the man on the door to let you in if you ask for him, and if there is any trouble to say you've come from the *Chronicle*, and will you sign this piece of paper for me anyway?" The boy almost pushed a pencil up Dodger's nostril, so Dodger relented and the boy got a squiggle and Dodger got the boy's pencil.

The boy said, "I don't quite know exactly where Mister Charlie will be right now, but you could always ask the peelers." He smiled. "You can be sure that there will be a lot of them about."

Ask a peeler! Dodger? But surely that was the old Dodger saying that, he thought. After all, because of two admittedly total misunderstandings he was a hero, at least to some kid with blobs of ink in his hair, and therefore a hero should be able to stand up and talk to a peeler man to man, shouldn't he? Because a hero would look the peelers directly in the eye and, besides, Simplicity had kissed him, and for another one of the same he would kick a peeler in the arse. All he had to do was keep on the square, life would get better, and it might be better still if he could enlist the help of Mister Dickens.

He looked at Simplicity and said, "Sorry, but it looks like we've got another journey to make."

Then there was nothing for it but to pick up another growler among the plenty outside and head for Parliament Square.

CHAPTER NINE

Dodger takes a cutthroat razor to Parliament,
and meets a man who wants to be on the right side

THE MEN WHO GUARDED the Houses of Parliament, in uniform or otherwise, were not very happy about letting them in, possibly because they could be French spies, or even Russian ones. Dodger wasn't either, but instead of telling them to go to blazes, which he would have done once upon a time before he had Simplicity hanging on his arm, he simply stood there, making himself look as tall as he could, and said, "I am Mister Dodger and I am here to see Mister Charlie Dickens."

This caused a certain amount of chuckling, but he stood straight and stared at them and then somebody said, "Dodger? Isn't he the man who wrestled the Demon Barber to the ground this morning, right down there in Fleet Street?" The first man who had spoken came closer and said, "Yes, the peelers were frightened to go in there, so people say! I heard that people have already subscribed nearly ten guineas for him!"

Now there was another crowd, and the only thing Dodger

could do was to keep saying, "I am here to see Mister Dickens on a very important matter." Then he told himself that all he would have to do would be to hang on, stand up, shake the hands that were proffered, nod and smile and wait until somebody came back with Charlie.

That worked, and a young man—a very smart, very dapper man—suddenly appeared and said, with withering scorn, "If this is the hero, *twice* the hero of Fleet Street according to the newspapers, then what kind of service are we giving him when he comes to see us, yes, what do you *think*?"

There was a kind of little hum on that last "think," and people started clapping and a couple of them said things like "Well said, Mister Disraeli, well done; where are our manners, after all?" And finally one of them said, "Well, I don't know about you, gentlemen, but it seems to me that a hero like that is just the kind of person to have that dreadful cutthroat razor about his person even now!" A statement which made Dodger's heart whine as his mind flashed through images of the repercussions of being caught with it until the very man who had said that burst out laughing, and added, "The very thought, indeed."

"The very thought," Dodger murmured in response, matching the man's laugh with one of his own.

And that was how Dodger and Simplicity got into Parliament, indeed with the cutthroat razor—and with a lie, which was fine, considering that's how so many people got into Parliament. Dodger still wasn't quite sure why he had taken Mister Todd's razor in all the confusion, but he had a feeling that the best place for it to be right now was close to him. Anyway, before he could do anything about it, Mister

Dickens was called for and arrived shortly afterward, taking good care to shake Dodger very theatrically by the hand and then looking at Simplicity and saying, "You are surely not the young lady I last saw fair beaten up three nights ago?" Then he said that he had urgent business with the young cavalier, whatever that meant.

They were escorted along carpeted halls and poured into a small room with a table in it. While Dickens was sorting out chairs and getting Simplicity settled, Dodger kept his eye on Mister Disraeli. He reminded Dodger somewhat of a much younger Solomon, and he also looked like a cat who had found a saucer of milk and had enjoyed every last bit. He was, yes, that was it: he was a dodger—not a dodger like Dodger, but another kind of dodger, and it took one to know one. He looked sharp as a knife, but probably the knife was his tongue; he was that kind of bloke—a smart person, but a definite geezer.

Dodger looked at Disraeli and caught his eye, and Mister Disraeli winked—a tribute from one dodger to another dodger, perhaps. Dodger let himself smile but didn't wink back, because a young man could get into trouble winking at gentlemen. Up until then this place—all these statues, all these soundless carpets, all these pictures on the walls of elderly men with white hair and expressions of acute constipation—had been preying on his nerves, pushing him away, telling him he was small, insignificant, a worm. That wink had broken the spell and told him that this place was just another rookery: bigger, warmer, certainly richer, definitely better fed to judge by the stomachs and the redness of the noses, but after that wink just another street where people jostled for advantage and power and a better life for themselves if not for everybody else.

Dodger couldn't stop grinning as he clutched this thought to himself, like a magic ring that gave you power and no one knew you had it. Then after this high came the low; this rookery was full of words, the place was full of books, and right now he could find no words at all.

At this moment there was a hand on his shoulder and Charlie said, "We, my friend, well, we have business to attend to. You can speak freely to me in front of my good friend Mister Disraeli, an up-and-coming politician of whom we have great hopes and who is aware of the certain current problem that we have. How are you, by the way? Would you like some refreshments?" As Dodger struggled for words, Simplicity nodded her head politely and Charlie walked over to the door and pressed a bell pull. Almost immediately a man came in, had a whispered conversation with Charlie, and went out again.

Charlie sat down in a big comfy chair, and so did Disraeli. Disraeli fascinated Dodger; there was no two ways about it. Dodger didn't know the word "insinuated," but he knew the thought, and Mister Disraeli insinuated himself, in some way never leaving anywhere until he was entirely somewhere else, whereupon he instantly became everywhere. This, of course, would make him dangerous, thought Dodger, and then he remembered what it was he had stuffed up his shirt.

With the servant off fetching drinks, Charlie said, "For heaven's sake, sit down, young man, the chairs don't bite! I am glad to see that our young lady is progressing slowly but surely, which is very good news."

Disraeli said, "Excuse me, but who exactly is the young lady? Is she . . . ? Would someone please introduce me?"

He rose to his feet and Charlie stood up and piloted Disraeli toward Simplicity, saying, "Miss . . . Simplicity, may I introduce Mister Benjamin Disraeli."

Dodger watched this from the edge of his seat with a certain incredulity. Then Charlie said, "Ben, Miss Simplicity is the lady who has been discussed."

And, very sweetly, Simplicity said, "What has been discussed about me, pray?"

Dodger almost leaped back to his feet, ready to defend Simplicity if necessary, but quite sharply Charlie said, "Sit back down, Dodger. Best if you let me handle this, if you don't mind, but feel free to break in." He looked across to Simplicity and said, "May I say that you can do the same." He cleared his throat and said, "The facts of the matter, as understood here in England, are that you lived out of the country with your mother—an English teacher, we believe, working abroad. Following her sad demise, sometime in the recent past you went through a form of marriage with a prince from one of the Germanys." Charlie looked at the girl as if fearing an explosion, but she just nodded, so he continued, "We also understand that a short time later, you, miss, fled the country and landed up here in England—where we understand your mother was born."

Glaring at him, Simplicity said, "Yes. And I left, gentlemen, because my husband became, as soon as we were married, a sniveling wretch of a man. He even tried to put the blame for our so-called marriage onto me, a trick as you gentlemen must know which is as old as Eden."

Dodger glanced toward Disraeli, who had turned his eyes up to Heaven. Even Charlie himself seemed somewhat awkward, saying nothing more about *that*, but continuing, "Subsequently, we have learned by means which I shall not disclose here that two farm workers who were witness to the marriage have been found dead, and the priest who conducted the ceremony apparently lost his footing one day while inspecting the roof of his church and plunged to his death."

Her face pale, Simplicity said, "That would be Father Jacob, a decent man, and I would say not a man who easily falls off roofs. The witnesses were Heinrich and Gerta. I was told about them by the maid who brought my meals. You seem, sir, to be lost for words, but I suspect that what you are going to try to tell me now in your long-winded British way is that my husband wants his wife back. Apart from the priest, Heinrich and Gerta were the only people who had knowledge of our wedding and I know they are gone. Now this"—she slipped off her ring and held it up—"is the only evidence of the marriage. I believe, sir, that what you are trying to tell me is that my husband, that is to say his father, wants to see this ring back, come what may."

Glances passed between Disraeli and Charlie, and Disraeli said, "Yes, madam, so we understand."

"But you see, sir, there is more evidence of the marriage. That, sir, is myself. But I will not go back there because I know full well that I could simply vanish. And that is if I even survived the journey—a journey by boat, gentlemen. Because, you see, if I am now the only evidence left, how difficult would it be for me to disappear along with the other evidence?"

She slipped the ring back on her finger and glared at them. "Two very nice people here in England, gentlemen," she continued, "not knowing my real name, called me 'Simplicity,' but I am rather more complicated. I know that my father-in-law got very angry when he found that his son and heir had married, he said for love, a girl who was not even fit to be a lady-in-waiting, let alone a princess. Well, sirs, that's what the fairy tales tell us, and I had thought I was *in* a fairy tale when I first met my husband. But in truth, I have learned that princes and princesses in the politics of Europe have a certain value when it comes to matters of state. People feel somehow that because 'our' princess has married 'your' prince, two countries that were likely to wage war on each other now might not do so. And my vain and stupid husband—and my stupid self for believing him—ruined a perfectly good opportunity for bargaining flesh for a treaty."

Dodger was staring at Simplicity with his mouth open. A *princess*!? You had to be a knight or something even to rescue one, didn't you? You never got this sort of thing in Seven Dials. Charlie and Disraeli shuffled uncomfortably in their seats. And at this moment there was a discreet knock on the door and a man appeared with cups of coffee and plates of small cakes.

"I believe, sir," Simplicity continued when they were alone once more, "that I am what is called 'a displaced person,' and that there are those who wish me harm in this country. They have twice tried to abduct me since my arrival in England, and it is only thanks to Dodger and, I believe, to you, Mister

Dickens, that I am here today and not on some boat back to my husband. My mother, who—yes—was English, said that in England everybody is free. I would be very happy to stay here, sir, though even here I fear for my safety now that I appear to be a person of some value. But if I should go back, I dread what might befall me. I am at a loss, gentlemen—safe nowhere. Not even in England, where no man, I am told, can be a slave. I trust, gentlemen, that this applies to ladies as well."

Charlie walked over and leaned on a mantelpiece and said, "What do you think about this, Ben?"

Mister Disraeli looked like a man after someone has thrown a very large rock at his head and seemed, if only for a little while, at a loss for words. Finally he managed, "Well, madam, I am very sorry to hear of your situation, but we, that is to say the British government, have been assured that if you go back, you won't be harmed."

At this point Dodger rose out of his chair at speed and said, "Would you trust them? Besides, not being harmed is one thing, being locked up where no one can see you is something else. I mean, you coves know about words. There's a lot of bad things lurking around 'won't be harmed.'"

"But how," said Disraeli, "could we be expected to guarantee Miss Simplicity's safety while she remains on our shores? We all understand how neither the government of which we speak nor our own can be seen to be . . . interfering in this matter. But this does not mean that either party might not consider employing others to, let us say, act on their behalf. Now, if Miss Simplicity should suffer harm while in our country, it might not bode well for . . . affairs between the two governments." He swallowed, as though fearing he had said too much.

Dodger turned to Charlie. "That, sir, is why I—I mean, we—have taken the liberty of removing Simplicity from the house of Mister and Missus Mayhew, kind though they have been to her, simply so that no harm befalls *them*. Whoever the people looking for Simplicity are, I don't think they're very nice. And you can trust me, sir, not to give up on this. If I can find those villains what treated her so cruel and make them pay, she won't *have* to go back, will she? I can protect her."

Mister Disraeli squirmed a little in his chair and looked knowingly over at Charlie before replying, "Well, you see, my dear sir, it is all rather complicated. Right now the government of which we speak is demanding the return of this lady, who is, after all, married and therefore the rightful property of her husband. There are indeed people, even here, who think it quite sensible to send her back for the sake of peace between nations." He saw Dodger open his mouth to protest. "Mister Dodger, be aware that we have had enough of wars lately—I believe you know this rather well after your run-in with our Mister Todd—and all too many of them started over trivial things and I am sure you can see why this matter is so difficult."

Difficult? Dodger thought, his temper rising. They were treating Simplicity like she wasn't a person, just some kind of bargaining counter in a game of politics. Even the Crown and Anchor man would give you better odds of winning! Suddenly his face was in front of Disraeli, who had been forced back in his chair. "There is nothing complicated, sir, not one thing," he cried. "A lady what has been beaten up by her old man and doesn't want any more of it ain't going back to where she is going to get more of the same. My word, that happens in the rookeries all the time and nobody waggles a finger exceptin' the old man who suddenly has to wash his own unmentionables."

Before Disraeli could speak, there was a welcome comment from Charlie, who said, "Ben, surely it is possible for you to delay a decision on this for a little time, give us all the opportunity to consider the best next move. But there is a matter that clearly does need to be resolved right now. Dodger here lives in Seven Dials with an elderly landlord and an . . . interesting dog. It is no place for a lady, and there is no doubt that we have a young lady here. One in fear for her life. If she's unlucky enough, she could even be killed in the light of day, because our Mister Dodger, swift as he is, cannot always be everywhere. So we have to make a decision right now, you understand? That is to say right now, Ben, as to where this lady—a *princess*, Ben—will lay her head in the certainty that she will have one when she wakes up. You and I know the one person we could call on in these circumstances."

Disraeli looked up as if someone had handed him a bucket of water when his foot was on fire. "You are, of course, talking about Angela?"

"But of course." Charlie turned to Dodger, now standing by Simplicity like a guardsman ready to strike at any moment and went on, "We have a useful friend, who I am sure will be delighted to offer shelter, faithful guards, and lodging, to Miss Simplicity. I, for my part, am absolutely certain that she will rise to the occasion, because I believe that she is a woman who never, ever has to care what politicians think, or kings for that matter. We could get there in a growler in less than an hour, if the traffic isn't too bad. You too must accompany us. I will come with the pair of you and explain matters."

"How do I know I can trust you, Charlie," said Dodger, "even if we can trust this mysterious lady?"

"Well," said Charlie, "on a number of matters you probably can't. I was telling you the truth of it. And the truth, you know, is a fog—but do you believe, truly *believe* that I am not trustworthy in *this*? Where else are you going to take the lady? Down into the sewers?"

Before another word could be uttered, the ringing voice of Simplicity said, "I must trust *you*, Dodger. Maybe it's time for a little bit of trust on your behalf."

There were always growlers waiting around the Parliament buildings, and they were soon heading west as far as Dodger could make out.

They traveled in silence until Simplicity said, "Mister Dickens, I do not much like your friend Mister Disraeli; he is like somebody who sees that there are two sides to every question. He kind of floats, if you get me; it's like everything was, well, like some cloth you could shake and pick up again. And my mother said such people were innocent but dangerous." After a pause she added, "I do apologize, but I think what I said was true."

Charlie sighed. "People must have invented politics as a means for preventing wars and in that respect politicians are useful, most of the time. It is very hard to see what else we have. But Ben's hands are tied. There are things he simply cannot do in his position, things that he would not wish to be known to be involved in. It may surprise both of you to know that agents of foreign powers roam around in this country all the time, just as we ourselves send people to spy on those other countries. Both sides know this happens and again, generally and unbelievably, a fragile peace is maintained. However," he added, "when the kings and queens find themselves in checkmate, a pawn might win the day."

This was all news to Dodger who said, "So we are always spying on our enemies?"

In the darkness of the coach there was a chuckle. "Generally, Dodger, no, because we know what our enemies are thinking; it's *friends* you have to be careful of. It can be like a seesaw. One day our enemies might be like our friends, and another day our friend may turn out to be an enemy. Oh, everybody knows about the agents. The *agents* know about the agents. I must confess, though, I am at a loss to see what even diplomacy can do in this case. Undoubtedly Simplicity could be allowed to live here, but I cannot believe that this would be the end of the matter, since the other government, on behalf of her father-in-law, seems to be very adamant. Perhaps we could smuggle her onto a boat to the Americas or possibly Australia, although this is me now thinking as a novelist."

Dodger burst out, "The Americas? I've heard about them! Full of savages. You can't possibly send her there! She won't have any friends! And I don't know very much about Australia, but Sol told me it's the other side of the world, so the way I see it that means that they must walk around upside down. And even if we did put her on a boat, there will be people who know that happened: you know that, Charlie;

there's people who watch everything that happens on the docks—I used to be one of 'em."

"I'm quite certain she could go in disguise," said Charlie. "Or," he added, "it might just be sensible to lie low until said father-in-law finally has an apoplectic fit. As I understand it, from what Disraeli has gleaned, the rather unpleasant son might be more easy to deal with."

In the corner where Simplicity was sitting, a voice said, quietly and firmly, "Excuse me, gentlemen. All I want to do is stay here in England where my mother was born. There are no other sides to this question, and talking about it won't create one. I have no intention of going anywhere else."

Dodger listened very carefully to this. Simplicity had been beaten up very badly, and she had been an invalid, and ever since then Dodger had thought of her in those terms, but now a distant memory struck him. He said, "Charlie, I remember someone telling me once that when the Romans were over here building the sewers, there was some girl who chased them around the place with chariots with wheels that cut their legs off; you're a reading type of cove—can you bring to mind what her name was?"

"Boadicea," said Charlie, "and I think you have made a point. Miss Simplicity is a young woman who knows her own mind, and she should be allowed to stand firm against those who oppose her."

Then the coach slowed, and it stopped outside what seemed to Dodger to be a very large and well-lit house. A butler opened the door when Charlie knocked. There was a whispered conversation; then Dodger and Simplicity were ushered into a small neat room by the door, while Charlie went away at some speed with the butler, whom he had addressed as Geoffrey.

Within less than a minute, Charlie was back, accompanied by a lady whom he introduced as Miss Angela Burdett-Coutts. She looked quite young, Dodger thought, but she dressed quite old, and what he could see was sharp. It was rather like Charlie. You saw at once with this lady that you would need to be either direct or silent: she had the look of somebody who inevitably won arguments.

The woman held out her hand. "My dear, you must be Simplicity, and I am very pleased to meet you." She turned to Dodger. "Ah yes, the Hero of Fleet Street. Charlie has told me about your exploits at the *Chronicle*, and everyone is talking of your bravery this morning, and you must believe me, I do have a notion as to what is going on—people can be so talkative. Clearly the thing to do right now is to get this young lady"—she corrected herself—"young *woman* a meal and a chance to sleep in a warm and, above all, secure bedroom." She added, "Nobody comes into this house without my leave, and any intruder who came in with malice aforethought would wish they had never been born, or perhaps if they were able to think more selectively, that *I* had never been born. Simplicity is entirely welcome or, I should say . . . I am welcoming the daughter of an old friend from the country, who is staying here in safety while she learns to navigate her way in this wicked city. I am sure that you, Mister Dodger, have all your work cut out as it is. Heroes are always such busy people, I have found, although I would be very grateful if you would attend me here at a dinner party tomorrow."

Dodger listened to this, openmouthed, until Charlie pushed past him and said, "Dear Angela, would it be in order to allow this young man, busy though he is, to come tomorrow with his friend and mentor, Solomon Cohen? An excellent and renowned maker of jewelry and watches."

"Capital. I would be most happy to meet him. I believe I have heard of him. As for you, Charlie, you know you are invited anyway, and I would like to have a quiet word with you after Mister Dodger has left."

The word "left" had an air of finality, but Dodger found that he had raised his hand, and since it was up there, he said, "Excuse me, miss, would you allow me to see where Miss Simplicity is going to sleep?"

"Why, pray?"

"Well, miss, I reckon I can get through most windows in this city, and if I can, then so can someone more nasty than me, if you see what I mean."

He was expecting a reproof, but what he got was a broad smile from Angela. "You acknowledge no master, do you, Mister Dodger?"

"I don't know what you mean, miss, but I want to know that Simplicity is safe, you see."

"Well done, Mister Dodger. I will get Geoffrey to show you the room and the bars on the window. I too do not like intruders, and even now I'm wondering whether I shouldn't employ you or some of your contemporaries to find a hither-to undiscovered way in. We might talk about this on the morrow. But now I must speak at length to Charlie."

CHAPTER TEN

Dodger uses his head

DODGER RAN TOWARD HOME feeling in some way buoyed up by the meeting, especially since Charlie had whispered to him as he left that Angela had more money than anyone who wasn't a king or queen. A nobby party sounded like a difficult crib to crack, though. He sped at a steady pace until he reached the first drain cover: an entrance to his world. A moment later, despite his smart attire, there was a distinct absence of Dodger and the sound of a drain cover falling back into place.

He got his bearings by feel, the echoes, and, of course, the smell—every single sewer in the city had a smell that was all its own; he could taste them like a connoisseur of fine wines, and so he plotted the way home, changing direction only once when his two-note tosher whistle was answered by another already working that particular tunnel. It was still light, which helped when you passed the occasional grid or grating, and the walking was easy—not so much as a trickle today—and he almost absentmindedly explored as he passed a secret niche. He found sixpence, a sign that somebody or something was watching over him.

Overhead in the complicated world was the noise of hooves, the echo of footsteps, and occasionally a carriage or a coach, and out of nowhere a sound that made him freeze: there was an eerie metallic squeal of metal in extreme distress, as if something was wrong, or maybe something had got stuck in a wheel, causing it to drag noisily over the stones with a sound that seared the soul and once heard could never be forgotten.

The coach! If he could find where it went, he might see the men who had battered Simplicity. He clenched his fists in anticipation—wait until they were on the receiving end of a set of brass knuckles. . . .

The coach was running along the street above him, and he cursed the fact that the next drain cover in that direction was some way away, luckily in a usually moderately clean sewer which he told himself would save wear and tear on the shonky suit. He ran along the sewer, not stopping at all, not even for a shilling, and didn't halt until he saw the gratings of the drain cover above him. He got out his crowbar, but just as he was about to fling the cover away, there was a sound of heavy hoofbeats and the jingle of harness. Something huge covered that little circle of light that had been salvation with a great and glorious smell of dung as a brewer's cart pulled up on top of the drain and settled down like an old man finding a privy at last after a long wait. The likeness was assisted by the fact that the great steaming shire horses that had been pulling the cart decided, as one, very hygienically to empty their bladders. They were large animals and it had been a long afternoon, and so the shower was not over in the space of a moment, but rather an elegant duet to the goddess of relief. Regrettably, since the only way was down, there was simply no time for Dodger to dodge out of the way, not now.

In the distance, gradually merging with all the rattle and clamor of the streets, the screaming wheel could barely now be heard. In any case, the beefy men who worked for the brewers were unloading the heavy casks down wooden ramps, and the rumble of the barrels drowned out every other sound that was left.

Dodger knew the routine of these men; once they had shifted all the empty barrels from the pub and replaced them with full ones, they would as sure as sunset drink a pint of beer. They would be joined in this cheerful enterprise by the landlord himself, the ostensible reason for this being that they all would agree on the quality of the nectar concerned, although in truth the likely reason was that after heaving great loads around for any length of time, well, a man deserves a beer, doesn't he? It was a ritual that was probably as old as beer itself. Occasionally, the brewery men and the landlords would have another beer, so great was their determination to make sure that the beer was in the best possible condition. In fact, Dodger could smell it, even above the scent of the horses, and even with a certain essence of horse to contend with, it still made him thirsty.

He had always loved the smell you got in the sewers by the breweries. A geezer called Blinky, who was a rat catcher by profession, had once told him that the rats in the sewers underneath the breweries were the biggest and fattest anywhere, adding that the rat-catching fancy would pay extra for brewery rats because they had a lot of fight in them.

Whatever he did now, though, Dodger knew he wasn't going to catch up with that damned coach. The men above him were being very assiduous in deciding on the quality of the beer, and while he could, of course, run along to the next grating, his quarry by then would have got lost in the street noise of London, as sure as heaven. All he could do was to seethe at an opportunity lost.

He trudged on anyway, mostly because the large shire horses also did other things than piss—that's why some of the street urchins used to follow them with a bucket. You often heard them shouting their wares among the nobbier houses, where people had gardens, with the refrain "One penny a bucket, missus, well stamped down!"

The only thing to do now was hurry along to the next drain cover and get out there. And so, after a day of dodging, he traipsed through the maze of streets, tired, hungry, and well aware that there was indeed *not one mark* on the shonky suit; it was now, in fact *made up* of marks. Jacob and his sons were pretty good at cleaning up things, but they would have their work cut out on this. No hope for it, though—he would have to take his lumps.

Gloomily he walked on, paying attention all the time for heads that dropped out of sight as soon as they knew that they had been made, or people who very swiftly disappeared into alleyways. This was what a geezer did; a geezer knew that most of the hurrying, scurrying crowd would be simply minding their own business, although with an option of minding somebody else's business as well if the opportunity arose. What Dodger was looking out for was the interrogating eye, the eye of purpose, the watchful eye, the eye that read the street.

And right now the street seemed clear, insofar as any street could, and at least Simplicity was safe for tonight, he consoled himself. Although not safe if she went out. It was dreadful, the things that could happen on the street, in full view.

Not so long ago, he remembered, he had dressed up as a little flower girl; he was young enough to pull it off with his auburn hair sticking out fetchingly from a scarf, and it wasn't even his hair because he had borrowed it from Mary-Go-Round, who had pretty good hair. Mary's hair grew like a mushroom and looked like it too. But she made good money every few months or so by selling it to the wigmakers.

The reason he had been doing this favor was that the flower girls, some of whom were as young as four years old, had been having a certain amount of . . . harassment from a particular kind of gentleman. The girls, who mostly sold violets and daffodils in season, were a decent bunch, and Dodger quite liked them and cared for them. Of course, they had to make a living as they grew older, just like everyone else, and it might be said that in certain circumstances a little bit of hanky-panky might just be acceptable to the older ones, provided that they were in control of the hanky, not to mention the panky. They were furiously protective of their younger sisters, however, at which point Dodger had been persuaded to don his first dress.

And so when the sharp-suited gentlemen, who liked to go down among the poor flower girls to see if there were any new blossoms they could pluck, came to ply them with strong liquor until they could have their wicked way with them, they would actually be subtly directed to the shrinking and simpering violet who was, in fact, Dodger.

Actually, he had to admit that he had been incredibly good at it, because to be a geezer was to be an actor and so Dodger was better at being a shrinking violet than any of the other flower girls who had, how could you put it, better qualifications. He had already sold quite a lot of his violets because his voice hadn't broken then and he could make himself a real little virgin when he wanted to. After a few hours of this, the girls tipped him off to the whereabouts of a particularly nasty dandy who always hung around the smaller girls, and who was heading toward him with his nice coat and his cane, jingling the money in his pockets. And the street applauded when a suddenly rather athletic little flower girl grabbed the smarmy bastard, punched him, dragged him into an alley, and made certain that he would never be able to jingle anything in his pockets for some time to come.

That had been one of Dodger's very good days because, well, firstly he had done a good deed for the flower girls, earning from one or two of them the likelihood of an occasional kiss and cuddle, as between friends. Secondly, since he had left a gentleman groaning in the alley without even his unmentionables, he had harvested one gold watch, one guinea, a couple of sovereigns, some small change, an ebony walking cane set with silver trimmings, and one pair of the said unmentionables.* And the bonus in the whole affair was that the man was never, ever likely to get in touch with the

---

* Rather soiled but nevertheless very well made, and which he had subsequently worn quite a lot afterward—that was, after some serious washing.

peelers. Also, he had forgotten this: there had been the gold tooth which the man had spat at him after the best punch that Dodger had ever laid on anybody. He had actually caught it in the air, much to the applause of the flower girls, making him feel for a while the cock of the heap. He had taken the older flower girls for an oyster supper, and it had been the best day a young man could ever have. It was always worth doing a good deed, though that had been before he had rescued Solomon, who wouldn't have approved of some aspects of the enterprise.

Since Dodger was now practically on his home patch, blackened by smoke though it was, he let his guard down and a hand landed on his shoulder with a grip that was surprising, given that its owner mostly used his strength to push a pen.

"Well, Mister Dodger! You will be amazed how much I had to spend on the growler to get here so quickly. And, may I say, your sewers have made short work of your suit. Any chance of there being a coffeehouse around here, do you think?"

Dodger thought not, but did volunteer that one of the nearby meat pie houses might have some of it on the go, adding, "Not certain what it will taste like. A bit like, probably very much like, the meat pies really; I mean, you have to be really hungry if you see what I mean."

In the end, he led Charlie to a pub where they could talk without being overheard, and where it was least likely somebody would try to pick Charlie's pocket. When Dodger went in, he was Dodger in spades. No, come to think about it, not just in spades, but also in clubs, hearts, and diamonds as well—a diamond geezer, the friend of everyone in the rookeries. He glad-handed Quince, the landlord, and a few of the other hangers-on of dubious repute with enough fire to send the word to those who had the eyes to see that this mark belonged to Dodger, and nobody else.

On the whole, Charlie was putting a good face on it, but nevertheless, here he was in the rookeries, where even the peelers trod carefully and never, ever went singly. Here was Charlie, as out of place as Dodger had felt himself at first in Parliament. Two different worlds.

London wasn't all that big when you thought about it: a square mile of mazes, surrounded by even more streets and people and . . . opportunities . . . and outside that a load of suburbs who thought they were London, but they weren't at all, not really, at least not to Dodger. Oh, sometimes he went outside the square mile—oh, as far as two miles away!—and he took great care to cloak himself with the full cocksureness of geezerdom. Then he could be all friendly with those people it paid to be friendly with, and geezer would call unto geezer; the geezers of the Outer Wastes, as Dodger called those streets, weren't exactly friends but you respected their patch in the hope and sureness that they would respect yours. You reached an understanding with looks, assumptions, and the occasional exchange of gestures which hardly needed words. But it was all a show, a game . . . and when he was not Dodger, he sometimes wondered who he really was. Dodger, he thought, was a lot stronger than he was.

Now and then a customer in the pub glanced at Charlie and then looked at Dodger, and instantly thought they understood and looked away. *No problem, 'nuff said, guv'nor, right you are.*

When it was clear that warfare would not break out, and

two pints of porter, for once in clean glasses what with there being a gentleman here, were put in front of them, Charlie said, "Young man, I made great haste to my office after finishing our business with Angela, and what did I find but that my friend Mister Dodger the hero is a very rich man." He leaned closer and said, "In fact, I have in my pocket, carefully wrapped so that they should not jingle, specie to the tune of fifty sovereigns and what you might now call small change, with the promise of more to come."

At last Dodger got control of his own mouth, which for a few seconds had totally been beyond him. He managed to whisper, "But I ain't no hero, Charlie."

Charlie put a finger to his lips and said, "Do be careful about protesting; you know who and what you are and I suppose so do I, although I suspect I am kinder to you than you are to yourself. But right now the good people of London have contributed this money to someone they consider to be a hero. Who are we to deprive them of their hero, especially since it might be that a hero can get things done?"

Dodger glanced around the bar. Nobody was listening and he hissed, "And poor old Todd is a villain, right?"

"Well, now," said Charlie. "A hero, one might think, is a man who might protest that the so-called villain is nothing more than a sad mad man in torment because of what war has done to him, and indeed suggest that Bedlam would be more sensible than the gallows. Who would deny a hero, especially if said hero sprang some of his newfound wealth seeing to it that the poor man had a reasonable time there?"

Dodger thought of Mister Todd in Bedlam, where the poor devil would presumably be locked in somewhere with his demons and with no comforts unless he could afford to pay for them. The thought made Dodger's flesh crawl, because surely that would be much worse than the gallows in Newgate, especially since they were getting the art of putting the knot in the rope in such a way that the neck was broken instantly, which saved a lot of hanging around for all concerned and meant that people no longer had to rely on their friends swinging on their heels as they danced the hemp fandango. Reportedly, a good pickpocket could get his lunch just by strolling behind people who were intent on making the most of the entertainment. Dodger had himself tried this out once and hadn't done too badly, but he had been surprised to find himself feeling a little ashamed at using such an occasion for profit and so he had redistributed the money he had expertly filched to a couple of beggars.

"No one's going to listen to me," he said now.

"You undersell yourself, my friend. And you undersell the power of the press. Now close your mouth before something flies into it, and remember, tomorrow morning you must come to see me at the offices of *Punch* magazine so that Mister Tenniel can make a very droll likeness of you, for our readers would like to see the hero of the day."

He slapped Dodger on the back—an action he immediately regretted as his hand encountered an especially fruity patch of Dodger's suit.

"The coach," said Dodger. "I heard it again. Nearly caught it too. I'll find them coves, Charlie. Simplicity will be safe from *them*."

"Well, she's certainly safe right now at Angela's." Charlie smiled. "And I believe I can keep Ben quiet for a day or so while I make further inquiries. We make a team, Mister Dodger, a team! The game is on, so let us hope we are on the winning side."

With that, he left the pub, heading fast for the next wide road that might contain a cab and leaving Dodger standing there with his mouth open and a pocket full of glorious, shiny specie. After a few seconds the goddesses of reality and self-preservation ganged up on him, and a man holding a fortune raced through Seven Dials and hammered on Solomon's door.

He gave the special knock, heard the joyful bark of Onan followed by the shuffling of Solomon's slippers, followed by the rattle of bolts. Dodger knew that at the Tower of London—a place he never wanted to see the inside of— there was a great ceremony of the Yeoman Warders, known by some as the Beefeaters, when the place was locked up at nights. But however complicated their ceremony was, it probably wasn't as careful and meticulous as Solomon opening or closing his door. This was, in fact, now at last open.

"Oh, Dodger, a little late. Never mind, stew is all the better for a really good simmer. . . . Oh dear, what *have* you done to Jacob's very nearly new suit!"

Carefully taking off the jacket, Dodger hung it at the insistence of Solomon on a coat hanger to await further attention before turning round slowly, opening the purse that Charlie had given to him, and letting its contents tinkle onto the old man's worktable.

He then stood back and said, "I think that Jacob would now agree with me that the suit is not really important at the moment. In any case," he continued, smiling, "everybody knows that a little bit of piss does no harm to a garment what-soever, so I think some of this specie would make everything as right as rain, what do you say?" And while the old man's mouth was still open Dodger went on, "I hope you've got some room in your strongboxes!"

Then he thought, as Solomon stood there in amazement and said nothing: Maybe it would be a very good idea to get these riches somewhere else, as soon as ever possible.

Sometime later, two empty bowls of stew sat on the table alongside a fortune made up of carefully stacked coins, which were ranged in order of denomination from one or two half farthings right up to the guineas and sovereigns. Solomon and Dodger stared at the piles as if expecting them to perform a trick or, possibly more likely, to evaporate and go back to where they came from.

As for Onan, he looked anxiously from one to the other, wondering if he had done something wrong, which to be frank was generally likely to be the case, although on this occasion he was blameless so far.

Solomon listened very carefully to Dodger's account of what had happened in the barbershop and all that had fol-lowed, right up to the dinner invitation from Miss Angela and the reward Charlie had given him in the pub, sometimes raising a finger to ask a particular question but otherwise not making a sound until finally he said, "Mmm, it is not your fault if people call you a hero, but it is to your credit that you recognize that if he was a monster, then it was other mon-strous things that made him so. The iron forged on the anvil cannot be blamed for the hammer, and I believe God would quite understand you took every opportunity to explain the situation to all those who listened. Mmm, don't I just know that onto the world that *is* people paint the world that they would *like*. Therefore they like to see dragons slain, and where there are gaps, public imagination will fill the void. No blame attaches. In the case of the money, one might feel that this is in some way a society trying to feel better. A healing action, which almost as a side effect makes you a very well-off young man who in my opinion definitely should put most of this money in the bank. You tell me of a lady by the name of Miss Angela Burdett-Coutts; she is indeed extremely rich, having received a very large legacy from her grandfather, and you would be very wise to deal with her family. The people at Mister Coutts's bank are your men, I think, and therefore I suggest that you put the money with them, where it will be safe and earn interest. A very good nest egg indeed!"

"Interest? What's money interested in?"

"*More* money," said Solomon. "Take it from me."

"Well, I don't want people to be very interested in me!" said Dodger.

The mmm from Solomon was an unusually full one, and he said, "Not so much interested in you, but very interested in your money. Mmm, you see, it is like this. Supposing one of these new-fangled railway gentlemen, let us call him Mister Stephenson, has a design for a wonderful new engine. Being a man interested in mostly bolts and atmospheric pressures, he might not be very well versed in the world of commerce. Mmm, now Mister Coutts and his gentlemen will find for him entrepreneurs—that is *you*, Dodger, in this case—who might lend him the necessary cash in order to get his good idea to a state of solid reality. Mister Coutts can take the measure of a man as to his trustworthiness and, in short, see to it that your money works for the aforesaid engineer, and also at the same time for you. Of course, they will take advice to ascertain that this gentleman with the shining eyes and grease down his breeches with a definite reek of coal dust about his person is a sound investment, but Mister Coutts and his family are very wealthy people who most certainly didn't get that way by guessing wrongly. It's called finance. Trust me; I'm Jewish, we know about these things."

Solomon was beaming happily, but Dodger said uneasily, "This sounds a bit like gambling to me. You can lose money gambling."

Under the table Onan whined, because nobody was paying him any attention.

"Indeed you can, but mmm you see there is gambling, and on the other hand there is *gambling*. Take poker, for example. Poker is about watching people, and you, young man, are incredibly good at that. You read people's faces. I don't know how you do it so well, it's a gift. So it is in finance; you have to be careful with the people you deal with, and so are Mister Coutts and Co."

"You make them sound as if they are on the dodge, like me!" said Dodger.

Solomon smiled. "Mmm, that is a most interesting philosophy, Dodger, but not one that I might suggest too appropriate to mention to the men at Coutts bank. Remember, it's very hard to stay in business with a bad name, and they certainly stay in business." He wrinkled his nose as the odors of the drying jacket managed even to overwhelm Onan's contribution to the air in the attic.

"I'm sorry about the shonky suit," Dodger managed, but Solomon waved this away with a sound like *phooey!*

"Don't worry about Jacob," he said. "Jacob would never be angry with a man who has a lot of money to spend. Anyway, horse urine is, as we know, very good for cleaning clothes—a fact not everyone appreciates, though everybody knows it has a smell like good cider, and is very fruity. Now I suggest an early night, once you have finished the washing up, because tomorrow we will be dining with very important people and I will feel ashamed if people were to say, 'Look at that overgrown street urchin, you can see that he has no manners at all.' They will say he might know how to use a knife and fork certainly, but he does not know how to use mmm a fish slice; and they will say to themselves, 'I suspect that he slurps when he drinks his soup,' which you, Dodger, if I may say so, do a lot. If people like Mister Disraeli are going to be there, then you must be a gentleman and mmm it would appear that I have less than one day to turn you into one. Money alone doesn't do the trick."

Dodger winced at this, but Solomon plunged on loudly with Old Testament firmness and waggled the finger of rectitude as if at any moment he would throw down the Ten Commandments. Given that the timbers of the property were already creaking and groaning with the weight of multiple families in that one building, this would mean that the building would surely collapse.

Sticking out his beard like an advance guard, Solomon mumbled on, "This is a matter of pride, Dodger, which I have and you must acquire. First thing in the morning we will go and visit Mister Coutts, and then see if it is possible to find in London a man who will do the very best haircut and shave for the customer without killing him with a razor. I know just the one."

Before Dodger could say a word the finger was raised again, seas parted, thunder rolled, and the sky darkened, making birds fly frantically for safety. Or at least, that is what happened in the privacy of the attic, and indeed in the mind of Dodger.

Solomon said fiercely, "Do not argue with me. This isn't the sewers. When it comes to finance, and banking, and smartening yourself up, I am a master. With the scars to prove it. I must tell you that just for once in your life I am insisting! This is not the time to argue with your old friend. After all, I wouldn't tell you how to work the sewers."

His finger stopped stabbing and joined its family on the hand, and the tide turned back, the dark sky became the peaceful if somewhat dirty glow of evening, and the terrible finger of thunder and lightning faded out of Dodger's imagination as Solomon became rather smaller and said, "Now, please take Onan down to do his business and we can shut up shop for the night."

There was still some light in the sky when Dodger got the dog downstairs. As is the protocol of these things, he let Onan off his leash, then looked around as if he had no idea what the dog was actually doing. There were a few lights to be seen, though not too many, candles being the price they were. Just the galaxies of London, the occasional star, or a candle in a window, wasting a part of its tallow on the ungrateful streets. When you saw a candle in a window at this time of night, it meant that some poor wretch had died, or some other poor wretch had been born. Lights were for when the midwife had to be called in, and lights were for a death. If, of course, it was the more heated kind of death—the kind that might make the peelers take an interest—that would be a job for the coroner and would bring forth a second candle.

With that in mind, Dodger called Onan to stop worrying whatever he was worrying, and a tiny bell rang in his mind as he realized that in the darkness someone had crept so silently toward him that they now had a knife at his throat.

A voice said very quietly, "There is something of considerable importance that you know the whereabouts of, Mister Dodger, and I'm hearing that some people are scared of you on account of everybody knowing, so they say, that you must be quite the lad to have put down Sweeney Todd. But me? I say no, that can't be true, can it, considering that all a cove needs to do is wait right here and threaten you when you comes out to take the air of a night, waiting for your stinking mutt to make the cobbles even more treacherous for law-abiding folks, such as what I am. Don't blame yourself, Mister Dodger; routines have been the undoing of many poor buggers, and I heard tell you was clever. Well, there's none here but you, me, and the mutt, and he won't last long when you've told me what I want and I'm done with you. You'll be just one very short scream in the rookeries, eh. And my employer, Mister Sharp Bob, will be all the happier. That is, Mister Dodger, if you can tell me of the whereabouts of that girl with golden hair; and if you don't I'll gut yer anyway."

Not one muscle had moved anywhere on the body of Dodger, if you didn't count the sphincter. But as the name

Sharp Bob rocketed through his brain, he said, "I don't know you. Thought I knew everyone in all the boroughs. Would you mind telling me who you are, mister? After all, it's not as though I'll be able to pass on the information, right?"

The blade just occasionally touched the nape of Dodger's neck. Onan would almost certainly attack if Dodger gave him the signal, but a knife at your neck is a great encouragement to careful thinking. The neck, Dodger knew, was tough and strong and quite capable of holding the weight of a very large man, as was demonstrated regularly at the Tyburn gallows, and sometimes difficult to puncture if you didn't get the place right. But what it was vulnerable to was, of course, the slice.

The unseen man had stopped talking; if it hadn't been for the sensation of his breath close to Dodger's ear, he almost wouldn't have known somebody was there. All this went through the brain of Dodger at speed. The man was enjoying the fact that Dodger was helpless and totally in his power; you got that sort sometimes, and the man would never become a geezer. If a real geezer wanted you dead, he'd have done it straightaway.

Now the man apparently decided that it was time for more tormenting of his victim. "I like to see a man take his time," he said, "so by now I reckon you've worked out you can't break my grip and I could do very nasty things to your neck before your doggie got to me. Of course, there would be a wee little set-to between him and me, but dogs is not too difficult if you have the knowing of it and take care what clothing you wear. Oh, I didn't spend years in the ring without knowing how to take care of myself in any fight you could mention! And I knows you can't get to your knuckles right now, nor that little bar you like to carry—not like the last time we met." The man chortled. "I'm going to enjoy this after the way you came at us in that storm. You might have 'eard tell that someone has taken measures since then so as my associate of that night is now no longer in the land of the living—and you're going to be joining 'im pretty sharp-ish, I reckon. And if I don't want to be among that happy crowd, I needs that information. Now."

Dodger gasped. So this was one of the men who had been beating Simplicity! And *Sharp Bob* was behind it! He had heard tell of the man—a legal cove, of sorts, widely respected by the unrespectable. Was he the geezer who had been talk-ing to Marie Jo?

Anger rose in him, a terrible anger that coalesced into one glittering shining certainty as the man's blade gently stroked across his neck. It whispered, "This man is not going to walk out of here."

Nobody was nearby. There was the occasional scream, shout, or mysterious sigh—the music of the night in the tene-ments—but for now Dodger and the unseen man were alone. Dodger said, "It sounds like I am in the hands of a profes-sional, then?"

The voice behind him said, "Oh yes, I guess you could say that."

"Good," said Dodger, and threw his head back so hard that he heard the reassuring noise of something breaking, and then spun around and kicked. It didn't matter very much what he kicked, or indeed on what he stamped, but he found a mul-titude of choices, and in his rage he kicked and stamped on practically everything. When it came to it, the only sensible thing to do was stay alive, and the chances of staying alive with a man threatening you with a knife were reasonably small. Better him with a bloody nose and a great big bruise than you being nothing but a memory. And goodness, the bloke had been drinking before coming out—never a good idea if you wanted to be really quick. But this was one of the men who had been *beating Simplicity* and no kicking now could be thorough enough for that.

The knife had been dropped, and Dodger picked it up, looked down at the man who was lying in the gutter, and said, "Good news is that in a couple of months you will hardly remember this; the bad news is that after about two weeks you will need to get somebody to break that nose proper for you again so's you look like your old 'andsome self."

The man snuffled, and by the sight of him in the gloom, the way his face looked now was quite probably better than it had been before: it was all scars. People thought that a ragged face was a sign of a professional boxer, but it wasn't—it was a sign of an amateur boxer. Good boxers liked to be pretty; it put the contenders off their guard.

Dodger kicked the recumbent man in the fork, as hard as he could, and while the man groaned, he rifled his pockets to the total account of fifteen shillings and sixpence ha'penny. Then he kicked him again for good measure. He also pulled off the man's shoes and said, "Yes, mister, I am the geezer that knocked you down in the storm. The geezer who stood up to Mister Sweeney Todd, and do you know what? I have his razor. Oh my, how it does talk to me. You tell Sharp Bob to come and ask me questions himself, right! I ain't a murderer, but I am on good terms with such as is, and I'll see you in lavender if I ever see you around here, or hear of you taking your fists to a lady again. You will float down the river without a boat, and that's the truth."

Above and around them there was the sound of windows being cautiously opened, cautiously because whatever it was that had just gone down in the street might be something that you really didn't want to see, especially if it was possible that the peelers might quiz you about it. In the rookeries you needed to develop a blindness that could be switched on and off.

Dodger cupped his hands and shouted cheerfully, "Nothing to worry about, folks, it's me, Dodger, and a bloke from out of town who amazingly enough fell over my foot." The "out of town" bit was necessary, to show to all those listening that the local patch, such as it was—and mostly it was mud and the remnants of Onan's most recent meals—was being defended, and it did not hurt, did it, to let everyone know that it was being defended by Dodger, good ol' Dodger.

In the gray light there was a sleepy applause from everybody except Mister Slade, who was a bargee by profession and not known for the gentleness of his speech, him being a man who also had to get up very early in the mornings. He had clearly had a bad day and shouted down, "Okay, now piss off and go back to bed."

Dodger decided not to take the invitation to piss off and go back to bed; instead, he half dragged, half carried the man off his patch, as the protocol of the streets demanded, then spent another ten minutes dragging him a further distance away from the tenement, just in case a peeler wanted to investigate. He propped the figure up against the wall and whispered, "You are a very lucky man. And if I ever see your face around here again, you will have what we in the business call a very close shave. Understand? I will assume that was a yes." Then

Dodger whistled to Onan, though not until after the dog had urinated on the man's leg: something that in fact Dodger hadn't intended, but that he thought in the circumstances was a perfect ending to that particular scenario.

And then . . . there was just Dodger, and it seemed to him that the events of the evening needed one last touch, one last little detail that a geezer could look back on and be proud about—a detail that would give his reputation even more shine too. After a few moments' thought, jingling the purloined coins in his hand, he walked back to his own streets, over to a small doorway, and knocked several times.

After a while a very cautious old lady in a nightshirt peered out, saying with the deepest suspicion, "Who's that? I ain't got any money in the house, you know." Then it was, "Oh, it's you, young Dodger. Cor blimey, I only recognized you 'cos of your teeth. Never known anyone with such white teeth."

Dodger, to the old woman's surprise, said, "Yes, it is me, Mrs. Beecham, and I know you haven't got any money in the house, but you have now." He dropped the booty into her astonished hands.

It felt good, and the toothless old woman perceptibly beamed in the darkness and said, "God bless you, sir, I will say a prayer for you at church in the morning."

This somewhat surprised Dodger; no one had offered him a prayer before, as far as he could recall. The idea that he might have one was, on this chilly night, a welcome warmth. Cuddling that to his bosom, he led Onan up the long stairs to bed.

CHAPTER ELEVEN

Dodger smartens up,
and Solomon comes clean

SOLOMON HAD BEEN WAITING up for him. He hadn't been in
the neighborhood audience because no room in the attic
faced the street. His windows instead looked out on one
side of some warehouses, which Solomon had considered a
much better view than the kinds of things you have to see
in the street itself. Only a very few words were exchanged in
the darkness before Dodger flopped down onto his mattress
and the last candle was snuffed.

As he snuggled down under his blanket in the knowledge of a day well filled, Dodger watched his own thoughts
swim past his eyes. No wonder the world spun—there were
so many changes. How long ago was it that he had heard a
scream and jumped out of a foaming sewer . . . how many
days was it? He counted—three days. *Three days!* It was as if
the world was moving too fast, laughing at Dodger to keep
up with it. Well, he would chase the world and take what
came and deal with it. Tomorrow he would be attending a

wonderful dinner at a place where there was certainly going to be Simplicity, and it appeared to him as tiredness built up that the important thing in all of this was how you seemed and he was learning how to seem. Seem to be a hero, seem to be a clever young man, seem to be trustworthy. That seemed to fool everybody, and the most disconcerting thing about this was it was doing the same to him, forcing him on like some hidden engine. And with that strange deduction still in his head, he fell asleep.

The following morning, the man whose job it was to open the doors of Coutts bank to the customers found himself looking at an elderly Jewish gentleman in a ragged gabardine coat, whose eyes gleamed with mercantile zeal. This apparition pushed past him, followed by a young man in an ill-fitting suit and a nasty-smelling dog. Among some of the other clients there was some murmuring about poor people coming in there until it turned out—after every coin above the rank of sixpence was duly bagged and signed for—that these were poor people with a lot of money.

A receipt and a shiny new bank book were received, the little party swept away as fast as they had come in, and the Red Sea closed again, the planets wobbled back to their rightful orbits, firstborn children once again played happily, and all was right with the world. Except that part of it now contained one of Mister Coutts's senior partners, who was realizing that somehow he had agreed to a rate of interest that they seldom offered, but he had considered cheap at the price if it got Solomon out of the building before he threw out the moneylenders. The suggestion was, of course, ridiculous and unfounded in every respect, but Solomon nevertheless was always a winner when it came to bargaining, and it tended to leave everybody somewhat dazed.

As soon as they got outside the bank, Dodger reminded Solomon, somewhat reluctantly, that he was due in the offices of *Punch* magazine, so that some artist or other could draw a picture of him for the front cover.

Mister Tenniel turned out to be a young man only a little bit older than Dodger and whose brown hair seemed closer to red. With Dodger in a seat in front of him, the two of them chatted away while the artist drew. Being drawn by Mister Tenniel wasn't all that difficult, and a lot less difficult, Solomon said, than being drawn and quartered, at least. That was apparently a Solomon joke: one he didn't explain to Dodger.

Perhaps, Dodger thought, he should have said that the process was not difficult but occasionally worrying, because Mister Tenniel would scribble and scribble and then suddenly dart a glance toward Dodger, which pinned him like a butterfly, and then just as soon disappear as Mister Tenniel got back to the scribbling again. Only the top of his head could be seen as the artist bent over his work, while Solomon sat drinking coffee and reading a complimentary issue of *Punch*.

To Dodger's amazement, being drawn didn't take very much time, and finally Tenniel made a sudden few last-minute adjustments to the portrait on his easel and turned it toward Dodger with a grin. "I'm pretty pleased with this, Mister . . . may I call you Dodger? I think I have your essence down pat, but of course the paper is always somewhat cluttered, and I will be expected to add a few other details to give the public some vision of what happened in Mister Sweeney Todd's shop. I need to draw Mister Todd too, you know—the public demands both hero and villain."

Dodger swallowed. "But Mister Todd wasn't really a villain, sir . . ." he tried.

Tenniel cut him off with a wave of his brush. "I hear that Talavera was a most dreadful battle. They say that Wellington simply threw men forward into the mouths of the cannons in abandon, and to great loss of life. One can only hope that the deaths were worth the sacrifice, if that could be possible." He shook Dodger by the hand and went on, "Mister Dickens told me the truth about what transpired on that day in Fleet Street, and it is wonderful, is it not, how the public perception of what is true these days seems always biased toward the macabre? It would seem that the common man likes nothing so much as an "orrible murder.'" He paused and added, "Is there something the matter, Mister Dodger?"

As often as Tenniel had closely scrutinized Dodger, so had Dodger in his turn scrutinized him. He had seen not what was there, but at one point seen something very subtly out of kilter. It took a while for him to see it properly and to find the words.

Embarrassed at being caught staring, he decided to make a clean breast of it and said, "I believe you have something wrong with your left eye, don't you, Mister Tenniel? I hope it ain't too much of a drawback in your profession?"

The artist's face froze and then thawed into a lopsided smile. "The scar is so small that I believe that you are the first man I have met to notice it. In fact, it was a trivial childhood accident."

Dodger, watching the smiling face, thought: Not, I think, so trivial.

"Charlie was right in what he said about you the other day!"

"Oh? Mmm, and what *did* Charlie say about my friend Dodger the other day, if you please, sir?" Solomon rumbled, standing up and packing the magazine into the depths of his coat. "I would very much like to know." He smiled, of course, but the wording was emphatic.

This was most certainly picked up by Tenniel, who blushed and said, "Since I have put my foot in it, sir, I can do no more than tell the truth—will you please not tell Mister Dickens that I mentioned it? What he said, in fact, was: 'Mister Dodger is so sharp that one day his name will be known on every continent, possibly as a benefactor of mankind, but also quite possibly as the most charming scoundrel ever to be hanged!' "

Mister Tenniel took a step backward in amazement when Solomon, laughing, said, "Well, at least Mister Dickens is a wonderful judge of character, and directness in a man such as himself is admirable. But should you meet him before I do, please tell him that Solomon Cohen is endeavoring to see that the first option will prevail! Thank you very much for your time, sir, but please excuse us now, because I must go with the young ruffian to a place where he will get cleaner than he's ever been in his life, because this evening we are due to go to a very important dinner engagement in the West End. Good day to you, sir, and thank you, but now we must really take our leave."

"No time to dawdle, Dodger," said Solomon as the door

closed behind them. "You know how keen I am on bathing? Well, we are today going to have a Turkish bath, with all the trimmings."

This was news to Dodger, but Solomon's wisdom and efforts at basic hygiene had kept him alive so far, so it was almost inconceivable for Dodger to thwart his friend on this occasion; he dared not argue for fear that Solomon's righteous zeal would cause him to drag Dodger there by the ear. Acquiescence was better than becoming a laughingstock in all the rookeries and stews. And so, putting a brave face on it, he followed the old man out into what was really a drizzle with smoke in its eye; they unhooked Onan from the lamppost where he had been tethered in the certain knowledge that nobody would ever want to steal him.

Dodger felt better when he cogitated on the word "Turkish." Somebody, probably Ginny-Come-Lately—a nice girl with a laugh that made you very nearly blush; they had been quite close once upon a time—had told him about Turkey. She had filled his mind with exciting images of dancing girls and light-brown ladies in very thin vests. Apparently, they would give you a massage and then oil you with what she called "ungulates," which sounded very exotic, although to tell you the truth, Ginny-Come-Lately could make anything sound exotic. When he had mentioned this to Solomon—Dodger had been much younger then, and still a bit naïve—the old man had said, "Surely not. I have not traveled widely in the countries of the Levant, but whatever else they do to their goats, I am quite sure they don't rub them all over their own bodies. The goat has never been distinguished by the fragrance of its aroma. I suspect you mean 'unguents,' which are perfumes distilled from fragrant oils. Why'd you want to know?"

The younger Dodger had said, "Oh, no reason really, I just heard somebody say the word." Right now, though, whatever way you put it, the word "Turkish" conjured up visions of eastern promise, and so he became quite optimistic as he strolled through the streets all the way to the Turkish baths in Commercial Road.

There were, of course, bathhouses all over the place, often used even by those who were really poor, when—as one old lady had put it to Dodger—"sometimes you need to knock the lumps off." Often, the baths were ordered just like the rest of the world, in that the more you paid, the more likely it was that you got the hottest and cleanest water which was, at least before the soap went in, transparent. Dodger was aware that in some of those places the water that the nobs had bathed in ended up in the baths habituated by what you might call the middle classes, traveling afterward to the great bath for the lower classes, where at least it arrived soapy which if you took the cheerful view meant a saving. Even though you might never sit down at a table with mayors and knights and barons, at least you could share their bath, which made you proud to be a Londoner.

The rain was falling faster now, rain that was undeniably London rain, already grubby before it hit the ground, putting back on the streets what had been taken away by the chimneys. It tasted like licking a dirty penny.

The door to the bathhouse was up some steps, although there was nothing much else to recommend it; it certainly didn't look like a haven for nubile Nubians of any kind.

Once inside, however, they were greeted by a lady, which sent Dodger's spirits up a bit, although the fact that she turned out to be quite old and had something of a mustache lowered them once again. There was a muted conversation between her and Solomon. The old boy would haggle over the price of a penny bun but had apparently now met his match in the old woman, whose expression suggested that the price was that well-known one "take it or leave it," and as far as she was concerned she would be very happy if he left it, as far away as possible.

Solomon was not often thwarted in his determination to haggle the cheapest price for everything, and Dodger heard him mutter the word "Jezebel" under his breath, just before paying for what turned out to be the keys to a couple of lockers. Of course, Dodger had been to the ordinary public baths many times before; but this one, he hoped, might be more adventurous. He was rather open to the prospect of being oiled.

So, clothed only in large towels, their feet slapping on marble, Solomon and Dodger stepped out into a huge room which looked rather like Hell would look if it had been designed by somebody who thought people deserved another chance. It was full of the strange echoes you get when steam, stone, and humanity are all in one place. To Dodger's dismay, there were no signs of the eagerly anticipated ladies in thin vests, but shadowy figures—male figures—were visible everywhere in the steaming gloom. At this point, Solomon put a hand on Dodger's shoulder and whispered, "Be careful of the Percys, a word to the wise."

This word to the wise left Dodger no wiser until the penny

dropped, and he said, as they were stepping down into the nearest bath, "This isn't the first bath I've been in, you know, but I think it's the prettiest. The Percys never bothered me before."

"God seems to have really taken against them," said Solomon as the hot water rose up their legs. "For myself, I can't see why, because it seems to me that, in a small way at least, they are doing this small planet something of a service by not helping to fill it with unnecessary people."

There wasn't just one bath in the baths; there were sweat baths, cold baths, hot baths; and right now, clambering down into the bath with the two of them was a gentleman wrapped in towels and with biceps bigger than most people's thighs, who said in a voice like a grinding mill, "Would either of you gentlemen require a massage? Very good, very thorough, you will feel the benefit and afterward you will be as right as ninepence, yes?"

Dodger looked at Solomon, who nodded and said, "You should try it, by all means. They tend to be rather brisk in here, but afterward you will feel the glow." He nodded to the man and said, "I will take a massage myself alongside my young friend, and we can talk and relax."

Afterward Dodger considered that the massage had not been relaxing, unless it was that you felt so much better when it stopped, but while the two masseurs twisted and pummeled with no other interest in their victims/clients, he unloaded his thoughts to Solomon, occasionally punctuated with an "ouch."

"I'm glad that Simplicity is safe where she is," he said, "but she will be in danger every time she goes for a walk, and as far as I can see there ain't nobody in the government who wouldn't do nothing to help her (ugh!)."

"Mmm," said Solomon. "That is because mmm the government thinks mostly about all the people—they are not very good at individuals—and undoubtedly there would be those in the country who consider that handing her back against her will might save any bad blood between two countries. And indeed, although I fear to say it, it would be a Christian act, since after all she is a wife in the eyes of God—although, Dodger, God sometimes appears to be looking the other way and I have often told Him so. The wishes of the husband are mmm invariably considered more important than those of the wife."

"That man last night was working for a cove called Sharp Bob, who is (ouch!) interested in Simplicity and me," Dodger said between blows. "Wants to know where she is, so there must be money in it for him. Do you know him? I heard tell he's a legal kind of gentleman."

"Sharp Bob," Solomon mused. "Mmm, I believe I have heard of him. And yes, he's a lawyer—for criminals, you might say. I don't mean getting them off in front of the beak. He does do that, certainly, but he is more a sort of mmm go-between, you might say. Someone will approach him and say, as it might be, 'There's a gent in our town who I might like to see inconvenienced.' Nobody would say anything about killing or chopping off an ear because it would be done simply by looks, and a touching of the nose and little signals like that—just so that Sharp Bob himself can say that he knew nothing about the matter or why somebody's dining room had blood all over it." Solomon sighed. "You say his men are those who attacked Miss Simplicity?"

"Yes, and now I need to find him," Dodger said, "soon as we've got this business tonight out of the way. I oughtta have got the whereabouts of this Sharp Bob off that cove last night, but I was (ouch!) kicking him in the crotch at the time and forgot to do anything about it. I think I had perhaps punched him heavily on the conk as well, flattened it over his face, so all he could say was grunts."

"Let that be a lesson to you," said Solomon. "Violence is not always the way to resolve things."

"Solomon, you have a six-barreled pistol back at home!" said Dodger.

"Mmm, I said, not always."

"Well, if you know where he might be, let me know 'cos tomorrow I'm after him anyway," Dodger said. "Maybe he reckons someone would be happy to hear that Simplicity was dead. Not because they hate her, but just because she is (ugh!) in the way."

There was a very long mmm from Solomon, which at first Dodger thought was because of an extra-special twist from the masseur, then Solomon said quietly, "Well then, Dodger, you have answered your own little conundrum. Let them hear that Simplicity is mmm dead. No one hunts a dead man. Mmm, just a point that crossed my mind, of course. No reason to take it seriously."

Dodger looked at Sol's expression and his eyes were shining. "What do you mean!?"

"I mean, Dodger, that you are a very resourceful young man, and I have given you something to think about. I suggest you think about it. Think about people seeing what they want to see."

A fist came down on Dodger with a thump, but he barely noticed it as his brain started to clamor and then began to spin. He looked back at Solomon and just nodded with a glint in his eye.

Solomon loomed up then like a whale and patted his arm, saying, "Time to go, young man—there is such a thing as being *too* clean."

No sooner had they got dried off and back in their cubicles than Solomon said, "We should sit here for a little while for a drink; it doesn't do to go out immediately after a bracing massage—you could catch a fever. After that, my boy, I intend to introduce you to Savile Row, where all the top men go for their clothing. We haven't got much time, but last night I sent a boy over to my friend Izzy, who will see you right. His place is no shonky shop, and I am certain that he will give a good deal to an old friend who incidentally carried him to safety when the Cossacks shot him." He added, "He had better. Running, I carried him for more than a mile before we lost them in the snow and none of the three of us had boots on, having been woken up at night. After that we went our separate ways, but I will always remember young Karl—I believe I have mentioned him to you before?— saying to me that all men are equal but they are downtrodden, though sometimes they do their own treading. Now I come to think of it, he said a lot of other things too. Worst haircut I have ever seen on a young man, and wild eyes too, reminded me of a hungry wolf."

Dodger wasn't listening. "Savile Row is in the West End!" he said, like a man talking about the ends of the Earth. He went on, "Do I really need toffs' clothing? Mister Disraeli and his friends, well, they know what I am, don't they?"

"Mmm, oh, and what are you mmm exactly, my friend? Their subordinate? Their employee? Or, I would suggest, their equal? That's what young Karl would certainly have said, and probably still does. Unless he's no longer alive." Dodger gave Solomon a strange look and Solomon hastened to clarify. "Mmm, as I recall, if you go around telling people that they are downtrodden, you tend to make two separate enemies: the people who are doing the downtreading and have no intention of stopping, and the people who are downtrodden, but nevertheless—people being who they are—don't want to know. They can get quite nasty about it."

Intrigued, Dodger said, "Am I downtrodden?"

"You? Not so you would notice, my boy, and neither do you tread on anybody else, which is a happy situation to be in, but if I was you I shouldn't think too much more about politics, it can only make you ill. As a matter of fact I certainly believe that some, if not all, of the people you will meet tonight will be considerably richer than you, but from what I have heard of the lady in whose house we will be dining, I have reason to assume that they will not think this means they are that much better than you. Money makes people rich; it is a fallacy to think it makes them better, or even that it makes them worse. People are what they do, and what they leave behind." Solomon drained his coffee cup and said, "Since it's a long way, and my feet hurt, we will take a growler, and behave like the gentlemen we are."

"But that's a lot of money!"

"So? I should walk all that way in this rain? What are you, Dodger? You are a king of infinite space—provided that said space is underground. You are a man who picks up money for a living, and because you have a wonderful eye for it, I think it makes something of an everlasting child of you. Life is fun with no responsibilities, but now you are taking on responsibilities. You have money, Dodger, as that shiny new bank book proves. And you hope to have a young lady, mmm yes? This is good for a man because responsibilities are the anvil on which a man is forged."

Just as soon as they were outside the baths Solomon had to rescue an elderly lady who had simply patted Onan. He helped her brush herself down, then when both her dress and Sol's handkerchief were cleaner, he hailed a cab, which stopped without the driver having meant to, his horse's hooves leaving sparks on the cobbles.

Once they were safe on the cushions inside, with the London rain and all its stickiness falling outside the windows, Solomon sat back and said, "I have never really understood why these gentlemen seem so hostile to their clientele. You would have thought that driving a growler was a job for somebody who liked people, wouldn't you?"

It was pouring down now and the sky was the color of a bruised plum. It was not a good day to be a tosher, but the night might be, when with any luck Dodger could be back after dinner where he belonged, underground. . . . With Solomon's recent lecture in mind, he amended it mentally to "the place where he sometimes chose to be."

He felt he would need to be there because he was once again feeling not entirely sure about himself. He was still Dodger, of course, but what kind of Dodger? Because he was most definitely not the Dodger he had been a week ago. And he thought, if people change like this, how can you be sure about what you get and what you lose? I mean, these days, well, getting into a growler . . . easily done, I'm the kind of lad who goes around in growlers, not the lad with the arse hanging out of his trousers who used to run up behind them and try to hold on. Now I actually pay; would I still recognize the boy?

It looked as if the weather was shaping up to be a storm akin to the one on the night when he had met Simplicity for the first time. In front of them, the coachman himself was out in all elements and weathers, which may have had something to do with the growling, and surely only the horse could be doing the navigating in this downpour. There was nothing in the world but rain, it seemed, and now, against all the rules of nature, it seemed some of it was even falling upward, since there was no room anywhere else.

At this point Dodger heard, only very slightly, the sound he had for days been subconsciously listening for—it was the squeal of metal in pain. And it was ahead of them. He dived toward the little sliding plate that enabled the inmates of a growler to speak to the coachman, if ever he wanted to listen to them, and water splashed on his face as he yelled, "If you overtake the coach in front of us—that one with the squeaky wheel—I will give you a crown!"

There was no answer—and how could you hear one in these crowded streets of vapor and flying water?—but nevertheless the speed of the growler suddenly changed, just as a puzzled Solomon said, "I am not at all sure we have a spare crown on us!"

Dodger wasn't listening; a growler had a lot of places where somebody with quick wits could grasp and pull their way to the roof of the thing, in this case much to the extreme annoyance of the driver, who swore like the devil and shouted out above the noise of the storm that he would be mogadored if a poxy upstart was going to climb all over his vehicle. Above the noise of the storm and the cursing, Dodger leaned down and said, "You must have heard of the man who brought down Sweeney Todd the Demon Barber? Well, cully, that was me, yes, Dodger. Now, you want to talk about it or shall I get angry?" Dodger worked his way down so that he could hang on while talking to the man, and said, "The person who owns the coach ahead of us is wanted for attempted murder, assault, and battery. Probably also kidnapping a young lady and responsible for the death of a baby!"

With water pouring off him in every direction, the captain of the growler growled, "The hell you say!"

"The hell I do indeed, sir!" said Dodger. "And if I find that person before the peelers do, it will be the worse for him, and incidentally of course there will be a reward in all of this for you."

The coachman, trying to keep the horse under control with lightning flashing around them, gave Dodger a sideways look in which was mingled anger, intrigue, and uncertain disbelief. "Oh, so he's got more to fear from you than the peelers, does he? They have damn big sticks, as I very well know!" He opened a mouth in which there appeared to be just one solitary tooth, adding, "We certainly know when they want to get their point across, those bastards." He spat, increasing the storm by the equivalent of about three raindrops, and gave Dodger a pitying look, then growled with another toothless grin, "Well, how will you be worse than the peelers, my little lad, do tell me?"

"Me? Because the peelers have rules. I don't firkytoodle around! And unlike the peelers, when it comes to bashing, I don't have to stop!"

The growler, though, *had* come to a stop. A dead stop, and its driver cursed under his breath. "Piccadilly Circus, guv, all fouled up 'cos of the rain. To tell you the truth, I can't tell which of these buggers is the one you're after, chief, 'cos people are cutting in like Christmas dinner. I don't know why they're always messing about with the roads, but I reckon it's the four-horsers that are causing this lot—they shouldn't be allowed in the city! People are walking around in the road too like they own it—ain't they got no sense?"

It was true; there were people dodging between stationary vehicles, and Piccadilly Circus was a pattern of umbrellas spinning through the growing host of rain-soaked vehicles, none of which could move until the others did. Now the horses were beginning to panic, and yet other coaches, cabs, and one or two brewers' drays were piling in. Then somewhere in the damp, jostling, frantic cauldron of frightened horses and bewildered pedestrians, someone must've stuck part of his umbrella up a horse's nose, causing what previous centuries would have called a hey-ho-rumbelow, but what the growler captain called it could not be put on paper because it would have immediately caught fire.

After that, there was nothing else for it. As the coachman said, "If they want to get everybody out of there, they need to drag out one or two coaches and dismantle the whole damn mess." With that, the sun came out, bright and shining in the clear blue sky, which made it even worse, because every human or horse who wasn't already so began to steam.

Even Dodger could see they had lost their quarry with very little chance of finding it now. No point. Solomon was looking at him from the vehicle's window, holding up his huge pocket watch and pointedly showing him what the time was. Dodger groaned inwardly. If he gave in, then maybe, just maybe, when this seething fiasco was eventually unraveled— and hopefully before any more fights started—he might be in the right place to hear the dreadful screeching wheel scream again. If he couldn't find out what he wanted from Mister Sharp Bob, of course. But right now it was Solomon who looked as if he was likely to be the one doing the screaming.

Dodger turned back to the coachman, shrugged, and said, "How much, mister?"

To Dodger's surprise, the man gave him a sly grin, waved his hands in the air to demonstrate that the progress of horse-drawn transport in this vicinity was a bucket of sheep droppings, and then said, "You really the geezer who brought down Sweeney Todd? You look like a liar to me, but then so does everybody else. Ho-hum, never mind, just give me your signature on this little page I have here, making a suitable mention of the fact that it was indeed you what done it, and we'll call it quits, how about that? 'Cos I think it'd be worth some money one day."

Well, thought Dodger, this was Charlie's fog again; if the truth wasn't what you wanted it to be, you turned it into a different version of the truth. But the man was waiting patiently, with a pencil and a notebook. Taking them up and sweating, Dodger very carefully scribed, one letter at a time:

It woz me wot took dahn Sweeni Tod. Dodjer and that iz troo.

As soon as he had handed it to the coachman, he was dragged to the curb by Solomon, who was frantically trying to open an umbrella—a black and treacherous thing that reminded Dodger of a long-dead, but nevertheless large, bird of prey and could take your eye out, if you let it. Dodger pointed out that right now, at least, it wasn't necessary—except, of course, for protection from the horses all around them, which were doing what horses regularly do and doing it slightly more because they were in a state of panic.

They headed on foot to Savile Row. The side streets were more busy with pedestrians than usual because of the tangle that they had thankfully left behind them. They arrived, wet and warm—which can sometimes as in this case be worse than wet and cold because it includes sticky and horsey—at the shining, polished door of Davies & Son, at 38 Savile Row, leaving Onan at a lamppost and on this occasion with a bone brought along for the purpose, in the company of which he was oblivious to the world.

Once inside, Dodger tried not to be awed at the world of schmutter. After all, he knew there were swells who had much finer clothing than he ever wore, but seeing such a lot of it in one place would have been overwhelming if he let it be so. As it was, he tried to look like somebody who barely glances at this sort of thing because he sees it every day—although aware that the cleaned-up but still quite *fragrant* shonky suit might be a clue that this was not entirely the case. But after all, a tailor is a tailor and all the rest of it is just shine.

Eventually, they were handed into the care of Izzy, small

and skinny but nevertheless possessed of some inner nervous energy that would in other circumstances have turned a mill. He appeared like an arrow between Dodger and Solomon and the front-of-house man who opened the door for them, talking all the time so fast that the best you could do was understand that Izzy would take care of everything, had anything, and everything was in hand and if everybody left it to Izzy, everything would not just be all right but also extremely acceptable in every possible way, and at a price that would amaze and yet satisfy all parties—if, and this was important, Izzy was allowed to get on with the job, thank you all so very much. He fussed Solomon and Dodger into one of the fitting rooms, never at any time ceasing to worry, fret, and to apologize to nobody in particular about nothing very much.

A long cloth tape measure was whisked around his shoulders and Dodger was pushed gently but firmly to the center of the room, where Izzy looked at him with the expression of a butcher faced with a particularly difficult steer, walking around him, measuring by the pounce-and-run-away method. And in all this time the only words he said to Dodger were variations on the theme of "If you would just turn this way, sir?"; and sir this, and sir that, until Dodger was seriously in need of refreshment. It didn't help matters either when the spinning, dashing Izzy, apparently now with no alternative left to him, finally stopped with his mouth in the vicinity of Dodger's left ear, and in the tones of a man inquiring after the whereabouts of the Holy Grail, whispered, "How does one dress, sir?"

This request was something of a problem for Dodger, who had never really given a thought to the aspect of putting his clothes on; after all, it was just something you did. But the little tailor was standing by him as if he expected to learn the location of hidden treasure, and therefore he made an effort, and said, "Well, normally I'd put on yesterday's unmentionables if they ain't too bad, and then I pulls on my stockings . . . No! I tell a lie; most days I put on my undershirt and then I put on my socks." It was at this point that Solomon crossed the room at the normal speed of a god intending that the ungodly should be smitten, only to whisper something in Dodger's ear, causing the latter to say, with some indignation, "How the hell should I know? I never bothered to look! Things find their own way, don't they? What kind of question is that to ask a man, anyway?"

Solomon laughed out loud, and then went into a huddle with an ever-vibrating Izzy, who seemed never to be actually still. Solomon and Izzy were chattering to one another in language that went all over Europe and the Middle East until at last, laughing, Solomon said, "The luck of the Dodger is holding; Izzy says he can do us a wonderful deal! It appears that another tailor was told to work on a frock coat and a very elegant navy-blue shirt, but regrettably one of Izzy's associates made a laughable mistake during the measuring, which meant that they would no longer fit the fine gentleman they were intended for, and so my friend Izzy," Solomon continued, staring fixedly at Izzy, "has a little proposition for you, my friend."

Izzy looked hesitantly at Solomon, and like a man throwing a bone to a lion about to eat him, turned to Dodger, and said hurriedly, "I could do you an excellent deal, young sir, on both those garments; they are happily only a stitch away from your requirements at a very spirited discount of . . . fifty percent?"

Oh, that little telltale question in the statement which told the world that Izzy was just slightly uncertain, and, even more worryingly for Izzy, he was uncertain in the face of Solomon's deadpan face.

The bargaining had only just begun, and rather wisely, Izzy, with an eye on Solomon, dived to, "I beg your pardon, seventy-five, sorry no, *eighty* percent. I will throw in two pairs of very elegant unmentionables as well?"

Solomon smiled, and Izzy looked like a man who had not only been pardoned on the very steps of the gallows, but also had been given a purse full of sovereigns to atone for the misunderstanding. And twenty minutes later a grateful Izzy sent Solomon and the Hero of Fleet Street on their way, with Dodger clutching his new schmutter, Solomon carrying the bag containing the unmentionables, and Izzy now in possession of some of the hero's reward. There was also, courtesy of the management, Solomon's umbrella, which had been dried and brushed; and there was a growler waiting for them in the street.

Well, not exactly; it was coming along the street right up until Solomon stood in front of it waving his finger of God in the air, and the horse began to slow even before the coachman had time to pull on the reins, because horses know trouble when they see it. Dodger was quite careful to put Onan and his bone in the cab before the man had a chance to object; Onan tended to leave a certain Onan-ness wherever he went.

Once inside, Solomon made himself comfortable and said to the driver, "Lock and Co. of Saint James, please, my man."

He turned to a startled Dodger and said, "They will almost definitely have a hat there for you, my lad. Everyone who is anyone, or at least thought by everyone to be anyone, gets their hats there."

"I've got a hat from Jacob!"

"That shonky thing? It looks like somebody used it as a concertina and handed it to a clown. You need a hat for a gentleman."

"But I am not a gentleman," Dodger railed.

"You will be much closer to being one with an elegant hat for special occasions."

And Dodger had to admit that the shonky hat, no doubt about it, was shonky. Generally, hats were not your friend when you were a tosher; they got knocked off your head far too easily. He often wore a thick leather cap, just good enough to save you from cracking your skull if you stood up too quickly in a small sewer, and easy to keep clean.

Everybody wore a hat of some kind, but the hats in the shop they stepped into now were extraordinary, and some were extremely high. And so, of course, Dodger pointed to the biggest one, which looked like a stovepipe and called to him with a siren voice which only he could hear. "I rather think that one will do me a treat."

When he looked at his reflection in the mirror, he thought, oh yes, a really sharp look, sharp as a razor. He would be no end of a swell, where recently he had been no end of a smell—because no matter how hard you scrubbed, the curse of the tosher would always leave its own cheerful mark on you.

Oh yes, this would do him! How amazed Simplicity would

be when she saw him in such a splendid hat! However, it didn't do for Solomon, who considered the price of one pound and eighteen shillings to be grossly extravagant. Dodger was firm. True, it was a lot of money for something that he really didn't need, but it was the principle of the thing. He didn't know exactly what the principle was, but it was a principle and it had a thing, and that was that. Besides, he pointed out that only the other day Solomon had said while he was working on one of his little machines that "this thing needs oiling" and, he continued relentlessly, only the day before *that* the old man had said that his little lathe had "wanted" oil.

"Therefore," said Dodger, "surely *want* is the same as *need*, yes?"

Solomon counted out the coins very slowly and in silence, and then said, "Are you certain you weren't born Jewish?"

"No," said Dodger. "I've looked. I'm not, but thanks for the compliment."

The last call before they went home was to a barber—a perfectly reasonable and careful barber who didn't include extras like having your throat cut. However, the poor fellow was unmanned when Solomon said, just as the barber was shaving Dodger, "It might impress you, sir, if I told you that the gentleman you are now shaving was the hero who put paid to the activities of the nefarious Mister Sweeney Todd."

This intervention caused the man to panic—only a fraction, but nevertheless not a thing to do when you have just put a very sharp cutthroat razor to a man's throat, and it nearly caused another hey-ho-rumbelow in the vicinity of Dodger's neck. The nick was not big, but the amount of blood was out of all proportion to the size, and so there was a great performance with towels, and alum for the cut. It would certainly leave a scar, which was something of a bonus as far as Dodger was concerned; the Hero of Fleet Street ought to sport something on his face to show for it.

Then, once his face was tidy and, of course, Solomon had negotiated in a friendly but firm way six months of free haircuts, they caught another growler home and there was just about enough time to get washed, dressed, and generally smartened up.

It was while Dodger was sponging himself down, including the crevices because, after all, this was a special occasion, he found part of himself thinking: What would I have to do to let someone die and then come alive again? Apart from being God, that is.

Then, for some reason, the dodger at the back of his head remembered the Crown and Anchor men with their dice, and the man with the pea that you never, ever found. Then tumbling on top of that there was the voice of Charlie, saying that the truth is a fog and in it people see what they want to see, and it seemed to him that around these little pictures a plot was plotting. He trod carefully so as not to disturb it, but wheels in his head were clearly turning and he had to wait until something went *click*.

The new clothes still fitted him exactly as promised and Dodger wished that he had something more than a tiny piece of broken mirror in which to see himself in his finery. Then he pushed aside the curtain to ask Solomon's opinion and was confronted by Solomon arrayed in all his glory.

A man who usually wandered around in embroidered slippers or old boots, and wore a ragged black gabardine, had suddenly become an old-fashioned but very smart gentleman with a black fine woolen barathea jacket, dark-blue pantaloon trousers, and long, dark-blue woolen stockings with ancient but well-kept court shoes sporting silver buckles that shone. But what amazed Dodger most of all was the large dark-blue-and-gold medallion around Solomon's neck. He knew what the symbols were on the medallion, but Dodger had never associated them with the old man: they were the seal and the eye in the pyramid of the Freemasons. Finally, since Solomon had washed his beard and primped it, the whole effect appeared to have an amazing power.

And Dodger said so, which caused Solomon to smile and say, "Mmm, one day, my boy, I will tell you the name of the august personage who was gracious enough to give this to me. And may I say, Dodger, as always you scrub up very well; one might almost take you for a real gentleman."

It only remained to very cautiously give Onan his dinner and equally cautiously take him for a little walk outside to do what he needed to. They left him in dog heaven with another bone; and then there was nothing for it but to find another growler, just as the evening fog was rising, and head back west to number one Stratton Street, Mayfair.

CHAPTER TWELVE

In which Dodger mixes with the gentry,
Disraeli accepts a challenge,
and Dodger proves to be a quick learner

DODGER STARED OUT OF the cab as they rattled westward
with the words "I'm going to see Simplicity again" etching
themselves on his heart, or so it felt, and suddenly he thought
of Simplicity being dead. Dead, and therefore no trouble to
anybody—no reason for wars, no reason for people to prowl
the streets with malice aforethought.

There had to be a way! Right now she was a girl whom
no one wanted; that was to say, no one other than him. As
the fog delivered the stink of the Thames to his nostrils, a
click in his brain signaled a successful conclusion, and all that
remained was the fine details. There were a few things he
couldn't quite see, but with the Lady on his side, he thought
they would drop into his hand.

"A remarkable woman is Miss Burdett-Coutts," Solomon
was saying. "She is an heiress, and also a major philanthropist,
which is somebody who gives their money away to the poor
and needy—which I must make clear to you, young man,

doesn't mean you, you being neither poor nor needy, just occasionally knee-deep in sewage."

Solomon seemed very taken by his little joke, and it would have been like kicking Onan to do anything other than applaud, and so Dodger pulled his mind away from Simplicity and said, "That was a good one! Why on earth does she want to give so much money away?"

They were passing through Leicester Square and Solomon said, "Because she feels that she should. She pays for the Ragged Schools, which give some children at least an elementary education and funds mmm scholarships and bursaries, which I must tell you means giving brighter pupils the chance to go to university for an even better education. That's all they know about her down at the synagogue, apart from the fact that she keeps bees, and you need to be a very mmm sensible person to keep bees—someone who thinks about things, plans ahead, and thinks about the future. A very thorough lady, in fact, who I assume does not wish to die rich. Which I've always considered to be mmm an admirable ambition. A very singular lady and a power in her own right."

He paused. "I wonder who else there is likely to be at this little soirée since she knows so many important people. In a sense, I rather suspect you might see tonight some more of the mmm powerhouse of politics. Of course, the lords and elected members debate the issues of the day in Parliament itself, but I strongly suspect that here in London the actual outcomes have a lot to do with the things that people say to other people over a drink. The process of ratifying what they have decided among themselves may be a variant of mmm what is known as *proportional representation*, but on the whole it all seems to work, if somewhat mmm erratically."

He warmed to his subject. "What I really like about the English is that they don't have theories. No Englishman would ever have said 'I think, therefore I am.' Although possibly he might have said, 'I think, therefore I am, I think.' The world can have too much order, alas. Ah, here we are at last. Mind your manners and remember what I told you about how to eat with so much cutlery* which, I have to reiterate, I would rather you did not attempt to steal. I know you to be a well-intentioned young man, but occasionally you get a little mmm absentminded around small light objects; please refrain from the habit of a lifetime, just for tonight, please?"

"I'm not a thief!" said Dodger. "I can't help it if things are left lying around." Then he nudged Solomon's arm and said, "Just kidding. I will be on my best behavior and a credit to my wonderful unmentionables—I've never had a garment that fitted so well in the groin. If I'd known what it feels like to be among the gentry, I would have applied for a ticket a long time ago!"

The driver stopped just short of their destination; private coaches and growlers were politely jostling to disgorge their passengers without their drivers having to swear at one another more than usual. They got out and walked up the steps of the very pleasant building Dodger had hardly noticed the night before. Solomon raised his hand to knock on the door and magically the door opened before he had touched it, to reveal Geoffrey the butler.

The important thing to do, Dodger thought, was to keep

---

* Frankly, most of the time Dodger ate using his fingers unless Sol told him off.

close to Solomon, who seemed to be entirely in his element. The guests were still coming in, and most of them knew one another and they certainly knew where the drinks were, and therefore Dodger and Solomon were ignored right up until Charlie and Mister Disraeli returned together from wherever it was they had huddled to exchange current information.

Disraeli made a beeline for Solomon and said, "How nice it is to see you here!" They shook hands, but Dodger read from their faces that here were two people who distrusted each other quite a lot. Then Disraeli, with a glint in his eye, turned to Dodger and said, "Oh, wonderful, the young tosher transmuted into a gentleman! Excellent!"

This slightly annoyed Dodger, though he couldn't exactly figure out why, but he said, "Yes, sir, indeed tonight I am a gentleman and tomorrow I might turn out to be a tosher again!" As the words dropped into Dodger's ears, his brain clicked again, telling him: this is the opportunity, don't mess it up! And so, grinning, he added, "I can be a gentleman, and I can be a tosher; can *you* be a tosher, Mister Disraeli?"

For just a moment, and probably entirely unnoticed by anyone else in the throng apart from the four of them, the world froze briefly, and then thawed the instant Mister Disraeli had decided what to do, which was to smile like the morning sun with a knife in its teeth. He said, "My dear boy, do you think I would make a tosher? Hardly a profession I had reason to contemplate, I must say!"

He had to pause because Charlie had slapped him on the back, saying, "It's just scrambling in the mud to find the hidden treasure, my friend, and I might suggest it is remarkably like politics! If I was you, I would take the opportunity to learn something very valuable about the world. I always do!"

Disraeli glanced at Dodger and said, "Well, now I come to think of it, quite possibly a reconnaissance of the underbelly of the city would be sensible at this time."

"And indeed," said Charlie, grinning like a man who has dropped a sixpence and picked up a crown, "it would show, do you not think, that you are being very careful of public opinion in the matter of drainage in this city, which is in fact antiquated and noisome, to say the least. A canny politician would, I am sure, like to show his concern for this scandalous state of affairs. Our friends in *Punch* magazine would certainly portray you as a forward-looking politician, careful of the city as a whole."

For a moment Disraeli looked rather solemn, playing with his little goatee beard as if lost in thought. Then he said, "Yes indeed, Charlie, I think you may have a point."

It seemed to Dodger that the two men were each hatching plans of their own; he could smell the smell of a man who scents an opportunity and was deciding how to bend it to his own advantage, just like he was. He thought, good old Charlie knows that whether Mister Disraeli comes out of the sewer covered in richards or covered in diamonds, Charlie will have covered a very good story.

Disraeli lit up like a very enthusiastic candle and his smile broadened as he turned and said, "Very well, Mister Dodger, let no one say that I am averse to a challenge. I will indeed, if you are prepared to be my Virgil, take a subterranean ramble with you in the public interest. Let me see—the day after tomorrow perhaps? After all, a politician should do more than just talk!"

He looked around approvingly, and Dodger said, "I'd like you to understand, sir, I ain't a virgin, you just ask Ginny-Come-Lately! But I would be quite happy to give you a little tour, sir. Not near the hospitals, of course. The breweries are pretty good; down there, even the rats smell good."

At that point Miss Burdett-Coutts passed, circulating among her growing crowd of guests, and Charlie said, "Here's a go, Angela. Ben and young Dodger here are hatching up a scheme to go down into our wretched sewers shortly, on a voyage of exploration for the public good. Don't you think that is a fine thing?"

"Are they? I certainly hope they tidy themselves up before they come back here!" Angela smiled at Dodger, held out her hand, and said, "So nice to see you again, Mister Dodger. I see you have raised your game considerably when it comes to your clothing. Excellent!"

Dodger took the lady's outstretched hand and kissed it, to her surprise and his own, but to the great edification and amusement of both Charlie and Disraeli; Solomon certainly hadn't told him to do this but, well, he was Dodger, and Miss Burdett-Coutts was smiling as if a favorite dog had done a good trick, but at the same time she would quite like the dog to know that it was allowed only one bite. The unspoken code was that once was fine and twice would be taking liberties, and she was sure that Dodger would not need telling twice.

She looked at Solomon and said, "Ah, the most learned Mister Cohen, I presume? I have heard so much about you. I believe the Papal Nuncio told me a wonderful story about your perspicacity." She turned back to Dodger and said, "Mister Dodger, I believe you might be interested to meet

Miss Simplicity Parish, a cousin of mine from the country."

Almost immediately, Simplicity stepped out from behind Miss Coutts, and for Dodger every single person in the room disappeared, leaving only Simplicity. After a moment, Simplicity, clearly realizing that if she didn't say anything, Dodger was likely to be there with his mouth open for the rest of the evening, held out her hand and said, "My word, so you are the famous Mister Dodger. I am very happy to meet you."

Angela, glancing at Dodger, said, "When dinner is announced, I would be happy for you to take Miss Simplicity through to the dining area. You may sit beside me so that the proprieties are maintained." Having neatly put Simplicity and Dodger together, Miss Coutts then cased the room, Dodger thought, like a burglar anxious to find every piece of silverware, scanning all the newcomers milling around. "Do you see that gentleman over there, by the fireplace?" she said with a small gesture of her head. "That is Sir George Cayley, who certainly has demonstrated to us exactly why birds are able to fly and I believe is determined to see that humans do the same, although I suspect that William Henderson might beat him to it—I have been hearing much about his prototype steam-powered aerial carriage. If things look promising, I might consider funding further progress. It would be such a boon for mankind. Just imagine if you could fly to France in one day!"

That would be like the railways, Dodger thought. If you had money, you find someone who is, you are sure, going to change the world, and get more money back if it works. After all, money doesn't do much when it's just standing still. It's when it's moving around that it really works. He felt quite pleased with himself for coming up with this observation.

One of the guests had cracked a joke on the other side of the room and there was general laughter, and then in a low voice Angela said to Dodger and Simplicity, "Do you see that rather taciturn gentleman over there who looks as if he lost a guinea and found a farthing? That's Charles Babbage, and he has made a machine that can add up, and that's very interesting and I am very fond of interesting people. Although in his case, he is not really very keen on other people at all, apart from having excellent taste when it comes to his lady friends. And I see that Mister Cohen is already in conversation with Mister Babbage and his friend, Ada Lovelace, who is a most elegant lady and a credit to her father. I am sure they will have a lot to talk about. If ever there is a man who introduces himself, it is Mister Cohen." Suddenly she said happily, "Ah, there's Sir Robert Peel. I'm so glad he could come. I had been told that he had been held up on a bit of business at Scotland Yard." She swept away into the chattering throng.

Sir Robert Peel? The boss of the crushers! Being a tosher wasn't exactly illegal—Grandad had told Dodger a coin was a coin, and if you picked it out of the mud, well, who knew whose coin it had been? Mind you, there was the little matter of *getting* into the sewers, that being a matter probably of trespass. Nobody bothered all that much though, except for the work gangs, who thought that loose coinage was their legal perk. The public at large didn't care a fig; toshers could scrabble in the dark and come up with a copper or two, or they could scrabble in the dark and die, at no extra charge.

But peelers, well, sometimes peelers had their own

interpretation of the spirit of the law, and some of them saw it as their duty to make life a little more tricky for those people on the edge of society, which was why they were having so many fights with the Cockney lads, which amounted to a small war.

Toshers were small fry, but in the rookeries, well, peelers were the *enemy*. Dodger didn't know the word "visceral," he just understood the situation: you would do yourself no good mixing with the peelers, and now here he was in the same room as their boss, and as sure as sixpence Angela was going to introduce Dodger to him. He told himself that he had done nothing wrong—well, maybe a few things hardly worth mentioning and mostly a long time ago—but if you came from the rookeries the peelers didn't listen for long.

On the other hand, of course, he thought, it was quite possible that Angela might object to people being arrested in her house.

He didn't panic, because people on the tosh who panicked would sooner or later knock themselves out and lose their bearings. But Simplicity was watching him with a slightly worried smile, and by sheer main force he calmed himself down as if nothing had happened, because in fact nothing *had* happened, and by degrees he was feeling better. All he had to do was not get excited and keep as far away as possible from Sir Robert.

To his surprise, Simplicity stroked his hand and said, "Are you all right, Dodger? I know you have had such a busy time, all because of me, and I am so very grateful."

Charlie and Disraeli had drifted off on another current in this room, where it appeared that nobody stood in one place for very long before seeing somebody else that they also wanted to talk to. So gossip and people oscillated through the air, with at the moment himself and Simplicity in a little bubble.

He managed to say, "Oh, don't worry about me, miss. How is life here?"

"Angela is very kind," said Simplicity. "Really very kind, and . . . how can I put this . . . ? Very understanding."

Dodger said, "I asked you this once before, and now things is different but there's no change in the question. What would you like to happen next? Do you want to stay here?"

Her face went solemn. "Yes, Angela is very kind. But I know I am here because I am a problem, and I do not wish to be a problem. Sooner or later, problems get solved. I wonder how that might happen."

Dodger looked around, but no one was paying them any attention so he plucked up his courage and said, "Supposing as you could go somewhere where you could be anybody you wanted to be? Not no problem to nobody. Because, you see, I think I might have a plan. It's quite a good plan, but I only got one part this evening so I'm still working on it. It might be risky and it could mean a bit of playacting, but if I trust in the Lady, I think it will work—she has never let me down this far." Then he had to explain to her who the Lady was.

At last, Simplicity said, "I see. I mean, I think I see. But, dear Dodger, would I be right in believing that the success of this plan will end up with you and me together somewhere safe?"

Dodger cleared his throat. "Yes, that is the plan."

She stared at him. There was always something delightfully

solemn in the way Simplicity spoke, and she said softly, "I think that would be an excellent plan, Dodger, don't you?"

Dodger said, "You agree?"

"Oh yes, indeed, you are kind, very kind. I don't know about loving; we shall see. I have had what I believed was love, but it was an untrue thing, what I think is called a forgery, a bad coin, and not what I thought it was." She hesitated. "What I thought of as a shining sixpence proved to be a farthing, as you would say. But I have found that kindness lasts a lot longer than love, because my mother always said that kindness was love in disguise. And, Dodger, where you are, the world seems to fizz. You make everything seem possible."

At a moment like this, for a boy like Dodger who would trip over his own mental feet, he said, "Of course we don't have to stay together if you don't want to."

Simplicity smiled. "Dodger, this may be hard for you to understand, but sometimes you should just stop talking."

And as Dodger blushed, dinner was announced.

Miss Burdett-Coutts led the party into dinner, accompanied by a tall man with a severe flinty look on his face and, Dodger noticed in horror, dressed in exactly the same clothes as Dodger—a fact that made him unaccountably nervous. What was it that Izzy had said before giving him and Solomon such a good deal? *Dodger, I've got a really good deal on this splendid new suit with wonderful and cherished unmentionables because some apprentice tailor got the sizes wrong the first time.*

Yes, his frock coat was exactly like Dodger's, and the man had opened the coat to reveal the wonderful blue silk shirt that was the spit and image, apart from a trifling matter of size, to the one which Dodger was wearing; and now, oh dear, because he had been looking at the man, the man was now looking at him with the same sharp expression, causing hairs to rise on Dodger in places where he had never known he had hairs. But they had paid for the clothes, hadn't they, fair and square? He knew that Solomon had most definitely got a receipt, Solomon being the kind of person who was almost as anxious about getting the receipt as he was about getting the relevant merchandise itself.

In this moment of slight panic Dodger recognized, coming toward them, Henry Mayhew and his wife, and indeed Simplicity was running toward Jane Mayhew to give her a hug.

While that was going on, Henry held out his hands to Dodger and said cheerfully, "The man of the moment. Mister Dodger, I have made a study of the multiple classes of people in London, and it does seem to me that you are climbing the ladder faster, if I may say so, than a chimpanzee." He smiled nervously and said, "No offense, of course." And indeed no offense was taken as Dodger had no idea what a chimpanzee was and made a mental note to ask Solomon later.

So Dodger took Simplicity somewhat nervously on his arm and followed the Mayhews into the dining room. And he succeeded in parking her exactly where Angela had intended, according to the smile of approval.

Then Angela turned to him and said, "Well now, Dodger, I wonder if you have met my very good friend Sir Robert Peel? I suspect you may have some things in common." Her eyes twinkled as she introduced the two men, as if she was actually introducing the two sets of matching trousers.

Sir Robert Peel smiled, although because of Dodger's

nerves, it seemed to him more like a grimace, and said, "Oh yes, the Hero of Fleet Street. I would very much like to have a quiet word with you."

Dodger looked into those eyes and they had "copper" all over them. He thought: Is that always how it's going to be? Always being the man who took down Sweeney Todd? Well, it was useful, no doubt about it, but somehow it was awkward as well, like wearing another man's trousers, which in a sense was what he was doing right now. And the man was still watching him carefully, as if sizing him up.

People were now sitting down. Dodger was urged toward the chair next to Angela, with Simplicity already seated on his other side and Solomon beside her. Sir Robert—or "Dear Rob," as Angela called him—sat on Angela's other side.

In a lowered voice, Angela said to him, "Does it hurt? You wince when somebody calls you the Hero of Fleet Street. Do you not notice that? Charlie tells me that you are quite clear that people should know that the facts of the matter are not as they seem, and I suggest that you feel that every commendation for you is a damnation for Mister Todd, and I must say that this is to your credit. One feels there was another kind of heroism, of the kind which is often ignored. I will bear this in mind because I do have some influence. Sometimes a word in the right place can do a lot of good." She smiled then, and said, "Do you like it, scrabbling in the sewers for money? Tell the truth now!"

"I don't need to tell a lie," said Dodger. "It's freedom, miss, that's the truth, and pretty safe if you keep your wits about you and use your head. I reckon I earns more than a chimney sweep any day of the week, and soot, well it's terrible stuff, miss, not good for you at all. Bad for you inside and out, my oath! But when I come back from the tosh, well, good old lye soap does the trick. Not what you would call fancy, but you do feel clean."

The conversation had to stop there as waiters came past, and after the noise of the plates and the—oh so much—cutlery, Miss Burdett-Coutts said, "You appear to be everywhere and into everything according to my informants, rather like the famous, or if you prefer, the *in*famous highwayman Dick Turpin. Have you heard of him, young man? What do you think about his extraordinary ride to York on his mare Black Bess? I believe they are doing plays about him now and the public just love him, because he was a scallywag."

Looking apprehensively at the meal put in front of him, Dodger said, "I have heard about the gent, madam, and I like the way he put a shine on the world. But I think he was clever, and far too clever to ride all the way to York. Too risky, and while I have to say I ain't—I beg your pardon, I *am not*—a horseman, I reckon that he would have knackered the horse within an hour if he'd done it as fast as they said. No, I reckon he rushed up to some of his mates what he knew to be not all that matey and shouted out something like 'Pray for me, my lads, for I am going to try to get to York this very night!' And o' course, you see, you can be certain that when you have a price on your head like he did, his mates would have instantly peached on him to the runners within ten minutes, by which time, I'd bet you a crown, our friend Dick would be in the West End with his mustache a different color, walking around with two sporting ladies arm in arm. That's what's *clever*; just legging it don't do the trick, though I know they got him in the end. If I was him, I'd've dressed up as a priest and just lay low somewhere until everybody had forgotten about me. Sorry for the lecture, miss, but you did ask."

Angela laughed. "Your reputation goes before you, Mister Dodger, as a young man of great courage and indeed understanding. Now it would seem you are a man of strategy and a breath of fresh air!" She put her hand on his arm and said, "Are you a churchgoing man at all, Mister Dodger?"

"No, miss. Take it from me, miss, Solomon does the believing for both of us, depend upon it! I reckon he tells the Almighty what to do. But don't worry, I heard that Jesus walked on water, so he might know a little bit about toshing, but I ain't seen him down there. I mean no offense; mind you, in the dark you don't see everybody."

He noticed Angela's smile become a little strained before coming back to normal, whereupon she said, "Well, Mister Dodger, it would appear that an unbeliever might put some believers to shame." He assumed from this that once again he had got away with it, even though he wasn't quite sure what the "it" was.

Now, at last, Dodger was able to pay attention to the food in front of him: a rather good bowl of vegetable soup, even better than the stuff that Solomon made, and he said so as soon as he finished it, noticing as he did that no one else had dived into the soup with the same alacrity.

"It's called julienne," said Angela. "I really don't know why that is so. I envy you your appetite!"

Cheered up by this, Dodger said, "Can I have some more?" Out of the corner of his eye he saw Charlie wearing the familiar expression of a man enjoying the fun.

Angela followed his gaze and said, "Charlie writes books, you know? I often wonder where he gets all his ideas from. As for the soup, I'm sure there is plenty more, but there is a very nice turbot to follow, after which there will be roast saddle of mutton and that will be followed by roast quails. If, young man, you haven't exploded by then, there will follow a compote of cherries—very sweet. I see you haven't touched your wine; it is quite a decent sauvignon blanc, and I think you would like it." As Dodger reached for the glass, she turned to answer a question from Sir Robert Peel on her other side.

Dodger did like the wine, and because he was Dodger he thought, well, this is pretty good stuff so I will drink it very slowly. After all, he very seldom drank wine, although Solomon used to buy some stuff at Passover which was so sweet it made your teeth ache. Dodger generally liked beer or stout, especially stout in the winter; they were simple drinks for simple people, and Dodger did not wish to become a complicated person, which he certainly would become if he drank more than one glass of this wine.

Solomon had told him beforehand that there could be a different wine with every course with meals like this; he had to wonder how on earth people would get back home. So, while Angela spoke to Sir Robert Peel and Simplicity delicately finished her own bowl of soup, he treasured the little glass, taking one small sip at a time. Oh, he had been rascally drunk occasionally, but while it had looked a good idea at the time, it never looked quite the same later on when you woke up, and it was very hard to go on the tosh without your mind being clear. Of course, not throwing up a lot helped too, and more than anything he didn't want to disgrace himself in any way in front of all these nobby people, and while Simplicity was watching. And she *was* watching.

So was the turbot, which came past on a silver tray before being distributed among the guests. It was big and fat, but you had never seen such a sorry expression on the face of a fish before, although perhaps it might have been cheered up by the fact that along with the rather piquant sauce it tasted very nice. Dodger was more at his ease now; the dinner was going well, people were chattering to one another, and it was all rather jolly. It was still jolly when the roast saddle of mutton turned up, slightly yellow and rather greasy, and to a lad as energetic as Dodger, pure pleasure, although he couldn't remember the last time he had eaten so much. In the attic, the meals prepared by Solomon were . . . wholesome, and enough. Meat came in small amounts, more a seasoning than the whole meal, and generally the basis of a thick soup or nourishing gruel. He was aware now of a general tightness of the stomach; but good mutton was the food of the gods, and therefore it would be totally unrighteous not to do it justice.

Things were going well; he had listened to Solomon on the subject of which knife and fork you should use for each course,* he had tucked his napkin in his neck, and he could definitely do this sort of thing every night. But he knew that he had been ignoring—how could he?—Simplicity, who was, he saw, very politely listening to one of Solomon's stories now, with every semblance of interest, which was right and proper because Solomon could surprise you every time.

---

* Solomon had said, "Don't bother about the fish slice; nobody bothers with the fish slice, it is there as an ornament, just to show people that you have a fish slice."

Just as he turned to look at her, she turned to look at him and said, "It's rather droll, Dodger, that you appear to be dressed like a slightly smaller version of Sir Robert." Here she lowered her voice to a whisper. "Much more handsome, and you don't scowl as much. But I must say you look like two peas in a pod."

Dodger said, "He's a lot older and bigger than me."

A remark which caused Simplicity to smile and say, "Sometimes I think English people don't always think about what they say; if you look inside any pod of peas, you will see that they are all sizes. The pea pod shapes them differently."

He stared at her with his mouth open. Because firstly, he realized he often shelled peas for Solomon and had never really bothered what shape any of them were, and secondly, here was Simplicity telling him something new. Not for the first time, he thought, yes, Simplicity is not simple.

She laughed softly. "You don't know anything about me, Dodger."

"Well, I expect that someone will let me find out some more at some time, please?"

"I have very fat legs!" she announced.

The chances of getting very fat at all in the rookeries were small, but Dodger had never heard of any girl saying that her legs were too thin, and so he said, in the silence that followed her remark, "I don't want to be indelicate, miss, but that is a matter of opinion—your opinion obviously, but alas, I have as yet been unable to form one for myself."

It wasn't quite an uproar, he thought, more like a halfway-up roar, but Dodger heard variations on the theme of "I'd say!" And quite a few examples of that hard-to-describe noise that people make when they are pretending to be shocked, but really are just rather amused and possibly also relieved. It was probably Charlie who said, "Excellent, worthy of the famous Beau Brummel himself!"

Solomon's face was absolutely blank, as if he hadn't heard, and Angela, God bless her, was chuckling. This was very useful, Dodger thought, because she was the hostess, and an incredibly rich woman, and quite clearly to everybody there she was perfectly happy about what was going on, thus defying anyone who thought otherwise. After all, who would want to disagree with one of the richest women in the world?

Around them there grew then a sort of comfortable buzz as people finished their drinks and in some cases started them again anew, and at this point Dodger realized that he certainly needed the jakes, and he had no idea where they would be, except of course they would be downstairs. In a world of unmentionables—real, erratic, and sometimes invisible—he was not going to ask a lady where he could go to take a piss.

Then he found himself looking into the eyes of Sir Robert Peel, who was grinning around Angela like a cat who has seen a mouse, and the boss of the peelers said, "Ah, Mister Dodger, I rather suspect from the way in which you are searching about that you are looking for a place of some easement; allow me to escort you, because I myself am noticing the same urgency."

Dodger was in no position to refuse. Sir Robert exchanged a nod with Angela and piloted Dodger out of the room and down some steps, ushering him eventually into something like a paradise made of mahogany and gleaming brass and copper.

It sparkled; it was a palace. The jakes in the rookeries were crowded, dark, and stank; you would be better off going outside, and many did—which meant that walking along an alleyway at night was a very big adventure. Solomon, always fastidious about this sort of thing, had his own portable bucket with a little well-scrubbed wooden lid for those moments when a man just wanted a nice sit-down. One of Dodger's chores was to take the bucket to the nearest cesspit, but these were overflowing most of the time; anyway, every night the honey wagons came around, which did a little something to improve matters when the workers shoveled up the stuff and away it went, along with the horse muck too. But however often the honey wagons came along, and however hard the dunykin divers scoured the septic tanks, you were never very far from yesterday's dinner. But this place, well, this was amazing, and although he knew what the hole in the shiny mahogany was for, it seemed like sacrilege to use it. And what was this? Sheets of paper, all cut out ready for use, just like Solomon did with the *Jewish Chronicle*, and there were mirrors too, and little soaps in a large bowl, soft and smelling nice on the hands. Dodger couldn't help pocketing some—despite the company—because there were so many of them.

He took a few moments to be stupefied, despite the pressure on his bladder and a certain nervousness about being cooped up in the same room as the boss of the peelers who, he noticed, was now sitting quite happily in a very expensive chair and lighting a cigar.

Sir Robert Peel smiled at him and said, "Please don't stand on ceremony, Mister Dodger; I am in no hurry and, of course, as you must have realized, I am also between you and the doorway."

This information, just as he was addressing himself to the

ornate and gleaming pan in front of him, dropped Dodger into a state where the business in hand was turning out to be impossible. He glanced over his shoulder. Sir Robert wasn't even looking at him but was simply enjoying his cigar, like a man with all the time in the world. But since nothing actually *bad* was happening now, Dodger got a grip on his . . . fears and had to admire the perfect workings of this wondrous new contraption. When he had finished, the voice of Sir Robert, still in his chair, said laconically, "Now you pull the porcelain knob on the chain to your left."

Dodger had been wondering what that was for. It was surely waiting to be pulled, wasn't it? But why? To let people know that you had finished? Did it ring a bell so that people didn't come in and disturb you? Oh well, he gave the nice little ceramic knob on the end of the chain a casual but hopeful pull, then backed away from the bowl, just in case this really was the wrong thing to have done and despite everything he was going to get into trouble . . . except the water gurgled around the pan, leaving the place spotless. Now that was a thing worth having!

He swung around and said, "Yes, sir, I know what to do. And I know you are having a little game, sir. I am wondering what you want from me."

Sir Robert looked at the tip of his cigar as if he had not seen it before and said very casually, "I would very much like to know how you did that murder in the sewers this afternoon."

Inside Dodger, the turbot and all his little friends rushed to escape the sinking Dodger, and for a moment he thought he would make a terrible mess on that shiny floor until he reminded himself, *I never murdered anyone, didn't want to, didn't have time*. So he said, "What murder would this be?"—quelling the turbot and telling it to mind its manners. "I never murdered nobody, never!"

The head of all the policemen in London said cheerfully, "Well now, it's funny you should say that, because I believe you, but sad to say we have a dead body in the morgue and two men who say you put the poor fellow in there. And the funny thing is, and you might laugh at this, I do not believe *them*. There is a corpse, certainly, reported to us by a gentleman known around and about as Manky Smith—probably known to you as well?"

"Manky Smith? He's a boozer, walks around all the time with wet pants. He would peach anybody for a pint of porter. I bet the other one was Crouching Angus, an old sweat with one and a half legs."

The man had said that he didn't think that Dodger had murdered anybody and that was a good thing, wasn't it? A very good thing, but nevertheless the chief peeler had that look about him you learned to recognize after you had had a few run-ins with authority. It said that authority wanted you to know that authority always had the upper hand, and that you had just better mind your manners for the moment, because you were the enemy of authority unless authority told you that you weren't.

Mister Peel was watching him with a slight smile on his face—you must never ignore the smile on the face of a peeler—and Dodger thought, this one is the king of the peelers, the big Peel himself, so even a dodger knows when not to dodge. He said, watching that smile, "You say that you don't think I murdered anybody, but there are two people saying I done it, right? Who's the body what was murdered? And why you ain't taking their word against mine?"

Very calmly, Sir Robert said, "Frankly, my men know them and say that they wouldn't take the testimony of those two if the Archangel Gabriel was standing beside them and had given them a reference." He smiled the smile of a policeman, which was only slightly better than the smile of a tiger, and said, "And I'm not taking *your* word as anything, Mister Dodger, but I *am* inclined to take the word of Solomon Cohen, who is very well thought of in the Jewish community. While I engaged him in conversation earlier this evening—and quite clearly he knew nothing of this accusation, nor did I say anything of it to him—he was kind enough to mention that you have spent almost the whole day in his company, a fact which can be verified by a number of reputable merchants, including my own tailors, which I can see with my own eyes. But I ask myself, if this murder took place only a few hours ago, why did this allegation reach me instantly, do you think?"

Before Dodger could say anything, Sir Robert continued. "I think that you have made enemies because, as Ben tells me, you appear to be compounding your heroic deeds by keeping a certain young woman safe while she is in our country. I salute you for that, but this situation cannot go on forever. There are indications that . . . others involved in this affair are growing increasingly impatient."

He drew on his cigar and lazily blew out a cloud of blue smoke; it drifted and curled around Dodger's head like an aromatic fog.

"There has clearly been a murder," the head of the peelers

stated, "and indeed I must make certain that somebody is brought to justice—despite the fact that the corpse concerned was a gentleman who was known as a man who got things done, for a fee, with no questions asked and certainly no questions answered. He was a lawyer until the other lawyers found him out, and then he became what we call an accommodator, and a particularly good one because he knew all the lawyers' tricks. He was very good at introducing people who needed crimes committed to people who wanted to be paid for committing crimes, and, of course, he would skim something off the top for his expenses without ever getting his hands dirty. Now he turns up quite professionally dead, meaning neat and clean and not involving any third party. A very neat job. And a very silent corpse. They might as well have done the washing up and fed the cat before they left. His name was Sharp Bob."

Sharp Bob was dead! So someone had got to him, Dodger thought. But now he had other questions. What had this Sharp Bob known? Had he been working on his own, just to make some specie . . . ? Or under the orders of someone else? For that government Mister Disraeli had spoken of?

"All the policemen know about you, Mister Dodger," Sir Robert was saying, "and the old Bow Street boys did as well: always suspected, never impeached, never had to stand in front of the beak. One old lad I know said some people believed you were protected by the Lady of the Sewers, and I believe that you may now need all the protection you can get. *We* are not the Bow Street runners, Mister Dodger; we are clever men—your friend Charlie Dickens is in fact quite fascinated by our procedures." Sir Robert sighed and went on, "Indeed, I sometimes suspect he would love to be a peeler if I let him; he'd make a good copper if he didn't scribble, scribble, scribble all the time, I am sure. We know what goes on, Mister Dodger, but sometimes we don't see the need to tell people everything that we know."

He paused to take another puff on his cigar before continuing. "I do know, however, that one or two people with associations to the aforesaid Sharp Bob are said to have recently run up against a gentleman known to all and sundry as Dodger, and ended up the worst for it. One . . . employee, shall we say, appears to have had an unfortunate and terminal accident only yesterday morning—the kind involving his being run over by a coach and four in a busy street not too far from your own neighborhood. Run over *twice*, it would appear . . . with no witnesses whatsoever."

Dodger's mind was racing. Someone else had got to the other cove who had beaten Simplicity, then—someone who *hadn't* held back from killing. Now it began to seem that everyone connected with this affair was ending up dead. . . .

"We are rather wondering," Sir Robert mused, "if there might be another player here now; people are getting restive and want to see this whole matter cleared up. Of course, a keen policeman would still automatically think that said Mister Dodger, being somewhat annoyed by the lackeys of Sharp Bob, might see that some harm came to him or his associates. However, as all London knows, you were otherwise engaged yesterday morning at Mister Todd's establishment. You appear to be a lucky man, Dodger. A man who is normally invisible has become surprisingly visible at just the right moments." He paused. "Although my informants do tell me there is a further known associate of both of these two late gentlemen who was seen sporting a broken nose this morning, while also walking in a rather peculiar fashion . . . this may need further investigation. Are you with me? I see that you are remaining quiet; very sensible of you."

The boss of the peelers stood up, knocking the ash off the end of his cigar into a small silver ashtray. "Mister Dodger, I am the head of the police force, which makes me a policeman, but I am also a politician. I am sure that someone as smart as you is aware that politicians—who in theory wield a great deal of power—can sometimes get somewhat tangled up when it comes to using it, knowing that their every move is going to be watched and questioned. Agents watch every port—good heavens, you yourself must know that; there isn't a mudlark or an urchin on every quay who wouldn't keep an eye open for anyone for a cost. But there are indeed some of us who, while publicly toeing the government line, feel that an innocent person who has sought sanctuary in Britain should not be sent back to where she does not want to go. Good Lord, man, we are British! We should not bow to the demands of anyone. There must surely be a way to resolve this situation without risking a war."

Dodger's mouth fell open. A war? Over Simplicity?

"Mister Dodger," the head of the peelers continued, "you and Miss Simplicity appear to be a reason why people are being killed. And why more people might be, unless we can resolve this, and very soon, since you must by now also realize that this affair has ramifications beyond Miss Simplicity and yourself. Now I know that you are very keen to see that the young lady in question comes to no harm, and as your friend

Charlie has said, when the kings and queens and knights and rooks find it difficult to move, the pawn may win the game. Like Charlie, I therefore believe that somebody not so readily associated with the government could indeed be the very man to help us find a solution." His voice dropped as he said, more softly, "You are the freest free agent that I can possibly imagine and frankly, Mister Dodger—and I will deny this if ever you repeat it publicly and you may be sure that my word will be taken against yours—one of the reasons I'm talking to you now is to tell you that whatever you may be planning, you must not break the law. Since I have just now stepped out of this room and any voice you may be hearing cannot possibly be mine, I must however point out to you that there are times when the law may be somewhat . . . flexible."

He moved closer to the door and said, "And now, without another word, we will both stroll back to the others as if we had just been discussing the very latest in modern sanitation, and I will find you again when I need to. We will"—he paused—"be watching you with interest." The head of the peelers looked at Dodger's panicked expression and smiled again. "Don't worry unduly; in the meantime, we have a homicide—that just means a dead body really. Who knows? He might have been meeting a client in rather insalubrious surroundings and banged his head on something and some people got the wrong idea. And, Mister Dodger, this conversation and everything to do with it has never existed. Do you understand?"

At last Dodger found his tongue and he simply said, "Understand what, sir?"

"You are a quick learner, Mister Dodger. Incidentally, you

appear to have no other name than Dodger, Mister Dodger. I know you were brought up in an orphanage, but surely they gave you a name?"

More than a name, Dodger thought, and I bet you already know it, Mister Peel. Then he said, "Yes, they did. They called me Pip Stick! Are you happy now? Because I'm not! How about that for a name? Think of all the fun people can have with that and a small boy; and they did, Mister Peel, they certainly did. It's writ down in the workhouse, all official like. Mister Pip Stick, just my luck. Hard luck. Mind you," he added, "now I come to think of it, Mister Pip Stick had to know how to fight. And to dodge. And to kick and bite. And run. Oh, and how he could run, and climb and twist." He hesitated and added, "Not that I'm sayin' that it was a good name to have, oh dear me, no."

The dinner was almost over when Dodger got back to his seat, and a few minutes later Angela tapped a wineglass with a spoon, very gently, and announced, "My friends, custom and practice these days is that ladies withdraw to the withdrawing room while all the gentlemen stay behind, and as you know I find this rather irksome because I'd quite like to talk to some gentlemen, and I'm sure some gentlemen might like to talk to some ladies. After all, these are modern times and we are all people of the world; I daresay none of us in this eminent company require a chaperone. I shall go to the drawing room and await all comers!"

To Dodger's surprise one of the richest women in the world then grasped his arm. "Now, Mister Dodger," she said, "I would like to talk to you about *reading*. Solomon tells me that you seldom make any attempt at reading and can barely cipher something approximating your name. This is not good enough, young man! A person of your caliber has no business being illiterate. Normally I would suggest that you should get enrolled in one of my Ragged Schools, but I fancy you would consider yourself too old for that, so instead, and so that I may begin to instill in you a love of words and the way they can be used, will you promise me that tomorrow night you will come with me and young Simplicity to the theater to see the new production of William Shakespeare's *Julius Caesar*?"

She straightened up and added, "Mister Cohen may accompany us too if he would be so kind. You must raise your play, Mister Dodger, because no man should waste his life tramping through sewers when he could be sailing through literature and the theater. Raise your play, Mister Dodger, raise your play! You already have the gingerbread, time to get the gilt!" She paused and looked at Dodger's expression. "You are looking at me with your mouth open," she added. "Is there anything that I have just said that you might not have understood?"

Dodger hesitated, but not for long. "Yes, miss. I am rather busy but I would like to go and see the play, and I have seen gingerbread with gilt on it in some baker's shop, but for the life of me I don't know what that has to do with anything."

"One day, Dodger, you should ask Solomon what a metaphor is."

"There's another thing I want to ask please, miss," said Dodger. "That is, how can you be sure that nothing bad could happen to Miss Simplicity in the theater? They are big places with lots of people in them."

Angela smiled. "Sometimes the best place to hide something

is exactly where no one would think to look. But if they do, then surely, Mister Dodger, we will be one step closer to reaching a happy conclusion to this affair? Simplicity will be in no danger—I have the ways and means to see that all of us will be able to enjoy the evening unmolested, you can be sure of that. My footmen have—you might say—hidden talents. But we may gain more than an evening's entertainment from the excursion."

She very carefully steered him then into yet another very well-appointed room in which comfy chairs were in abundance and so, on the whole, was everything else. Up in the attic Solomon had nothing that was not practical. The old man had his worktable and a very narrow bed, and behind his curtain Dodger had a bedroll and a number of blankets, and if it was a cold winter sometimes Onan as well; the smell could get bad, but Onan was polite enough not to acknowledge it. But this room was full of . . . well, things! Things that as far as Dodger could see were there just to be seen, or perhaps things that were designed to have other things put on top of them, or inside them. It also had enormous displays of flowers in great big vases, and the place looked like Covent Garden. He wondered why people needed all these things, when he himself could carry everything he owned in quite a small bag, not counting the bedroll. It seemed to be something that happened when you were rich, like in the Mayhews' house but with more knobs on.

But he pushed that aside in his mind to make way for his plan. It was a good plan, a shiny one, and it had come together finally because Mister Disraeli had tried to make fun of him. All evening long he had been piecing it together,

trying to figure out which parts were likely to be straight-
forward—such as the breeches—and which parts there were
where you would just have to trust to your luck—and the
Lady, of course.

Tomorrow was going to be a very busy day.

He was looking around for Solomon when somebody else
tapped him on the shoulder and said very politely, "I'm very
sorry to intervene, but I hear that you habitually frequent the
sewerage system."

The unwanted inquirer was a young man some ten years
older than himself with the beginnings of a very curly mustache in the current fashion, and the way the question was
asked made Dodger suspect that the man might be something
of an enthusiast when it came to drains. He was a gentleman who wanted to talk about drains and he—that is to say,
Dodger—had to be polite, and so there was nothing for it
but to smile nicely and say, "I'm no expert, sir, but since you
ask, I am a tosher and I reckon I've been down every drain
anybody can get down in the Square Mile, and then some.
And you, sir, are . . . ?" He smiled so as not to give offense.

"Oh dear, how remiss of me. Bazalgette, Joseph Bazalgette;
here is my card, sir. May I say that if you are thinking of a
journey into the sewers, I would be most pleased if I could
come with you. Indeed, I would be honored!"

Dodger turned the card over and over in his fingers, gave
in, and said, "I was planning an . . . expedition with Mister
Disraeli and Mister Dickens. The day after tomorrow, I
believe. Perhaps one more . . . ?" After all, he thought, it
could fit in very well with his plans, especially if one of the
aforesaid gentlemen should change his mind, or find himself

"otherwise engaged," as he believed it was described.

Mister Bazalgette was beaming with delight. Yes, he was an enthusiast for sure. A man who liked numbers and wheels and machinery, and quite possibly sewers. Mister Bazalgette, Dodger thought, might just be a gift from the Lady. "You must surely know," Bazalgette burbled, as if reading his mind, "although perhaps you don't, that the first people to undertake the work of building these sewers were the Romans. Indeed they believed in a goddess of the sewers, who I believe is commonly known as 'The Lady,' and gave her a name—Cloacina. You may be interested to learn that not so long ago a gentleman here in England called Matthews wrote a poem to her, following the example of the Romans, imploring her to help him with—how can I put it?—a way to make smoother his bodily functions, which the poem suggests were something of a morning trial to him."

From what Dodger had heard, the Romans were sharp coves and had built other things besides sewers, like roads. But now, without any warning, it turned out that they had also worshipped the Lady. Those Romans, according to Solomon, were tough and rough and merciless if you went up against them . . . and they had believed in the Lady. Well now, Dodger had prayed to the Lady to be sure, but he was never, well, definite when he did—sort of only half believing. Now it turned out that all those big warriors were once upon a time in this city kneeling down to her to make their richards a bit more squishy. There could be no better endorsement. Now more than ever, Dodger—admittedly via a roundabout route—was a believer.

Mister Bazalgette was coughing. "Are you all right, Mister

Dodger?" he queried. "You looked a bit faraway for a while."

Dodger hustled back to reality, smiled at the man, and said, "Everything is fine, sir."

Then a hand dropped on his shoulder, and gleefully Charlie said, "Excuse me, Mister Bazalgette, I thought I must remind our friend about that trip into the sewers. Benjamin, too, because those of us who are his friends would love to see what the dapper chappie will make of the subterranean experience, especially if he slips over in it, and of course I sincerely hope that does not happen. I wonder what shoes he will wear." Charlie was smiling, in Dodger's opinion with a certain touch of cheerful malice—not the nasty sort as such, but maybe the sort you use to tell one of your chums that he is getting too big for his boots. Dodger wouldn't mind betting that Charlie's mind was suggesting that the sewer excursion could just possibly be very entertaining as well as instructive.

As people milled around him saying their good-byes to one another, Dodger said to Charlie, "I expect you gentlemen are all very busy, so for this trip let us meet at the Lion in Seven Dials. It won't be a difficult walk from there to where we start, and you could keep the growler there. The day after tomorrow, wasn't it? Maybe seven o'clock? The sunlight will be low and you will be amazed how far it reaches into the sewers, like it was trying to fill them up." Then he added, "No offense to you, gentlemen, but if I take you down there and something nasty happens to any of you, I will be very upset and so will you. So I'll do a little walk around there early in the day to make sure there ain't going to be any problems because you never know. If it ain't on, I'll make shift to let you know so that it's postponed."

Charlie grinned with glee. "Now that's a sensible precaution, Dodger. What a shame Henry is unable to join us! But I for one cannot wait to join this little odyssey. How about you, Mister Bazalgette?"

The engineer's eyes sparkled. He said, "I will bring along my theodolite, my most waterproof boots, my most expendable trousers, and, knowing something about sewers, good stout leather breeches will be your friend. Thank you so much for this, young man. I very much look forward to seeing you the day after tomorrow. And if possible to meeting your Lady."

As Mister Bazalgette headed off to find his coach, Charlie turned to Dodger and asked, his face a mask, "What lady might that be?"

Dodger hurriedly explained. "I was talking about *the Lady*, our Lady of the Sewers, sir, and if you reach for your notebook now I think I would just about pull your fingers off, sir, 'cos this is stuff that should not be known, sir."

Charlie said, "Are you telling me, Dodger, that you truly believe that there is some kind of a goddess in the sewers?"

"No, sir, not a goddess, not for the likes of us," Dodger continued. "Gods and goddesses are for the likes of people who go to church, sir. They laugh at people like us, but *she* doesn't. There is no salvation, sir, not with her, because there is nothing to be saved from, sir. But, like I say, if you get on well with her, then one day she might show you something of great worth. Everybody has got to believe in something; that's all it takes. That's why, because of this, I decided to rescue Simplicity, you see. I mean, how could I have heard all the screaming above the noise of the storm? But I heard it right enough. And so I have to think that I have been guided on a journey, and I don't know where all the steps are, and I know the people who are my betters would like to see Simplicity shut away in some bleak house somewhere, so as she would cause no trouble. I won't stand for it, sir, whoever they are. *I said I didn't want you to write things down!*"

This came out fast and Charlie's pencil fell away from his notebook and, flustered, he said, "My apologies, Mister Dodger. My attempt at jotting a thought down had nothing to do with Miss Simplicity, I can assure you."

Dodger jumped as Angela appeared at their side and said, "Changing times, Mister Dodger. A young queen on the throne and a new world of possibilities. Your world, should you choose to make it so." She leaned closer and whispered, "I know that Sir Robert has spoken to you, and I know why. There are wheels within wheels. Make certain now that you're not crushed between them. I admire men of resource who are prepared to make some difference in the world, and on occasion, as you know, I like to help them up. And, Mister Dodger, like you I cannot abide bullies. I do not like men who trample on others." She paused and handed him a slip of paper. "Something my dear friend Sir Robert just said to me makes me feel that you could find this place very interesting."

Dodger glanced at the piece of paper, feeling embarrassed. "Excuse me, miss," he said. "Is this the way to one of your Ragged Schools?"

He saw her eyebrows narrow until she looked quite fierce. "Not exactly, Mister Dodger; it is where I think you might like to teach someone a lesson. But do please feel free to call on me at need."

And now Solomon loomed like a revelation, a pink one, and slightly fatter than Dodger remembered. "Have you said all of your good-byes and thank-yous? Say good-bye to Miss Simplicity, and then you and I must be going; Onan will be pining."

Dodger turned round and there was Simplicity, who simply said, "How very nice to see you again, my hero, and I look forward to going to the theater with you tomorrow, I really do."

As he and Solomon were leaving, Simplicity, standing next to her new hostess in the doorway, blew him a kiss and Dodger was suddenly floating on air.

CHAPTER THIRTEEN

The clock is ticking as a mysterious
old lady crosses the river

SOLOMON WAS SILENT UNTIL the growler was well on the way, and then he said, "Rather a forward young lady, I feel, and so there must be something in the saying that 'like attracts like,' and mmm you Dodger were Dodger, which I believe is a skill unto itself. But you must be careful; you are in the center of things now, if you did but know it. Although there are agents of other powers in this country, I suspect they would think twice before doing any harm to Mister Disraeli or Mister Dickens, but I think the life of a tosher is one they would snuff out without a second thought."

Dodger knew Solomon was right. After all, tangled up in this there was politics, and where there is politics there is money and power, which probably can be considered more important than a tosher and a girl alone.

"Tomorrow," Solomon was saying, "remember, you must be smart and in your best clothes again when you go to the theater. Incidentally, what is that piece of paper rolling up in your hand? Unusual for you to try to read . . . ?"

Dodger gave up the unequal struggle and said, "Tell me what this means, Sol, 'cos I think this one is important. I think these people are the people what mean Simplicity harm."

The speed with which Solomon drank information off a page always seemed wondrous to Dodger, and the old man said, "It's the address of an embassy."

"What's an embassy?" said Dodger.

It took a minute or two for Sol to explain the concept of an embassy to Dodger, but by the end of the explanation Dodger's eyes were ablaze and he said, "Well, you know me and writing. Can you just tell me where it is?"

"I wonder if I dare," said Solomon, "but I know you will not be satisfied until you find out. Please promise me, at least, that you won't kill anybody. Well, unless they try to kill you first." He added, "A remarkable woman, Angela, isn't she?" He glanced out of the window and continued, "As a matter of fact I think I might be able to persuade the growler to go past the address."

Five minutes later, Dodger was staring at the building like a pickpocket fixes his gaze on a lord's trouser pockets. He said, "I'll come back home with you now to see you get in all right, but then don't wait up."

He itched with impatience all the way to Seven Dials as they rumbled through the darkened streets, and as they arrived home he apparently took no notice of the single man lurking in the shadows and the man paid them no apparent attention as they climbed up the stairs, a grumbling Solomon complaining about being so late for bed. Dodger spent some time feeding Onan and taking him for his usual nocturnal walk. When that was over, the dog followed him upstairs, and very shortly after that the watcher down in the street below saw the solitary candle go out.

On the other side of the building, Dodger—now dressed in his working clothes—climbed down the rope he utilized whenever he wanted to get back to ground level without being noticed. Then he slid around to where the watching man was still watching, silently tied his bootlaces together in the darkness, and then kicked the man's feet from under him, saying, "Hello, my name's Dodger, what's yours?"

The man was at first startled, then extremely angry, saying, "I am a policeman, you know!"

"I don't see no uniform, mister policeman," said Dodger. "I'll tell you what, 'cos you have a nice face I'll let you go, okay? And tell Mister Robert Peel that Dodger does things his way, all right?"

But he was, he thought, if not exactly in trouble with Scotland Yard, nevertheless certainly in a stew of sorts, and it was bubbling, wasn't it just! Once the peelers from Scotland Yard got ahold of you they tended to hang on, and if the news got about that he had spoken to the peelers—especially the big Peel himself!—then the street people would think he was getting into bad company, and probably likely to peach on them.

Even worse, he was being *spied* on. Plainclothes policemen! There ought to be a law against it; everybody said so—it was, well, it was unfair. After all, if you saw a peeler walking around, well, maybe you would think once or twice about dipping into someone's pocket or dipping into something that didn't really belong to anyone really, when you came to think about it, or just possibly knocking off something from a barrow when the owner wasn't looking. After all, seeing policemen around kept you honest, didn't it? If they were going to lurk around like ordinary people, they were basically asking you to commit crimes, weren't they? It was entirely unfair in Dodger's opinion.

It had been a long night already indeed, but there were things that had to be done quickly, or else he would burst. So he ran through the dark streets until he came to the abode of Ginny-Come-Lately.

She answered the door on the third knock, and in something of a bad temper until she said, "Oh, it's you, Dodger, how nice. Er, can't invite you in quite yet, you know how it is, don't ya?"

Dodger, who certainly did know how it was because it was always what it was, said, "Nice to see you, Ginny. You know that little package of tools I once asked you to keep for me when I promised Solomon I wasn't going thieving anymore? Still got it?"

She smiled at him for a moment, then ducked back in and came out with a small package wrapped in oilcloth. She gave Dodger a peck on the cheek and said, "I'm hearing a lot about you these days, Dodger. I hope she's worth it!"

But at that point Dodger was already out of the door and running at speed; he had always liked running, which was just as well, since a thief who couldn't run fast was soon dead, but now he ran like he had never run before. He was running through the streets in what seemed like a frenzy of acceleration, and occasionally an alert peeler, noting that someone was running, would shout or blow his whistle and then feel rather stupid since Dodger was a rapidly dwindling bit of darkness in a city full of the stuff. He didn't simply run; he *sped*, legs pounding much faster than his heartbeat. Disturbed pigeons flew away. A man who tried to waylay him as he ran down a useful alleyway was punched and then trodden on, and Dodger kept going, not looking behind him because, well, by now *everything* was behind him as he channeled rage into his legs and simply followed them . . . and then, suddenly, there it was again. That building.

Dodger slowed down and disappeared into darkness and spent some time in getting his breath back; after all, now he was here, he would have to take his time. By the light of his dark lantern, he unrolled the green baize parcel wrapped in the oilcloth, and the light glistened on all his little friends—the half-diamond pick, the ball pick, and the torsion bar—but of course there were the others; there was always some lock or other that was slightly different, and he had spent many a happy hour with the rakes and picks, bending and filing them into exactly the right shapes. It seemed to him that they were saluting him, ready for combat.

Shortly afterward darkness moved within darkness and this particular darkness found, on the more insalubrious side of the building, a metal cover to a cellar. When he had given it just a little bit of oil and a little tinkering, Dodger was in at the enemy's throat. He grinned, but there was no fun in the grin; it was more like a knife.

The building was mostly in shadows and Dodger just loved shadows. He was pleased to see that there were carpets—not really a sensible choice if you were running an embassy and might like to know if there were some unwelcome people walking about, because marble floors were much to be recommended, as Dodger well knew; sometimes if you stepped on them in the nighttime they could ring like a bell. Whenever he'd found them, he had always got down and very carefully slid himself over them, so that no sound could be heard.

Now he listened at doors, he stood behind curtains, and he made sure not to go too near the kitchens, as you never knew when a servant might be up. And all the time he stole. He stole in the same methodical way that Solomon made beautiful small objects, and he smiled when he thought that, because now Dodger was making small beautiful things disappear. He stole jewelry, when he found it, and he opened every lock and rifled through the contents of every drawer, in every boudoir. On two occasions he robbed rooms in which he could just make out people sleeping. He didn't care; it was as if nothing could stop him or, maybe, it was as if the Lady had made him invisible. He worked fast and methodically and everything was wrapped up in its own little velvet bag, within the main bundle, so that nothing would ever go *clink* just at the wrong moment because if there was a clink then the clink was where you spent your days until they hanged you. It was a little joke among thieves.

At one point, in the middle of the building, in a large desk that took one hell of a long time to yield its secrets to his busy fingers and their little friends, he found ledgers and a series of small books. They had a complicated look about them, and manuscripts and scrolls with red wax on them, which always looked expensive. He recognized the crest on some of the documents, he surely did.

As he stood in this busy, important room, he thought, I wish I could do something so that they would know. And then he knew what he would do. I'll let them know who it had been, he told himself, because, well, I could have brought the place down in flames. After all, all those oil lamps around? All those curtains? All those stairs and all those people sleeping up there? He was so angry, but, in the warm darkness of the room, what he was not—whatever else he had been—was a murderer. I shall make them pay in my own way, he decided, and at that moment all of them were saved from a fiery death, if they only had known it, and were only living because Dodger, silent in this sleeping world, allowed them to.

Put like that, it made him feel a little better. Padding away silently, he thought, I've always said I wasn't a hero, and I ain't, but if I've ever been a hero, then as sure as Sunday I'm a hero now, because I've stopped an embassy full of people from being burned alive.

And so at last, not long before the first crack of dawn, he was down and outside and into the mews by the side of the embassy. He knew there would be ostlers and grooms hanging about here any minute soon but, nevertheless, moving even more stealthily, he found the coach house, and yes, there was a coach there with a foreign crest painted on the side. Dodger carefully knelt down beside it and felt around near the wheels. Close to one wheel it seemed that a length of metal had been thrown up on one occasion and got stuck, scraping on the rim of the wheel. Dodger tried to pull it free, but without any success until a very useful little crowbar caused it to spring out, and Dodger caught it in the air, whereupon he straightened up, went to the coat of arms on the coach, and scratched, as deeply as he could inscribe them, the words

MR PUNCH

Then, with his face dark and his purpose ironclad, he walked from loose box to loose box, driving the occupants into an adjacent mews and carefully shutting the gate behind them, because everybody knew that horses were so stupid that if there was a fire they would rush into their stables because that's where they thought they would be safe, a habit that showed you why horses didn't rule the world. They wandered about aimlessly while Dodger struck up a light and dropped it into a large bale of hay and then walked in earnest down the nearest alleyway with the virtuous feeling of having done something right, by virtue of not doing something wrong. He jogged his way toward the river, where the crackling of wood and the shouting of humans grew louder in the distance behind him.

Of course, Solomon shook him awake not long after the usual time, with the certain allowance for the fact that Solomon himself had slept in somewhat, after that wonderful meal. Solomon had also decided to let Dodger sleep on, and meanwhile had taken a look at the contents of Dodger's useful bag, because he wouldn't have been Solomon if he wasn't inquisitive. So that when Dodger did in fact find himself shaken awake, and he came around the curtain, he saw a beaming Solomon sitting at the table with the jewelry in one neat pile on a velvet cloth and some of the books and ledgers beside it.

"Mmm, Dodger, I do not know for certain what you think you were doing last night, but I think I can perceive, because as you know Solomon does himself have a certain wisdom of his own, that you thought you had a score to settle with somebody. Though you know that I do not mmm tolerate thievery of any kind, I've had a word with God and he agrees with me that in the circumstances you might have wanted to set fire to the place."

Dodger looked embarrassed for a moment and then said, "Actually, Sol, I did torch the stables, because the bloody coach was in there."

Solomon's brow wrinkled in distress. "Mmm, I trust you let out all the horses."

"Of course," said Dodger.

"And mmm after all," the old man continued, brightening, "what is jewelry? Just shiny rocks. And you have an excellent eye. Quite excellent. But I daresay that some of these ciphers and code books might be of considerable interest to the government. There are things here in several languages that would do a great deal of damage in some quarters, and cause a great deal of rejoicing in others."

All Dodger could find to say at that moment was "You . . . don't mind?" And, "You could read them all?"

The old man gave him his most supercilious look. "Mmm, I can read in most languages of Europe, with perhaps the exception of Welsh, which I find a tad difficult. One of these documents is a copy of a message about the Tsar of all the Russias who mmm apparently has done something quite naughty with the wife of the French ambassador—oh dearie me, such goings on; I wonder what would happen if more people knew about it. Dodger, if you don't mind, I think it would be a very good idea if somebody like Sir Robert was privy to this startling information, which is only one of the many things which Her Majesty's government would be very interested to know about. I will see to it that he gets them in a mmm covert way."

He paused. "Of course, I see no reason to mention anything to him about the jewelry. Incidentally, it's worth a king's ransom, even for the rubies alone. Or perhaps a gift from a prince and his father mmm? As you know, I am not a fence, but I think I know one or two associates who might take the stuff off our hands, and I am sure I will be able to negotiate an acceptable price. Indeed I shall, because they go to the synagogue as I do, and sooner or later every man has to bargain with the Devil, and in those circumstances God is inclined to help him achieve a good price. You won't, of course, get the full value, but I believe that after I have negotiated, you will have a second fortune. As a dowry for your young lady, perhaps?"

He plucked one of the documents from the pile. "And mmm all I will ask from you, my friend, is that I am allowed to take this document concerning the tsar, and quite possibly make some use of it one day, when the occasion ever presents itself, especially if my young friend Karl is still alive. . . . Mmm, and incidentally, in another one of these packages is a scurrilous piece of information about a member of our own royal family. I suppose I should throw it into the fire. . . ." He hesitated for a moment. "But perhaps I will just keep it in a place of safety mmm so that it never comes to the attention of unfriendly eyes." He grinned again. "And, of course, gentlemen like ourselves would have nothing to do with such things, but nevertheless there are times when a little leverage is worth having."

With that, the old man carefully stowed away both the

jewelry and the precious information somewhere inside his voluminous jacket, and turned to his workbench while Dodger sat and stared at nothing. He thought, If you put Solomon in a room full of lawyers, how many would come out, and in what condition would they be as they crawled along the floor?

He took this opportunity. "Solomon," he asked, "could you do a little job of work for me, please? Could you melt out some gold from this haul and make a gold ring? With a decent ruby maybe? And possibly a sprinkling of diamonds to set them off?"

Solomon looked up. "Mmm, I would be delighted to do that for you, Dodger, and at my very best price." He laughed at Dodger's expression and said, "Honestly, my friend, what must you think of me? You must understand that was just my little joke, and I do not make many of them." He added, "Mmm, by any chance would you like an engraved inscription?" His expression looked sly as he went on, "Perhaps something relating to a young lady? We can agree the exact wording later, yes?"

Dodger blushed and said, "Are you a mind reader too?"

"Mmm, of course! And so are you, the only difference being that I have had far more chances to read them than you have, and some of the minds that I have fathomed were very tangled and convoluted minds indeed."

Dodger stood back and said, "I have never asked you this before, but you know so much and you can do so much. Why then do you spend most of your time fiddling with bits of old jewelry and watches and so on down here in the rookeries when there are many other things you could be doing?"

And Solomon said, "That in itself is a convoluted question, but surely you know most of the answer mmm? I enjoy my chosen trade and receive good remuneration. That is to say, for your benefit, *money* for doing something that gives me great pleasure." He sighed and went on, "But I suppose the main reason is that I can no longer run as fast as I once could, and death is, well, so final."

This last piece of information caused Dodger to sit up straight. But it was a call to arms, the starting of a clock, which meant Dodger wasn't so free as he had been because now time itself was his master, so he got dressed in a hurry.

He had to be careful about this; there were quite a number of people whom he could trust, but there were, as it were, several stages of trust, ranging from those he could trust with a sixpence to those he would trust with his life. There weren't all that many of the latter, and it was probably a good idea not to trespass on their goodwill, because: a) goodwill, if trespassed on too often, might have a tendency to lose some of its bloom; and b) because it didn't do for anyone to know too much about Dodger's business.

Now he made his way once again to the stall of Marie Jo, who probably wouldn't be too busy at this time of day, since most of her customers would be out there on the streets, begging, stealing, or—when all else failed—earning enough for their dinner. But she was there, as reliable as the peals of the Bow bells—and Dodger made sure *he* was reliable too, and paid her the promised few sixpences more for the children's soup—and then there were not many around to hear them so he lowered his voice and told her what he wanted.

When she laughed and said something in French that he

didn't understand, he said, "I can't tell you why I need to, Marie Jo."

She looked at his face and laughed again, giving him the expression that a certain type of woman has when they are dealing with a saucy young gentleman such as Dodger, and he recognized this as he had spent a lot of time analyzing it in the University of Dodger; it was accusing and forgiving wrapped up together in a complicated parcel, and her eyes twinkled and he knew that she would do anything for him. But knowing that, he also knew that he shouldn't ask for too much.

Looking him up and down, she said, *"Cherchez la femme?"* Dodger knew this one, and very carefully looked embarrassed. She laughed, that laugh which somehow came from her childhood, and she insisted that he run the stall and chop up some onions and some carrots while she ran this little errand for him. How embarrassing! In the full light of day, passersby could see Dodger—yes, *Dodger*—working in a stall; he was glad that there weren't too many people about.

Fortunately, Marie Jo soon came back with a small package, which he carefully stowed away, and in good faith he spent half an hour cleaning and chopping vegetables and welcomed it, because the attention to detail meant the inner Dodger could think about what he was going to do next, which was to take a walk among the shonky shops and pawnbrokers. He knew what he needed but was careful not to get it all from one single shop, although he was particularly fortunate in one old shop smelling of not quite properly laundered clothing to find just what he wanted, and the proprietor smelled of gin and appeared not to know Dodger at all.

But the clock was still ticking and he was short of time.

By midafternoon, though, after a trip to the Gunner's Daughter and a couple of pints of porter with a few mates, and one in particular—good ol' Dodger, never forgot his friends now he was in the money after his exploits with the Demon Barber—he was ready, though Solomon chuckled rather too much for his liking.

Dodger had heard that God watches everything, although he thought that around the rookeries, He tended to close His eyes. If God wasn't available today, and since people didn't look too much, just in case they saw anything, possibly only a watcher on the moon would have seen an elderly lady—an extremely pitiful one, even by the standards of the rookeries—shin down a length of rope, land like an athlete, and then, very slowly, hobble away.

Dodger wasn't particularly bothered about this bit; there were only a few places you could stand to see the rope in any case, but being an old lady meant that you couldn't travel fast. Regrettably, little old ladies—rather unwashed ones, at that—didn't often have enough money to hire a growler, but since he would be damned before he hobbled all the way to the river, the old lady did manage, by the frantic waving of her walking stick, to hail a cab. Unusually, given the pitiful condition of the old girl who seemed to be a jolly playground for warts, thanks to the theatrical help of Marie Jo, the growler captain, thinking about his old mum, carefully helped the old girl up and didn't shortchange her.

Indeed, she was a very pitiful old lady; she smelled six days away from a good wash. And warts? Never before had he seen such terrible warts. She wore a wig, but that wasn't unusual knowing the sensitivities of old ladies, and goodness, he thought, it was a terribly bad wig even so, about the worst a shonky shop could offer.

He watched her walk away, and it looked as if her feet were in a terrible way, and this was true because Dodger had put a piece of wood in his boot that hurt like the blazes. By the time he reached the nearest wharf, his feet were killing him. Once upon a time, Marie Jo had told him that with his skills, he should be on the stage, as she had been, but since he knew that actors didn't get paid very much, he had always reckoned that the only reason to be on a stage would be to rob it.

A waterman, coincidentally one with whom Dodger had chatted earlier in the day—Double Henry, a regular at the Gunner's Daughter—gave a lift to the dear old lady with the warts and *terrible* bad teeth, and kindly helped her out quite near the morgue at Four Farthings, London's smallest borough. Possibly somebody on the moon watching the old lady from that point on would have watched her progress all the way to the coroner's office. It was pitiful, absolutely piti-ful. So pitiful, in fact, that an officer in the morgue, generally not well disposed to living people and with something of a temper, actually gave her a cup of tea before directing her to the coroner's office, some distance away.

The coroner was a kind man, as generally the coroners were, which was quite remarkable given that so often they saw and knew things that decent people should neither see nor know, and this one listened to the old lady, who was in floods of tears about her niece, who had gone missing. It was a familiar tale, a tale just like one Dodger had heard from Messy Bessie: the sweet girl had come up from somewhere in Kent, seeking to improve herself and get a better job in

London. A dreadful engine, if she did but know it, that took the hopeful, the innocent, and ultimately the living, and turned them into . . . something else.

The coroner, hardened though he was to this sort of thing, was overwhelmed by the tears and the lamentations on the lines of "I told her, I said we could manage, we could run along all right." And, "I told her not to talk to any gentlemen on the street, sir, I certainly did, sir, but you know how it is with young girls, sir, ever the prey of a dashing gentleman with money to spend. Oh dear me, if only she had listened. I shall always blame myself." And "I mean, the country ain't like the city, that's for God's certainty. I mean, generally, if a lad and a lass got to grips and she started to swell around the waist, then her mum would have a word with her, wouldn't she? And then her mum would talk to her dad and her dad would talk to the boy's dad in the tavern and everyone would sigh and say, 'Oh well, but at least it shows that they can have kids.'" According to the old lady, the young couple would very quickly then go and see the vicar, and all in all there would be no harm done.

The coroner, not only a man of this world but in some sense of the next one too, was not certain it was always as easy as that, but he took care not to say so. Eventually, the old woman explained about the girl running out of the house and how she had gone as best she could from bridge to bridge in search of the runaway. The coroner nodded gloomily at that point, because this was the same old tragic story. He knew that there were always Christian people who patrolled the London bridges at twilight, looking out for these unfortunate "soiled doves." Generally, they were given a pamphlet and urged not to do it; sometimes this even worked, but then it was going to be the workhouse, and most likely after the birth the poor girl would never even see the child for more than the time it took to be delivered.

You had to develop the hide of a rhinoceros to deal with this sort of thing on a daily basis and, alas, he found himself not very good at it, but he listened to the old woman's description of her niece with a glum countenance. In between sobs were the words "A blue dress, sir, not very new, but very nice underthings, sir, very good with the needle, so she was. . . . Just an iron ring made out of a horseshoe nail like the blacksmiths make, 'cos it's a ring, you see. Ain't got no jewels, but a ring is a ring, ain't it, sir. Maybe this is important, sir; she had yellow hair, lovely yellow hair. Never cut it, not like the other girls who would cut it every year or so and sell it when the wigmakers' man came round. She wouldn't have none of that, sir, she was a very good girl. . . ."

After hearing all this the coroner brightened a little, and so did Dodger on seeing his expression. It had been worth the time spent to locate Double Henry and the two pints of porter had got every single detail out of him.

The coroner said, "It would be invidious of me to use the word 'luck' in this context, madam, but fortuitously it may just be the case that your niece is even now lying in our mortuary and has been there for a few days. She was drawn to my attention when I visited there yesterday morning, and indeed the officer on duty and myself were much taken by the wonderful color of her hair. Alas, all along the lower Thames this sad tableau is reenacted far too often. In the case of this lovely young lady, I must say that I was beginning to despair that anyone would claim her as their own."

At this point the old lady broke down whimpering, "Oh

dear, whatever am I going to tell her mother! I mean, I said I'd look after her, but young girls these days . . ."

"Yes, I fully understand," said the coroner hurriedly, and continued, "Do let me give you another cup of tea, my good woman, and I will take you to see the corpse in question."

There was another wail at this, and another flow of tears and they were real tears, because by now Dodger was so wrapped up in the drama that he might have had a fainting fit. But he, or strictly speaking at this point *she*, carefully drank the proffered tea, taking great care not to knock off a wart. Shortly afterward the coroner, having taken so much pity on her dreadful state, led her by the arm to the mortuary. One glance from the old lady at the girl on the slab, who had been cleaned up a little to the point where she looked as if she was sleeping, was enough. There was no more acting now, or perhaps the acting was so good, so perfectly in the role, that there should have been a gallery of theatergoers cheering to the rafters.

The old lady turned a face lined with hairs, snot, and tears to the kindly coroner and said, "I ain't rich, sir, really I ain't. Seeing my Arthur neatly away on Lavender Hill left me fairly skint, sir, so I reckon it will take me some time to get the wherewithal for seeing her decent, sir. Do you reckon they will have her at Crossbones?"*

"That I cannot say, madam, but I hardly think that your

* The Crossbones cemetery in the borough of Southwark was known as the single women's churchyard, after the single women in question plied their single women's trade under license from the Bishop of Winchester, who owned that part of the riverside, which was why they were humorously named "Winchester Geese." Delicacy, of course, prevents the author from describing what exactly they were trading. Although it does suggest that the church of the time had an understanding and, one might say, very forward-thinking approach to the matter.

dear niece so fresh from the country was anything like a"—
and here the coroner cleared his throat, embarrassed, and
went on—"a Winchester goose." Most unusually, he took
out his handkerchief to wipe away a tear and continued,
"Madam, I cannot but be very moved by your plight and
your determination to do the very best for the soul of this
unfortunate young lady. I will guarantee you that—we have
no shortage of ice, after all—your young niece can remain
here, not forever, but certainly for a week or two, which I
reckon should be enough for me to contact those others who
may be able to help you in your plight."

He took a step backward as the old woman tried to throw
her rather smelly arms around him saying, "God bless you, sir,
you truly are a gentleman, sir. I will turn over every stone, sir,
so I will, right away, sir, thank you so much for all your kindness. Got a few friends I could talk to. Might help me write a
letter to her mum, on the postage, and I'll move heaven and
earth not to put you to any trouble, sir. Can't be said that
we will let one of our own go into a pauper's grave, sir." At
which point tears actually were pouring down the coroner's
face. And Dodger meant it. The man had been a decent cove;
that was something to keep in mind.

The coroner deputized his officer to assist the old lady back
to the wharf, and before saying good-bye pressed into her
hand enough money for the waterman, and so the unknown
watcher on the moon watched the poor old lady work her
way through the naughty city until, as she walked down an
alley, she suddenly appeared to drop into the sewers where
the old woman died but was instantly, possibly to do with the
Lady, reincarnated as Dodger, and a shaken Dodger at that.

He was used to playing roles; to be Dodger was to be a man of all seasons and seasonings, everybody's friend, nobody's enemy, and all this was fine, but sometimes that all went away and it was just Dodger, alone in the dark. He realized that he was shaking, and down in the hospitable sewers he heard the sounds of London floating through the grating. He carefully packed up the trappings of the old lady into a bundle, endeavoring to memorize the placement of every single wart. Then he set off.

He was still as upset about the drowned girl as the old lady had been. It was a shame, and he would have to see to it that when all this was over the poor unknown girl did indeed get a decent burial, rather than a pauper's grave or worse. He absentmindedly toshed his way across the city, more or less instinctively, becoming sixpence richer in the process.

Well, he'd got the coroner sorted out, but corpses need careful attention and there was nothing for it—he would have to go and see Mrs. Holland. That meant going to Southwark, and even a geezer like Dodger had to be careful there. But if ever a geezer was careful, it was Dodger.

Mrs. Holland. She had no other name; well, she was a gang all by herself, and if that wasn't enough there was her husband, Aberdeen Knocker, known to his friends as Bang, who had in all probability never seen the city of Aberdeen, which was somewhere up north, like maybe in Wales. The soubriquet had settled on him as such things did on the streets of London, indeed as the name Dodger had landed on Dodger, but Bang's skin was as black as your hat and a very black hat at that, and he had been married, theoretically at least, to Mrs. Holland these past sixteen years. Their son, known to everybody for some reason as Half Bang, was as smart as a dungeon full of lawyers and really of use in the family business, which was basically property and people.

But Mrs. Holland was a great organizer with a very fertile imagination. Probably every sailor who had docked in the port of London had gone to Mrs. Holland's League, as they called it, usually to meet the young ladies who adorned the upper floors of the building while Mrs. Holland took charge of everything in her office downstairs. Of course, Mrs. Holland being Mrs. Holland, sometimes it was rumored those sailors, once they were rascally drunk, were shanghaied and sent on a lovely cruise whose destination might be round Cape Horn, or possibly Davy Jones's locker. But when not giving sailors nice long holidays, Mrs. Holland arranged things.

Around the docks Mrs. Holland was queen, and nobody questioned the fact when Bang was by her side. It would be difficult to pinpoint her actual occupation these days, though Dodger was well aware that once upon a time she had been both a nurse and a midwife, and apparently had made a living by causing things to turn up or more often to disappear. If you were the kind of person who would come seeking more definite information about her activities, you were the kind of person who was likely soon to be inspecting the Thames bridges from underneath.

Dodger got along with the family, of course—especially Bang, who had once fascinated a young Dodger by showing him the scars where his shackles had chafed him most cruelly, and the place where he had been branded by the slavers like an animal. Despite his history, he was a gentle and very amiable person, although right now, answering Dodger's knock, he was holding back the growling slavering dog of Satanic proportions which was the family's frontline security. They also had a blunderbuss the size of a French horn and famed to be packed with black powder and rock salt and, on occasion for very special customers, miscellaneous nails as well for the hard of understanding.

There was Mrs. Holland herself, all chins and smiles, and that meant a lot of smiles, above the blunderbuss. Mrs. Holland had bright-blue eyes which, Dodger had often noticed, twinkled with sincerity every time she told you an outright lie. As she put down the blunderbuss, she said cheerfully, "Dodger! As I live and breathe! Welcome! Welcome!"

Very shortly afterward, in her little private room, with the dog, name of Jasper, lying there peacefully in front of her but nevertheless ready to leap and snarl on command, she listened to Dodger's story. She looked thoughtful for a moment, then said, "Ah well, it's amazing how lively a corpse can be after it is dead. Stiff one day, and playful as anything the next. What you are suggesting ain't no journey for the unprepared, but I have the knowing, oh yes indeed. I ain't no stranger to corpses, as you are aware. So just you listen to your favorite aunty, right? Well, first of all, what you are going to need is . . ."

Dodger learned things quickly, and after a few minutes said, "I'm in your debt, Mrs. Holland."

She smiled at him and said, "You know, I always thought you were one of my smart boys, Dodger. As for being in my debt, well, who knows? One day you will have an opportunity to pay me back. And it's all right—I know you are not a killer, so you wouldn't be my chosen in that respect, but in other matters. Well, as they say, one hand washes the other."

Dodger glanced down at her podgy hands; it looked as if neither of them had been washed in a week, but he understood the meaning and accepted it. Favors were currency down here, just like they were on the street. He also knew she always had a twinkle in her eye for Dodger, although it didn't do to rely on a twinkle.

Just as he was leaving, she suddenly went all solemn and said, "I reckon you've been stirring things up, my little lad. And there's some people that I don't like the stink of the moment I hears about them, and one of them is a cove by the name of the Outlander—ever heard of him?"

Dodger shook his head and Mrs. Holland began to look uneasy. She glanced at her husband and then back at Dodger and said, "I don't know if I've ever met him, don't know what he looks like, but by all accounts he is your dyed-in-the-wool, stone-hard killing cove. I think it might be his first time in England, but I'm getting word that he's been asking questions about 'somebody called Dodger' and some girl. Don't know much about him. Some say he's a Dutchman, sometimes they say he's a Switzer, but always they say he is a killer, who comes out of the dark and goes back into the dark and gets his money and disappears. No one knows what he looks like, no one knows him as a friend, and the only thing that anyone knows is that he likes the ladies. They say that he will always have a girl on his arm, never the same one twice." Her brow wrinkled. "Don't know as why I ain't seen him here yet, given that liking. Maybe we will. But no one can tell you what he actually looks like. I mean that: sometimes they say that they've met him and he's tall and thin, and other times that he's a fairly short cove. From what I understand, I reckon he must be a master of disguise, and if he wants to talk to you he sends one of his ladies with a message."

Mrs. Holland stared down at the small and smoky fire in the grate and looked unusually troubled. "I cannot say he is in my league, the Outlander; he's more like a nasty dream. Mostly, of course, he stays in Europe where they deserve people like him. I don't like the idea that he's turning up here. I quite like you, Dodger, you know that. But if the Outlander gets on your tail, you're going to have to order up a whole new bag of smarts."

Dodger checked that his face was as cheerful as he could make it. "And no one's ever really seen him, yes?"

"No," said Mrs. Holland. "Like I said, lots of people have seen him, but they never seem to see the same man."

Her concern was palpable; Dodger could feel it pouring off her, and this was a woman who would have no great compunction about sending a drunken sailor to, quite probably, a watery grave. Now it seemed that there were some things that even she got nervous about, and she said, "It might surprise you, my boy, that a nasty old creature like me has got some standards, and so if I was you, I'd keep my eyes open even if I was asleep. Now give me a great big kiss, 'cos it may be the last one I'll ever have off of you!"

Dodger did so, much to the amusement of Bang, and he was careful not to wipe his face until he was well away. Then he went back home via the sewers, as much as that was possible.

So somebody that you couldn't really describe was out there after him and/or Simplicity. . . .

Well, they would have to wait in line.

CHAPTER FOURTEEN

A lighterman gets a surprise,
an old lady vanishes, and Dodger knows nothing,
hears nothing, and—unsurprisingly—
was not even there

THERE WAS SO MUCH that needed doing, he thought as he hurried home. He had to get ready to go to the theater later on,
but first of all and most importantly, what he had to do was
pray. Pray to the Lady.

Dodger had been in churches occasionally, but on the
whole the street people kept clear of them unless the promise
of food was in the offing; after all, a cove could put up with
quite a lot of "Come to Jesus" for the sake of a full stomach,
so now he was down in his beloved sewers wondering how
to go about a prayer.

He'd never seen the Lady, although Grandad had always
talked about her as if she was a friend—and he had seen her
before he died, and if you can't trust the word of a dying
man, then who can you trust? Oh, he'd always halfheart-
edly asked her for help almost automatically, but he'd never
really prayed from the guts upward, and standing here with
the sounds of London overhead and apparently a real assassin

looking for him, he needed a prayer.

He began in the time-honored way by clearing his throat and was about to spit when he hesitated, because at a time like this you didn't want to offend *anybody*. Kneeling down was not something you generally did in the sewers, so he straightened up instead and said, "I'm sorry, I don't know what to say, Lady, and that's the truth. I mean, it's not like I'm a murderer, is it? And I promise you that if Simplicity is spared, that poor girl up in the mortuary in Four Farthings will get a place in Lavender Hill; I will see to it, and flowers too." He hesitated and continued, "And she will get given a name, so that at least *I* can remember her, and that's it, Lady, because the world is rather bad and extremely difficult and all you can do is the best you can. And I'm just Dodger."

There was the tiniest of noises. Dodger glanced down and saw a very small rat run over his boot. Was that a sign? He really wanted a sign. There *ought* to be signs, and if there was a sign there should be a sign on it to show that it was a sign so that you *definitely* knew it was a sign. To be frank, a rat running over your boots in the sewer did not, when you thought about it, seem that much like a sign. Was it a sign, or was it just a rat? Oh well, what was the difference? The Lady always had rats around her, and he had half hoped to see a beautiful face magically appear on the dripping bricks of the sewer.

The traffic rattled overhead and the usual punctuated silence remained distinctly empty, and so Dodger added, "Grandad, who you most surely have heard of, told me that you always had a pair of shoes on—I mean, not boots but real shoes, so if you would be so good as to smooth my way, I will give you the best pair of shoes that money can buy. Thanking you in expectation, Dodger."

That afternoon Solomon pretended to be amazed at how much care Dodger was taking to get ready for the theater.

Dodger scrubbed out every crevice and corner several times while thinking about the Outlander. He'd never heard of him, but then you don't get to hear about everybody and it was certainly unlikely that anybody would try anything at the theater, wasn't it? But later, in his little private world behind the curtain, as Solomon went through his own ablutions with a considerable amount of splashing and grunting, Dodger carefully took Sweeney Todd's razor from its hiding place and stared at it.

It was a razor, *just* a razor. But it was also a fear and a legend. He could slip it into his pocket quite easily. Izzy had done some magnificent work; in fact, the jacket had an inner pocket which just did the job perfectly, and Dodger wondered whether, since this jacket had originally been intended for Sir Robert Peel, Sir Robert Peel had required there to be an inner pocket for those items that a gentleman walking the street might need to get hold of in a hurry—brass knuckles, perhaps.

He sighed and put the razor back in its hiding place. He was uncertain if he wanted to sit next to Simplicity with that so close, and as soon as he had that thought, he felt a little shocked and told himself, Mister Todd killed, but he wasn't a killer. Maybe if he'd never had to go to that blessed war, he wouldn't have gone right off his head. But however he looked at it, today at least was not the day for Sweeney

Todd's razor to be on the streets.

Angela had told Solomon to expect a coach that would take them all to the theater. Dodger found himself looking out for it at least an hour before it was due to reach them, and was gratified that when it did arrive, there were two brawny footmen with it, well spruced up. Their well-set jaws and knowing eyes indicated that they were more than happy to take on anyone in the rookeries who got closer to the coach than they wanted them to.

Solomon got in first. When Dodger stepped in behind him, he was totally crestfallen not to see Simplicity inside, but one of the coachmen poked his head into the coach, gave Dodger an uncharacteristic smile, and said, "The ladies are still getting ready for the performance, sir, and so we were told to pick you up first. I'm also to tell you that there are refreshments that you may wish to savor during the journey." Then, and in a far less nobby voice the footman said, "The man that battled Sweeney Todd. Oh my, I can't wait to tell my old mum!"

While Solomon critically inspected the little well-stocked bar inside the carriage with, as it turned out, great approval, Dodger was thinking hard. Never mind about the Outlander, he thought, but there was something at the back of his mind that was playing over and over again the words that Mrs. Holland had told him. Something wasn't right: what she had told him sounded like, well, a story, rather like Sweeney Todd's razor, and Dodger knew the truth about Sweeney Todd's razor, didn't he? Admittedly, he thought ruefully, he had made up parts of that story so now he was some kind of brave warrior to a lot of people while in his heart he knew himself only as a smart young man.

Swift as a knife, the thought came back. How much of that is the same for this Outlander? Him with all his ladies? Does that sound quite real? he thought. He answered himself: No; even Mrs. Holland is pretty well terrified of him, and maybe the Outlander had spun a little spell that made him bigger and more dangerous than he was. Ah yes, that made Dodger feel better. It was like showmanship; it was always showmanship that got you through, and he had a show of his own to prepare.

He reminded himself that he would have to have a very important conversation with Miss Coutts, dear Miss Coutts. He knew that she was a most unusual woman with more money than practically anybody and no husband, and he smiled at himself and he thought, hmm, a woman with loads of money who isn't interested in a husband. After all, if you've got the money—your own money—a husband is sort of in the way. Solomon had told him that she had once proposed marriage to the Duke of Wellington. Wellington, known to have been a good tactician, had carefully and respectfully declined. Dodger thought, there's a man who knew there was one battle he would never be able to win!

Solomon put a stopper in a brandy decanter with a happy sigh, and Dodger said, "Solomon, there's something I must tell you."

It was less than fifteen minutes before the coach got to its destination, and Dodger spent a lot of that time looking nervously at Solomon, who seemed lost in thought right up until the old man said, "Mmm, well, Dodger, I must say that you are very thorough. You are looking at a man, old and creaky as he is now, who once got out of a jail by garroting a jailer with his bootlaces. It is something I regret now, while at the same time reminding myself that because of that act I am now here to tell you about the escapade—and frankly the bastard deserved it because I had seen what he had done to others. My people are not known as fighters, but should it be necessary, we try to be very good at it. As for your plan, it is bold, daring, and in the circumstances you describe quite possibly something that will work. Although, my dear friend, do reflect that you will have to get this past Angela, who sees herself at the moment as the protector of our Simplicity."

The coach was slowing down now, and Dodger said, "I know what you mean, but the only person who can order Simplicity to do anything, according to the rules, is her husband, and you must understand that what he says is not going to happen, because he is a pox of a prince. A right royal richard."

Another flunky opened the door even before Solomon's hand had touched it, and Solomon and Dodger were shown into a sitting room that contained Angela, but alas, not Simplicity. Angela must have noticed Dodger's expression, because she said cheerfully, "Simplicity is taking her time, Mister Dodger, because she is going out to a theater with you." She patted the sofa next to her. "Do take a seat."

So the three of them sat there, in that rather strange silence of people who are waiting without very much to say to one another, until a door was opened and a maid came in, fussing alongside Simplicity, who smiled when she saw Dodger and turned the whole world into gold.

Miss Coutts said, "How nice to see you looking so beautiful, my dear, but I think we are going to be late for *Julius Caesar* if we do not hurry. I know we have a box at the theater, but I always think it looks so discourteous to be late."

Dodger was allowed to sit next to Simplicity in the coach; she wasn't saying very much at the moment but was apparently somewhat excited at the prospect of the theater, while Dodger thought things like: a theater box—that means quite a lot of people in the theater can see you, oh dear.

But shortly after they arrived at the theater, in sufficient time not to be too embarrassing, the footmen—or a pair just like them—took their places behind the four of them. It must have been the original two, Dodger thought, because as he turned to look at them he recognized the one who couldn't wait to tell his mum about Dodger. For just one moment, as he recognized said Dodger, the footman proudly let him glimpse a shining display of brass knuckles, which magically disappeared again into his dressy outfit. Well, that was something.

Dodger had been in theaters before, unofficially, but it took him some time to get the hang of what was going on. Solomon had earlier tried to give him some inkling of what *Julius Caesar* was all about, and it seemed to Dodger to be about something like a gang fight, except that everybody talked too much. But the words flew over his head and he tried to flap after them, and after a while the play began to enter him. Once you'd got used to the way they were speaking, and all the bedsheets and so on, this was about nasty people, and the moment he thought that and wondered on whose side he should bet, he remembered that these Roman coves had built the sewers and called the Lady "Cloacina."

Although Julius Caesar and the other coves were not actually building any sewers on the stage, Dodger wondered if he should call the Lady by the name they had given her; it might be worth a try. So as the speeches rolled over him, he shut his eyes and trusted his luck to the Roman goddess of the latrines and opened his eyes again as a voice declaimed, "There is a tide in the affairs of men, Which, taken at the flood, leads on to fortune." Eyes wide open, he stared at the players. Well now, if you were going to have a sign, something like this was certainly better than a little rat on your boot!

Miss Coutts, his hostess, was sitting beside him for propriety's sake, leaving Simplicity chaperoned by Solomon, who being an elderly gentleman could in theory be guaranteed not to think about hanky or panky. Now Miss Coutts nudged him very discreetly and said, "Are you all right? I thought you were sleeping, and you nearly jumped out of your seat."

"What?" said Dodger. "Oh yes, I just know that it's going to work, no doubt about it."

He cursed himself for being stupid then, because Angela whispered, "What is going to work, pray?"

Dodger mumbled, "Everything." And suddenly he paid more attention to the stage, wondering why it took so many Romans to kill one man, especially since he didn't seem to be a particularly bad cove.

It was what Solomon called "a repast." Which was apparently something much more exciting than a meal. There were glorious potted meats and cold cuts and pickles and chutneys to make your eyes water and Solomon's eyes gleam. As they finished eating, Dodger said quietly to Angela, "Where are your servants now?"

"Why, in the servants' hall. I only have to ring if I require them."

"Can they hear us?"

"Absolutely not, and may I remind you, young man, that you already know that they have my full trust. I would not employ them otherwise."

Dodger stood up. "Then I must tell all of you what I hope will happen tomorrow, if you agree."

The thing about secrets is that they are usually best kept by just one person. That was the special thing about secrets. Some people seemed to think that the best way to keep a secret was to tell as many people as possible; what could possibly go wrong for a secret when there were so many people defending it? But sooner or later he did need to tell it, and the time was now. He also needed an ally, and it needed to be Angela. It seemed to him that a woman who had more money than God, and was still happy and alive, must be a very clever woman indeed. So he told them, quietly and carefully, covering every detail, including what Mrs. Holland had told him about the Outlander, and when he stopped there was absolute silence.

Then Angela, not quite looking at Dodger or Simplicity, said, "Well, Mister Dodger, much as I admire you, my first inclination was to utterly forbid you to attempt this curious and dangerous scheme. But even as I summoned up the breath to do so, I realized, having seen the looks that passed between the two of you and reminding myself that Simplicity is not a child but a married woman, that the best I can do is to thank you for allowing me into the secret. And frankly, even if I have to pick up the pieces, in truth this matter is one between the two of you." She turned to Solomon and said, "Will you tell us your thoughts, Mister Cohen?"

After a few seconds there was "Mmm, Dodger has told me of the Outlander, and it is unlikely that he would find Dodger before Dodger's plan comes to fruition. As a plan it seems to me it does have certain beguiling aspects, because if it works it is unlikely anyone would wish to delve into the matter subsequently. And, of course, my spirits rise when I consider that this plan will take place on a battlefield absolutely familiar to my young friend, who, as I am aware, knows every inch of the terrain. In the circumstances mmm, I don't think Wellington himself could do better with an army."

Dodger's eyes had remained on Simplicity through all of this. Once he saw her frown and his spirits had plummeted, rising again when she grinned—not a smile but a grin, quite a saucy one like somebody contemplating a weak adversary.

Angela said, "Well, my dear, you are your own woman and will have my support against any man who suggests otherwise. Pray tell me what you think of this harebrained scheme, eh?"

Quietly Simplicity walked over to Dodger and took him by the hand, sending a quiver down his spine so fast that it bounced up again. She said, "I trust Dodger, Miss Angela. After all, look at the things he has done for me already."

With this ringing in the air, Dodger said, "Er, thank you. But now you've got to give up your wedding ring."

Instantly her hand touched the ring, and the silence in the room thundered great peals of absence of sound while Dodger waited for the explosion. Then Simplicity smiled and said, quite softly, "It's a pretty ring, isn't it? I loved it when he gave it to me. And I thought I was married in the eyes of God. But what do I now know about being married? The poor priest who conducted the ceremony is dead, and so are two good friends, so I think that God was never in this marriage. He was never there when I was beaten, or when I was dragged into that coach, and then there was Dodger. Angela, I trust my Dodger, completely." With that, she looked into his eyes, then dropped the ring into his hand and gave it to him with a kiss, and of the two he considered the kiss to be truly twenty-four-karat.

Angela looked at Solomon, who said, "Mmm, I think there is no doubt about it, Angela. What we have here is a rather unusual *Romeo and Juliet*."

"So you say," said Angela, "but as a practical woman, I think we will also need a dash of *Twelfth Night*. Mister Dodger, you and I must talk about particulars before you leave."

Angela's coach carried Dodger and Solomon back to Seven Dials, and they barely exchanged a word until after they had got back from Onan's late-night run and even then, still lost in their own thoughts, they spoke little in the gloom. Finally Solomon said, "Well, Dodger, I have faith in you, Miss Burdett-Coutts may have some faith in you, but Miss Simplicity has a faith in you which I venture to suggest is greater than that of Abraham's."

In the darkness, Dodger said, "Do you mean your friend Abraham, the slightly suspect jeweler?"

And the darkness came back with, "No, Dodger: the Abraham who was prepared to sacrifice his son to the Lord."

"Well," Dodger said, after a moment, "we are not going to have any of that sort of thing!"

After that he tried to sleep, seeing, as he tossed and turned, the face of Simplicity repeating again and again the words that she had said during that last discussion: *"I trust my Dodger, completely!"*

The echoes of it bounced among his bones.

In the morning, he counted what he took to be three plain-clothes policemen, trying to be surreptitious and as ever not doing it properly. He pretended that he didn't see them, but Sir Robert Peel obviously meant what he had said; two nights in a row there had been someone outside his crib and now they were here in the daytime too! They were, in a policemany sort of way, trying out new ideas, such as having no man visible near the tenement but putting a couple just around the corner, where he might run into them. Was Sir Robert getting nervous?

Long before daylight, Dodger had already been a very busy boy while the fogs, steams, and smoky darkness gave him lots of cover. And now, as the world woke up, some little way away a poor old woman could be seen hobbling past the policemen—if there was anyone about who cared to look at poor old women, who were in reality something of a glut on the market, owing to the fact that they tended to outlive their husbands and generally speaking had nobody who cared about them very much. Dodger thought it was sad; it always was, and sometimes you saw the old girls scraping a living by scrabbling around in the dust heaps and sieving household dust for anything remotely usable.* Of course, it was outdoors work but you hardly ever saw one of them in anything like a

---

* Sights like this were commonplace. Henry Mayhew's research is full of details of this level of poverty, nowadays unimaginable in cities such as London.

decent coat. And they were scary; they really were. Terrible bright eyes some of them had as they held out a claw for a farthing; toothless old ladies with that fallen-in look to the face that made you think of witches, and you found them everywhere—anywhere a body could get out of the rain.

But on this occasion, moving through the lanes and alleys, there was a now rather more spry old woman towing a handcart—a vehicle of high status on the streets—and she was fussing over it as elderly ladies did. If there was indeed a watcher on the moon, looking down on London, they would have noticed her zigzagging her way to the Embankment, whereupon she hazarded a penny on a boat that took her and her little cart across the Thames, although on this occasion she paid no more than a farthing—not the official sum for the trip, the watcher would have noticed, but the lighterman himself had never seen an old girl in such a sad old dither. Having an old mother himself, he felt a little generous today and even agreed to wait to take her back across the river, only to find that when she came back from her errand, on her cart was strapped a corpse in a winding sheet. This, to tell the truth, was a problem, but then one of his mates stopped on the landing to disembark a fare and, waving vaguely toward the old girl who was still in such a terrible state, the lighterman got his mate to help him with the cadaver. Fortunately, it was still bendy.

Dodger—because the old lady was indeed Dodger—felt rather happy about all of this. And also slightly ashamed since, after all, the coroner of Four Farthings himself *and* his officer had come out to help the old lady with the cart and had assured her that the remains of her niece had been treated with veneration at all times. It warmed the cockles of your heart, so it did.

Then of course there was the return journey, this way against the tide, and the lighterman could see he was not, as it were, going to become a rich man in this situation, so he said gruffly, "Okay, dear, in for a lion, in for a lamb, a farthing each and let's call it even."

The journey across the water wasn't that long, although it was a bit choppy, and after the man helped the fussy old lady to get the little cart over the cobbles, he was amazed beyond belief when the old girl handed him three shiny sixpences, calling him the last gentleman in London. For a long time afterward he remembered the incident fondly.

Once back on the right side of the Thames, a watcher would have seen, the old lady pulled her cart in a haphazard way along a dark and foggy alley where there was a shadow and a great smell of gin, and a very drunken, very dirty, and very nasty-looking man who said, "Got anything for me in your bag there, Granny?"

This little tableau was witnessed through the gloom by a bootblack who was sitting down on the curb to eat his breakfast. Just as he began to think that he should do something about the ambush farther on, something very strange eventuated in which the old lady seemed to vanish in a whirl and the man was on the ground while she was kicking him merrily in the fork crying out, "If ever I see you around here again, sonny, I'll have your giblets on my griddle, just you see if I don't!" Then, after adjusting her dress somewhat, the old lady once again became, well, an old lady in the eyes of the bootblack, who had watched with his half-eaten baked potato neglected in his hand. Then the old dear waved at him cheerily and said, "Young man, who's doing potatoes around here today?"

This led to Dodger continuing his journey with quite a lot of baked potatoes in his bag, which he distributed to any old ladies he saw sitting pitifully on the curb; it was a kind of penance, he thought. And someone—perhaps that watcher on the moon—who must surely have looked kindly on this act of charity seemed to have arranged it that a lavender girl had set up right in the next street, which meant that Dodger was spared the chore of going out to find one, not a difficult task since in the stink of London everybody liked to buy some lavender now and again. In this case the lucky girl sold all of her stock to the old lady with grateful thanks and went to the pub, while the old lady, smelling far more fragrant, trundled on her way.

Moving a dead body is never easy in any case, but in the murkier part of Seven Dials Dodger treasured an alley with a drain in it that was just the job; and of course, once he was in the sewers he was in his element. He could go about his business unrecognized by the people walking about above, and the chances of meeting another tosher were small. Anyway, as the king of the toshers, he could do as he pleased. In sewers, if you knew where to look for them, there were places that would make a good-size room—places the toshers had given wonderful names to, like Top and Turn Again.

Splashing his way into one of the tunnels, Dodger set about the nastier piece of the enterprise. This particular stretch had so far never been given a name; it got one now: Rest in Peace. Death was always around in the darker places of London, and it was an unusual day when you didn't see a funeral procession, so this engendered a kind of pragmatism: people lived, people died, and other people had to deal with it. At this point, because he very much wanted to live, Dodger pulled off his disguise to reveal his normal clothes hidden beneath the rags, and pulled on a pair of large, well-greased leather gloves, just as Mrs. Holland had advised. And he was grateful for the advice, and grateful too that he had spent so much on the lavender, because however you looked at it the dull, heavy, cloying smell of death was something that you didn't put up with for any longer than you had to.

So with traffic a few feet overhead he pulled, pushed, and levered very thoroughly until he had got things looking just right. All was well right up until, as he was just positioning the remains of the young lady in her nook, she sighed as her head moved. Dodger thought, if something like *that* is going to happen, it's a good job you are standing in a sewer. It was nothing; he knew the dead could be quite noisy at times, as Mrs. Holland had said. What with gases and so on, corpses might be said to speak long after they were dead. He opened his carefully prepared little bag of camphor and cayenne pepper, which ought to keep the rats away, for long enough at least.

As he stood back to look at his handiwork, he was glad, very glad that he wouldn't have to do it ever again. Then there was nothing more to do, apart from packing up his gloves, but he also took great care to leave the sewer at some distance away from the scene of the crime—if such it could be called, he added to himself. Finding a pump, he washed his hands in London water, which he knew was always slightly suspicious unless you boiled it, but good old lye soap was a reliable if caustic companion. Then he strolled back to Seven Dials with the air of a young man just enjoying the sunshine which, in fact, was rather strange today, as if something was going on in the upper air.

He didn't think very much about this, however, for as soon as he got home, two peelers were waiting for him, and one of them said, "Sir Robert would like a word with you, my little lad." He sniffed at the leftover lavender that Dodger had chosen to take home because it was always welcome around Onan. "Flowers for your girl, hey?"

Dodger ignored him, but he had been expecting something like this, since once the peelers had got interested in you, they kept on being interested in you, apparently thinking that sooner or later you would break down and confess to everything. It was a sort of game, and the worst of it was when they tried to seem to be friends. And so, like the upstanding citizen he was, he accompanied the two men to Scotland Yard but made sure that he went with the swagger of a geezer and everyone in the rookeries could see that this wasn't something he was in agreement with—for Dodger had a reputation to keep down; it was bad enough to be an official hero, but he would be damned if he was going to be seen to go willingly into anywhere where peelers lurked. It wouldn't be the first, third, or tenth time the peelers thought they had got Dodger and would have to think again.

Sir Robert Peel was waiting for him. Even now Dodger didn't trust him—he looked like a swell, but had a street gleam in his eye. The head of the peelers regarded him over his desk and said, "Have you ever heard of the Outlander, my friend?"

"No," lied Dodger, on the basis that you always lied to a policeman if at all possible.

Sir Robert gave him a blank look and said that the police forces of Europe would very much like to see the Outlander behind bars or, for preference, swinging from the gallows. "The Outlander is an assassin. He is a sharp man, Mister Dodger, and so are his knives. We presume from as much information as we can glean that he is very much interested in the whereabouts of Miss Simplicity. And, by association, you. We both know the facts of the matter, and I must assume that someone somewhere is getting extremely impatient, as evinced by the murder of Sharp Bob and his employee. We appear to be running out of time, Mister Dodger. You must understand that the British government would be doing nothing wrong in the eyes of many people if a runaway wife was sent back to her legal husband." He sniffed. "Distasteful as that would seem to many of us who are cognizant of the circumstances of this whole sordid matter. The clock is ticking, my friend. People in power do not like to be continually thwarted, and can I at this stage also draw to your attention the fact that I am one of them."

There was a tapping noise and Dodger glanced down at Sir Robert Peel's left hand, the fingers of which were drumming on a pile of documents that seemed rather familiar.

Sir Robert looked at his face and said, "I know, because it is my job to know these things, that a certain embassy was broken into two nights ago, with a great deal of documentation and miscellaneous jewelry stolen. Subsequently it appears that the miscreant, whom we are under some pressure to bring to justice, then saw fit to set fire to a coach house."

Dodger's face was all innocent interest as Sir Robert continued, "Of course, my men had to go to check up on the details of this theft and this willful vandalism and it seemed that even before the fire one wheel of this coach was damaged, but the perpetrator appeared to have scratched across the crest of this coach the name Mr. Punch. I must assume that of course you know nothing about any of this?"

"Well, sir," said Dodger brightly, "as you know, we were at a jolly dinner party that night. I went home with Solomon, who I am sure will testify should you require it." And he thought, I wonder if Solomon would lie for me to a policeman? Swiftly the thought came back: Solomon must have lied to policemen all over Europe, and with God on his side, and would be very unlikely in the presence of a peeler to know if the sky was blue.

Sir Robert smiled, but the smile had no warmth in it, and the drumming of his fingers became a little more insistent. "Mister Dodger, I am absolutely certain that Mister Cohen would say exactly that. And since we are on the subject, would you know anything about a Jewish gentleman who called in at our front desk this morning with a little package of documents for me? The sergeant in charge said he placed them on the desk and scuttled off at some speed and most certainly without leaving his name." There was the unfunny smile again, and Sir Robert went on, "Of course, generally speaking, all elderly Jewish gentlemen in their black clothing look very similar to everyone except their nearest and dearest."

At this point Dodger piped up and said, "Indeed, I never really thought of it." He was enjoying this and so, in some twisted way, was at least part of Sir Robert.

"So you know nothing," said Sir Robert. "You know nothing, you heard nothing, and you weren't there, of course." He added, "These are very interesting documents, very interesting. Especially in the light of the current discussions taking place. Which is why the embassy wants them back. Of course, I don't know where they are. Surely Solomon must have pointed out to you the worth of what you brought home?"

"What, sir, sorry, sir. Solomon ain't mentioned to me anything about any documents and I ain't seen them," said Dodger, thinking, What's he think I am? A little baby?

"Ye-e-s," said Sir Robert. "Mister Dodger, have you heard the phrase 'you are so sharp that you might cut yourself'?"

"Yes, sir, very careful with knives, sir, you can be sure of that."

"I'm so glad to hear it. You may go now." And as Dodger had his hand on the doorknob, Sir Robert said, "Don't do it again, young man."

Dodger said, "Can't, sir, haven't done it once." He didn't shake his head except in the privacy of his brain. Yes, they always wait until you think you are out of trouble and then they fly one on you. Honestly, I could teach them a few tricks.

He left Scotland Yard, calling out cheerfully as he did so, "Told yuz! You'll never find anything on me, my lads." But he thought, So there are clocks ticking. A government's clock. The Outlander's clock. And mine. It will be best for Simplicity if mine chimes first.

As for the Outlander? Here he paused. A man whose only description was that he never seemed to be the same man twice? How could you ever find a man like that? But he comforted himself as he thought, We are so close now, and he's got to learn all about me and find out where I am. That's going to be very difficult for him. This didn't entirely satisfy him, because the thought that came after was that the Outlander was a professional killer, apparently of important people, so exactly how hard would it be for him to wipe a snotty-nosed tosher off of the world?

He considered this and then said aloud, "I'm Dodger! It will be very hard indeed!"

CHAPTER FIFTEEN

In the hands of the Lady

As seven o'clock neared, Dodger went over all his precautions and preparations and came up out of the sewer a little way away, in order to be seen cheerfully walking to the Lion public house.

He was not surprised to find Mister Bazalgette sitting on a bench outside, wearing what might be called serviceable clothes for someone who is going to perambulate underneath the streets of London. The young man looked like a kid waiting for the Punch and Judy show to begin, and had festooned himself with various instruments and a large notebook, and had also very thoughtfully come with his own lantern, although Dodger had made certain to borrow three of these already. It meant calling in a few little favors, but that was surely what favors were for.

The young engineer was primly nursing a pint of ginger beer, and right there and then he struck up a conversation with Dodger about the nature of the sewers, with reference to the amount of water that Dodger had seen in them, the prevalence of rats, the dangers of being underground, and other things of interest to a gentleman as enthusiastic as Bazalgette.

"Looking forward to seeing your Lady, Mister Dodger?" he asked.

Dodger thought, yes, both of them, but smiled and said, "I ain't never seen her, ne'er even once. But sometimes, you know when you are by yourself, you get a feeling that someone's just walked past, and there is a change in the air and then you look down and all the rats are running very fast, all in the same direction; and then sometimes, as it might be, you look at a bit of rotted old sewer wall and something tells you that it might *just* be worth fumbling around in the crumbling bricks. So you take a look, and glory be, there's a gold ring with two diamonds on it. That's what happened to me one time." He added, "Some toshers say they've seen her, but that's supposed to be when they are dying, and I ain't intending to do that right now. Mind you, sir, I'll be happy to see her right now if she points me to a tosheroon."

There followed a conversation on the legendary tosheroons and how they were formed. Fortunately, at this time a growler pulled up and disgorged Charlie and Mister Disraeli, who was bright and shining and somewhat nervous, as a sensible citizen tended to be in the general vicinity of Seven Dials. Charlie sat him down on the bench and headed into the pub, coming back shortly afterward with a man carrying a couple of pints of beer on a tray, and Mister Bazalgette rubbed his hands and said, "Well now, gentlemen, when do we start?"

"Very soon, sir," Dodger replied. "But there's been a slight change of plan. Miss Burdett-Coutts wants one of her young footmen to come down with us because she wants to encourage him to better himself." He added brightly, "Maybe he might become an engineer like yourself, sir."

Dodger stopped, because a very smart coach with two beefy coachmen had spun into the pub's yard, and its doors opened to disgorge the aforesaid young footman, somewhat plumper in certain regions than the average footman, and remarkably—yes, thought Dodger—the signs of shaving around his jaw. Simplicity, and just possibly Angela, was really taking this charade seriously. The rest of them were taking it on the chin.

It wasn't at all a bad disguise and quite a lot of young serving men were on the plump side, what with all the leftovers, but to anyone who had seen her in a dress she was Simplicity, absolutely Simplicity, and if you were Dodger, looking more beautiful—even if unshaven—than ever before. But she had been wrong; her legs were not fat! No, in Dodger's mind they were perfectly shaped, and he had to fight to take his mind off her legs and back onto the task ahead of him.

He wasn't sure what Joseph Bazalgette was thinking, but quite possibly he was thinking about sewers and couldn't have seen that much of Simplicity at the party in any case. And since Angela was right there, Charlie and Disraeli were seeing—my word, yes!—what they were supposed to see. It was, thought Dodger, a kind of political fog.

Miss Coutts leaned out of the coach window and said, "I will return for my young footman in an hour and a half, gentlemen. I trust you will take care of him because I have no wish to answer for him to his grieving mother. Roger is a good boy, rather shy, and does not talk much." She added meaningfully, "If he is sensible."

The coach window closed again, and Miss Angela was gone. It was left to Charlie to say, "Well, gentlemen, maybe we should start? We are in your hands now, Mister Dodger."

All things planned in the rookeries had to be carefully thought through, Dodger knew. That was why, just before they left, he threw a handful of ha'pennies and farthings down where they were standing, so that the urchins around the place had more interesting things to do than follow them, so engrossed as they were as they struggled against one another for this sudden storm of wealth.

Dodger kept the pace brisk with a number of unnecessary twists and turns and doublings back until he got to the sewer entrance of his choice, and proceeded to help the party down one at a time with the young footman first.

When they were all assembled, staring around at the rotting bricks and the curious unnamed growths that hung from the walls, he put a finger to his mouth to indicate silence, walked a few steps, and gave out a two-tone whistle, which floated along the pipes. He waited; there was no answering call. He wasn't expecting any other toshers today, but if there had been any, they would have responded; generally speaking, it was common sense to know if other people were working down there as well.

"And now, gentlemen," he said jauntily, "welcome to this, my world. As you can see, in this light sometimes it even seems a little bit golden. It's amazing how the sun gets through. What do you think of it, Mister Disraeli?"

Disraeli, who Dodger was slightly unhappy to see had

come in proper useful boots for the occasion, wrinkled his nose and said, "Well, I cannot recommend the smell, but it is not quite as bad as I expected." This was probably true, Dodger knew, because for quite some time in the last few hours he had done his level best to prepare the most salubrious bit of sewer there had ever been. After all, Simplicity was going to be walking in it.

"It used to be nicer, in the old days," he said cheerfully. "Not so good now that people are banging holes through from their houses, but just step carefully and please, if I ask any of you to do anything, please do it with alacrity without question." He was pleased with "alacrity"; every so often Solomon hit him with a word he didn't understand and Dodger had a good memory. He let them walk for a little while and then, like a tour guide, glanced down and said in the gluey tones of a Crown and Anchor man, "Now here's an interesting place that's occasionally kind to toshers." He stepped back and said, "Mister Disraeli, will you now try your luck as a tosher? I noticed you have clapped your eyes on what might be generously called a 'sand bar' on the floor over there by that rivulet, and may I say, well done, sir, and so I will give you this stick and suggest you have a go."

The group moved forward as Disraeli, with the fixed grin of someone who wants to seem a good sport and dare not seem to be a bad one, took the stick from Dodger and approached the pile of miscellaneous debris with caution. He hunkered down and stirred about fastidiously until Dodger produced a pair of small gloves and handed them to the man, saying, "Try these, sir, very useful in certain circumstances if you can afford them." He thought Disraeli almost giggled at this point—the man did have some gumption after all—but the politician put on the gloves, rolled up his sleeves, and trailed one hand in the pile, being rewarded with a clinking sound.

"Hello," said Dodger. "Do we have some beginner's luck here? That's the sound of specie, right enough. Let's see what you've got."

They crowded around and Disraeli, almost in a daze, held up a half crown, as shiny and as untarnished as the day it had been coined.

"My word, sir, you have the luck of a tosher and no mistake. I see I had better not let you down here again, hey? If I was you I would have another go, sir; where you find one coin, you tend to find another one. After all, it takes two to make a clink. It's all to do with how the water's running, you see; you never quite know for certain where the specie might turn up today." Again they craned as Disraeli, this time with every evidence of enthusiasm, rummaged in the heap of litter, and there was another clink and he held up a gold and diamond ring. "Oh my word, sir." Dodger reached for the ring and Disraeli pulled his hand away until he realized that was bad manners, so he allowed Dodger to handle the ring and was told, "Well, sir, it's gold, that's true. It ain't diamonds though, just paste. Shocking, isn't it, but there you go, sir, first time out and you've already earned a workingman's daily wage." Dodger straightened up and said, "I think we ought to be getting on because of the light, but maybe our young man here would like to try next time? Would you, Master Roger? You could make a day's wages like Mister Disraeli here!"

Dodger was rewarded with a wide smile, and Disraeli, smiling just as much, said, "This is rather like a lucky dip, isn't it?"

"Yes, sir," said Dodger, "but there aren't many rats around at the moment, and it's not particularly wet. I mean, you are seeing it at its best."

Bazalgette and Disraeli began talking about the construction of the sewers, with the former tapping the brickwork occasionally and the latter trying not to be drawn into expressing an opinion, such as paying for something better. Charlie followed behind, noting and observing, his sharp eyes worryingly everywhere.

Now as they strolled carefully, sometimes bending where the roof seemed to sag, Dodger pointed to a couple of broken bricks and said, "There's a place that might trap a coin or two. It's like a little dam, see? The water goes past, heavy stuff gets trapped. This one is yours, Master Roger. I have another pair of gloves." He handed them to the footman with a wink.

He was entirely elated when she kneeled down in the muddy gloom and stared at the brickwork, then pushed and pulled for a while and came up holding something. She gasped, and so did Disraeli, who said, "Another golden ring? You must live like a lord, Mister Dodger. Well done, Miss Simplicity."

Suddenly the sewers were silent except for the occasional drip. At last Charlie cleared his throat and said, "Ben, I cannot for the life of me understand why you confused this young man, handsome though he is, with the young lady in question. Quite possibly the vapors here must, I suspect, alongside your evident joy in your newfound profession, have just for a little while gone to your head."

Disraeli had the grace to say, "Yes, yes indeed. How silly of me." Joseph Bazalgette simply smiled nervously, like a man who knows someone has cracked a joke that he hasn't understood, and returned to his detailed inspection of the sewer wall.

It was Charlie who worried Dodger, Charlie who held back and watched and had leaned forward and perhaps had noticed Simplicity's gasp as she saw the inscription on the ring, and almost certainly must have noticed that she turned wide-eyed to look directly into Dodger's face. He wasn't quite certain about Charlie; he always had the feeling that here was a man who could see through Dodger and out the other side.

Quickly, he said, "I'll tell you what, friends, let me go ahead. Tosh all you want to and I will point out some matters of interest to Mister Bazalgette. Of course, anything you find is yours for the keeping. And if I was you, Master Roger, I'd put that ring in your pocket for safety right now."

He knew what would happen next. It happened to every new tosher; once you'd found your first coin, the toshing fury was at your throat. Here was money for the taking, and already Simplicity and Disraeli were fascinated by holes in the brickwork, interesting holes, small mounds of rubbish, and anything that seemed to sparkle.

Mister Bazalgette, on the other hand, was grumbling and measuring at the same time. "These bricks are useless," he said from a nearby corner. "They are rotten—they should be taken out and put back and faced with ceramic tiles; that can be the only way forward. It would keep the water out."

"Alas, we don't have the money," said Disraeli, staring intently at what turned out to be one half of a dead rat.

"Then if you don't have the money, you have the stink," said Bazalgette. "I've seen the river at low tide, and it is as if the whole world has taken a purgative. It surely cannot be healthy, sir."

They walked on while the light allowed, and the total yield to the two would-be toshers was a further one shilling and a farthing which, to give him his due, Disraeli handed over to Simplicity with a bow. And Charlie watched, with his hands in his pockets and a curious and calculating smile, occasionally taking out his damned notebook and scribbling, occasionally cheering a find, sometimes staring around at the debris and the smaller outlets.

Now the light was beginning to go. Not a problem; there were lamps galore—Dodger had made certain of one each, even though he could generally get around without one. But the lamps lit only small pools in the darkness, and as the light changed, the sewers began to take on their own life. Not sinister, exactly, but little noises became more acute; the rats which were otherwise minding their own business fled out of the way, the dripping of water from the ceiling seemed louder, shadows seemed to move, and it was then that the thought might creep up on a person that if you tripped over some of these crumbling bricks, or took the wrong turning at those places where sewers met and merged, you were suddenly a long way away from what you knew as civilization.

Dodger thought, well, Simplicity shouldn't have any problem; he had been very careful about the special route, with the occasional brick lighter than the others and debris and other rubbish masking every wrong turn. He noticed her watching him intently now and it was no time to lose his nerve. A few more minutes would do, he thought. Once you lose the sun, then that's when you really become a tosher.

Then Charlie said, "There's a likely-looking place over there, Dodger. You can just about make out something like an entrance?"

Dodger bustled back to him quickly and said, "Do not go any farther down there, sir. It is very dangerous; the floors are washed out. All very, very nasty, and all jammed up too, lots of places like it in the sewers—they just don't get cleaned out enough. Now since we really haven't got much light left, could we all agree that Mister Disraeli, although a gentleman, is also a tosher. Hurrah!"

Simplicity, that is to say Master Roger, burst out laughing, as did Bazalgette, and Charlie clapped, and as the clapping came to an end there was another sound—a scraping sound, the unmistakable sound of a crowbar somewhere ahead of them opening a drain cover, and Charlie said, "What was that, Dodger?"

Dodger shrugged it off and said, "Could be anything, sir. A trick of the sewers, you might say. The sun has gone down, things expand and contract, like they say, and you get all kinds of little noises then. It's been quite a hot day really; sometimes you could think there was someone else down here with you, and if we simply turn around it's an easy stroll back to where we came in. It's not as though we've gone all that far, to tell you the truth."

Mister Bazalgette, waving his lamp, said, "I would really like more time, if you don't mind." In the end, Dodger pacified him with the promise to take him farther afield on the following day, possibly in the company of Mister Henry Mayhew, who had been unable to join this little excursion.

After saying that, he once again delivered the two-tone whistle of a tosher. It was not returned and this worried him, for any tosher would have whistled back. . . . Even the rat catchers knew enough to shout out when a tosher whistled— that saved embarrassment all around. Well, he thought, it was quite a good plan, it really was, but I can't do it if there is somebody else stamping around down here. Inwardly he groaned. Well, maybe tomorrow he could come up with another plan.

He had not, he thought, heard any more noises since that scraping, apart from those made by the company, and that meant that somebody was trying to keep quiet. So right now it was important to get Simplicity out of here. It could be a very young tosher who hadn't yet learned the ropes. Or it might be something else . . . but it wasn't worth taking the chance. Nothing must happen to Simplicity.

Keeping his tone cheerful, he ushered his little flock back along the way they had come, silently cursing every step. It was not as easy as might have been thought, even by the lamplight, which didn't penetrate all that far.

"Gentlemen, if you don't mind, there are a few things I'd like to look at down here," he said as they approached the sewer exit. "When you are aboveground I hope that you can take care of . . . Roger until the coach turns up. Sometimes you get undesirables down here, well, more undesirable than what's down here already. I'll just have a quick glance around and then come back. I'm sure it's nothing, but with Mister Disraeli here as well, I feel a little caution is sensible."

Simplicity was watching him intently, Mister Bazalgette was looking somewhat dismayed, and Charlie was just strolling carefully back the way they had come. Mister Disraeli, quite surprisingly, took Simplicity's hand. "Come along . . . Miss . . . young man. Frankly, I could do with a breath of fresh air."

As they climbed up and out, Dodger took care to say again, "Probably nothing at all, nothing at all, but I had best check." Then he dropped back into the sewer and was free, free of other people. Someone else had got into his sewer, and if it were any of the work gangs there would have been a shout on the lines of "Bugger off, you toshers!"—not exactly a cheerful greeting, but at least something human. No, someone *was* there. It couldn't be the Outlander, could it? That would be too glib. But the Lady knew there were still a number of people after Dodger, and everyone knew where Dodger could usually be found. Oh well, at least he was on his own ground, sticky and stinking though it was.

In the dark now, he heard the rattle of a coach overhead, and the sounds of voices, one of which was unmistakably that of Simplicity. He breathed a deep sigh of relief. Well, whatever happened now couldn't happen to her. Of course, he told himself again, it almost certainly wasn't the Outlander, who was surely just a bogeyman, after all . . . though try as he might, his thoughts dived from being optimistically cheerful to: *I'm a bloody fool.* If the Outlander has been so successful in his trade, then he must surely know just about everything concerning Dodger and Simplicity.

That was just the start of the terrible scenarios jostling for space in front of his eyes. Pictures flashed across his mind at speed, nasty pictures. Well, would someone like the

Outlander go down into the sewers? Perhaps someone had paid him enough money. And then what further scenarios could near-panic throw up? Everybody knew Dodger had gone into the sewer with his group. Who did the Outlander know? How fast did news travel? And how clever must someone like the Outlander have been still to be alive when by now he must have so many enemies in so many countries? Just how stupid had Dodger, good old Dodger, been to have thought that the threat was something he could just brush off? But perhaps it was someone else?

Well, Simplicity was safe, for now. Then the sensible thing for Dodger to do would be to get up and out of the sewer as soon as possible before the stranger caught up to him, but with his heart pounding most unusually against his ribs, he considered his limited options. He *could* get out of the sewer by another drain farther along, but if he took the time to go there, anything could happen, and if he tried to leave by the nearest one, whoever it was—and suddenly he felt certain that it *was* the Outlander and he was trapped down here with him—could come out right behind him.

Then the last of the sunlight faded. He thought, this is my world. I know every brick. I know every place where if you put a foot wrong, you are up to your waist in stinking mess. He thought, Here I am. Maybe he could use this to his advantage. Make a *new* plan, a plan with a different way of getting to the same end. And Julius Caesar appeared in his mind, admittedly sitting on a jakes (an image which would stay with him for a long time)—and Dodger thought, He was a warrior, wasn't he? A cove who was difficult to kill too. He whispered, "There!" and said aloud in the gloom, "Come along. Here I am, mister; maybe you want to be shown the sights."

Looking down, he realized that someone was most definitely on his way, because the rats were running straight toward him, trying to keep ahead of whoever or whatever was coming up the sewer. Dodger, by now, was up against the sewer wall, mostly in a little alcove where several ancient bricks had fallen out (and where, he recalled fondly, he had once picked up two farthings and one of the old-fashioned groats that you didn't see around these days).

The running rats clambered over and around him as if he wasn't there, and he thought, they see me nearly every day. He had never hunted them, slammed his boot on them, or even tried to shoo them away. He left them alone and so they left *him* alone. Besides, he didn't know how he would stand with the Lady if he was nasty to her little subjects. Grandad had been very firm about this, saying, "Tread on a rat and you're treading on the Lady's robe." Dodger whispered to the silence and said, "Lady, it's Dodger again. About that luck I mentioned? If you can see your way clear, thanking you in expectation, Dodger."

And up there in the darkness, there was the scream of a stricken rat. They were capable of dying quite noisily, and there was another squeal, and even more rats were pouring past him, surrounding him.

There, suddenly, barely visible in the grimy light, was the intruder, crawling with commendable stealth along the sewer, actually passing Dodger in his stinking hideaway, since Dodger was clearly invisible, being the same color and certainly the same stink as the sewer itself. The rats were running over the intruder too, but he was hitting out at them with something—Dodger couldn't quite see what—and the rats were screeching and most certainly the Lady would be listening.

Now, in his hand Dodger had—yes!—Sweeney Todd's razor; he had brought it with him not so much as a weapon but as a talisman: a gift from fate that had changed his life, just as it had changed that of Sweeney Todd. On a day like this, how could he have left it behind?

In the darkness, Dodger's dark-accustomed eye saw the gleaming stiletto dagger in the man's hand. It was an assassin's weapon if ever he had seen one. No decent murderer would use something like that. The thought came to him fast and all at once: He had nothing at all to fear down here. It was his world, and he could feel the Lady helping him, he was sure of it. No, the person who ought to be afraid was the man stealthily crawling along the drain just where Dodger could see him . . . and Dodger jumped on him, pinning him down immediately, and assassin or not, it is hard to use your dagger when you are splayed in the muck of a sewer with Dodger sitting on your back.

He was a wiry boy, but he held the man more or less fixed to the ground as if he had been nailed to it, and pummeled every bit of the man that could be pummeled. Even as the man struggled, Dodger pressed cold steel to his throat and whispered, "If you know anything about me, then you know that pressed to your neck is Sweeney Todd's razor, wonderful smooth so it is, and who knows what it could cut off?" He allowed the prone man to at least lift his mouth and nose out of the muck for a moment, and added, "Upon my word, I was expecting rather more of an assassin than this. Come on, speak up!" Dodger grabbed the stiletto and flung it into the darkness.

The man below him spat out mud and a piece of what might have once been part of a rat and tried to say something that Dodger couldn't understand, so Dodger said, "Come on, what was that again?"

A voice—a female voice—said, "Good evening, Mister Dodger; if you look carefully, you will see that I am holding a pistol, quite a powerful one. You will not make a single move until my friend here stops throwing up so unpleasantly, whereupon I expect he will wish to do unto others that which hath just been done to him. In the meantime, you will stand where you are and I will pull the trigger if you move so much as an inch. Later I will kill your young lady friend. . . . By the way, I can't say I like that gentleman very much, not the best assistant I've ever had. Oh dear, oh dear, why is it that everybody assumes that the Outlander is a man?" The owner of the voice stepped nearer and Dodger could now see both her and her pistol.

There was no doubt about it. The Outlander was attractive, even in this gloom, and Dodger could not pinpoint the accent. Not Chinese, certainly not European, though very fluent in English. He had Sol's pistol strapped in his boot; that had been for use later, for the plan which was now of course in tatters, and so he said, "Excuse me, miss, but why do you want to kill Simplicity?"

"Because I will then be paid quite a considerable sum of money, young man. Surely you know that? Incidentally, I have no particular quarrel with yourself, although Hans—once he can stand up straight—almost certainly would quite like to have a brief, very brief, conversation with you. We just have to wait for the poor man to recover."

The girl—and the Outlander looked like a girl not much bigger than Simplicity and, he had to admit, slightly thinner—gave him a charming smile. "It won't be long now, Mister Dodger. And what is it that you are staring at, apart of course from myself?"

Dodger, almost swallowing his tongue, said, "Well, miss, not staring, miss, just praying to the Lady." And indeed he was praying, but also watching the shadows shift. They lingered even here.

"Ah yes, I have heard tell of her . . . the Madonna of the sewers, the goddess Cloacina, the lady of the rats, and I see so many of her congregation here with us this evening," the Outlander continued.

The shadows behind her quite subtly changed again. And hope, which had disappeared for some time, suddenly returned—although Dodger made certain to keep it out of his face.

"You are a fervent believer to turn to the darkness in supplication, but I am afraid it will take more than rats to save you, however hard you stare into the darkness. . . ."

"Now!" screamed Dodger, and the quite hefty lump of wood in Simplicity's hands was already in flight, hitting the Outlander on the back of the head and knocking her straight to the ground. Dodger jumped and slid and snatched up the pistol, banging his head on the side of the sewer in his haste as the rats ran and squeaked in panic.

He gave Hans another swift boot to ensure he stayed on the

ground a little longer, and Simplicity, with great presence of mind, sat on the woman. Dodger thought, Thank goodness for all that heavy German sausage. Then he shouted, "Why did you come back here? It's *dangerous!*"

Simplicity gave Dodger a bewildered look and said, "You know, I looked at the ring that I found, and on it I saw it said in tiny writing: 'To S, with love from Dodger.' So of course I had to come back, but I kept quiet, because you said we should keep quiet in the sewers. I told them I was going to wait until I saw you come out of the sewer, and I thought something was wrong. Well, you told me that the Outlander always had a good-looking lady with him, and I thought, well, a good-looking lady who went around with somebody like that assassin would be a very powerful woman. I wondered if you realized that; it would appear, my dearest Dodger, that I was right."

In the echoes of that little speech, for just one bleary moment, Dodger thought he heard the voice of Grandad with its cheerful toothless sound, saying, "Told yuz! You is the best tosher I known. You got your tosheroon now. That young lady there—she's your tosheroon, lad!"

There was nothing for it. Treading heavily on the Outlander, he grabbed Simplicity, gave her a hug and a kiss, one which regrettably couldn't go the optimum distance because now, surely, there was so much to do.

Simplicity had hit the Outlander quite hard; there was certainly a pulse, but also a bit of blood here and there, and the assassin definitely wasn't going to get up for a while. The man, however, was, but not with much enthusiasm, since a mouth full of mixed sewer water can slow down anybody. He was groaning, swaying, and dribbling—dribbling green slime.

Dodger grabbed him and said, "Can you understand English?" He couldn't understand the answer, but Simplicity stepped forward and after a brief interrogation said, "He's from one of the Germanys, from Hamburg, and he sounds very scared."

"Good, tell him that if he is a good boy and does what we ask, he might see his home country again. Don't tell him that what he's likely to see there could be the gallows, 'cos I wouldn't want him to worry. Right now, of course, I need to be a friend to this poor man led astray by a wicked woman. So he will, I reckon, be very very helpful. . . . Oh, and tell him to take his trousers off, quickly!" They were foreign and pretty good, but as the man sat there, naked, Dodger tore the German trousers to shreds and used them to bind the recumbent Outlander and her employee.

Simplicity was wreathed in smiles, but a cloud passed over her face and she said, "What should we do now, Dodger?" and he replied, "It's like the plan. You know the place I told you about. We call it The Cauldron, 'cos that is what it is like when there is a real storm, but at least it means it's a lot cleaner than most of the places down here. You remember all the lighter bricks? There's food up there, and a bottle of water too. And people will come running down when they hear the gunshot." He gave her Solomon's pistol and said, "Do you know how to fire one of these things if necessary?"

"Well, I have seen men shooting, with my . . . husband, and I think I can."

"Right!" said Dodger. "You just point the bit at the end at anyone you don't like, and that generally works. If all goes well, I think I should be able to come and find you around about midnight. Don't you worry; the worst thing in these sewers right now is me, and I'm on your side. You will hear voices, but just lie low and keep very quiet and you will know it's me that's coming to find you when you hear me whistle; just like we planned. . . ."

She kissed him and said, "Do you know, Dodger, your first plan would have worked too." Very pointedly she put on her finger the ring she had "found" on the tosh, then she left, following the slightly lighter bricks in the darkness.

Dodger worked fast now. He scurried at speed back down through the sewers to the place he most emphatically had stopped Charlie going into and with care pulled out from hiding—and from the sheaves of lavender—all that remained of the unfortunate girl, yellow haired and wearing exactly the same breeches and cap as Simplicity was wearing. He slid the wonderful ring on her cold finger—the gold ring with the eagles on the crest.

Now there was the worst bit. He drew out the Outlander's pistol, took a few breaths, shot the corpse in the heart twice, because the Outlander as a matter of course would use two shots to make sure, and—horribly, and almost without looking—once in the side of the face where the rats had begun to . . . well, do what rats usually do to a nice, fresh corpse. He whispered, "I'm sorry." Then he took from another hidey-hole among the junk in the sewer a bucket of pigs' blood. He tipped it out, trying all the time to not exactly be there, trying to become a disembodied spirit watching somebody else doing all these things, because as often as he told himself that he had done nothing really bad, there would always be a little part of him that would argue.

And then he walked back along the tunnel, sat and sobbed and listened to the noise of splashing feet coming at speed down the sewer, led, interestingly, by Charlie, followed by a couple of policemen. They found Dodger curled up in tears, tears that right now came of their own accord.

"Yes," said Dodger, crying. "She's dead, she's really dead. . . . But I did my best, I really did."

A hand landed on Dodger's neck and Charlie said, "Dead?"

Looking at his boots, Dodger said, "Yes, Charlie, she was shot. There was nothing I could do. It was . . . the Outlander, a right proper assassin." He looked up, tears glistening in the lamplight. "What chance would the likes of me have against someone like that?"

Charlie looked angrily at Dodger and said, "Are you telling me the truth, Dodger?"

Now Dodger looked up with his head held high. "It all happened so quickly that it's all a bit of a fog. But yes, I'd say that's the truth of it, all right."

Charlie's face was suddenly much closer to Dodger's. "A fog, you say?"

"Yes indeed, the kind of fog in which people see what they want to see." Was that just a hint of a grin in Charlie's eye? Dodger had to hope so.

But the man said, "Surely there is a corpse?"

Dodger nodded sadly. "Yes, sir, I can take you to it right now—indeed, I think I should."

Charlie lowered his voice and said, "This corpse . . . ?"

Dodger sighed and said, "A poor girl's corpse . . . and I have the culprits and will bring them to justice with your help, Charlie, but Simplicity, I am afraid, you will never see alive again."

He said these words very carefully, eyes glued to Charlie's, who said, "I cannot say I am pleased by what I hear, Mister Dodger, but here is a constable and we will follow your lead." He turned to Disraeli, who almost stepped back, and said, "Come along, Ben, as a pillar of Parliament, you should witness this." There was an edge of command in that suggestion, and a few minutes later, they had reached the sad corpse of "Simplicity," lying in a pool of sewerage and blood.

"Good lord," said Mister Disraeli, doing his best to appear shocked. "It would appear that Angela's footman is really . . . Miss Simplicity."

"If you don't mind me saying so, sir, what was a girl doing down here dressed as a man?" the constable asked, because he *was* a policeman, even though right at this minute he looked like a constable who found himself in a position that needed a sergeant at least.

Charlie turned to him. "Miss Simplicity was a girl who knew her own mind, I believe. But I beg of you all, please, for the sake of Miss Coutts, let it never be known that the girl was dressed like this when she died."

"I should think not," Mister Disraeli pronounced. "The death of a young girl is appalling, but a young girl in breeches . . . whatever next?" There was a hint of politician in this little speech; a whiff of wondering, What would the public think if they knew I was here, down here, mixed up in all this?

"Perfect for a working girl," Dodger said. "You don't know the half of it. I've seen girls working on the coal barges, and strapping big girls they were too. Nobody told them they shouldn't, 'cos I remember seeing one that had a fist on her that many a man could wish for."

Charlie turned back to the corpse. "Well," he said, "we are all agreed that this lady, who is wearing breeches, is Miss Simplicity. But her death—what do you think, constable?"

The policeman looked at Charlie, and then at Dodger, and said, "Well, sir, that's a bullet wound and one more at least with no doubt about it. But who done it? That's what I'd like to know."

"Ah well," said Dodger, "for the answer to that, I must beg you gentlemen to follow me over here. If you would be so good as to keep your lanterns bright, you will see trussed up a lady who I think you will find is the Outlander."

Even Charlie looked surprised at this, saying, "Surely not!"

"She told me she was," said Dodger, "and lying down there is 'exhibit B,' her accomplice. Speaks German, that's all I know, but I rather feel he will be very anxious to tell you everything, since I must tell you to the best of my knowledge he had no part in the death of Simplicity and, as far as I am aware, hasn't committed any other crime in London. Apart from trying to murder me." Then he held up the pistol and said, "This was the weapon, gentlemen, and there wasn't much I could do to stop her shooting Miss S . . . Miss . . ."

Dodger began to cry, and Charlie patted him on the shoulder and said, "Well, you couldn't have stopped a pistol, and that's the truth of it. But well done for catching the miscreants." He sniffed and went on, as an aside, out of the hearing of the constable, "You know, clearly you've told us the truth, but I have seen a corpse or two in my time—oh, haven't I just—and this one appears to me to be possibly . . . not very fresh . . . ?"

Dodger blinked and said, "Yes, sir, I think it's the miasmic effusions, sir. After all, the sewers are full of death and decay, and that finds its way in, sir, believe me it does, most egregiously, so it does."

"Miasmic effusions," Charlie repeated, louder this time. "Hear that, Ben? What can we say? I think that all of us know that Mister Dodger would never have hurt Simplicity, and we all understand that he was very caring of her. So I hope that you will join me in sympathy for this young man, who despite the loss of his lady love has managed to bring a dreadful killer to justice." Then he added, "What do you think, constable?"

The policeman looked rather stern and said, "Well, sir, so it seems, sir, but the coroner will have to be informed. Has the corpse any next of kin that you know of?"

"Alas, no," said Charlie. "In fact, officer, I am aware that nobody really knows who she is, or where she came from. She was somewhat unfortunate—an orphan of the storm, you might say. A girl whom Miss Coutts had taken under her wing out of the sheer goodness of her heart. What do you say, Ben?"

Mister Disraeli appeared horrified by the entire business and looked nervous, saying, "A dreadful matter indeed, Mister Dickens. All we can do is let the law take its course."

Charlie nodded in a statesmanlike way and said, "Well, Mister Dodger, I think that all you need to do is give the constable here your particulars, and of course I can vouch for you as a pillar of the community. As you may know, Constable,

Dodger is the man who set about the infamous Sweeney Todd, and may I add my own dismay at how our innocent little excursion came to such an unhappy end."

He sighed. "One can only speculate as to why this poor, unfortunate girl was the target of this madwoman. But I have taken note, Constable, that the dead girl is wearing a fine gold ring, very ornate and with a ducal seal on it too. This may or may not be of interest, but I must ask you to take it as evidence that may be very germane to the investigation. But then," he added, glancing again at Disraeli, who still looked appalled, "in the circumstances, Constable, I am sure you and your superiors, when of course they have satisfied themselves about the sad facts of this matter, will see to it that the whole business does not lead to unnecessary speculation because, of course, surely the facts speak for themselves."

He looked around for agreement. "And now," he concluded, "I think we should leave, although I think that some of us"—and here he glanced meaningfully at Dodger— "should wait until the coroner's officer comes along. May I say, Constable, you should approach him in all haste."

To Dodger's amazement the policeman saluted, actually saluted, and said, "Yes indeed, Mister Dickens."

"Very good," said Charlie. He then added, "But you do have here these killers, and if I was you I should right now make an immediate report and have the wagon here as soon as possible. I will wait with Mister Dodger and the pistol, if you don't mind, until you and your colleagues return." He turned to Mister Bazalgette. "Joseph, how do you feel?"

The surveyor looked a bit unnerved but said, "Honestly, Charlie, I have seen worse things."

"Then would you be so kind as to see that Ben gets home safely? I think he is rather shaken by all of this; I am sure that it wasn't the happy little jaunt we were all expecting."

Two more policemen arrived almost immediately, and then others soon followed suit, and by now a crowd was forming around the entrance to the sewer, and more policemen were called in to hold the crowd back. Every policeman at some time went down into the sewers just so they would have something to tell their grandchildren. And the newspapers were already churning . . . another "'*orrible murder!*" would be front-page news tomorrow, oh yes.

It was indeed a very strange evening for Dodger, who was interrogated several times by different policemen, themselves watched like a hawk by Charlie. It was embarrassing when some of the policemen came up to Dodger to shake his hand, not because the Outlander had now been captured—after all, who could believe that a *girl* could be a dangerous assassin?—but because of Mister Todd, and how Dodger now appeared to be a hero in more ways than one, even though a young girl had died. And all the time the fog spilled over everything, finding its way in everywhere, silently changing the realities of the world.

They took away the Outlander and her accomplice. Then the coroner's officer came and the coroner as well, and there were coaches and carts, and everywhere there was Charlie, and eventually the last remains of the poor dead girl were put into a coffin for the final destination at Lavender Hill.

The coroner, said Charlie afterward, had taken the view that since the girl had no friends or relatives to speak of, except a young man who clearly loved her very much and a lady who had kindly given her shelter and tried to stop her from following other young girls down the wrong path, then surely this was an open and shut case if ever there was one. Even if there were a few little mysteries.

The killer was now under lock and key, despite the fact that the wretched woman now denied shooting anybody, an assertion belied by her confederate who, it must be said, was talking his heart out in the hope of salvation.

Dispatches were sent to Downing Street, along with the ring for examination, once the crest on it was noted, this being political. And indeed the word "political" seemed to hover like the fog over the case as a warning to all men of goodwill, with the meaning that if your masters are satisfied, so you had better be as well.

Now it was nearly midnight, and there was only Charlie and Dodger. Dodger knew why he himself was there, but since Charlie had already filed his copy to the *Morning Chronicle*, he had no idea why the other man was still there.

Then, in the gloom of midnight, Charlie said, "Dodger, I think there is a game called Find the Lady, but I am not asking to play it. I simply wish to know that there is a lady to be found, in good health, as it might be, by a young man who can see through the fog. Incidentally, both as a journalist and as a man who writes things about things and indeed people who do not exist, I rather wonder, Mister Dodger, what you would have done if the Outlander had not turned up?"

"You were watching me all the time," said Dodger. "I noticed. Did I give very much away?"

"Amazingly little. Am I to assume that the young lady we all saw so emphatically dead did not die by your hand, if you will excuse me for being so blunt?"

And Dodger knew that the game was up but not necessarily over, and said, "Charlie, she was one of those girls who drowns herself in the river and no one cares very much. She will get a decent burial in a decent graveyard, which is more than she would have got in other circumstances. And that's the truth of it. My plan was simplicity itself, sir. Simplicity would have excused herself, being a very 'shy lad.' Alas, she would have wandered into the sewers, where I would rush to find her. In the dark there would be a great noise of a scuffle and a scream as I fought valiantly, I'll have you know, as I came to blows with an unknown man who must have heard of our little excursion and may even now be still at large. Whereupon I would rush to meet yourself and the others and implore you all to help the dying Simplicity, and not least chase the dreadful assassin through the sewers. It would be a terrifying but fruitless pursuit."

"And where would the living Simplicity be, pray?" said Charlie.

"Hidden, sir. Hidden in a place where no one but another tosher would ever find her—a place we call The Cauldron on account of the way the waters wash it clean—with a waterproof packet of cheese sandwiches and a bottle of boiled water with a dash of brandy to keep the cold out."

"Then, Mister Dodger, you would have made fools of us all."

"No, sir! You would have been quite heroic! Because I would never tell and nor would Simplicity, and then one day everyone would know the name of Charlie Dickens."

It seemed to Dodger that Charlie was trying to look stern,

but in fact Charlie was rather impressed, saying, "Where did you get a pistol?"

"Solomon has a Nock pepper-box pistol. Dangerous brute. I think I thought about everything, sir, except for you, that is."

"Oh," said Charlie. "Those bricks over there look so beguilingly higgledy-piggledy. I wondered why they were there. Also, I am wondering now why you are hanging around here? Would it help if I say that I won't pass my suspicions on to any third party because, frankly, I don't think that I would be believed!" He smiled at Dodger's discomfiture and said, "Dodger, you have excelled yourself, by which I mean to say you have done exceptionally well, and I salute you. Of course, I am not a member of the government, thank goodness. Now I suggest that you go and find Miss Simplicity, who I imagine must by this time be feeling a little chilly."

Caught unusually unawares, Dodger burst out, "Actually, it can be quite warm down here at nighttime—tends to hold the heat, you see."

Charlie laughed out loud and said, "I must be off, and I suspect, so should you."

"Thank you, sir," said Dodger, "and thank you very much for teaching me about the fog."

"Oh yes," said Charlie. "The fog. Intangible though it is, it is a very powerful thing, is it not, Mister Dodger? I shall follow your career with great interest and, if not, with trepidation."

When he was absolutely certain that there was no one else around, Dodger made his way through the sewers until he

came to the little hidey-hole where Simplicity was waiting, and he whistled softly. No one noticed them leave, no
one saw where they went, and the veil of night spread over
London on the living and the dead alike.

CHAPTER SIXTEEN

A letter comes from York,
and the skills of the dodgerman
win approval in the highest quarters

FOG, OH YES FOG, the fog of London town, and it seemed to Dodger, once Charlie and Sir Robert Peel got to talking, that the fog was shaped to a purpose, or so it appeared. There were a number of meetings in offices around Whitehall, where Dodger was asked questions about his little excursion into the embassy and the paperwork which he had brought back, and they listened carefully, nodding occasionally as he explained that he had taken it then simply to get back at whoever it was who was making life so difficult for Simplicity and himself.

He didn't mention the jewelry, now carefully concealed in Solomon's strongboxes, those pieces, that is, that weren't already stealing their way into the welcome fingers of Solomon's jeweler friends. He did not want to get into trouble, and it appeared, amazingly enough, that it was beginning to seem that he was not going to get into trouble for *anything*.

At one point, a friendly-looking cove with silver hair and a grandfatherly kind of face beamed at him and said, "Mister

Dodger, it is apparent that you got into the well-guarded embassy of a foreign power and roamed at will among its floors and the inner sanctums without ever being challenged. How on earth were you able to do this? Could you please elucidate, if you would be so good? And may I ask if you would be amenable to repeating this singular feat another time, at some other place, should we ask you to do so?"

It took a little while, and a certain amount of translation with the help of Charlie, to give an explanation about the working practices of the snakesman. It culminated in Dodger's handing back Charlie his watch, which he had taken from him just for fun, and then he said, "Do you want me to be a spy, is that it?"

This comment caused a certain frisson around the men in the room, and they all looked at the silver-haired man, who said, smiling, "Young man, Her Majesty's government does not spy, it merely *takes an interest*, and since both Sir Robert and Mister Disraeli have told us that while you are a scallywag, you are the right kind of scallywag, of which we may wish we had a few more, Her Majesty's government might have an interest in occasionally employing you, although having employed you, they would emphatically deny ever having done so."

"Oh, I understand that, sir," said Dodger cheerfully. "It's a kind of fog, isn't it? I know about fogs. You can trust me on that, sir."

The white-haired gentleman looked affronted at first, and then smiled. "It seems to me, Mister Dodger, that no one can teach you anything about fog."

Dodger gave him a cheeky salute and said, "I've lived in the fog all my life, sir."

"Well, you do not need to give me an answer now, and I suggest you talk it over with your friend Mister Dickens, who I'm bound to say is something of a scallywag himself, being a newspaper gentleman, but who I suspect has your best interests at heart. May I say, Mister Dodger, that there are some slightly worrying details about what happened in the sewer the other day which might in other circumstances have led to more investigation, were it not for the fact that you most certainly did bring to justice the notorious Outlander, a circumstance that will cause great relief among our European friends, while at the same time showing them what happens to assassins who dare to come to England. I believe some rewards might be coming your way."

The white-haired man stood up, and the action broke the tension in the room; Dodger saw smiles all round him as the man, his face now looking a little sorrowful, added, "I'm sure we were all upset to hear of the death of the young lady known as Simplicity, Mister Dodger, and may I say you have my condolences."

Dodger looked at the old man, who probably wasn't all that old but instead had been made old by the white hair. He was totally certain the face in front of him knew everything or, at the very least, as much of anything that anybody could, and most certainly knew everything about the uses of a fog. Dodger thought he'd be the kind of cove, for example, who might pick up the detail that a body, having apparently just been shot, seemed very like somebody who had been dead for almost a week, and never mind about noxious effusions.

"Thank you, sir," he said carefully. "It has not been a very pleasant time lately, and I was thinking of taking a little trip out of London so that I don't see anything that reminds me of my girl."

And he cried real tears, which was quite easy to do, and it shocked him inside, and he wondered if there was anything in the boy called Dodger that was totally himself, pure and simple, not just a whole packet of Dodgers. Indeed, he hoped in his soul that Simplicity would embrace the decent Dodger and put him on something approaching the straight and narrow, provided it was not all that straight and not all that narrow. Ultimately, it was all about the fog.

He blew his nose on the nice white handkerchief that he had absentmindedly removed from the pocket of one of the other gentlemen around the table and said, "I was thinking of going up to York, sir, for a week or two."

This revelation caused a little excitement in the room, but after a few minutes' discussion, it was agreed that Dodger, who after all had committed no crime and, indeed, quite possibly the reverse, should of course be allowed to go to York if he wanted to.

The meeting broke up, and Charlie put a hand on Dodger's arm as they were leaving and escorted him at some speed to a nearby coffeehouse, where he said, "It would appear that all sins are forgiven, my friend, but of course it's such a shame that Miss Simplicity, despite all your best efforts, is now deceased; how is she, by the way?"

Dodger had been expecting something like this, and so, giving Charlie a vacant look, he said, "Simplicity is dead, Charlie, as well you know."

"Oh yes," said Charlie, grinning. "How foolish of me to have forgotten." His grinning face went as blank as a board;

then he held out his hand, saying, "I am sure that we will meet again, my friend. It has, I must say, been a privilege of sorts to meet you. I am as unhappy as you are perhaps about the death of poor Simplicity, the girl that nobody really cared about, except for you. And, of course, dear Angela, who seems suspiciously unmoved? I expect, nay assume, that you will before very long find another girl quite like her. Indeed, I might even bet on it."

Dodger tried to keep any expression away from his face and then gave up because no expression at all is an expression in itself. He looked into Charlie's eyes and then said, slowly and deliberately, "Well, I don't know nothing about that, sir." And he winked.

Charlie laughed, and the two of them shook hands, then went their separate ways.

The day after this conversation, a coach left London bound for Bristol, with the usual cross-section of passengers to endure the raggedy road. However, in this case the coachman reckoned that one of the passengers was the most unpleasant he had had that year, and it was all the worse because it was an old lady with a voice as crackly and demanding as a cauldron full of witches; nothing would please her—the seats, the ride, the weather, and, as far as he knew, the phase of the moon. When the passengers were allowed off for a mercifully quick meal at one of the coaching inns along the way, she found fault with every dish put before her, including the salt, which she declared was not salty enough. The old baggage, besides smelling too much of lavender, also bullied incessantly a rather pleasant-looking young lady who was her granddaughter.

She, at least, lit up the atmosphere in the coach a little, but mostly the coachman remembered Grandma, and he was very glad to see the back of the old besom as she almost fell off the coach when they got to Bristol. Of course, she had complained about that too.

A cheerful-looking young man then went to a pharmacist's at Christmas Steps, near the center of Bristol, where he discussed certain things to do with pigments and similar, in a very useful discourse that included words like henna and indigo. Shortly afterward quite a pretty young lady with beautiful red hair and a dark-haired young gentleman hired a coach and a driver to take them out of the city and all the way to the gaunt gray Mendip Hills, whereupon they told the driver that they wished to continue the journey along the turnpike past the pub at Star, where they had lunch consisting of excellent cheese and the type of cider that was so strong it might have been fortified by lion's piss, and all the better for it apparently, because even the young lady had a second half pint of the scorching stuff.

After their lunch they dismissed the coachman, telling him to meet them at the same place in precisely one week's time. The man happily agreed, because he had already been paid quite a considerable sum by the young man, who had handed him a beautiful amount of money, whispering that he would be grateful if nobody was told about this little excursion since they would both be in trouble if her father found out. The coachman was not unfamiliar with journeys of this sort, and he therefore saluted and tapped the side of his nose with a greasy little grin that said, "Me? I know nothing, I am totally blinded by the shine of money, and God bless you, sir."

The following day a man in the local pub, a carrier by trade, was induced by means of a jingling purse to take the young couple on a shortcut to the small town of Axbridge, on the other side of the Mendips. The couple came down the southern slopes and took lodgings near the watermill. It was an unusual arrangement, however, since the young man made it clear that the young lady was to sleep in the best bedroom, such as it was, and he himself would sleep on a straw paillasse outside the door, covered with a horse blanket. This caused a little bit of talk locally with the ladies of the village, who took the view that the runaways (which everyone agreed was what the nice young couple were) were being very careful about things as decent Christians should be.

Christian or otherwise, that was in fact the case. The communication had passed between Simplicity and Dodger almost by telepathy; this had to be a time to relax, heal, and, well, enjoy the world. And the world itself seemed to enjoy them, because they were quite free with their money, and although the girl was rather modest as a maiden ought to be, she took every opportunity to chat to people. She seemed very keen to speak like they did in the Somerset accent, which might have been called bucolic because it was slow. It was indeed slow, because it dealt with things that *were* slow—like cheese and milk and the seasons, and smuggling and the brewing of fiery liquors in places where the excise men dared not go—and in those places, while the speech was slow, thought and action could be very fast indeed.

And Dodger learned fast, because on the streets a quick uptake was the only one to have and you never got a second chance. At first his head ached with a language that seemed made up of corn and cows. But the learning was helped along by the drink the locals called scrumpy, and after a while he was talking like them as well. His head filled up with words like "Mendip," "priddy," and "bist," and conglomerations of a language whose rhythms were not the staccato of the town but practically had something which you could call a melody. There are more types of disguise, he thought, than just putting on a different kind of shirt or changing your hair.

One morning, as they walked by the river, he said to Simplicity, "I never asked you before. But why did you have the game of Happy Families?"

The Somerset accent wobbled a little as she said, "My mother gave it to me and, you see, I always wanted to have one thing—something that was mine, when nothing else was. I used to look at it and think how one day things would be better, and now I think they are, after the wretched time I had."

She beamed at him, and the little speech, combined with the smile, warmed the cockles of Dodger's heart and carried on going farther down.

It was about this time that in London—a place where people spoke so fast that you never saw where your money had gone—a lady called Angela stepped out of a coach in Seven Dials, the coach then being immediately guarded by two strapping footmen, and climbed up a set of stairs and knocked gently on the door to an attic.

It was opened by Solomon, who said, "Mmm, ah, Miss Angela, thank you so much for coming. May I tempt you to some green tea? I am afraid you have to take us as we are, but

I have cleaned up as best I can, and don't mind Onan; the smell does disappear after a while, I can assure you."

Angela laughed at that and said, "Do you have any news?"

"Indeed, mmm," said Solomon. "I have had a letter—surprisingly well written—from Dodger, from York, where he went to grieve, because there he won't see anything that reminds him of poor dear Simplicity."

Angela picked up the spotlessly cleaned teacup and said, "York, well, yes indeed, how very fitting. Has anyone else inquired of you of Dodger's whereabouts, pray?"

Solomon filled her cup meticulously, saying, "I got these in Japan, you know? I am amazed that they have survived as long as I have." He glanced up and, with a face as straight as a plumb line, said, "Sir Robert was kind enough to send two of his constables to visit me two days ago, and they did ask about Mister Dodger's whereabouts, and so of course mmm I had to tell them all that I knew, which is of course my duty as a good citizen." His smile broadened and he said, "I always think one should lie to policemen; it is so very good for the soul and, indeed, good for the policemen."

Angela grinned and said, "You may or may not be surprised, Mister Cohen, that I too have had a communication from a nameless person, giving me details of a place in London and—isn't this quite exciting?—a time as well. This is rather fun, isn't it?"

"Yes, indeed," said Solomon, "although I must say my life has been altogether too full of this kind of fun, so I now prefer working here in my old carpet slippers, where fun does not usually interrupt my concentration. Oh dear, where are my manners? I do have some wonderful rice cakes here, my dear.

Bought them from Mister Chang, and very excellent they are too. Do please help yourself."

Angela accepted the proffered cake and said, "Should you meet the young Mister Dodger again, please do tell him that I have reason to believe that the authorities would indeed like to speak to him, not because he has done anything wrong, but because he has the capacity, they think, to do some things very right, and for the good of the country. The offer is open." She hesitated for a moment and added, "When I mention the word 'authorities,' I mean the highest authority."

Most unusually Solomon looked surprised, and said, "When you say 'highest,' you mean . . . ?"

"Not the Almighty," said Angela, "at least not as far as I know, but definitely the next best thing—a lady who could make some parts of Mister Dodger's life somewhat easier. I rather think that this is an invitation that would not be repeated if ignored."

"Mmm, really? Well, in that case I'd better get my morning dress suit from Jacob and have it cleaned, shall I?"

Quite apart from the cider, the fresh air, the cheese, and the stars, the young couple making friends with everybody in the town of Axbridge also got a taste for wall fruit, which the girl had told them was called by the French *escargots*, while in Somerset they were snails and be damned if they tried to be anything else.

All in all, the pair were a source of amiable mystery to the townsfolk, and everyone seemed to have their own anecdote about the couple, and speculated about them; the lady who did the church flowers said she had seen them in the lane by the river with some kids, teaching them a game called Happy Families. And a farmer declared that he had seen them sitting on a gate with the girl teaching the lad to read, or so it seemed, correcting his pronunciation and everything, for all the world like a schoolteacher. But, the farmer maintained, the lad seemed to enjoy the whole business and one of the farmer's mates then mentioned to the regulars in the pub that he had seen the lad every night lying on the warm grass and watching the stars. He said, "It were as if the poor devil had never seen them before."

On the last day, as they said their good-byes, one of their new friends, who had a pony and trap, took them back up the road to the pub at Star. He took a minor detour on the way to show them the field wherein there was a stone which, it was said, possibly by people who drank all that cider, came alive on some nights and danced around the field.

At that point, just after they had finished watching the stone, in case it was inclined to attempt a little jig for the tourists, Dodger said to his girl in the pure, rustic tones of Somersetshire, "Oi reckon we oughtta be moving along now, moi goyirl."

She, smiling like the sun, said, "Where bi'st to, my lover?"

Dodger smiled and said, "Lunnon."

And she said, "Where folk be so queer, not like ussun."

Then she kissed him and he kissed her, and in tones more like those of Lunnon than Somerset, he said, "My love, do you thinks it possible that a stone could dance?"

She said, "Well, Dodger, if anyone could make a stone dance, it would have to be you."

After that, two locals from Somerset, who nevertheless had

enough money to travel by coach, arrived in London from Bristol. Entirely disregarded, they disappeared into the throng and paid for accommodation for a single lady in a respectable boardinghouse while the young man set off to Seven Dials.

The following morning, Dodger took Onan out for a run and then disappeared down into the sewers. Anyone watching might have noticed that he was rather solemn and carrying a bag, although it is questionable whether rats can tell how solemn a human being is, or indeed know the meaning of the term "solemn." The rats might have been surprised later to find, tucked away in the debris of the sewers, carefully placed high above the normal levels of the water, a pair of shiny new shoes.

What Dodger did subsequently nobody saw, but he was most certainly on London Bridge at noon. There he was, staring at the boats going past, when a girl with long hair said in a voice that made his bones tingle, "'Scuse me, mister, can thee show me the way to Seven Dials, where my aunty lives?"

Dodger, if anyone was watching—and they certainly were—brightened up and said, "Are you new here? Capital! Allow me to show you around—it would be my pleasure."

At that moment a coach pulled up, to the consternation of the drivers of some vehicles behind it. But the coachmen paid them no attention as a woman stepped out, smiled at Dodger, looked intensely at the Somerset maiden, and said after an almost forensic examination, "Well now, how surprising, my friend, one might be mistaken in thinking that this young lady was Simplicity herself, but alas, as we both know, the poor girl is most dreadfully deceased. But clearly you, Mister

Dodger, are a resilient gentleman—I am aware of that. Since the three of us have strangely met on this bridge, perhaps you would allow me to take you and your new friend to Lavender Hill cemetery, where I was intending to go today, because the stonemason will by now have finished poor Simplicity's gravestone." She turned to the girl and said, "What is your name, young lady?"

The girl smiled and said, "Serendipity, miss." And Angela had to put her hand over her mouth to conceal laughter.

And so they went, all three, to Lavender Hill, where flowers were laid and not surprisingly tears were shed, and then Dodger and the young lady called Serendipity were dropped off again at one of the other bridges, where he had been told the Happy Family man had positioned his rather strange cart.

It was, in short, one quite large cage in which was a dog, a cat, a small baboon, a mouse, a couple of birds, and a snake, all living together in harmony, like real Christians, as the old man put it.

Serendipity said, "Why on earth doesn't the cat eat the mouse, Dodger?"

"Well," he said, "I think the old man is not one to tell you his secrets, but some people say if they are brought up together with some kindness, they become just that, a happy family. Although I have been told that should a mouse who has not yet been introduced to the snake come in through the bars, it would become the snake's dinner very quickly."

She held his hand then, and they walked along across the bridges and saw all the entertainments thereon: the men who lifted heavy weights, and the Crown and Anchor men, and the man who sold ham sandwiches, and the man who could stand on his hands upside down. Finally, as the golden light of evening made London look more like a pagan temple, all bronze and shiny, and turned the Thames into a second Ganges, they went home, totally ignoring the Punch and Judy man.

The following morning began with pandemonium outside. When Dodger crept down the stairs and peered out at the street, he saw two men wearing plumed helmets, and a smaller man looking at the same time both self-important and also slightly terrified about where he was. Dodger managed to get the window open and shouted down, "What do you want, mister?" He didn't like the look of the smaller man, who was obviously the boss—because whenever you see a big man alongside a small man, the little man is generally the boss. The little man now demanded, "A gentleman by the name of . . . Mister Dodger?"

Dodger gulped and shouted down, "Never heard of him."

The man looked up and said, "Well, sir, I am sad to hear that. But if you do in fact meet the said Mister Dodger, perhaps you would tell him that Her Majesty Queen Victoria has summoned him to Buckingham Palace tomorrow afternoon!"

From behind Dodger, Solomon said blearily, "Mmm, Dodger, you cannot ignore a summons from Her Majesty."

And so Dodger was short of anywhere to dodge to, and he stepped gingerly into the street. People were already gathering, much to the chagrin of the two men with the plumed helmets, because the rumor had run around that Dodger was being taken to the gallows at last and one or two people were talking about fighting back; and naturally, when you have one rumor, it buds little extra rumors. Just for the fun of it.

Now Dodger stood there, blinking, and said, "Okay, mister, now tell me the truth."

The small, rather harassed man, trying to maintain a dignified image in a world that had no dignity at all, handed Dodger a document. "Make yourself available at the gates of Buckingham Palace at four thirty tomorrow," he said, "and you will be welcomed in. You may bring members of your family, to the number of three. I shall of course relay to Her Majesty that you have humbly accepted."

It was a strange, mysterious day after that, even when people lost interest and went about their business, or in some cases as much of anyone else's business that they could steal. Dodger started it by going for a walk, forsaking the sewers but simply crisscrossing London with Onan, who was overjoyed at this lengthy outing, trotting happily beside him. Eventually Dodger's legs, who knew him better than he did, took him through Covent Garden and into Fleet Street.

Charlie wasn't there, but when Dodger asked to meet the editor and said who he was, he was instantly ushered upstairs, where he was told that another seven guineas was accrued to his account. Dodger said that he would like the remaining money in that wretched subscription to please be diverted to make life comfortable for Mister Todd who, he understood, was now incarcerated in Bedlam hospital, a place not suitable for those of a delicate disposition.

Mister Doyle agreed, and moreover promised to see to it that the money would actually get to where it should go. That made Dodger feel better. Then he continued his walking, pausing only to buy a bone from the butcher's shop for

Onan's lunch. Then he went to a bottle shop and procured a bottle of good brandy and carried it with him down to the river, where he hailed a waterman to take him down to the wharf at Four Farthings.

The coroner was not there, but his officer promised to see to it that this gift, ostensibly from the son of an old lady he had helped, would get to its intended owner; alas, there were times when you had to hope that people were as good as their word. There really wasn't much in Four Farthings that wasn't soon going to be swept up by the bigger boroughs, but Dodger did take a look in the church of Saint Never, a little-known saint who was in charge of things that didn't happen, which was why so many young ladies prayed there. He dropped a shilling in the offertory box but heard the coin hit wood, where he suspected it was likely to be lonely for quite some time.

He found the time to make a detour to the house of Mister and Missus Mayhew, shaking hands and thanking them for their condolences, and for all the help they had given to the poor late Simplicity, who, said Dodger, if she was alive now, would be very grateful. He was absolutely certain of that, he told them, as certain as if he had heard it from her very own mouth. Then, when he was shown along to the main entrance, he waved the suggestion away and headed down past the green baize door, where he had a cheerful smile even for Mrs. Sharples and a pneumatic kiss from Mrs. Quickly.

As he wandered back across the river, he wondered why he was doing all this, and quite rightly so did Onan, who was having the time of his life, never having had such a long walk in one go. It struck him that there was one person who could tell him. That led to the hiring of another waterman to take him upstream for a while, and then a reasonable walk took him to Miss Serendipity's boardinghouse and a growler took the two of them to Angela's home. The door was opened very respectfully by the butler, who said, "Good afternoon, Mister Dodger, I will see if Miss Angela is in."

In fact, it was less than a minute before Angela appeared. Then, brightening, Dodger told them his news over coffee and asked Serendipity to accompany him.

Serendipity took the news in a very feminine way, which was to panic that she wouldn't have anything to wear to the palace, at which point Angela chimed in happily, saying, "My dear, you hardly have to worry about that. Perhaps we could have a little visit to my dressmaker; it's very short notice, but I am sure something can be done." She turned to Dodger and said, "Talking of dresses reminds me of rings, and so I should like you, Mister Dodger, to tell me exactly what your intentions are? I understand the two of you are engaged; when do you believe that you will be wed? Personally I have never seen the point of long engagements, but there may be . . . difficulties?"

Dodger had thought long and hard about Serendipity and marriage. Officially, as Simplicity, she was still a married lady, but as she herself had said, God could hardly have been at that wedding or He would not have allowed it to turn from love to something so awful. When he'd asked Solomon, the old man had stroked his chin and mmm'd a few times and then said that surely any Almighty worth believing in would agree. And if not, Solomon would explain it to Him for them. Dodger had chimed in then and said, "I don't know if God was in the sewer, but the Lady definitely was."

After all, he thought, other than the prince who would surely keep silent, the only witnesses to the wretched marriage now had been Simplicity and the ring. The ring was gone and Simplicity was dead. So where was the evidence that Simplicity had ever been there at all? It was in a way another kind of fog, and in that fog, he thought, people might make their way to some sunlit uplands.

Now he said firmly, "Simplicity was married. But Simplicity is dead. Now I have Serendipity—somebody new, and I'll help her. But I'm someone new too, and before we marry, I've got to get a job, and a good one—I shall have to save the toshing for a hobby. But I don't even know how to get proper work."

He paused there, because Angela's smile spoke volumes, which at the moment he could not interpret. "Well now," she said, "if I can believe tittle-tattle, I rather suspect, young Dodger, that shortly in your life you will see again a cheerful but friendly old man with silver hair who might like to give you a holiday in foreign parts. Congratulations to you, young man, and to you too, Miss Serendipity."

The following day the coach arrived exactly on time and with Serendipity on board. When they set off again, Solomon, who seemed to know everything about these matters, said, "This is, of course, a private audience. But just remember, Her Majesty is in charge. Do not speak until you are spoken to. Never, ever interrupt and—and I stress this, Dodger—don't get familiar. Do you understand?"

Some of this information was imparted as they were

walking through the palace, which was to a part of Dodger the most target-rich environment he had ever encountered. Even Angela's place was put to shame. Room followed room, and it was an overpowering panorama for someone who had been a snakesman, but he told himself it would never work. No one would have a sack big enough to take away those great big pictures or those great big chairs.

Then suddenly there was another room, and the queen and Prince Albert were here and indeed, Dodger noticed, there were flunkies everywhere; standing still in the way a good thief does, because people are quick to notice movement.

Dodger had never heard the word "surreal" but would have used it when Solomon, dressed in all his glory, bowed so low before the queen that his hair nearly touched the floor. There was a little click and a sudden stillness in the room, and Solomon was frantically waving a finger at Dodger, who knew the drill and so stepped forward, smiled nervously at the queen, wrapped his arms around Solomon, stuck a knee in his back, then brought him upright. To his own dismay, he heard himself say cheerily, "Sorry about this, Your Majesty, he gets the twinging screws when he tries that, but no harm done, I've knocked him into shape again."

A splendid-looking girl, he thought—very nobby, of course; that went without saying. Her face was a blank and Prince Albert was looking at Dodger like a man finding a codfish in his pajamas. So Dodger took a step back, let Solomon find his feet, and tried to look invisible, and at that point the queen lit up and said brightly, "Mister Cohen, it is a great pleasure to meet you at last; I've heard so many stories about you. You are not in pain in any way, are you?" she added in a less royal tone of voice.

Solomon gulped and said, "Nothing damaged except my self-esteem, Your Majesty, and may I say that some of the tales they tell about me are not true."

Prince Albert said, "The king of Sweden tells a very good one."

Solomon blushed under his beard—Dodger could just make that out—and said, "If it was the one about the race-horse in the lodge, Your Royal Highness, alas it was true."

"Nevertheless," said the prince, "I feel quite privileged to meet you, sir." He held out his hand to Solomon, and Dodger watched the handshake very carefully and recognized the Masonic hand of freedom.

The queen, her eyes on her husband, said, "Well, my dear, there is a nice surprise for you." Although it was quite a pleasant sentence, it had a little clip on the end, to remind everybody that *that* conversation at least was at an end. She turned to Dodger and said, "You, then, must be Mister Dodger? You do very well around desperate criminals, I believe. Everyone is still talking about Sweeney Todd. That must have been such a terrible day for you."

Dodger recognized that it might not be a good idea to deny this fact, even though the day had been more astonishing than terrible. And so he took refuge in: "Well, Your Majesty, there he was and there I was, and there the razor was, and that was it really. To be honest, I felt sorry for the poor man."

"So I have heard," said the queen. "It is a disquieting thought, but it is to your credit, at least. I believe that the young lady beside you is your fiancée, is that not so? Do come here, Miss Serendipity."

Serendipity stepped forward and suddenly Dodger found himself somehow outside the room looking down on it, watching how expressions changed and changed again, and then he was back in himself and everything was cheerful and someone had just brought in some tea and there was a definite feeling that things were satisfactory.

Who would dare lie to a queen? he thought. How much did she know? For that matter, how much did Prince Albert know? He was from one of the Germanys, wasn't he? But that would start him thinking about politics again, and so he chased the thought out of his mind, and as time floated back, Serendipity curtsied—rather better than Solomon had bowed—and the room began to be even more cheerful.

"When do you think your wedding will be, my dear?"

Serendipity blushed and said, "Dodger says he will have to get a new job first, Your Majesty, so we don't know yet."

"Indeed," said the queen. "What is it you do, Mister Dodger, when you are not thwarting criminals?"

Dodger didn't answer that, not being entirely sure what thwarting meant, but Solomon was in there fast with "He assists with the proper running of the drainage, Your Majesty."

Prince Albert rolled his eyes and said, "Oh, drains, we have them here and they never seem to work properly."

Dodger opened his mouth, but the queen, anxious to get drains out of the way, said, "Well, sir, I wish you well in whatever post you eventually take. And now . . ." she added, glancing at a flunky, "we think that bravery such as yours should be recognized, and so I would like you to step forward here and get down one knee. See the cushion here, and it would probably be a good idea if you took off your hat." A flunky stepped forward holding a sword, and quite a shiny one at that. The queen took it and then said, "What is your full name to be, Mister Dodger? I have been advised that you would like to see the last of Pip Stick."

Dodger stared at her, and then Serendipity said, "If it's any help, Your Majesty, I've always thought that Jack is a very nice name."

Jack Dodger, thought Dodger. It sounded slightly nobby, but he didn't know why. The queen looked at him expectantly and said, "If I was you, sir, I would take the advice of your lady." She glanced at Prince Albert and added, "As sensible husbands do." All Dodger could do now was say, "Uh, yes please," and then there was a breath of air over his scalp and the sword was back in the arms of a flunky again and Sir Jack Dodger stood up.

"It makes you look taller," said Serendipity.

"Indeed it does," said Queen Victoria. "Incidentally," she went on, "I am told, Sir Jack, that you have a very intelligent dog as a pet?"

Dodger grinned. "Oh yes, Your Majesty, that would be Onan; he's a very good friend, but of course we couldn't bring him along here."

"Quite so," said the queen, and she cleared her throat. "You mean Onan, as in the Bible?" Out of the corner of his eye Dodger could see Solomon stepping backward, but nevertheless he said, "Oh yes, miss."

"Why did you call him that?"

Well, Dodger thought, after all she did ask. So he told her,*

---

*If you want to know more about Onan, a well-known biblical character, I am sure that many of my readers know their Bible from one end to the other. And if not, Google, or any priest—possibly a slightly embarrassed one—will help you.

and the young queen glanced at her husband, whose face was a picture, and then burst out laughing and said, "Well now, we *are* amused."

Like some sort of clockwork, the tea then disappeared as quickly as it had turned up, and there was a certain signal that this audience was at an end. Greatly relieved, Dodger took Serendipity by the arm and led her away, and was slightly surprised as they left the room that the white-haired man he had met before walked boldly up to him and said, "Sir Jack, allow me to be the first to congratulate you. May I trespass upon your time for a moment? Have you perchance had the opportunity to consider my proposal?"

"He wants you to be a spy," murmured Solomon behind him.

The white-haired man made a *tsk, tsk* noise and said, "Oh dear no, Mister Cohen. A spy, sir? Perish the thought. Her Majesty's government, I can assure you, has no dealings with spies, oh my word, no. But nevertheless we like the kind of people who help us . . . take an interest."

Dodger took Serendipity to one side and said, "What should I do?"

"Well, he does want you to be a spy," Serendipity replied. "You can tell that by the look on his face when he says that he doesn't. For someone like you, Dodger, it seems to me to be the perfect occupation, although I suspect it will mean learning one or two foreign languages. But I have no doubt that you will find learning them quite easy. I myself know French and German, as well as a little Latin and Greek. Not too difficult if you put your mind to it."

Not to be outdone, Dodger said, "Well, I know some

Greek. Παρακαλώ μπορείτε να μου πείτε που βρίσκονται
η άτακτες κυρίες;"*

Serendipity smiled at him and said, "My word, Dodger,
you do lead a very interesting life, don't you?"

"My love," he replied, "I think it's only just beginning."

And that was why two months later, Jack Dodger was running through the boulevards of Paris with the gendarmerie
lagging far behind him. He was carrying a pocket stuffed
with coins and bonds, a tiara that had once belonged to
Marie Antoinette and would look very good on his wife,
Serendipity, and last but not least, the plans for an entirely
new type of gun. Whistles were blowing all over the place,
but Dodger was never where anyone thought he would be.
He had been most interested to find out that the Froggies
had drains too, pretty good ones, which you wouldn't have
expected from Froggies, and so he jigged and dodged and ran
on to the safe house he had sorted out last night, and he was
having the time of his life.

---

* Please direct me to where the naughty ladies are.

Author's acknowledgments, embarrassments,
and excuses with, at no extra cost,
some bits of vocabulary and usage

DODGER IS SET BROADLY in the first quarter of Queen Victoria's reign; in those days disenfranchised people were flooding into London and the other big cities, and life in London for the poor, and most of the people were the poor, was harsh in the extreme. Traditionally, nobody very much bothered about those in poverty at all, but as a decade advanced, there were those among the better off who thought that their plight should be known to everybody. One of those, of course, was Charles Dickens, but not so well known was his friend Henry Mayhew. What Dickens did surreptitiously, showing the reality of things via the medium of the novel, Henry Mayhew and his confederates did simply by facts, lots and lots of facts, piling statistics on statistics. Mayhew himself walked around the streets chatting to little orphan girls selling flowers, street vendors, old ladies, workers of all sorts including prostitutes; and he exposed, by degrees, the grubby underbelly of the richest and most powerful city in the world.

The massive work known as *London Labour and the London Poor* ought to be in every library if only to show you that if you think things are bad now, they were oh so much more worse not all that long ago.

Readers may have heard of the movie *Gangs of New York*; well, London was worse and getting even more so every time fresh hopefuls arrived to try their luck in the big city. Mayhew's work has been shortened, rearranged, and occasionally printed in smaller volumes. The original, however, is not heavy going. And if you like fantasy, in a very strange way fantasy is there with realistic dirt and grime all over it.

And so, it is to Henry Mayhew that I dedicate this book.

Dodger is a made-up character, as are many of the people he meets, although they are from types working, living, and dying in London at that time.

Disraeli was certainly real, and so was Charles Dickens, and so was Sir Robert Peel, who founded the police force in London and became prime minister (twice). His "peelers" did indeed replace the old Bow Street runners who were, more or less, thief takers and not known for excessive bravery. The peelers were a very different kettle of fish, being drawn from men with military experience.

Readers will recognize other personages from history along the way, I expect. Most fantastic of all was Miss Angela Burdett-Coutts, heiress of her grandfather's fortune when she was still quite young and at that time the richest woman in the world, apart perhaps from a queen here or there. She was an amazing woman who did indeed once propose marriage to the Duke of Wellington. But more importantly, for me at least, she spent most of her time giving her money away.

But she wasn't a soft touch. Miss Coutts believed in helping those who helped themselves, and so she set up the Ragged Schools, which helped kids and even older people to get something of an education, wherever they were and however poor they were. She helped people start up small businesses, gave money to churches—but only if they were in some way assisting the poor in practical ways—and all in all was a phenomenon. She plays a major role in this narrative, and since I couldn't ask her questions, I had to make some informed guesses about the way she would react in certain circumstances. I assumed that a woman as rich as her without a husband would certainly know her own mind and generally not be frightened of anything very much.

The Romans did build the sewers in London; they were haphazardly repaired as the generations passed. The sewers were mostly intended for rainwater, rather than human waste, cesspits and septic tanks effectively doing that job, and it was when these overflowed, simply because of too many human beings, that you were in the land of cholera and other dreadful diseases.

There were indeed toshers, whose lives were anything but glamorous, but the same applied to the mudlarks and the young chimney sweeps who had nasty diseases of their very own. Dodger, then, was very lucky to find a landlord who was in receipt of four thousand years' worth of food safety information. But even then, I have to admit, as Mark Twain did many years ago, that I may have put a little touch of shine on things.

I didn't need to put a shine on Joseph Bazalgette, who appears in this book as a young but keen man. He was the leading light among the surveyors and engineers who changed the face, and most importantly the smell, of London sometime after the story of Dodger takes place. The new London sewers and sewer works were one of the technological miracles of the new Iron Age and so, with some maintenance here and there, they remain.

"Boney," of course, was the nickname of Napoleon Bonaparte, and if you don't know who he was, I am quite certain, alas, that your keyboard will sooner or later let you know.

A note about coinage. Explaining the British predecimal coinage to generations that haven't had to deal with it is difficult, even for me, and I grew up learning it. I could talk at length about such things as thrupence ha'penny, and tanners and crowns and half crowns and the way it drove American tourists, in particular, totally nuts. So all that I can say is that there were coins made of bronze, of all sizes, and these were the cheaper coins; and then there were the coins made of silver, which, as you might expect, occupied the middle ground finance-wise, and then there were the gold coins which were, well, gold—and in Dodger's day were truly golden, not like the coins you get today, mumble, mumble, complain. But in truth, the old currency had a certain reality to it that the modern "p," God help us, does not; it just doesn't have the same life.

Then there was the wonderful thrupenny bit, so heavy in a little kid's pocket . . . No, I'd better stop here, because if this goes on, sooner or later I'll be talking about groats and half farthings and someone might have to shoot me.

In the wonderful world of slang, if you like this kind of

thing, it is interesting to note that once upon a time the word "crib" meant among many other things a building, or place where you lived, and quite recently for some reason it has come back again in the English-speaking countries.

Victorian slang, and there was such a lot of it, can be a minefield. Looking at the world from Dodger's point of view means that you can't say "posh," because that word had not yet been created. But nobby does the trick. It would be possible to fill up this book with appropriate slang, but sooner or later, well, it's not there to be a textbook of slang and so I've left in some of the ones I liked. Unfortunately, I cannot find a place for my favorite piece of slang, which is "tuppence more and up goes the donkey" because, alas, it's just a little bit too modern.

And short though *Dodger* is, I've been helped time and again by friends with particular expertise, and my thanks go out to Jacqueline Simpson, Bernard Pearson, Colin Smythe, and Pat Harkin, who stopped me putting a foot wrong. Where one *is* wrong is probably my own dammed foot.

I have to confess ahead of the game that certain tweaks were needed to get people in the right place at the right time—students of history will know that Tenniel didn't illustrate his first *Punch* cover until 1850 and Sir Robert Peel was home secretary before Victoria came to the throne, for instance—but they are not particularly big tweaks, and besides, *Dodger* is a fantasy based on a reality. It was the devil's own job to find out where the headquarters of the *Morning Chronicle* was. It seems that they changed offices periodically, so I've stuck them, for the purposes of *Dodger*, in Fleet Street—where they ought to have been anyway. This is a historical fantasy—and certainly not a historical novel—simply for the fun of it, and also too, if possible, to get people interested in that era so wonderfully cataloged by Henry Mayhew and his fellows.

Because although I may have tweaked the positions of people and possibly how they might have reacted in certain situations, the grime, squalor, and hopelessness of an under-class that nevertheless survived, often by means of self-help, I have not changed at all. It was also, however, a time without such things as education for all, health and safety, and most of the other rules and impediments that we take for granted today. And there was always room for the sharp and clever Dodgers, male and female.

Terry Pratchett, 2012